BEAUTIFUL LIES

THE BEAUTY IN FLIGHT STORIES

ROBIN PATCHEN

JDO PUBLISHING

ACKNOWLEDGMENTS

No story comes together without help. Thank you to my critique partners, Normandie Fischer, Kara Hunt, Jericha Kingston, Candice Sue Patterson, Sharon Srock, Pegg Thomas, and Terri Weldon. Great writing is ten percent talent, ten percent hard work, and 80 percent having friends like you.

Thank you to my editor, Ray Rhamey, and to Misty Beller and Lacy Williams for all your marketing advice.

Thank you, Alanna Rodriguez, for your insights into caring for the elderly.

Thank you to Eddie, Nick, Lexi, and Jacob for supporting me in this journey.

Mostly, as always, my thanks go to Jesus Christ, my Salvation and my Strength. You know the battles I faced as I wrote these books, and You helped me overcome each and every one.

I

BEAUTY IN FLIGHT

For my sister, Jennifer.
My playmate, my secret-keeper, my champion.
No matter how far apart we live, you'll always be my best friend.

CHAPTER ONE

Two years out should have been enough. Cell mates no longer shoved her, fellow inmates no longer raised their fists, and guards no longer leered. A year ago, she'd been released from parole. Harper Cloud was free.

Except her heart didn't believe it.

At least the icky, creepy, somebody's-watching-me sensation she'd had since she left her house that afternoon faded as soon as she walked through the doors of the nursing home. Among these beautiful residents, Harper felt safer than she did anywhere else in the world.

"Harper, Miss Estelle's asking for you." Teresa, the LPN who worked the six-to-two shift, tossed the words over her shoulder as she lumbered behind the counter at the nurses' station.

"She feeling all right?"

"As good as can be, all things considered." Teresa typed something into the computer, then looked at Harper again. "New guy in Room 104. Peanut allergy."

"Got it." Harper had been trained as an LPN and had once hoped to become a registered nurse. Prison had changed all that.

She was lucky to have landed this job as a nursing assistant. While she delivered meals, mopped floors, cleaned bedpans, she focused on how much she loved caring for the elderly, these patients who'd become her closest friends, and ignored the fact that she barely made enough to pay her bills. She helped Mr. Jenkins to the restroom and pushed away a moment of self-pity. She was free to work where she chose. So what if she had to work weekends at the grocery store to pay for the classes she was taking at the local community college? Money wasn't important to her. Being free—that was what mattered. And the feeling of safety was certainly a plus.

But was it an illusion?

The fear she'd walked to work with tried to worm its way into her mind, but she pushed it away. In here, among her friends, she was safe.

After she checked on all the other patients, she pushed into Miss Estelle's room. "How you feeling today?"

The old woman's wrinkled face split into a big smile, and Harper raised the bed so Estelle could sit up. Her puffy blue-gray hair was flattened on one side from a recent catnap. Her brown eyes sparkled in her pale skin. "I wondered when you'd finally get around to me."

Harper leaned in and kissed the woman's cheek. Estelle looked grayer today. The pneumonia had taken a lot out of her. "You're not my only patient, Estelle, just my favorite. You need anything?"

"Went to the bathroom all by myself just a few minutes ago." Harper tried to show her disapproval with a glare, but Estelle only laughed and waved toward the chair beside her bed. "Been doing it since before you were a twinkle in your daddy's eyes. Sit down, honey."

Harper glanced at the door, then took the chair. "Just for a minute."

"But you saved me for last, right?"

"Don't I always? Everybody's settled. Now, tell me. What'd the doctor say?"

"Pfft." She waved off the question as if it were a black fly. "Told me I'm on the mend, but we know better than that."

Estelle's hand was cold when Harper took it. "Don't say that. If he says you're improving—"

"We both know I'm not long for this world. I'm not complaining. I'm ready to go home."

The thought of this place, of the world, without Estelle made Harper's eyes prickle. She was the closest thing to family Harper had. "This is your home." Her voice cracked on the last word, and she looked down, blinking furiously.

Estelle squeezed Harper's hand. "You listen to me, honey."

Harper looked up and sniffed.

"I love you, too. You're a good girl."

Harper started to protest, but the woman's grip tightened, silencing her. "Don't you argue with me. I'm an old woman, and I know what I'm talking about. You're not perfect. You've made mistakes. Join the club. But you got a God who loves you and wants you back. And you got a family who loves you—"

"They don't."

Estelle stared at her with those aged brown eyes. "They're not perfect, either. So they screwed up. You never going to forgive them, after everything?"

"I don't have to forgive them, Estelle. I'm the one who went to prison."

"And they should have been there for you. That's what family does. They screwed it up, and I bet they know it now. Call your mother, hon. I promise she wants to hear from you."

Hot tears dripped onto their gripped hands. "As soon as I have something to tell her. As soon as I... as I feel like I'm worthy—"

"Worthy. Pfft. You think you can do something to make yourself worthy? What did you do to make your folks love you when you were born? You earn that somehow?"

The question threw her off. "When I was an infant? What could I do?"

"Nothing. You were probably cute, but mothers even love their ugly babies. Babies do nothing to earn love. They scream and poop and eat." Estelle chuckled. "Not that I do much more than that now."

"Stop that. You're—"

"The point is, nobody's worthy. Or maybe everybody is. I don't know. I only know your mom doesn't need you to be perfect. She just wants you home."

Harper pictured her mother, the disappointment on her face that last time Harper had seen her. Mom and Dad had come to Vegas to surprise her and had gone to the club where she'd been a dancer. That's how she'd described her job to them, but they'd figured out what she really did by looking at the posters of the nearly naked women on the blacked-out windows. Her parents hadn't gone inside, thank God. But they knew what she'd become. The shame, the horror had been written all over their faces. And that was before Harper'd gone to prison.

"You have to give them another chance," Estelle said.

The desire to hear her mother's voice was so strong that she considered calling right then. But their last conversation ricocheted in her brain like a gunshot. She'd called from the jail right after they'd taken her into custody. Her father's words had never been far from her mind. "Don't call here again. Ever."

So she hadn't. What was there to say? *Hey guys, I'm not a stripper anymore. Drugs...? Kicked that habit. Prison was a long time ago. I know I said I was going to become a nurse, but I love my minimum wage job.* No, she wouldn't call them, not until she had something worthwhile to report. She wouldn't call until she could tell them something they could be proud of. Assuming she ever called at all.

The fact that she had a huge hole in her heart seemed irrelevant but fair, all things considered.

Estelle let go of her hand and coughed again and again. She couldn't seem to stop.

Harper helped her lean forward, soothing her until she could breathe again. Finally, Estelle lay back and took a few breaths.

"Should I get the nurse?"

Estelle shook her head, recovering a moment longer. Harper busied herself tidying the room. When she'd tossed the last of the tissues that hadn't quite made it into the trash, she said, "I'll go and let you rest."

"One more thing." Estelle paused to take another deep breath.

Harper returned to her spot at the beside, and Estelle turned her piercing eyes on Harper once again. "On your way here, did you get the feeling again?"

The fear came back like a bad virus. "I shouldn't have told you about that."

"Honey, God gave you instincts for a reason. You trust 'em. You think somebody's following you, then you take care, protect yourself. You get that pepper spray like I told ya?"

"I keep it in my pocket when I'm walking alone."

"Good, good." The woman reached toward the end table on the far side of her bed and snatched a cardboard box barely big enough to hold a lighter. "I got you this."

Harper took the box. "How did you—?"

"Amazon. They got everything. Open it."

Harper broke the seal at the end of the box and slid out the contents. She slid the keyring over her finger. Dangling from it was a Swiss Army knife about two inches long.

"Go ahead," Estelle said.

Harper pried out the small blade and showed Estelle. What was she supposed to do with this?

"It won't kill anybody, but it'll hurt like the dickens if you stab somebody with it."

"I could never—"

"Yeah, you're too sweet for your own good. But you do as I say. The mace in one pocket, the knife in the other. And don't be scared to use either one if you need to. Got it?"

"Yes, ma'am."

"Don't *ma'am* me. I'm not that old." The woman started to laugh, but it turned into a cough.

Harper stood. "Let me get someone."

But Estelle grabbed her hand and shook her head. When she'd settled again, Harper said, "Where I come from, we *ma'am-and-sir* our elders."

"Kansas." Estelle clucked her tongue as if being from Kansas were akin to being from Jupiter. "Just can't imagine. Now, tell me about your young man. Have you made a decision?"

Harper sighed. "I don't want to leave you."

"Nonsense." Estelle's New York accent came out more when she was vehement. "The question is, do you love him?"

"I don't know." Harper pictured Derrick Burns, his kind eyes, his gentle demeanor. "He's nice to me. We have great conversations on the phone. When we're together, it's as if I'm the only person in his whole world."

"You feel that way about him?"

She'd been burned by so many guys, it was hard to trust. "Maybe, someday."

"Hmph." Estelle pinned Harper with her gaze. "But you'd leave your stalker here. Surely he wouldn't follow you across the country."

"I don't have a stalker."

"Don't you poo-poo it. Even if not for the creep following you, there's the job. If it doesn't work out with the guy, the job would be good. You gotta think of your future."

"Assuming Derrick wouldn't fire me if we broke up."

"That'd be up to his grandfather, though. Not your boyfriend. And you'll win over the old man in about five minutes. Then, whatever happens with Derrick, at least you'll have that job."

"Is it wrong to go there for the job, not for him?"

"It's not like he proposed. Right?"

"He just wants me closer to him so he doesn't have to come to Vegas to see me."

"What's wrong with Vegas? It's a far sight better than where he's from. Who wants all that cold and rain and humidity, anyway?"

Harper didn't argue with Estelle, but after living in Las Vegas for years, she'd tired of the heat and sunshine. There were days she longed for cloudy and rainy and cold. Those kinds of days made the sunny ones that much more special. No, it wasn't moving to Maryland that made Harper hesitate. And to work as a private nurse for a wealthy old man would be much better than this job, even if she did love her patients. The job would be the first step in claiming the life she wanted—a real job, one her parents could be proud of.

If she moved to Maryland, she'd live with Derrick's grandfather rent-free and have the money to attend college and finish her Bachelor's degree. Assuming she could ever figure out what she wanted to do with her life now that being an RN was off the table. She wasn't going back to performing. She knew too well where that path led.

But what about Derrick? He'd sworn he didn't have expectations for their relationship, but she'd never met a man who didn't give without expecting something in return. What would he expect from her?

Right now, he acted as if she were his lifeline. He called her every night before bed and again on his way to work every morning. Flew to Vegas to visit her every chance he got.

"You're my anchor," he'd told her. "My salvation."

The words worried her. She could barely take care of herself. How could she be another person's salvation?

And what did he need to be saved from?

But every reservation was drowned under the sea of gifts and flowers and words of devotion.

She took Estelle's hand. It was wrinkled and cold. "I can't imagine leaving you."

"I got a date with Jesus, and I think it's coming soon."

"Don't say that."

When the old woman laughed, her face glowed, and Harper saw the young beauty she'd surely been. "I'm not afraid to die, Harper. Dying's the easy part. It's living that's hard. You gotta figure out how to live." Estelle squeezed Harper's fingers. "Not for a guy, not to feed and wipe the bottoms of a bunch of old people. You need to figure out how to live for you."

CHAPTER TWO

It was after ten that night when Harper bid Estelle and the rest of her patients good-night and left the nursing home. She hated walking alone after dark, hated the fear that haunted her. She'd been saving for a car and could almost afford a decent junker. But not yet.

She hitched her purse onto her shoulder and stuck one hand in her jacket pocket to grip the pepper spray. The other hand closed over her new key chain. Wouldn't Estelle be proud?

Air that had been hot earlier had dropped to the fifties. There were people about, despite the late hour and the fact that it was a Wednesday. Nightlife never ended in Las Vegas. She was thankful for all the city lights and thankful that the Las Vegas nightlife had played a part in her meeting Derrick.

A few months before, exhausted from a long night of partying with his friends, he'd come to the grocery store where she worked weekends. He'd chatted with her and taken her to breakfast. Something had clicked. They'd talked for hours that day. It had been the start of a conversation that never seemed to end. She'd told him the truth about her past, and he'd hardly blinked. It had made her nervous, the way he'd accepted her so quickly, but over the months she'd known him, those nerves had been buried beneath his acts of kindness.

Sometimes, she wanted to slow things down with Derrick. Other times, she wanted desperately to escape this life she was leading, and Derrick seemed like the answer. He'd been begging her for months to move to Maryland to take care of his grandfather. It was too soon, though. Wasn't it? To move across the country for a guy she barely knew?

A guy, she thought... Could she love him? Could she ever trust a man again after her last boyfriend? Emmitt had ruined her life.

It was probably the thought of her ex-boyfriend that had the hair on her arms standing on end. A feeling that someone was there, someone was watching, waiting. The fear that had plagued her for months, years, prickled her skin.

Foolishness, of course. She hadn't reconnected with any of her friends from before—not that they'd been real friends, anyway. Back then, only Emmitt, her ex-boyfriend, and Barry, his best friend, had felt like true friends. Felt like it, but look what they'd gotten her into. Both of them were still in prison.

Aside from Derrick, Harper hadn't connected with anyone except Estelle since she'd been released. Oh, there were familiar faces on campus where she was taking a few classes, but those bright-eyed college students wouldn't want to be her friend if they knew the real Harper Cloud. They didn't have a past like hers. They didn't have her sins, her criminal record. Compared to her, they were innocent.

There was nobody in Vegas who cared enough about Harper to follow her. She'd been telling herself that for weeks. She was safe. Of course she was safe.

Adrenaline flooded her veins anyway.

She walked faster, past a loud group of tourists who smelled of cigarettes and marijuana and liquor. Since prison, she had no desire for that kind of life. She passed an off-the-strip hotel, where the dings and beeps of the slot machines in the lobby carried through the open door, she kept her head down and crossed the street.

The fear crossed with her.

The sound of footsteps behind her seemed to get louder, closer, until they pounded in her ears.

The narrow alley that led to the back door of her apartment building was just ahead. She could walk around to the front, but to get there she had to pass a very dark stretch of sidewalk before reaching the floodlights and street traffic. Or she could cut through the alley.

A stalker could hurt her on the sidewalk or in the alley.

She'd be inside faster if she cut through the alley.

She was crazy. Nobody was following her. This insanity had to stop. Whoever was behind her was just a tourist or one of the millions of workers who kept this town running. This feeling was just her own anxiety chasing her like demons, mocking her. She was fine. She was safe. She was practically invisible these days.

Outside the nursing home, nobody even saw her anymore.

Great. Now she was being maudlin.

She squared her shoulders and turned down the alley.

The footsteps followed.

Adjusting her key so it would be ready for the lock, she moved faster. She was nearly there when something moved at the far end of the alley. A man in the shadows walked toward her.

Two men were closing in. One behind, one in front.

Her hands were trembling by the time she reached the door. She tried to slide the key into the lock. Fumbled it, and the keys clattered to the concrete. She passed the pepper spray from her left hand to her right and started to turn. A hand clamped on her upper arm, kept the pepper spray aimed at his knees.

She gasped, desperate to scream but unable to force the sound past her terror.

"Hey!" A deep voice. A familiar voice. It came from the man on the far end of the alley. He was running their direction.

The man with his hand on her arm turned and bolted.

The other man, the one with the familiar voice, chased him.

Stunned, confused, she watched as the first man rounded the corner and disappeared. The second followed him.

She stared into the darkness.

Had that just happened?

Had she lost her mind, conjured danger where none existed?

Danger... and salvation?

She snatched her key from the asphalt, pepper spray still gripped in her fist.

Her hands trembled, slick with sweat, but she managed to slip her key into the lock on the outer door of her building. She was turning the knob when she heard footsteps again.

Please, no.

"Harper?"

She turned toward the familiar voice she'd heard before.

"Barry?"

He jogged down the alley and stopped beside her. "I thought that was you. I saw you walking..."

His words faded. Or maybe she did. Suddenly, the dark night got darker, and her legs turned to jelly. She gasped as if she hadn't taken a breath in minutes. Maybe she hadn't.

"Hey." Barry gripped her upper arms. "You okay? You look like you're about to pass out."

"If you hadn't been there..." But she couldn't finish the statement.

"But I was." He pulled her close and wrapped his arms around her back. "You're safe."

Safe. She was safe. She took a deep breath, straightened. She was all right. She'd survived worse.

He let her go, turned the knob, and pushed the door open. "This is your building?"

"I'm fine. I'll be okay now."

"I'm walking you to your door anyway. Just to be sure. What if that guy went around to the front and got someone to let him in?"

The thought had her heart dropping. "Okay. Thank you."

She led the way into the building and up the narrow staircase, down the hall and to the door of her tiny studio apartment. "Oh." She'd left her key dangling from the keyhole downstairs. When she turned to Barry, he lifted his hand, and her keyring hung from his index finger, her key swinging beside the new knife.

"Here"—he nodded to the keyhole—"let me."

She stepped out of the way while he unlocked her door and pushed it open.

"Thank you."

"I'm just glad I happened by when I did."

The hair on her arms rose. Nobody *happened by* this part of town. Just a few blocks off the strip, but it might as well have been miles and miles. Suspicion had her stepping into her apartment, never taking her eyes off him. She kept one hand on the doorknob, prepared to slam it shut. "What were you doing in the alley?"

His smile seemed natural enough. "I saw you at end of the block. I was on the other corner. I was going to cut through the alley, see if I could catch up with you. When you turned in, I wasn't sure if it was you or not. I was getting closer to make sure. Then I saw that guy behind you."

Seemed reasonable, but... "What were you doing on the street?"

"There's a little bar on the next block. I met some friends there. My car was parked in that lot on the corner."

The story sounded plausible. And it definitely hadn't been Barry following her into the alley. If Barry hadn't been there, she hated to think what would have happened.

She held out her hand, palm up, and he dropped the keys in it. "Will you be okay?"

She nodded, then shook her head. "I'm a little..." But she couldn't find the word.

"Discombobulated?"

The sudden chuckle surprised her. "Yeah. That."

"Want me to come inside, make sure it's safe?"

"No, no. I'm sure it's..." She cocked her head, focused on him again. "When did you get released?"

He shrugged. "They let me go. A technicality."

Let him go? He'd been convicted of accessory to murder. How could that have happened? "And Emmitt? Is he...?"

"He's still in."

Thank God. The last thing she needed was Emmitt back in her life. Or Barry, for that matter.

"How long have you been out?" she asked.

"Couple months. I got a good job developing apps for this..." He chuckled and ducked his head. "It doesn't matter. Suffice it to say, that part of my life is over." He took in her apartment, the little dinette set beside the tiny kitchen, the loveseat that faced the TV she'd bought used for fifty bucks, the twin bed, unmade, pushed against the far wall. "And what about you?"

"I work, I go to school, I work some more."

"Nursing?"

"You remember."

"You're hard to forget, Harper."

She ignored the remark, not sure what to make of it. "I'm taking general ed classes until I figure out what I want to do."

"You don't want to be an RN?"

"With a felony? I'm lucky I got hired as a nurse's assistant." She smiled, yawned. "I'm sorry. It's been a long day. I owe you so much more than a thank-you, but that's all I have to offer."

He took her hand in both of his. They were warm and clammy. "Please be careful. You can't be walking down alleys by yourself at night. It's not safe."

The memory of that man... How long had he been following her? What would he have done if Barry hadn't been there? "I know. You're right. Next time, I'll stick to the main roads and go in the front."

He tilted his head to the side. "No car?"

"I'm saving for one."

"You need—"

"I appreciate your concern, Barry. Truly. I'll manage." She showed him her pepper spray. "See, I had it well in hand."

He didn't even crack a smile. "If you ever need anything..." He reached in his pocket and pulled out a business card. It was crisp, professional. So was he. The long hair he'd worn before had been cut to a respectable length. He wore crisp trousers and a long-sleeved golf shirt, tucked in. He looked like the young professional he'd been before he fell in with Emmitt. Nobody would ever guess Barry was an ex-con.

Good looks were about as trustworthy as a heroin junkie.

She pictured Derrick, his smile. No. He was a good guy with a good job. He treated her like gold.

She took Barry's business card, though she knew she'd never call. He'd saved her tonight, no doubt. But Barry was in her past, and she didn't want to bring anything from that life into this one.

CHAPTER THREE

Harper was slipping on the oversize T-shirt she slept in when her phone rang. She snatched it up and crawled into bed. "Hey."

"You're home safe?" Derrick's voice brought tears she hadn't expected.

"I'm home."

A beat passed, then, "Did something happen?"

Was she really that easy to read over the phone and across the miles? "Sort of. When I was walking home..." She told him the story. Though he was silent on the other end, tension radiated through the phone. She finished with, "I'm safe now."

A moment passed. She held her breath, waited for his reaction.

Finally, he said, "That's it. I can't..." A deep breath. "I can't do this anymore. Harper, I care for you. I feel like you and me... We've both messed up, and we're not perfect, but I care about you more than you know. I need you. I feel like, with you on my side, I can do anything, conquer anything. You're my...my lifeline. My salvation." His words were pleading. "I'm terrified something is going to happen to you. And tonight—"

"I was fine. Tonight was an aberration." But even as she said the words, fear tingled up the back of her neck. Was Derrick the answer?

When he spoke again, his words were measured. Angry. "Tonight proves it. You're not safe there. It's time for you to come to Maryland."

The tone of his words, the vehemence behind them. Was she imagining the anger?

Of course she was. Derrick only wanted what was best for her. And as if to prove it, he blew out a long breath. "I'm sorry. I don't have any right to tell you what to do. But Gramps needs somebody to take care of him." Derrick's voice was back to its kind and considerate tone. "I don't think he's been taking his meds consistently. And I can't put off hiring a nurse any longer. I trust you. I want you taking care of him."

Derrick had told her all about his grandfather, certain she'd love him. But what about Derrick, could she love him? "I'm just not—"

"Not for me. Don't move here for me." Though she couldn't see him, she could imagine him pacing, running his fingers over his short hair. "I promise, I won't ask anything of you. I don't expect anything of you. Just... I need to know you're safe. Move here for you. To be safe. To keep my grandfather safe. To start fresh."

To start fresh. The words reverberated like a promise.

Estelle was right. Derrick was right. She'd never be able to start over if she stayed in this city filled with memories. She needed a fresh start. Derrick's job offer was the perfect solution.

"Harper...?"

"Yes."

"Yes, as in—?"

"As soon as I finish my exams and give my notice, I'll move to Maryland."

Harper couldn't believe she'd actually done it. She'd sold most of her belongings and collected her security deposit. Then, she'd driven all the way across the country in a beat-up VW Jetta, praying as the car coughed and sputtered into a gas station in southern Utah, as the fan belt broke in Kansas, and when she needed a tire change during rush hour outside of Indianapolis, Indiana.

But she'd made it. And here she was.

Yes, she still missed Estelle. The woman had been right. A week after Harper told her she was moving, Estelle died in her sleep. Her last words, spoken earlier that very evening, had resonated with Harper ever since. "You've got a family who loves you, hon. But no matter what they say or do, you've got a God who loves you more, and always has."

She'd purchased a Bible the next day, and she'd been reading it ever since. It had become a good way to kill the long hours alone in motel rooms on her cross-country trek. She'd even bought a journal, which was mostly filled with questions about what she was reading.

Now here she was, driving a Cadillac, pulling up to the

house that had become her home. The house was enormous, bigger than the four-bedroom she'd grown up in back in Kansas. The neighboring houses—all equally grand and pretty—weren't so close the neighbors could spy for evening entertainment. And the trees! After the barren sand of Las Vegas, the vegetation felt as lush as a jungle.

She marveled at her good fortune. How had she landed here, in this amazing place? Nobody deserved it less.

Maybe God really did love her.

"What's the holdup, girl?"

She turned to her passenger and smiled. "Just admiring the view."

Red Burns mashed the button to open the garage door, and Harper glided the luxurious car into place beside her little Jetta. As soon as she shifted into Park, Red opened his door.

"If you'll just be patient," she said, "I'll come around."

"Don't need your help."

He shifted to get out of the car while she rushed to help. He waved her off and stood on his own. He beamed at her as if he'd finished a marathon. "Told you I had it."

"The physical therapy's helping after all."

He harrumphed, as she'd known he would. He'd balked at the suggestion, but she and Derrick had insisted he at least give therapy a try. He was moving better and with less pain since he'd begun the twice-weekly sessions, but he'd never admit it.

She knew better than to press the point.

Inside, she settled him in a chair in the eat-in kitchen. "I have that leftover fettuccini we ordered yesterday, or I could make you a—"

"Pasta will work," he said.

She took out the creamy dish and spooned the leftovers into a pan. While it warmed, she fetched Red a bottle of yellow

Gatorade, his favorite, unscrewed the top, and poured it into his glass. "Here you go."

He sipped the liquid, then leveled his blue-gray eyes on her. "Where's that grandson of mine?"

She pasted on a smile. "Derrick's been working hard lately." Working *and playing* hard, she knew. She cared for Derrick, but she wasn't impressed by how little time he made for his grandfather, his only living relative. At first, he'd driven up to Red's from his Baltimore condo every weekend to visit. But lately, things had changed. He'd quit visiting as often, and when he did, he seemed stressed. Worried.

Whatever it was, Harper saw no reason for him to neglect his grandfather. Maybe Derrick had only brought her here so he wouldn't feel as guilty about it.

Not that Harper had the right to judge. She hadn't spoken to her own parents in years. Hadn't spoken to her brothers, either. Sure, Dad had told her not to call, but she would someday. When things here were settled, when she knew the job would last. When she could handle their rejection.

"Works all the time, that boy," Red said.

She spooned helpings onto two plates and carried them to the table. "Maybe I should learn to cook fettuccini Alfredo."

Red smirked. "Stick to what you're good at."

She set the plates down and opened the silverware drawer. "You saying I'm a bad cook?"

"The worst." His lips twitched with the insult. "But you're the best nurse."

She set forks on the table and plopped into her chair. "That's because I have the best patient."

"Humph. Don't know about that." He held out his hand, and she took it. She'd gotten accustomed to the grace he said before every meal. He uttered a quick prayer, let go of her hand, and dug into his meal, flashing his bald head at her as he focused on getting the pasta to his mouth. Red had a point about her cooking. She'd tried, truly she had, but she hated it. Apparently it hated her, too. Anything beyond grilled cheese sandwiches and canned soup seemed to revolt at her incapable hands.

She was no cook. But caring for Red? That came as naturally as breathing. Maybe because she loved the old man so.

Harper felt so fortunate to be working for him, living in this lovely house. The thought from earlier returned—maybe God really did love her.

Could it be true? Estelle had been so sure.

And now Red. And the pastor at the church Red attended.

"What you thinking on, girl?"

"The pastor's message yesterday."

He wiped his mouth, nodding. "Good message. Got a question?"

She didn't have a question, not really. She just wasn't sure about it. "You believe all that? That we have to forgive because God forgave us first?"

"Course I do. Which part bothers you? The forgiving or the being forgiven?"

"Second part, I guess," she said. Because forgiveness for *all* her sins? All of them? Seemed too good to be true. When things seemed too good to be true, they usually were. Like this move to Maryland. Sure, the job was perfect, better than she'd ever imagined. But Derrick? She was starting to wonder if it was time to end the relationship. Not that he was doing anything wrong, certainly nothing she could put her finger on. He just seemed... tetchy lately. Short-tempered. When she'd asked about it, he acted as if she were the one with the problem.

More than that, she'd been very clear before she moved that she wasn't going to sleep with him until she was sure they would stay together, until she was sure he could be trusted. She'd also been clear that the move to Maryland had been about taking care of Red, not about making promises to Derrick. He'd agreed at the time.

But lately, he'd been pushing her. Not just to sleep with him, but also to make promises she wasn't ready to make. Promises about her love and devotion. Promises about their future. Between his making fewer trips to Red's house and the way he'd pushed her when he did come, she didn't know what to think.

Maybe she was too cautious. Maybe she'd been burned too often. And maybe she needed, like Derrick had told her over and over, to trust him. He hadn't hurt her, hadn't lied to her. He'd gotten her this great job.

Frustration pulled like a too-tight jacket. She needed to be sure about Derrick, sooner rather than later. But so much of the time they spent together, Red was with them. How could their relationship progress if they didn't spend more time alone with one another? How could she learn to trust him when he was absent so often?

Because she wasn't sure about him, she wouldn't sleep with him, and she wouldn't make those promises. Not yet.

Which brought her back to the pastor's message the day before.

"And the first part," she said. "The part about how, if we forgive others, we don't let them off the hook."

"We let ourselves off the hook," Red said. "That's the part that stuck with me, too. We forgive for our sake, not anybody else's."

"Right." Harper needed to forgive Emmitt and Barry for what they'd done, for the crime that had landed all three of them in prison. Maybe if she could forgive them, she could trust Derrick. Maybe that's what was holding her back.

"The second part's more important." Red set down his fork

and stared at her across the table. "The part about how God forgives all our sins. You get that part?"

She shrugged. "Seems too good to be true."

"That's God for you," he said. "Good, glorious, beautiful, perfect, and full of love for us."

"Why, though, when people are so messed up?"

One eyebrow lifted. "People, in general?" he asked. "Or someone in particular?"

"Fine. Why would He forgive me? You know my past. Why would God forgive what I've done?"

Red's smile lit his face. "He created you, didn't He? He knows all your frailties. His love is big enough for all your junk."

"I don't get it."

Red patted her hand. "You will. I believe soon, you will."

CHAPTER FIVE

Harper was scrolling through the website of the local college Friday afternoon when the front door opened.

"Who's that?" Red asked, as if she could see through walls and around corners. Not that there were many options. Most folks knocked.

She stood from her seat on the sofa. "I'll go check." She was halfway across the living room when Derrick stepped into the room. He saw her, and his face split into a huge smile.

"Surprise."

"What are you doing here?" She crossed the room, and he pulled her into a hug, then gave her a quick kiss.

"I took the afternoon off."

Red put down the footrest on his recliner and pushed himself to standing. "Great to see you, son."

The men hugged briefly. Then Red settled back in his seat, and Derrick sat on the sofa. "How you feeling, Gramps?"

"Couldn't be better," he said. "Got the best care a man could ask for."

Both men looked at her, and warmth rushed to her cheeks. "Can I get you anything? Iced tea?"

"Half-sugar tea, you mean?" Derrick asked.

"If I'd known you were coming," she said, "I'd have left the sugar out."

"Don't know why she needs so much," Red said. "She's sweet enough without it."

She ignored the remark and focused on Derrick. "I have Coke."

"Water's fine," he said.

"You hungry?"

"Depends. Did you cook?"

She forced a stern look. "Ha-ha."

He chuckled. "Not hungry. And I really can take care of myself."

She ignored him and went to the kitchen to get him a glass of water. When she returned, Red and Derrick were deep in conversation. She paused at the threshold, tuned out their words, and focused on the men.

They didn't look a bit alike. Derrick's features were more like Red's late wife's. Her photos were all over the house, and Harper could see the resemblance in the hazel eyes. She imagined when Red was a young man, he must have been built like Derrick was now. Not quite six feet, trim, healthy. Derrick had a full head of dark brown hair that he wore combed away from his face, which accentuated his widow's peak—or maybe it was a receding hairline. He played golf and tennis and worked out regularly, and he looked so professional and impressive in his dark suit. On weekends, he looked just as good in khakis and golf shirts. His wire-rim glasses only added to his charm.

Right now, he was leaning toward Red, nodding as the old man told a story, laughing with him. She loved how Red lit up when Derrick visited.

Too bad Derrick didn't come more often. So why was he here now?

He looked up and caught her eye. "Don't just stand there. Join us."

She stepped into the living room and handed him the ice water. "I didn't want to interrupt."

He focused on Red again. "I told you she was great, didn't I?"

"Gotta hand it to you," Red said. "You picked a winner."

She shook her head at their teasing.

Derrick focused on Red. "You think you can live without her for a couple of days?"

Based on Red's surprised expression, he didn't know what Derrick was talking about any more than she did.

"What's going on?" she asked.

"One of my clients has a summer house on Rehoboth Beach, and they're having a party tomorrow. They want us to come for the weekend."

A weekend on the beach. That sounded marvelous. And a weekend away, with Derrick? Maybe this would be a good opportunity to find out what was going on with him. See if the two of them could reconnect. They'd had a closer relationship when she'd lived in Vegas than they did now.

But what about Red?

She looked at the old man, then focused on Derrick. "I'm not sure I should leave him."

"Bah," Red said. "I survived without you for more'n eighty years." He picked up the photograph of his late wife and stared at it. "I got my memories of Bebe here to keep me company. I can manage two days."

"Yeah, but your medication, and—"

"Girl, I'm not a child. I can fend for myself for two days. You kids go, have a good time."

Derrick's smile only widened. "How would it make him feel if you refused now?"

What did Derrick expect from her? Promises she couldn't make? Commitments she wasn't ready for? Or a physical relationship she'd sworn she wouldn't give in to. She wiped sweaty hands on her jeans and held Derrick's gaze. "And what would the"—she cleared her throat and cut her gaze to Red—"*arrangements* be?"

Derrick's smile faded. "They have seven bedrooms. If they don't have an extra place for me to sleep, I can stay at a hotel down the beach."

It was clear that hadn't been his intention. But he held her gaze, and that one eyebrow rose again. "Please?"

"Good Lord, girl," Red said. "I told you, I can fend for myself."

With Derrick's pleading and Red's cajoling, how could she refuse? A weekend at the beach sounded heavenly, and as long as Derrick was willing to keep his promise about giving her time, what was the downside?

She smiled at both of the men now staring at her. "When do we leave?"

"As soon as you're ready."

CHAPTER SIX

Harper pulled her smallest bag from the closet. She could do nothing about its shabbiness, the splitting seam or the rickety wheel. With a sigh, she turned to study her wardrobe.

She'd need a dress for the party. Knowing Derrick's friends, she'd need something at least a little dressy. She didn't have a lot of options, but she found a pretty skirt and a peasant top that seemed suitable for a party on the beach. Derrick had bought both for her shortly after she'd moved. She added a pair of strappy sandals to go with that outfit. After throwing her bathing suit and cover-up in the bag, she added a couple pairs of shorts and a pair of patterned capris, a few of her nicer T-shirts, and her ugliest pajamas—just in case she was tempted to break her own rules.

She freshened her makeup, gathered her toiletries, and added them to the suitcase.

When the suitcase was zipped—no easy task considering the shape it was in—she opened her bedroom door to find Red sitting on the chair she'd put at the top of the stairs, a place for him to rest after climbing to the second floor.

She froze. "Are you all right?"

"Course." He glanced toward the back staircase, at the bottom of which Derrick was probably pacing, waiting for her. He lowered his voice. "I've been thinking... Can I talk to you for a second?"

She backed into her bedroom, and Red stepped just far enough inside to close the door. He hadn't been in her room since the day he'd showed her to it when she moved there, but this was his house, and he was practically family. "What's up?"

He rubbed his bald head. "Got the feeling you weren't excited about this trip."

"It'll be fun."

He studied her a moment. "Something tells me it won't."

Hadn't he just urged her to go? "What's that mean?"

He stared past her, out the window to the sunshiny day beyond. Took a deep breath and blew it out. Then, he focused on her. "I love my grandson. But... I don't know. I'm afraid..." He half-smiled. "Maybe I just don't want you to go."

She stepped toward him. "I can stay. If it makes you nervous—"

"Nothing like that." He waved her words away. "Just... Don't let Derrick talk you into anything. I know how you kids are these days, and I'm not judging. I'm just saying, that boy of mine, he doesn't have the best..." He seemed to falter, then shrugged. "Morals, I guess. His father didn't, either. Good man, my son, but he made a lot of mistakes. Derrick has, too. He's a decent kid, and I know he cares about you. But don't you let him talk you into anything you don't want to do."

That this man she'd only known for a couple of months would haul himself up the stairs to say this to her... Her eyes tingled, and she stepped closer. She set her hand over his where he leaned on her bureau. "If Derrick's half the man you are, any woman would be lucky to have him."

The man's cheeks reddened. "Just saying, you don't owe

that boy nothing. He brought you out here for this job, but I hired you, I pay you, and I decide if you stay or go." His bushy eyebrows pushed up on his forehead. "You understand what I'm saying?"

"Thank you." She kissed his cheek and squeezed his hand. "I love you, too."

"Bah." His cheeks turned an even darker shade. He huffed out the door. The sweet, grouchy, beautiful old man. He'd meant every word, and so had she.

Harper had never been to the beach on the East Coast. Red's house wasn't far from Chesapeake Bay, but this was different.

While Derrick maneuvered his Mercedes toward the beach house that afternoon, cursing the traffic, Harper stared across the sand to the ocean beyond. The sky was blue, and the steel-gray water seemed to go on forever. The waves were high—higher than usual, Derrick said, thanks to a storm a few hundred miles south. It was predicted to head out to sea long before it reached the Delaware coast. Funny how the waters churned and battered the shore because of a storm she couldn't even see.

"Come on, buddy!" Derrick hammered the steering wheel when the car in front of them stopped for a yellow light. "At this rate, we'll never get there."

He was more keyed up than she'd ever seen him. He'd spent most of the bumper-to-bumper three-hour drive on the phone with clients. Because, apparently, stockbrokers didn't get to take time off, not even lazy Friday afternoons in July. When Derrick wasn't on the phone, he was yelling at other drivers.

She turned to him and smiled. "How can you be so

grouchy? Look around. It's beautiful!" Her voice hitched on that last word, excitement and joy bubbling up and over. When was the last time she'd had a vacation? Gone anywhere fun?

Derrick glared at her, but the expression only lasted a moment. Then his lips drew tightly across his teeth. "You're right. Sorry. We're just late."

"Late for what?"

"Russell told me to be there by dinnertime, and it's"—he glanced at the clock on the dash—"nearly six-thirty."

"I'm sure he'll understand."

His plastic smile faded to a scowl. "I'm sure you *don't* understand. Russell is my biggest client. Not only that, but he's recommended me to a lot of his associates, and if this weekend goes well, he'll recommend me to more. I think his friend will be there this weekend. Constantine. The guy's loaded and swears his lineage goes back to Aphrodite." He smiled at that. "Or so goes the story he likes to tell. I've been trying to get his business for a couple of years. If I can impress him..." The promise of riches lay at the end of that unfinished sentence. But Derrick didn't smile at the thought of it. No, his lips tightened at the corners, and he focused on the road as they inched along.

There was that stress again. That worry. What was going on with him?

There was something he hadn't told her, something that mattered. Maybe this weekend, she'd get to the bottom of it.

One thing was sure. She'd need to do her best to impress this Russell guy and his buddy, Constantine.

Who traced his lineage back to a goddess.

No pressure there.

The phrase *delusions of grandeur* passed through her mind, but she pushed it away. She had to be charming and pleasant, which would be a feat in itself, more so if she were silently judging everyone.

As if she had the right to judge another living soul.

Despite Derrick's dire predictions, they arrived at the house ten minutes later. She wasn't sure what she'd expected. Derrick had told her the house had seven bedrooms, so she'd assumed it would be palatial, would have land and tended grounds and plenty of parking. All her assumptions had been wrong, though. She stared up at a three-story structure with a screened-in porch on the bottom floor and balconies on the upper two. The house was so close to its neighbors, there was barely room for a car between them, much less a garage. All the houses had been packed onto this beach like crackers in a sleeve. But the ones behind this didn't have views of the ocean. This one did, and for that the owners must have paid more than she'd earn in a lifetime.

Derrick found a parking spot, popped the trunk, and climbed out of the car. She snatched her purse from the backseat and joined him, inhaling the salty, briny scent of the Atlantic.

Funny how different this was from the beaches on the West Coast. The people were different here, too. Not all perfectly sculpted as they'd seemed in California. Not all blond and beautiful. They were normal people, her kind of people, and they were everywhere. Walking along the sidewalks in bikinis and T-shirts and flip-flops. Sitting side-by-side or standing in groups on porches and balconies, sipping adult beverages and laughing, grilling burgers and hot dogs, enjoying a perfect Friday afternoon in the summertime. A small family clad in dripping suits and gritty sand wandered past. They looked sunburned, exhausted, each holding a snack. The scent of fried dough and cinnamon had her stomach growling.

She turned when the trunk slammed. Derrick smiled at her, eyebrows up, and lifted their suitcases. "You ready?"

Could she pull this off? Pretend to be a normal person, someone who belonged among Derrick's high-society friends?

At least, if nothing else, she could always escape to the beach.

"Let's go."

Even with a suitcase in each hand, Derrick outpaced her so that she had to practically run to keep up.

At the door, Derrick set the suitcases down and knocked.

A moment later, a man answered. He was slender and tall and looked to be in his early fifties, despite his nearly bald head. He had a strong chin, and though he wasn't physically imposing, he radiated power and confidence. He had piercing blue eyes that regarded Derrick with a look she couldn't discern before they focused on her.

He held out his hand. "Russell Caldworth. Harper, isn't it?"

She took it. "Pleasure to meet you."

"I've heard a lot about you."

She glanced at Derrick. "Good stuff, I hope."

"Every word." Russell turned to Derrick and shook his hand. "Great to see you again. Glad you made it. Traffic bad?"

"The worst."

Russell chuckled. "Friday at the beach. Apparently we weren't the only ones with this idea." He led the way through the living room. In the kitchen on the far side of the great room, a few women were chattering, slicing, stirring. Harper picked up the scent of garlic.

"My wife and some friends are fixing dinner. It'll be ready soon."

"Can I help?" Harper asked.

Derrick's laugh seemed forced. "Please, no. Don't let her cook."

Russell focused on her, eyebrows lifted. "Did you earn that remark?"

"Unfortunately, yes."

He smiled and continued through the living room. Beyond a wall of windows and sliding glass doors, Harper saw two men in the screened-in porch seated on wicker furniture, beer bottles in hand.

Russell climbed a staircase, and she and Derrick followed. Though the staircase went up another level, Russell stopped on the second floor, led them down a short hallway, and pushed open a door. "This'll be your room, Harper."

She stepped inside, barely glanced at the queen-size bed and, beyond it, an attached bath, then walked to the door that led to a balcony. She took in the beach and the gray waters of the Atlantic. "Wow."

Behind her, Russell said, "Derrick, are you staying here with her, or do you need another space?"

Harper tensed. She hoped Derrick would give the right answer.

"Uh," Derrick said. "Well, I was thinking—"

"Another space, then." Russell's tone left no room for argument.

She blew out a breath and turned. The older man winked at her.

"There's a kids' room upstairs that should accommodate you. I'm sorry we don't have another like this to offer, but if I know you, you won't sleep much, anyway."

"That'll be great. I'll be happy"—Derrick seemed far from it when he cut his gaze to her—"as long as Harper's comfortable."

Russell nodded toward the door, and Derrick stepped back into the hallway. "We'll eat in about an hour," Russell told her over his shoulder. "We're really casual tonight, so what you're wearing is fine. Come down whenever you're ready." With that, he closed the door.

Harper turned again to the view, then opened the slider and stepped outside.

The evening was perfect. Laughter and chatter from the men below joined the sound of the surf like a lovely serenade. A warm breeze blew her hair into her face, and she pushed it behind her ears.

The sun was setting behind the house, casting shadows on the beach and the few folks who lingered there. One couple strolled hand-in-hand along the boardwalk that seemed to stretch forever in both directions.

The ocean was breathtaking. Waves crashed against the sand, then slid back out, just like they'd done for thousands of years. Just like they'd do for thousands more. The thought made her feel small and insignificant.

Estelle's final words reverberated in her mind. Red's words, too. That God loved her. That despite all evidence to the contrary, despite the pile of mistakes she'd made, the sins she'd committed, she had a God who loved her.

Loved *her*.

It was inconceivable.

Yet, look at all He'd done. Brought her to this job and, through Derrick, to this amazing place.

Harper looked toward the endless blue sky. If God was there, she wanted to know Him. She wanted to believe. She imagined walking the beach, asking all her questions to the God who'd created all of this. If only she'd remembered her journal.

Laughter drifted up from downstairs and snapped her out of her musings. Derrick would expect her to go down and mingle, so that's what she'd do, despite her desire to stay here, to soak in this view. She was at the beach to have fun but also to help Derrick impress Russell and his friends.

Back in her room, she opened her bag, grabbed her toiletries, and carried them to the attached bathroom. After she'd brushed her hair and applied some makeup, she surveyed her reflection. Before they'd left Red's house, she'd put on white capris with a teal sleeveless blouse that accentuated the blue of her eyes. Russell had said this outfit would do, so she wouldn't change. She was pretty, but she'd long since given up the belief that her looks were a blessing. Her looks had only led to trouble.

She'd trade all her beauty to get back those wasted years. But that deal wasn't on the table tonight and never would be.

Harper opened her bedroom door and listened. She heard women's voices, but no men's, which meant Derrick was either outside or still in his bedroom. Which meant she had to go downstairs and face a bunch of women she'd never met before, all by herself.

Which wasn't uncomfortable at all.

Right.

She stepped out of her room and closed the door behind her. Then she went down the stairs, resisting the urge to tiptoe.

The sound of women chattering mingled with the beeping of a timer, the humming of a vent fan.

At the bottom of the stairs, Harper peered beyond the long dining room table, which had been set to seat ten, to the screened-in porch, where Derrick was sitting on the arm of a chair. He held a brown beer bottle in one hand, a chip in the other. The other men held drinks, too, and talked. Russell was reclining, watching with those piercing eyes. She barely knew the older man, but after the way he'd handled Derrick upstairs, she liked him.

She debated for only a moment, then pasted on a smile and walked around the corner toward the kitchen.

The conversation came to an abrupt halt.

"You must be Harper." A fifty-something blonde with a short, relaxed haircut crossed the space, wearing an inviting smile. Over capris and a T-shirt, she wore an apron that read *I'm still hot. It just comes in flashes now.* She took both of Harper's hands in hers and squeezed. "It's such a pleasure to meet you. I'm Russell's wife, Betts."

With that wide smile and those joyful eyes, this woman seemed genuinely delighted. "Nice to meet you."

"I'm so sorry I didn't greet you at the door. I was in a critical moment with the bruschetta toast."

Another woman stepped beside Betts. Her hair was also blond, though the dye-job wasn't as professional, nor the haircut. "You know how finicky bruschetta toast can be."

Harper's chuckle surprised her. "I'm not even sure I know what bruschetta toast is."

Both women feigned gasps.

"We'll need to educate you!" Betts nodded toward the woman beside her. "This is my dear friend, Kitty Williams. She goes with Keith, who's outside."

Kitty shook Harper's hand. "Glad you could join us."

Harper nodded, focused on Betts again. "I appreciate the invitation."

Betts waved the thank-you off and stepped to the side. Harper focused on the other woman in the room, a thin, perfectly polished brunette with a plastic smile.

Betts said, "And this is Marjorie Slater."

Marjorie's smile tightened. She wore a black sleeveless turtleneck—which set off a long strand of pearls perfectly—over black slacks and black sandals that had two-inch heels. Even with the extra height, Marjorie didn't stand more than five-four, yet she still managed, somehow, to look down her nose at Harper. "Lovely to meet you, Harper... What's your last name?"

"Cloud."

Marjorie glanced at the others, then back at Harper. "What an unusual name. Where did it come from?"

Harper wasn't sure how to answer that and was saved when Betts interrupted. "It came from her father, I assume." She turned to Harper. "Unless it's an ex's name."

"No ex—"

"Of course she's not divorced," Marjorie snapped. "Nobody would *choose* to keep Cloud as a last name."

Kitty's laugh was forced, and she focused on Harper. "Don't mind her. She's had a rough day."

Marjorie sipped from the red liquid in her martini glass. "And not nearly enough alcohol."

Silence settled among the women until Betts sighed and returned to the counter where she'd been working. "Kitty, get Harper a drink, would you?"

"Sure!" She turned to Harper. "We have beer, wine, and Marjorie made up a pitcher of cosmopolitans." She cut her gaze to the brunette. "Which I'm sure she wouldn't mind sharing."

"No, thank you," Harper said. "Just water for me."

Kitty's eyebrows lifted.

Marjorie uttered a little *pfft*.

Betts said, "Kitty, get the girl a glass of water. She's had a long drive. Then, could you finish up with that salad?"

Kitty jumped to action. Betts was stirring some kind of cream sauce on the stove.

Marjorie leaned against the counter and sipped her cosmo. When their gazes met, the woman gave her a saccharin smile.

She'd known her five minutes, and clearly the woman hated her.

The kitchen had been remodeled with granite countertops

and had fresh paint on the cabinets, but it was no designer space. Just a normal kitchen to fix normal meals, which matched the kind woman currently preparing their dinner.

Dishes and pots and pans and various food items covered the counters. "Can I do anything to help?"

Betts turned to her with another big smile—the woman seemed as happy as anyone Harper had ever known—and nodded to a cookie sheet where slices of toast covered with some sort of tomato mixture were lined like soldiers. "You can transfer the bruschetta to a serving dish, if you don't mind."

"The serving dishes are where?"

Betts focused beyond Harper, and Harper turned to see Marjorie glaring at her back.

Betts said to Marjorie, "Grab her that blue dish from the cabinet, would you?"

Marjorie slid a pretty blue platter from the glass-fronted cabinet, handed it to Harper, and then settled back against the counter.

Harper pulled a spatula from a jar of utensils on the counter and shifted the little pieces of toast to the plate.

Kitty snatched one and took a bite. "Seriously, you should try it."

Betts said, "Go ahead."

Harper took one and bit into it. She tasted toast, tomatoes, garlic, basil, olive oil, and a sprinkling of some sort of white cheese. "This is delicious."

When she was halfway through her third and, sadly, last bite, Marjorie said, "So what do you do?"

Harper swallowed quickly, trying not to choke on her food. She sipped her water and met the woman's cold gaze. "I'm a private nurse. I care for Derrick's grandfather."

Marjorie's smirk seemed satisfied, though Harper had no idea why.

"A nurse!" Kitty sounded downright jubilant at the news. "I'm a doctor."

Harper faced her over the huge bowl of salad Kitty was tossing. "What's your specialty?"

"Pediatrics."

"You like your job?"

"Mostly, I love it. I only work part-time right now, so I can be home with my kids." She carried the salad to the dining room table around the corner. When she returned, she said, "But pediatrics is hard. Children aren't supposed to get sick."

Betts said, "It's so sad sometimes."

Harper turned to her. "You work there, too?"

"I'm just a volunteer at the hospital," Betts said. "I hold the babies and play with the kids."

"What a wonderful way to help," Harper said. "I bet you're universally loved."

Betts shrugged, and Kitty said, "She is. And you focus on geriatric patients?"

"I was working at a nursing home when Derrick and I met. I've always felt so comfortable with older folks. I can't imagine doing anything else."

"But it's sad, too," Kitty said. "In a nursing home, there's never a happy ending."

Harper shrugged. "I don't know. Death is a step in the natural order of things, isn't it? I lost a patient, a dear friend, right before I moved. She never talked about death, just about going home. I love that sentiment."

"If you know God," Betts said, "it's not just sentiment. It's truth."

Kitty's smile was indulgent before she turned back to Harper. "And Derrick's grandfather? Is he a good patient?"

Harper chuckled. "He's not always a *patient* patient, but he's a kind, sweet man. I've never had a better job."

Behind her, Marjorie *hmm'ed*. Harper made sure her smile was in place when she turned to face her. "And what do you do?"

"Nothing so *important* as what you do."

Harper was amazed at the woman's ability to make the word *important* sound like an insult.

Marjorie continued. "I work for a fashion designer in Manhattan."

"Oh. Sounds like a fun job."

"Fun." She sipped her drink. "Loads."

Betts poured a huge pot of pasta over a colander in the sink. "Get the guys, would you, Kitty? It's time to eat."

"Constantine isn't here yet." Marjorie's voice held more animation than it had yet. "Shouldn't we wait?"

Betts glanced at the clock. "It's seven-thirty. If he gets here, he gets here. I'm not waiting any longer."

Marjorie's tight lips told Harper what she thought of that.

Kitty passed the dining room table and opened the slider. "Soup's on."

The men walked into the house carrying their drinks and their conversation.

Derrick crossed to her side, took her hand, and leaned in. "Having fun?"

"Sure. They're nice." Her gaze cut to Marjorie, but Derrick didn't notice.

Harper turned to Betts, who was mixing cream sauce into pasta. "What can I do?"

Betts got her husband's attention. "Russell, make sure Harper meets everyone."

He nodded to his wife, then stood beside Harper. The two men she hadn't met were deep in conversation when Russell led her to them and interrupted. "Gentlemen, this is Harper Cloud."

Both men turned to her. One had longish brown hair, brown eyes, and dark skin. He was older and barely cracked a smile. "Keith Williams."

Kitty's husband. He couldn't be more different from the friendly woman Harper had met.

Russell said, "Keith's a police detective in Baltimore."

The word *police* had her stomach dropping, but only a little. She had nothing to fear from this man. She'd not so much as rolled a stop sign since she'd gotten out of prison. "Nice to meet you."

"You, too." His voice was gruff, and as soon as he'd spoken, his attention shifted elsewhere.

Russell turned to the other man. "And this is Marjorie's husband, Carter Slater."

Carter's gray eyes met her gaze with an intensity that made her want to step back. He took her hand in his, then covered it with his other hand. He moved closer, too close. "It's a great pleasure to meet you, Harper Cloud."

Adrenaline pumped into her veins as if he'd flipped a switch.

"Careful, Slater." Derrick's voice, right beside her, held a hint of warning beneath the forced chuckle. "She's spoken for."

Carter held her gaze a moment longer, then dropped her hands. "Just getting to know our new friend."

She flushed, and this time, she did step back. Marjorie glared at her from the far side of the room.

Great. They hadn't even eaten dinner yet, and she'd cemented her status as the enemy. Wouldn't this be fun?

The food was passed around the table. Fettuccini with a seafood cream sauce, angel-hair with a meat sauce, bruschetta, salad, and various side dishes. Harper loaded her plate, ravenous after the long day.

"Must be nice to be able to eat such rich and fattening foods." Marjorie, sitting on the other side of the table, eyed Harper's plate with disdain. "I can't imagine."

Harper snatched a couple of olives off the antipasto plate before she handed it to Carter. "It is, actually. I can eat whatever I want and never gain a pound."

At the look Marjorie gave her, she wondered if the woman knew how to do anything but glare.

Two seats down from Harper, Kitty laughed. "Every woman's dream!"

Betts added, "Men think our dream is to find Prince Charming. But no. It's calorie-free food."

Harper, Kitty, and Betts shared a laugh. Marjorie's lips tipped up in a feeble attempt before she helped herself to a bird-sized portion of angel-hair pasta.

Carter, who'd snatched the seat beside Harper, leaned in. "Whatever you're eating or not eating, it's working."

Harper shifted her attention to Derrick, sitting opposite her, hoping for some support. But he was focused on Russell.

Derrick asked, "How's business been? I read in the *Wall Street Journal* about that big merger—"

"Let's not talk shop tonight." Russell set the bowl of seafood pasta in the center of the table. He leaned over to Betts and kissed her on the cheek. "Looks delicious, babe."

She beamed at him. "I hope it tastes good."

They dug into their meals, and for a few moments, the only sounds were the scrape of silverware and the appreciative *mmms* of the diners.

"Wow." Keith lifted his fork, which was piled with pasta and tomato sauce. "This is awesome."

"Thank you," Betts said. "It's Russell's mother's recipe."

"Good cook, your mother?" Harper asked.

"Second best." Russell smiled at his wife, who blushed. They acted like newlyweds. Harper was about to ask how long they'd been married when a knock sounded at the door a moment before it opened.

A man stepped into the room. He was short, heavy-set, and had white hair and a white beard. He wore a sport coat over a polo shirt and slacks.

All the men stood. "Constantine," Russell said. "Glad you could make it."

Constantine surveyed the dinner table, and his eyes narrowed the tiniest bit. "I see you waited for me."

Russell just laughed. "Betts's house, Betts's rules."

Betts stood and produced a smile, though it was tight on the corners. "And Betts was hungry. Grab a seat."

Only when Constantine headed toward the table did Harper notice there was a woman behind him. She couldn't have been more than twenty-five. Blond, blue-eyed, slight, and beautiful.

Russell must've just noticed her, too. He crossed the room, and Betts followed. Russell held out his hand. "I'm Russell Caldworth. This is my wife, Betts. Welcome."

The woman glanced at Constantine before shaking Russell's hand. "Hi. I'm Jenny."

Russell introduced her to everyone, then introduced Constantine to Keith, Kitty, Derrick, and Harper, while Betts set another place at the table. The man barely nodded at any of them. He turned to the girl. "Come in and sit."

Jenny followed Constantine to the table.

And that's exactly what it was—obedience. In fact, except for Russell and Betts, everyone in the room seemed to fawn over Constantine. It wasn't shocking, really. The man emanated strength and power and authority. But did he wield those over this tiny, cowering woman?

Constantine sat at the end of the table, though Jenny hadn't reached her seat yet, the empty chair beside Harper. The rest of the men, Derrick included, waited until Jenny and Betts sat before they resumed their seats.

When the food had been passed to the new guests, Harper leaned toward Jenny. "I'm Harper. In case you missed it."

Her gaze flicked to Constantine, then to her plate. Then, for an instant, they focused on Harper. "Nice to meet you."

Constantine dominated the conversation, telling them about his latest business ventures, but Harper barely listened. She ate her dinner, tried to ignore Carter, who occasionally whispered comments in her ear that made her skin crawl, and focused on Jenny. Something about her didn't sit well. Harper had seen that vacant look in people's eyes before. Jenny reminded her of so many women she'd known back in Vegas, woman who'd latched on to some man thinking they'd hit the jackpot only to discover they themselves had been the prize. Women who'd gotten stuck with horrid men in horrid relationships and didn't have the courage to break free. Harper had seen that expression in the mirror. She knew it well.

Harper didn't know much about the world of finance and big business. But women being cowed and used? Unfortunately, that was a world she knew very well. She'd been there, and she'd met a lot of women who'd been there. If she'd come out of prison with nothing else, she'd come out with the determination to help women who were trapped in relationships with cruel men. She didn't know if Jenny was in that category, but she intended to find out and, if she could, to help.

Derrick caught her eye across the table. She could see the need there. The need for her to help him schmooze Constantine. She didn't think she'd be helping Derrick much tonight. Maybe if he knew what she did, he'd understand.

Something told her he wouldn't.

CHAPTER TEN

Constantine regaled them with stories like a king with his court. Harper couldn't deny the man was compelling. Marjorie even forgot to give Harper hate-filled glances when he was talking. Unfortunately, Carter didn't forget about Harper. Instead, when Constantine's stories alluded to the many women he'd known, Carter whispered comments under his breath that only Harper could hear, comments that had her hands clenching beneath the table. She said nothing in return, refusing to acknowledge his presence, though even if she could have pretended not to hear, his beer-and-garlic scented breath was impossible to ignore.

She glanced at Derrick a few times, hoping for some help, at least an encouraging smile, but Derrick, like Kitty, Keith, and Marjorie, had fallen under Constantine's spell.

Not Russell and Betts, though. They didn't interrupt him or try to steer the conversation elsewhere, but they shared the occasional lifted eyebrow or quiet laugh as though witnessing the scene as spectators, not participants.

Jenny barely glanced up from her plate.

Finally, when the serving dishes had been emptied of pasta, when the forks had been put down and Constantine had paused for a breath, Betts stood. "Anybody want a cup of coffee with dessert?"

When nobody but Harper took her up on that offer, Betts said, "Or another drink?"

Russell stood beside his wife, kissed her cheek, and said, "I'll manage the drinks. You get the pie."

"Who can possibly eat pie after such a heavy meal?" Marjorie spoke to the table but gave Harper a pointed look.

"I'd love some." Harper stood and began gathering dinner dishes.

Kitty helped, too. "Maybe if you moved more and drank less, Marjorie, you could eat dessert."

"Now, Kitty," Betts said, "I don't need anybody's help. Marjorie's our guest."

Kitty met Harper's gaze and rolled her eyes. For the first time since they'd sat for dinner, Harper felt a glimmer of amusement. When she reached for Jenny's plate, she smiled at her. "Want to join us?"

Jenny's gaze cut to Constantine. His nod was tiny, nearly imperceptible. Jenny pushed back her chair and took his plate.

They headed for the kitchen and started scraping dishes. Jenny went to the sink and ran the water.

"Oh, honey," Betts said. "I'll do the dishes if you'll just help clear the table."

Jenny's pale cheeks reddened just a bit. "I'll just wash the pots and pans, if you don't mind."

Betts regarded her with kind eyes, then snatched her apron off the counter. "Wear this so you don't get your pretty outfit dirty."

Jenny slid it on and settled in with sudsy water and a sponge.

Harper returned to the dining room to gather more dirty dishes.

"I can't imagine why you don't hire help for these gatherings." Constantine's remark was directed at Russell, who was carrying a few bottles of beer to the table. "I'm sure your wife would appreciate it."

Russell laughed. "You know Betts better than that." He looked at his wife, who was halfway to the kitchen with an empty platter in each hand. "I offered, believe me."

"My house, my rules." She winked at her husband and disappeared around the corner.

Harper snatched the remaining dirty dishes from the table.

"Her house?" Derrick took the offered beer, eyebrows lifted. "Did you give it to her?"

"Not even close, my friend," Russell said. "Unlike me, Betts came from wealth. This was their family's beach home when she was growing up. Her parents gave it to her when they relocated to Florida."

"Russell married up, to say the least." Constantine's words seemed laced with indulgence, superiority.

If Russell noticed, he didn't let on. "I married up in every conceivable way."

From the kitchen, Betts said, "And don't you forget it!" Then she rounded the corner and kissed his cheek. "And so did I." To everyone else, she said, "More water? Constantine, you need some Scotch?"

He nodded, and Russell headed toward the wet bar and poured the drink.

Harper took the remaining dishes to the kitchen. She'd never seen such a strong bond between a married couple as the one Russell and Betts shared. Harper's parents loved each other, but they'd never been quite so *in* love.

Though Betts had been focused on everyone at the table,

her focus had always, first, been on Russell. And he'd been the same way.

So unlike Derrick, who'd not only not sat beside her but who'd barely looked at her all night. Derrick had been too busy sucking up to Russell and Constantine to pay any attention to her. Did he have any idea how he looked to outsiders? How desperate he seemed?

Desperate.

That was the word, the only word to describe what had changed with him in the previous few weeks. Now that she thought about it, it was crystal clear. It was the reason he'd barely spared her a glance all night, apparently hadn't even noticed how Carter had come on to her. The realization had her stomach dropping for the second time that evening. Because desperate men couldn't be trusted.

She'd learned that the hard way.

"Would you see who wants pie?" Betts asked.

"Sure." Harper pushed her worries about Derrick aside and returned to the dining room.

When everyone who wanted a slice of Bett's apparently famous cherry pie had some—that was to say, everyone except Marjorie and Jenny, who was still in the kitchen—Harper poured herself a cup of decaf and took her seat. She'd offered to help Jenny, but the girl shooed her away. She seemed in no hurry to return to the dining room.

Carter leaned close and whispered in her ear. "What's this I hear?"

She'd had it with his whispered remarks. Whatever Derrick's issue was, it wasn't her problem. She didn't have to put up with these comments from Carter or anybody. She turned to face him, let her voice rise. "What did you hear, Carter?"

The chattering at the table stopped. She felt their gazes on her, but she didn't break eye contact with the jerk.

His face flushed, and his smile got tight at the corners. He glanced at Marjorie, and Harper followed the gaze. The woman was glaring at them both.

Harper didn't have to put up with that, either. She ignored her.

"What's this?" Derrick's eyes narrowed as if he'd just realized what was going on.

"I hear you two are sleeping in separate bedrooms." Carter said it with a hint of humor and an undertone of spite.

Marjorie said, "Oh, for the love of—"

"What about it?" Derrick's face flushed, and his gaze flicked to Constantine and back to Carter.

"Just thought it was curious."

Russell's hand clamped down on Carter's shoulder. "Doesn't seem like that's any of your business, my friend." He focused on Marjorie. "Are you two planning anything special for your anniversary? That's coming up, right?"

"Five glorious years in September." Her expression said her marriage had been anything but, and Harper's animosity toward the woman shifted to sympathy. Who could blame her with a husband like Carter? "We were considering Florence."

"Wonderful choice," Betts said.

Harper focused on Marjorie. "Have you been there before?"

The woman blinked, focused on her, seemed to forget to scowl. In fact, she looked wistful. "When I was a little girl, my father took me. I've always wanted to go back."

Harper was about to ask a follow-up question when Constantine cleared his throat. "Yes, Florence is lovely, all that art. Have you ever been to Mykonos?" And he launched into stories of Greece, which he called his homeland, though based on his accent, he'd been born and raised in New York.

Finally, dessert was finished, the dishes cleared, and Constantine seemed to run out of stories. He pushed back in his chair and stood. "Let's play cards, shall we?"

CHAPTER ELEVEN

Harper poured herself another cup of decaf and glanced at Derrick, who stood beside Constantine at the wet bar, pouring two glasses of Scotch.

Just what Derrick needed—to get a little drunker, suck up a little more.

This was not the man she'd met in Vegas.

She'd come on this weekend away because she'd wanted to get to know him better. So far, she didn't like what she saw.

Harper joined the rest of the ladies on the screened-in porch. After the cool of the air conditioning, the warm muggy air wrapped around her like a blanket. Hot coffee had been a bad idea.

A white wicker sofa and a couple of matching chairs were arranged to form a seating area. Betts, Kitty, and Marjorie were on the sofa. Jenny chose one of the chairs, so Harper settled into the other and stared at the surf beyond the boardwalk. "It's beautiful."

"It's my happy place," Betts said. "I have a lot of good memories in this house."

"And you're making a lot more," Kitty said. "Are you missing your kids tonight?"

Betts smiled. "A little, but they're having fun with my folks in Florida. They'll be back next week."

"How old are they?" Harper asked.

Harper learned about Betts and Russell's two teenagers, then about Kitty and Keith's three kids—all under four. Apparently, Marjorie and Carter didn't have any children, though whether by choice or not, she didn't know.

"Do you want children?" Betts asked Harper. "Assuming you find the right man." She laughed and added, "Not that Derrick isn't the right man. That's not what I meant."

Harper smiled. "I knew what you meant. Yeah, someday, I'd love to have kids. I never thought I'd want them, but you reach a certain age—"

"What are you," Marjorie asked, "twenty-one?"

If only she could be that young again. If only she could go back and make better choices and change the previous seven years. "I'm twenty-eight."

"Really?" Kitty said. "You're just two years younger than I am." She focused on Marjorie. "Take a good look, honey." She pointed back and forth between Harper and herself. "This is what kids'll do to you." She regarded Harper again and added, "Not that I ever looked like that."

Harper waved off the comment. "Don't be silly. You're beautiful."

Kitty looked at Betts and feigned a sympathetic tone. "So young to be losing her eyesight."

Betts bumped Kitty's shoulder. "You're the only person who thinks you're not beautiful."

"These pregnancy pounds—"

"Only add to it." Betts turned to Jenny. "And what about you? Do you want kids someday?"

The young woman shrugged and glanced inside. "Probably not."

"You don't want them," Betts said, "or you don't think you'll have them?"

"Constantine has children from his first wife. He doesn't want more."

Betts's smile faded. "But what do *you* want?"

Jenny swallowed, shrugged. "I don't know."

"How long have you two been together?" Kitty asked.

"A few years."

Betts's eyebrows disappeared behind her blond bangs. "Years? I had no idea."

Jenny looked toward the surf. "I prefer to stay at home when he travels. He's always so busy."

"Pfft!" Marjorie slammed her glass on the table. "He treats you like dirt."

Jenny's face paled, and she glanced through the screen toward the men inside. As if Constantine paid her any attention at all. The men had gathered around the smaller kitchen table and were in the middle of a game of poker.

"My dear friend." Betts reached across Kitty and patted Marjorie's leg. "I'm not sure you ought to be throwing stones." She pulled her hand away and focused on Jenny again. "I'd love to hear your story."

Marjorie said nothing, just studied Jenny.

The woman seemed to wilt under their gazes.

Harper cleared her throat and worked up her courage. Being candid was not her strong suit. "I've been there."

All the gazes turned to her.

"Dated a guy back in…" She swallowed. Decided not to share that much. "Before I met Derrick. He started out being so nice to me, treated me like gold—for the first few months. After that, I was window dressing. Brought along because I looked good on his arm."

Had she just complimented herself? How ridiculous she must look. But it was true, so she continued. "Looks are liars, let me tell you. I was a mess. After a while, you start believing you're equal to the way you're being treated. As if you're a reflection of everyone else's opinion of you. He treated me like dirt until I believed I was dirt."

Jenny leaned forward. That interest was enough to keep Harper talking.

"Then one day, I'd had enough. I broke up with him."

"What happened?" Jenny asked.

"It's taken me a long time to stop seeing dirt in the mirror." She reached across the space to Jenny and squeezed her hand, then let it go. "Dumping the guy was the first step. I wish I'd had some good friends before I did it. I ended up with another guy who treated me exactly the same, and the cycle started all over again."

"Not that it's any of my business," Marjorie asked, "but is that the reason for the separate bedrooms?"

The question surprised her, but not as much as the person who'd asked it. "That's exactly the reason. I don't trust men very easily. I doubt I'll ever trust a man again. Right now, I need to know I'm not some guy's hobby or decoration. A little something to brag about when people aren't impressed with his new car or new watch. I'm not just the dirt clinging to some man's shoes."

"Amen." Betts lifted her water glass in a sort of salute. "You're smart to wait, to make sure it's real."

"How will you know if he can be trusted?" Marjorie asked. "How can anybody ever know?"

If Harper had the answer to that, she'd have found Mr. Right long before—and skimmed over all those Mr. Wrongs. Clearly, Marjorie, too, had trusted the wrong man. She'd been married for five years to a man who'd flirt with another woman right under her nose. A man who'd rub her face in it.

Betts sighed. "Maybe I just got lucky."

"You did," Marjorie said.

"I did, too," Kitty said. "Keith's a good guy. He's never strayed. He's made some stupid decisions." A shadow crossed her face. "But I know he loves me and the kids."

Betts said, "He does. The rest of it, he'll get figured out."

Apparently Betts knew the story, whatever it was.

The women were quiet a moment as a few young men wandered down the boardwalk, laughing and ribbing each other. Their voices faded until only the sound of the surf and the muted noise of the men inside filled the silence.

An enjoyable moment, not just because of the beach and the women who surrounded her, but because she realized she didn't feel nervous. Didn't feel like somebody was watching her. Even at Red's house, she sometimes got that prickly feeling on her arms. That's how she knew she was crazy. What kind of stalker would follow her across the country?

None. Obviously.

But she felt safe tonight. Maybe the fear was wearing off. Maybe that's all it had ever been.

The man in the alley back in Vegas must have just seen her and followed. Bad luck on her part, nothing more.

"I think..." It was Jenny who spoke, and the rest of the women turned to her.

Harper leaned in, willed her to continue.

Jenny swallowed. "I think maybe I've trusted the wrong man."

Betts stood, crossed the small porch, and crouched beside Jenny's chair. "I've known Constantine since he and Russell were at school together. They've been friends for thirty years. Constantine is a great businessman. He used to be a good man. But the wealth, the success... He's changed. And not for the better." She patted the young woman's knee. "I don't say this to hurt you, Jenny, but to help, okay?"

"Okay."

"You say you've been with him for years?" At Jenny's nod, Betts continued. "We've seen him many times in the last few years. He's never without a woman. And he's never mentioned your name."

Jenny's expression didn't change except for the tears that filled her eyes. She opened her mouth, then closed it again.

"Where does your family live?" Harper asked.

"I'm from Missouri."

"Go home," Harper said. "That's what I did wrong. I was too proud to go home after I dumped loser number one. If I had..." If she had, everything would have been different.

Jenny nodded, tried a smile. "I could do that."

Could. The telltale word. "You need money?" Not that Harper had it to give, but she'd scrape it up if she had to. "For a plane ticket?"

But Jenny wiped her eyes, sat straighter. "I'm okay."

"Whatever you need," Betts said. "It's yours."

"Constantine gives me everything I need." She smiled at Betts. "I'll think about what you said."

She'd think about it, but she wouldn't leave. Because sometimes, the evil you shared a bed with was better than the great alone. Harper understood the lie. She'd lived it.

Marjorie stared at the surf. It seemed she'd allowed herself to believe the same thing. That the familiar trumped the unknown.

Neither of them understood. When you were alone, when you didn't trust anybody, then nobody could hurt you.

CHAPTER TWELVE

It was nearly midnight. With all the alcohol, Marjorie turned maudlin, Jenny got quieter, and Kitty cracked jokes that became stupider—and somehow funnier—by the minute. Betts, who'd hardly had a drink all night, observed the scene with patient indulgence, like a fond parent.

Harper bid them all good-night. Inside, she crossed the great room to the kitchen table, where the men were still engaged in their poker game. Constantine and Carter had piles of chips in front of them. Derrick looked to be nearly out. His scowl told Harper as much as the lack of chips did. She stopped beside his chair and bent to kiss his cheek. "I'm going to bed."

He barely glanced at her. "Fine. Good night."

She stepped back, surprised at his rudeness.

His expression shifted from irritated to apologetic. "I'm sorry. You okay?"

"She's fine." Carter's words were slurred and slushy. "More than fine."

Derrick glared at the man, started to push back in his seat. "You need to learn to keep your mouth shut."

Russell's hand clamped down on Derrick's shoulder, but he glared at Carter. "Maybe it's time for you to go to bed."

"No." Derrick scooted back to the table. "He's not going to bed until he gives me a chance to win my money back."

Harper stood another moment, then realized Derrick had forgotten she was there. Forgotten he'd been about to defend her, take up for her. Not that she wanted anyone to fight, but to see that he cared about her might have been nice. Right now, all he cared about was winning back his money.

Gambling. She'd never understood the allure of it. Money was hard to come by and too easy to lose. She'd seen a lot of people in Las Vegas who'd been destroyed because of gambling.

She headed for the stairs. The heat of someone's gaze warmed her. Maybe Derrick felt a twinge of remorse for his rudeness. But when she turned to look, it was Carter whose leer had followed her across the room.

She climbed the stairs quickly. Once she got to her bedroom, she closed the door and turned the lock. Then she tested it.

The door pulled open.

She tried again, but though the lock engaged, the door didn't close completely, rendering the lock useless.

Fear rose like flames, but she tamped it down. Nobody was out to get her. Carter wouldn't dare come into her room uninvited, not with his wife under the same roof. Not after Harper had shut him down at dinner.

She wouldn't let fear keep her from sleep. So the door didn't lock. So what? She was safe here.

She'd spent far too much of her life living in fear. Besides, nobody could hurt her. She'd learned in prison how to defend herself—or at least how to make enough noise to alert the guards.

She'd be fine.

Ten minutes later, she'd scrubbed off the makeup and pulled on the yellow pajamas she'd had since high school. They had tiny pink bunnies all over and were frayed at the hems. Happy to be alone after the long day, she slipped beneath the sheets, wishing she could open the patio door and listen to the surf. But the air conditioner was humming, and she didn't want to warm up her cool room.

She didn't know how long she'd slept when she woke. The house was quiet now, no murmurs from the party downstairs. She opened her eyes. What had woken her?

She heard a creak, saw through the darkness as the door inched open. She couldn't see who it was, but she had her suspicions.

Carter. The creep.

Harper flashed back to night after night of sleeping with one eye open. Most of her cellmates had been scary but not terribly dangerous. But she'd had one she hadn't trusted. Harper had learned to be ready.

She should have grabbed her pepper spray and her little keychain knife. Stupid. Hadn't she learned better?

She stayed still, clenched her hands into fists. Waited for him to get close enough. She'd hit him, hard, and then she'd scream. In prison, no guards would have cared. But in this house, she'd get everyone's attention.

The man inched across the hardwood floor to the far side of the bed, then pulled back the covers.

"Don't even think about it." Her words reverberated in the silence. The man froze.

"I thought you were sleeping."

"Derrick?"

A pause, then, "Who else would it be?" His words were barely a whisper.

She matched the volume. "I thought..." She sat up and faced

him where he stood on the far side of the bed. The moonlight beyond the gauzy curtains in front of the sliding door offered just enough to make out his silhouette.

"You thought what?"

She shook off the fear, unclenched her fists. "Nothing. What are you doing?"

He sat heavily on the bed and stared toward the glass. "Rough night. I just thought... I needed to be with you."

She shifted to face his back and rested her palm there. "Did something happen?"

"I lost. Big time."

She patted his shoulder. "That's not the end of the world, is it?"

His laugh was short and filled with bitterness. "You don't understand."

"Explain it to me, then."

He said nothing, just stared toward the sliders.

"It's okay," she said. "You can tell me about it tomorrow. Why don't you go on to bed, sleep it off?"

He shifted so that he was facing her, his bare feet on the bed with the rest of him. He leaned on one arm, pulled her against his chest with the other. "I need you, Harper." He leaned in and kissed her. He tasted like booze.

She knew what he *needed*, and it had nothing to do with her. Any warm female body could have satisfied that need. She rested her palms against his chest and pushed. "No. You're drunk, and I'm not interested."

He pulled her close again, nestled his face against her neck. Kissed the skin there. "Don't you understand? You're the only one who can save me."

She waited for some twinge of desire, but all she felt was annoyance. Maybe a little fear. She scooted away, tossed the covers back, and slipped out of the bed. "Save you from what?"

"From... from myself." He leaned toward her, held out his hand. "Please, let me hold you."

She flipped on the light.

They both blinked in the sudden brightness. Derrick seemed to shrink from it.

"This isn't going to happen tonight," she said.

"I'm not... We don't have to do anything. Just, can I please stay with you? I don't want to be alone."

Right. He'd just lie there and let her sleep? Even if he did manage to keep his hands to himself—which she highly doubted —she'd never be able to relax with him there.

But he looked so sad, so lost.

He needed her. She understood that need, that bone-deep desire to be held, to be loved. It wasn't sex he needed but affection. This man who'd lost both his parents, who had no siblings, whose only relative was an octogenarian grandfather.

Derrick felt alone. Lonely. He needed her.

She was being selfish.

"Please." His arm was still stretched toward her.

She started to reach for him, then let her arm drop while the words he'd uttered earlier came back. *You're the only one who can save me.* What did he need to be saved from, and why would he think she could do it?

She flashed back to those sweet counselors who'd visited the prison. They'd taught her that her biggest addiction wasn't substances, but people. Her need to love and be loved. She remembered the pattern they'd pointed out and how she'd spent years of her life spinning around a jagged triangle among the roles of rescuer, prosecutor, and victim. Right now, Derrick was playing the victim and asking her to play the rescuer.

Tomorrow, after she'd rescued him, she'd slide into prosecutor mode, and he'd stay right there as the victim. Only then he'd consider himself her victim, because she'd be angry.

And maybe none of that was on his mind right now. Maybe all he wanted was what all the men she'd known since she left home had wanted from her. It might be as simple as that. Well, that was an ugly, potholed road she'd traveled before. She knew exactly where it led.

But she saw something else in Derrick.

Something darker. Something... there was that word again. Desperate.

He said, "Please come back to bed."

"You need to go."

He let his arm drop to the mattress, turned his back to her, and stood. When he faced her again, his expression had shifted. His mouth was tight and angry, his eyes blazing. "You're serious? I can't stay?"

"You're not yourself. I don't know what happened or why, but if we ever do"—she waved toward the bed—"that, it'll be when you're acting like the man I met in Vegas. Not when you're behaving like this."

His eyes narrowed. "I had a difficult night. And you didn't help. You barely paid any attention to Constantine, even though I told you how important it was that I impress him."

"He's a blowhard who treats his girlfriend like dirt. I'm not about to suck up to a man like that. Apparently, that's your job."

"Yeah, it is my job." His whisper became vehement. "To ingratiate myself with wealthy people so they'll invest with me. That's what I do."

"Doesn't your work stand on its own?"

"Men like Constantine need to be respected."

"Brown-nosed, you mean. Why would you want to work with someone like that?"

"You have any idea what his account would be worth?"

"Money isn't everything. Not if it makes you behave like this."

His expression hardened into something she'd never seen on his features before. He moved toward her.

She took a step back and clenched her fists for the second time in ten minutes.

He froze. Blinked twice. His shoulders sagged, and he sat on the bed. "I'm sorry. You're right. I'm not myself."

She released her breath. After a moment, she sat beside him. "Go. Sleep. Things will be better tomorrow."

He said nothing as he stood and walked toward the door. He opened it, turned to face her, started to say something. Then, he clamped his lips shut, stepped out, and closed the door softly behind him.

Harper collapsed onto her pillow and thought about the man she'd just witnessed. If you examined anything long enough, you'd see all its facets. And its flaws.

CHAPTER THIRTEEN

The next morning, Harper slid the curtains back to discover clouds had moved in. She checked the weather on her cell. Apparently, the storm Derrick had assured her was supposed to move offshore had changed its course. So much for the day at the beach.

She dressed quickly in shorts and a T-shirt and tiptoed down the stairs. The house was quiet except for some gentle sounds coming from the kitchen. Maybe she could get in a walk on the sand before the rain started, but it would be rude to leave without at least saying good-morning. She headed toward the voices and found Russell and Betts at the table enjoying a cup of coffee. Russell was reading the *Wall Street Journal*, and Betts had a Bible open in front of her. She looked up. "How'd you sleep?"

Of course Betts would be sweet, even before eight a.m. Harper figured she'd better not tell them about her middle-of-the-night visitor. "Very well, thanks."

Russell set the paper down and pushed back in his chair. "Can I get you some coffee?"

"No, thanks."

He settled again. "If you change your mind"—he pointed to the pot and the cups beside it—"help yourself."

"I thought I'd take a walk before the rain sets in."

Betts's gaze shifted to the wall of glass on the far side of the room. "It's not the weather we'd hoped for. You need anything before you go?"

"Nope. Just... should I go out the front?"

Russell said, "The porch door's unlocked."

She thanked them and left. The air was cooler than it had been the night before but thick with moisture and the scent of rain. She crossed the boardwalk and headed for the water. She hadn't bothered with shoes. Beaches were for bare feet. Once she hit the damp sand, she turned south. Despite the clouds, the morning was beautiful. The gunmetal-gray water, the slate-colored clouds. It wasn't idyllic, but it stirred her. Storms always did that. Reminded her of the thunderstorms that used to roll across the prairie when she was a little girl. She'd look out her window and gaze at the lightning, then count until the boom of thunder hit. She'd eagerly watch the news for reports of tornados, even after watching *The Wizard of Oz.* When she was a kid, Harper'd secretly wanted to be in a tornado, to experience what it would be like to have the wind lift her from her feet, to throw her off balance.

She hadn't been afraid of storms. No, she'd loved them. The interruption of normal life. The drama.

What a foolish child she'd been. Today, she knew what real storms were. She knew what it was like to have life lift you off your feet and smash you into the wall. She knew what it was like to look around and realize you had no idea how you got where you were, and you had no way out.

Oz had lost its allure.

The wind shifted. The hair on her arms stood, though not from a chill. She resisted the urge to look behind her, to study the dunes and peer between the shingled houses that lined the beach. Because, of course, nobody was watching her. Of course, she was safe here.

The energy of the storm—that's what had caused her nerves to fire like that, the hair to stand on end.

Even if she'd had a stalker back in Vegas, he wouldn't have followed her to the East Coast. Even if he'd wanted to, how would he have known where she was? Besides, there were plenty of women in Vegas. Why would anybody bother to trail her across the country?

She was safe.

The words became the beat she walked to as she continued down the shore. She repeated them until she almost believed them.

A drop of water plopped on her hand. She looked at it, then at the surf crashing just a few yards away. Ocean water, not rain. But a second plop landed on her bare shoulder. A third on her nose.

She turned back toward Russell and Betts's house. The more raindrops that landed, the faster she walked until she was running on the packed sand. The house came into view just as the deluge began. She sprinted the last fifty yards, but it was no use. By the time she reached the door to the screened-in porch, she was soaked.

Betts was waiting for her inside, a beach towel slung over her arm. "I was worried."

She took the towel and dried off, shivering. "Wow, it got cold fast."

Russell stepped onto the porch beside his wife. "The water in the atmosphere is a lot colder than it is down here."

Suddenly, he reminded her of her father. The newspaper, the coffee, the weird facts added at just the right moment. She wanted to tell Russell that, tell him and Betts both how much she liked them, but it would sound silly and corny, so she settled for a huge smile. "I'll take that coffee now."

"I bet you will." His chuckle followed her as she headed inside.

"I'm just going to run upstairs and change, and I'll be right back."

Harper took a quick shower, brushed out her wet hair, and added a little makeup. By the time she returned to the kitchen, Russell had disappeared, and Kitty and Betts were at the table.

She headed toward the coffee and poured herself a cup. "What's going on?"

"We're cooking up a plan," Kitty said, "since the beach is out."

Harper added sugar and cream, then looked beyond the glass to the darkness that had settled outside. "What were you thinking?"

"The outlet mall!" Kitty seemed giddy at the prospect.

Harper tried to match her enthusiasm, but the thought of spending all day in and out of shops didn't appeal at all. Even if she had money to spend, which she didn't, she hated shopping.

Betts shook her head at her friend's glee, then focused on Harper. "Does that sound like fun, or do you have another idea?"

"Shopping is fine." She slipped into a chair at the table.

"We'll have a nice lunch out," Betts said, "my treat. That'll break up the day a little."

"Will the guys go with us?" Harper asked.

"Geez, I hope not," Kitty said. "Shopping with Keith is like dragging around a two-hundred-pound bag of sand all day long. Grouchy sand."

Harper giggled. "Derrick likes to shop, but if the rest of the guys aren't going, he probably won't either."

Betts said, "Considering how late they stayed up last night, I think most of them will sleep the day away."

"Did Russell stay up?" Harper asked. "Because he was awake early."

"Until about twelve-thirty. He'll wake up at six, no matter what time he goes to bed. We're alike in that way."

"You two are alike in a million ways," Kitty said. "Was it always like that, or did you grow more alike as the years went by?"

Betts seemed to consider the question. "I think... Hmm. We're alike in some ways. Our sleeping habits, for one thing. We both love to entertain. Neither of us likes to watch TV very much. We're both pretty high-energy. I guess we've grown more alike. But we didn't start that way. Our relationship was built on some pretty sandy soil when we first got married."

Harper leaned forward. "That's hard to believe, seeing you now. What changed?"

Betts shrugged, smiled. "We met Jesus."

"Oh." Harper hadn't expected that.

Kitty sighed. "Now you've done it." But her words were amused. "You've opened the door, and Betts never ceases to go through that particular door."

Betts just laughed. "She asked."

"I did." Harper kept her focus on Betts. "We went to church when I was a kid. It didn't seem to make much difference in our lives. I've been going lately with the man I take care of."

"Going to church and walking with Jesus are two very different things," Betts said. "Nothing against church, of course. We go faithfully when we're home. But going to church for a lot of people is about looking good on the outside. Walking with Jesus is about getting good from the inside out. It's about giving God access to your whole heart."

Her whole heart? Why would God want that? The thought

of Him seeing everything in her heart made her shudder. But Betts seemed so peaceful. "And that helped your marriage?"

Betts's nod was emphatic. "As we both sought to be closer to God, we couldn't help but get closer to each other."

"Seems simplistic," Kitty said. "No offense."

"Like a lot of things in life," Betts said, "walking with God is simple, but it's not easy." She sipped her coffee and stood. "You ladies want some breakfast?"

"Not if we're going out to lunch," Kitty said. "Because I know you'll serve a yummy dinner at the party."

"Mostly appetizers tonight," Betts said. "I'm having the party catered so I won't have to cook all day."

Harper's stomach growled at the mention of breakfast. "I don't want you to have to cook for me. Maybe just some toast?"

A few minutes later while Betts and Kitty planned their shopping excursion, Harper nibbled her toast and thought about what Betts had said.

Good from the inside out.

Red's words had been different, but the sentiment was similar to what he'd been telling her. That Jesus could forgive her sins. He *wanted* to forgive her. He *wanted* to wash her ugliness away.

Could it be true? Could Harper really be free of her past?

Russell came into the kitchen and kissed his wife on the cheek before settling into a chair. They shared a smile. Then, he picked up the newspaper, and Betts went back to her conversation.

The love between the two of them, the love that seemed to glow all around them, couldn't be denied. Did God have something to do with that?

Was God the key? With Him, would it really be possible for Harper to know that sort of love?

CHAPTER FOURTEEN

Shopping was more fun than she'd thought it would be, thanks to the company. Kitty not only oohed and aahed over everything, but she cracked jokes and kept them laughing from the moment they left the house. Jenny had joined them. She'd barely spoken in the morning, but as the day went on, she came out of her shell. Turned out, she had a flair for fashion, and she and Marjorie bonded over that. Harper'd planned to just browse, but Jenny convinced her to try on clothes. In one store, she and Marjorie dressed her up and accessorized her like a mannequin. They had a great time doing it. Harper pretended to enjoy it until she found she actually did.

She hadn't had real female friends since high school. She'd forgotten how fun they could be.

When they got back to the house that afternoon, the guys were sitting on the porch watching the rain outside, already sipping from bottles of beer.

"Constantine's holding court again." Marjorie dropped her purchases on the floor by the stairs.

The woman had done a complete turnabout in her opinion of Constantine. Harper followed her gaze and looked again.

Sure enough, Keith, Carter, and Derrick were nodding as Constantine spoke.

Russell was staring at the surf, sipping from a glass of what looked like water.

"Constantine's got charisma." Betts filled the coffee carafe with water. "Always has."

Jenny's *pfft* had them all looking at her.

She realized all eyes were on her and reddened. "What?" When nobody spoke, she said, "He can be charming. When people are watching."

Betts set the carafe in the coffee maker and focused on Jenny. "And when people aren't watching?"

Jenny shrugged. "It's nothing."

But it wasn't nothing. After they filled their coffee cups, Harper pulled out a kitchen chair and nodded to it. Jenny slid in, and Harper sat beside her and rested her hand over Jenny's. "Does he ever hurt you?"

"No. Not like that. Just... He can be cruel."

Betts took the chair on Jenny's other side. "Charming, charismatic, but when Constantine doesn't get what he wants, he's mean. He was like that in college. I never kowtowed to him, and he didn't like it. He made some cruel remarks about me. Some cutting remarks *to* me. Honestly, I didn't think his friendship with Russell would survive it."

"It did, though," Kitty said. "How come? Russell doesn't seem like the type of guy who'd put up with that."

"He didn't. He told Constantine to knock it off or they were through. Impervious though he seems, Connie needs Russell. Russell keeps him grounded. Years ago, after Connie made his first few millions, he came to our house all braggadocios. Russell wasn't impressed and told him so. And Connie... I think he needed to hear it. I think that's why he came."

Jenny's gaze hadn't wavered from Betts's face. "That's my

problem. That's why he doesn't take me seriously or treat me with respect. I always... how'd you put it? I kowtow to him. I cower. I never stand up for myself. I never argue with him. I never call him out when he lies to me or treats me badly. I just put up with it."

Harper could relate. She'd allowed herself to be treated like property. Like decoration. Shame inched its way into her heart, but she forced it out. She wasn't that woman anymore.

She never would be again.

"And as long as you put up with it," Betts said, "he'll continue to treat you like he does."

The doorbell rang, and Betts left to answer it. A moment later, women in chef's coats carried platters and trays into the kitchen. Betts followed. "You girls might want to go into the living room. It's about to get busy in here."

Kitty and Marjorie headed upstairs to get ready for the party. Betts stayed in the kitchen with the caterers. Harper sat on the comfy brown sofa and gestured for Jenny to join her.

Jenny settled in and set her coffee on the table, then turned to Harper. "I know what you're saying, you and Betts. And I know you're right. But what if I stand up to him and he dumps me?"

"No man is worth losing yourself over."

"You say that as if you're sure."

"It's a lesson I paid a really steep price for." Steep didn't begin to cover it. The things she'd done, the way she'd sold her soul for some counterfeit version of love. She'd trusted men, and one by one, they'd all let her down. The only exceptions were bald or gray-headed, too old to do any damage. And even them she had a hard time trusting. "I'll never allow myself to be used by a man again. Never."

Jenny sat back and swallowed. She reached for her coffee cup and took a long sip. Her hand was shaking.

Harper squeezed her hand and pushed her own demons aside. She needed Jenny to understand all of it. "It's very likely he'll dump you at some point. I wish I could tell you differently, but what I see in your relationship isn't love. It's power on his part, submission on yours. I can't see how he's going to take you seriously at this point, no matter what you do. You have to decide if you'd rather live like this or live without him."

"I was destitute before I met him. Now..." But her words trailed off.

"Now, you have a lot of nice stuff. Beautiful clothes, lovely jewelry. But life isn't about stuff."

Jenny swallowed, looked at the blank TV screen, and said nothing.

Harper looked beyond Jenny to the men on the porch. Constantine's gaze locked with hers. He narrowed his eyes. She broke the eye contact.

The hair on her arms stood again, and it wasn't from the cold.

That night, people kept coming until the beach house looked like it might burst at the seams. Of course, when Betts and Russell had invited all their friends for the party, they'd thought the weather would be nice. Harper imagined how different it would be if guests could gather on the patio and on the beach. That kind of party would be lovely. But this... She surveyed the huge crowd. There were well-dressed people sitting on every chair and standing on nearly every square foot of floor space. Harper stood a few steps up on the staircase and tried to talk herself into continuing down. She'd already been in that mess, had been introduced to so many people that all their faces were blending together. Perfectly coiffed blondes and brunettes dripping with jewelry, dignified gentlemen with open collars and sports coats, all holding drinks and nibbling appetizers and talking about people Harper didn't know and businesses Harper didn't understand.

Who could have blamed her for escaping to her bedroom for a few minutes of privacy? She wondered, had she stayed up there, if anybody would have noticed her absence. Not that she minded. Aside from Jenny, whom she hadn't seen, Harper's new friends were having fun. They knew the people here tonight. They enjoyed this kind of thing. Harper would rather be home with Red.

Near the front door, Jenny and Constantine were engaged in a private discussion. It was the first time Harper'd seen the man not surrounded by sycophants, though plenty seemed to be hovering nearby. That morning, before they'd left for shopping, she and Derrick had found a few moments alone on the porch, and she'd asked him about Constantine, trying to understand why the man was so well respected.

Derrick had rolled his eyes. "You're the only person here who doesn't know the answer to that question. He's worth hundreds of millions of dollars."

Hundreds of millions? No wonder people hung on his every word. Apparently, he'd invested in offshore oil and drilling technology. Not to mention real estate.

Apparently, being rich recommended a person to this crowd. She didn't belong here.

Jenny didn't fit in, either. The woman dressed the part, but she certainly didn't act it. It seemed she and Constantine were embroiled in a battle. By her feet... was that a suitcase?

Indeed it was. A moment later, Jenny snatched it and walked out.

Good for her.

Harper wanted to shout her support. All her boredom whooshed away with the closing of that door.

Jenny'd done it. And maybe, just maybe, Harper had given her a little encouragement.

All the junk she'd gone through, maybe sharing it had made a difference. Maybe all those years and experiences hadn't been a complete waste.

Constantine stared at the closed door a moment, then turned, a plastic smile on his face. Not ten seconds went by before people surrounded him. She couldn't hear them, of course, but she could imagine the flattering and fawning. He responded, but then he saw Harper on the stairs. Their gazes met.

She turned away, noticed Derrick and Keith on the porch. Harper started to head their way, then paused and looked closer.

They were arguing, too. Derrick was red-faced. Keith jabbed his finger in Derrick's chest. What was going on?

It couldn't be good. And Keith was a cop. Was Derrick in some sort of legal trouble?

If he was, Harper needed to know immediately. She'd had her fill of people living on the edge of the law. What else could it be?

Derrick slammed out the screen door and into the night.

What in the world? She hadn't gotten the feeling he and Keith had known each other that well. And now... there was definitely something there, something Harper knew nothing about.

When Keith turned back toward the party, Harper thought about following Derrick. Except that by the time she shouldered her way through the crowd and to the door, he'd probably be long gone. And he seemed angry. Maybe now wasn't the best time to talk. She'd ask him about it later.

Harper tried to find someone to talk to and watched Kitty as she snatched a blanket off the back of the couch, wrapped it around her shoulders, and joined her husband on the porch. A moment later, they, too, were involved in a serious discussion.

What was that about? Did it have something to do with Derrick?

Why was Harper the only one who didn't know?

Harper was just about to escape back up the stairs when she

heard someone behind her. She turned and saw Betts heading down.

"You all right?"

"Just trying to work up my courage."

Betts laughed. "Come on. I'll introduce you around."

It was the last thing Harper wanted to do, but she followed anyway, met Betts's friends, and made small talk. Usually, when people realized who she was (nobody important) and what she did (nothing impressive), they nodded politely and looked for the bigger, better deal. Betts wouldn't realize that, of course. She saw the best in everyone. Saw it when it wasn't even there to see.

Not thirty minutes had passed when Harper found herself alone, again, in a sea of bodies. She leaned against the living room wall, sipped a glass of tea that needed more sugar, and watched, wishing like crazy she'd escaped when she had the chance.

A moment later, she felt a presence beside her and turned. Constantine.

He was no taller than she was, though his presence seemed to loom large over the room. She hadn't been this close to him all weekend, and she didn't like it. Didn't like the strength he emanated, the confidence. The anger. She looked around for his ever-present posse, but he was alone.

He stared out at partygoers. "Having fun?"

She followed his gaze, happy not to have to look into his eyes. There was something...menacing there. "Sure."

"You're lying. You hate it."

She glanced at him, forced a smile. "Okay, I hate it. You seem to be enjoying yourself."

He shrugged. "You know what I don't enjoy?" He paused, seemed to wait for her to answer. She couldn't imagine and couldn't care less. He leaned closer and whispered, "Sleeping alone."

Acid pooled in her stomach. She didn't react to his words. She'd known men like this one. Like dogs, they could smell fear. "Sorry to hear that."

"Good to know, considering it's your fault."

She turned to face him then, tamping down the fear in favor of the irritation that rose. "How do you figure?"

"Jenny left."

Harper turned toward the crowd so he wouldn't see her satisfied smile. "Good for her."

Constantine's hand slithered around Harper's wrist. Soft and smooth, strong as cushioned handcuffs.

She considered trying to yank her arm back, but she knew it would do no good. Better to pretend she didn't care.

"Not so good for me," he said.

"That's not my problem."

He shifted closer. "It's your opportunity." Instinct had her yanking at her hand, but he tightened his grip. "Your boyfriend needs me. He needs my money. Tonight, you can make all his troubles go away."

How dare he? Did she look like a prostitute? Or did he think everyone was for sale if you had enough money. She clenched her hands into fists and contemplated a good, loud scream.

People would probably accuse her of harming their hero.

And then, the rest of his words registered.

Derrick's troubles? What did Constantine know that she didn't?

That he had troubles that money would solve, obviously.

She pushed that thought away. First, she had to deal with this... this... She couldn't even come up with a bad enough word.

She forced herself to think. She didn't want to make a scene. She wanted this man away from her. Now. She took a calming breath and blew it out. Then she faced him full on. "So you're saying that if we spend this one night together, you'll move your investment accounts to Derrick?"

"Some of them."

"For how long?"

A slow smile spread across his lips. "I guess that depends on how much fun we have."

She forced a laugh, leaned very close. Waited until he'd become quite sure of her. The slithering snake. "I've done a whole list of bad things in my life, *Connie*."

He flinched at the name.

"Things I'm not proud of. But I've never been a whore, and I'm not about to add that to the list tonight."

His smile faded. "Not a whore. An opportunist."

"Here's the deal," she said. "You're going to release my wrist or I'm going to scream and embarrass us both. And if you set one foot near my bedroom tonight, you'll regret it."

"Like you could stop me."

"You want to risk it?" After a little shrug, she added, "I spent a couple of years in prison."

His eyes widened, and his jaw dropped.

"I learned a few tricks there." She glanced toward the kitchen doorway. "Have you seen Betts's knife collection?"

He released her arm and stepped back.

She smiled at the doubt in his expression. The wavering confidence in his eyes. "You have fun now, Connie."

CHAPTER SIXTEEN

Back in her bedroom, Harper changed out of her party clothes and scrubbed her face. Before she climbed into bed, she perched her ratty old suitcase against the door. If anybody opened it, the thing would topple over.

At least she'd have a moment's notice before anybody got in. If she'd brought her keys, she'd have pulled out the little keychain/knife Estelle had given her. Like a fool, she'd left her keys on the bureau in her bedroom at Red's.

She couldn't get back home fast enough. The sooner she put this night behind her, the happier she'd be.

Not that she'd be able to sleep after Constantine's proposition. The disgusting creep.

She was reading while the party raged downstairs when she heard a soft knock on her door.

"Who is it?"

Derrick called, "You came upstairs without saying good-night."

She'd seen him once after the incident with Constantine. He'd been across the room, dripping rainwater and talking to someone she hadn't met. He'd laughed as if his walk in the rain had been a lark.

He hadn't noticed her, and she hadn't gone to him.

Now, she crossed the room and moved the suitcase to open the door. He stood on the other side in his green shirt and khakis. At least they were dry. He looked... defeated. "You all right?"

He stepped past her and sat on the end of her bed. He was silent a moment too long. When he spoke, his words were measured. "I just need to ask you..."

When his voice trailed off, she cocked her head to the side. "What?"

"Did you think of me at all when you told Jenny she should leave?"

"Oh." She hadn't. She didn't realize Derrick knew anything about that. She closed the bedroom door and stood in front of him. "What did Constantine tell you?"

Derrick swallowed, and his lips flattened. He took a deep breath. "He said you talked Jenny into leaving him, and she did. He was laughing when he said it, like it was all so funny, so we all laughed with him. But I could tell by the way he looked at me... He didn't think it was funny. And he blames you."

"It's not my fault he treats his girlfriend like dirt."

"So you did tell her—?"

"I suggested that he'd never respect her if she didn't respect herself."

Derrick smoothed the bedspread, nodded slowly.

She thought about telling him about Constantine's proposition. Maybe he'd be angry. Maybe he'd be indignant that the man would dare. But she feared there'd be a little spark of something else in his response. Hope, maybe. As if he wouldn't mind trading her for a solution to all his troubles.

She kept her conversation with Constantine to herself. Her

opinion of Derrick had fallen enough this weekend. The wrong reaction from him would make that opinion plummet beyond repair. Besides, she had something more pressing to say.

"What were you and Keith arguing about?"

He blinked, looked up, then back at the blankets. "Nothing, really. Nothing important."

"Looked important from where I stood."

He met her gaze with narrowed eyes. "Where was that? Were you listening?"

"I was on the stairs. I saw you guys through the windows. Why? Was it something you wouldn't want me to hear?"

"I'm managing it."

"Managing what? Are you involved in something illegal? Because if you are—"

"It's nothing like that."

"I can't be involved with you if you're doing something illegal. No way."

"It's nothing to worry about." He reached forward, took her hands, and looked up at her. "I promise. It's nothing to worry about."

"But he's a detective. What else—?"

"He does some work for a guy on the side."

"What kind of work?"

Derrick sighed, took off his glasses, and rubbed his eyes. "It's a long story."

"I have nowhere to go."

He slid the glasses back on. "I owe some money to this guy, and Keith works for him."

"You owe money... like, to a banker?"

"Not exactly."

And then she got it. She jerked her hands free, paced toward the bathroom, and turned. "A bookie?"

"No. Sort of." The slump of his shoulders told her much

more than his words could. "I didn't want you to find out. I'm trying to fix it."

"How much?"

He shrugged. "A lot."

"Are we talking hundreds or thousands?"

He stood and stepped toward her. "It's not your problem, Harper."

The pieces were falling into place. All the trips to Vegas. This summer, Red had gotten sick, and she'd called Derrick and told him not to come up for the weekend. He'd gone to Atlantic City instead.

He'd been back a number of times. He said he had clients there he had to visit. But maybe he'd only gone to gamble. And then there was the poker game the night before.

The truth held her in place like lead shoes. "You're addicted."

"Not addicted. Not like that." He ran his fingers through his hair. "I can fix it. You have no idea how good I am at poker. I'm the luckiest guy you've ever met." He offered his charming smile. "Obviously I'm lucky. I won you, didn't I?"

She wasn't stupid enough to fall for that. She crossed her arms and waited.

He sighed. "I'm working on it."

Right. He had it under control. He could get a handle on it. It wasn't a problem.

She'd been there before. She'd seen addiction. She wasn't going back to that circus. No way. "That's what this weekend was about, trying to get more business so you can pay off your gambling debts."

His mouth closed, tightened. He said nothing

She crossed the room and pulled back the curtains to stare at the darkness outside. To think. Waves smashed against the sand as if they had a grudge. The murmur of voices and laughter from the party filtered up through the floor and added to the loneliness infecting her like a virus. Because Derrick was with her. But his heart didn't belong to her.

It belonged to gambling.

How pathetic, for both of them.

At least now she knew Derrick's *troubles*. The reason he'd seemed desperate all weekend was because he was desperate.

Constantine knew about it. Keith knew. Who else? Did everybody know but Harper? Had they all been feeling *sorry* for her? Because she had such lousy taste in men. She'd been so proud, trying to help Jenny, when she should have been taking her own advice. They probably thought Harper was a fool. Why did she always do this, let herself believe?

At least she hadn't slept with him.

She let the curtain fall and turned. "How much?"

"I'm going to have to ask Gramps for the money. I was trying to avoid it, but I don't see that I have any choice now."

"How much?"

"A lot, okay?" His voice rose in volume and pitch—anger and embarrassment. "A lot."

"And then last night... Was that a friendly game of poker, like you said? Or was it high-stakes?"

He met her eyes. "It started friendly." And then his gaze slid away.

"And you went deeper into debt."

He said nothing, just stared at the floor.

"Do you owe money to anyone downstairs?"

"I paid Carter off. I had a little in my account."

She sat on the side of the bed. She felt sorry for him, she did. Except that he'd lied to her all along.

He circled the bed and sat beside her. His arm slid around her back.

She had to force herself not to pull away.

He hung his head. "I'll get help. I'll start going to those stupid meetings. Maybe do the twelve-step program."

She nodded, stared at the gauzy curtains, imagined the beach outside. If only she could sail away, avoid all of this.

He turned to her, and she forced herself to return the gaze. Everything about his expression said *trust me*. Round face, warm brown eyes, nerdy glasses. He dressed impeccably and had a good job. He'd been kind, treated her with respect. But he couldn't be trusted.

"I'm going to fix this," he said. "I've gotten myself into a mess before, and I've always managed to get myself out. But without you... Please, don't leave me." He took her hands and squeezed. "I need you, Harper."

"I can't be involved in anything illegal."

"You're not. You won't be. I'll get myself together. You and me, we'll be strong together. Promise me you won't let this come between us."

"You've let it come between us. All weekend, it's come between us. For weeks, it's come between us."

He nodded along with her words. "You're right. I didn't know how to tell you, but now I have. Now, we can be a team. You can help me with this, the way I helped you with the job for Gramps."

Wait, what? What was he suggesting, some sort of quid pro quo?

Her feelings must've shown on her face, because he said, "Not like that. Not like you owe me. I'm just saying, I trusted you, despite your past, because I knew you. I know you. And you know me. You know I'd never hurt you. You know I care for you. Yes, I have a problem, and I need to fix it. But I'm more than just a gambler." He released her hands and brushed her hair away from her face. "I'm a good guy, Harper. You know this about me."

"I know. You are."

He leaned closer. "I have a good job, a solid future."

She smiled. "I don't care about that."

"I know. That's one of the reasons I love you."

"Oh." He'd never said that to her before. He'd told her he needed her. She knew he wanted her. But love?

"You don't have to say it back." He rested his palm against her cheek. "You're not ready. It's okay. But just know, despite all the stupid stuff I've done this weekend, I love you. My love for you is the best thing about me."

Love? Was that what this was? Wasn't love supposed to be honest, selfless?

"You're not there yet." He traced her hairline with the tip of his finger. "It's okay. I'm willing to wait for you as long as it takes."

He leaned in and kissed her, slowly at first, then with a passion she couldn't resist. He lowered her to the bed, never releasing her from the kiss.

It would have been so easy to let it happen. He loved her. He'd said so. And look at all he'd done for her.

But he had a problem, a serious problem.

And she wouldn't be a fool again.

She pushed him away. "No. I'm not—"

"Please. Please don't send me away."

"I can't do this."

"You can. It'll be different with me." His hands roved and roamed, and she squirmed, tried to keep them in safe places. "Come on. You can trust me."

Could she? He'd kept his addiction from her. He'd kept the truth about his debt from her. Which proved she couldn't trust him.

"No."

He dropped his face to her shoulder. "Please. Don't send me away."

"Go to bed, Derrick."

He stood and stared down at her. "To bed?" He raked his fingers through his hair. "You think I can sleep now?"

"I'm sorry. I just—"

"Whatever." He yanked the door open, stepped into the hall, and slammed it behind him.

She listened to his footfalls until they faded. Then, she crossed the room and leaned her suitcase against the door again. To heck with Derrick. With Constantine. With Carter. If the suitcase fell, she'd scream her head off.

CHAPTER SEVENTEEN

Harper woke to sun streaming in through the curtains. She pulled them back and gazed out at the morning. Amazing what a difference a few hours could make. The blue of the sky was broken up by a few big, puffy clouds. There were already families and joggers on the beach. Although the weather was lovely, waves still pummeled the shore.

She dressed in a T-shirt and shorts and slipped out the patio door before anybody saw her. Even though the weather was tranquil and the people cheerful, she couldn't settle her thoughts. She wanted to regret coming on this trip, but she couldn't quite get there. She was glad to have met Russell and Betts. Their marriage was so filled with peace. Like Red, they were content. But what was special about them was that they were happy together. At peace together.

Could she ever find that with a man?

The question was so foolish, she scoffed. She'd come on this trip to find out what Derrick was hiding. Well, now she knew.

Every man she'd ever trusted had let her down. Her first serious boyfriend had hired her for his show in Vegas and had fired her when she'd broken up with him. Her second boyfriend had landed her in prison. Derrick had kept his gambling addiction from her. Then there were all the other men she'd met along the way, the drunk, drooling, disgusting men who frequented the club where she had worked. Men like Constantine, who treated her like a shiny toy in a storefront, available for purchase for the right price.

She wanted the sea breeze to carry the next thought away, but there it was. Even her father had failed her. He'd raised her in the church, taught her right from wrong. He'd thrown around words like *love* and *grace* and *mercy* all her life. But when she'd chosen wrong and ended up in prison, he'd rejected her. *Don't call here again.*

Men like Russell, men like Red... They might be out there, but they were taken or too old. Definitely too scarce. She'd never met a man like that who was her age, available, and attracted to her, and based on her track record—and her baggage—she never would.

Which left her with men like Derrick.

It wasn't his addiction that bothered her. Yes, that was an issue. Living in Vegas, she'd seen the effects of a gambling addiction. Formerly successful people reduced to poverty and, often, homelessness. People whose blind hope that the next game would be the game that saved them from all their troubles. She'd seen panhandlers take their meager funds into casinos, certain this would be the day for their big score.

She'd also known and heard of plenty of people who'd overcome the addiction. If Derrick were willing, he could overcome it, too. But the fact that he'd lied about it said a lot about where he stood. So did the fact that he thought Harper could rescue him.

She knew better than to think she could pull him from the deep water. She was barely surviving herself. Derrick might just take them both down.

She was nearing the house, hoping Derrick was awake so they could head back to Red's, when she heard people on the porch. With the bright sun beating down on her, she could barely make out who was there. When she heard Derrick's voice, she paused.

"Look." The pitch was too high, too eager. "I know it looked bad this weekend. I've just hit a rough patch. But that doesn't affect—"

"I'm sorry." Russell, so calm and steady. "Not forever. Just until you grow up a little, settle into your success."

Harper stepped around the corner of the house and out of their line of sight. She shouldn't eavesdrop. On the other hand, maybe this was her only opportunity to find out what was really going on.

Derrick said, "I'd never gamble with your money."

"I believe that," Russell said, "but when people dig themselves into holes, they do things they wouldn't otherwise do. And from what I overheard last night, you're in deep."

Overheard? Had he heard the conversation between Derrick and her? No, probably not. So maybe he'd overheard the conversation between Derrick and Keith on the porch. Maybe he knew more than Harper did.

"None of that affects the kind of stockbroker I am. I'm good at what I do."

"One of the best I've ever worked with," Russell said. "But when I give someone access to my money, I need to know I can trust them. Unfortunately, after your behavior last night, I don't trust you anymore."

"It was just one game!"

A cloud drifted in front of the sun. Harper peeked around the corner and saw inside the screened-in porch. Derrick was seated on one of the chairs, his head rolled forward. Russell stood beside him, his hand on Derrick's shoulder.

"Here's the thing," Russell said. "This is not the end for you. You need to get yourself together, keep working hard, and quit gambling. Go to Gamblers Anonymous and seek that higher power they talk about. In fact, do more than that. Seek God, the only real God. He can help you overcome this. If you ever have any questions about God, don't hesitate to call me."

Derrick might have said something, but she didn't hear it.

Russell walked into the house and closed the slider behind him.

At that moment, Derrick looked up. His gaze locked with hers.

She took a few steps toward him but froze at the expression on his face. Despair mixed with pure fury.

After a deep breath, she stepped inside the porch and sat beside him.

"I guess you heard everything?"

"Just the end."

"Not only did I not get Constantine as a client, I lost Russell's business."

"I'm sorry."

He nodded slowly, staring beyond her. "I guess none of it matters to you."

"What's that supposed to mean?"

"You cost me my shot with Constantine."

She sighed. "I didn't mean to hurt you. It never crossed my mind that Jenny would tell him I'd told her to leave. I didn't. I just told her to stand up for herself."

"Whether you meant it or not..." His voice trailed off. "And then last night, after you kicked me out, I went back downstairs."

"And played poker," she guessed.

He said nothing, which was as much of an admission as anything.

"And lost big," she said.

He shrugged.

"And you blame me."

His gaze snapped to hers. "If you'd let me stay—"

"You don't get to blame me for your bad choices, Derrick. You could have gone to bed. You should have."

"I was too keyed up."

"You could have gone for a walk. You could've read a book. You could've gone back downstairs and not gambled. You could've done a lot of things besides play poker."

"I know that." He raked his hands through his hair. "Don't you think I've gone over all the things I could have done differently? Don't you think I regret it enough? Thanks for piling on."

She didn't like this Derrick one bit. She liked the sweet, generous man she'd met in Vegas. She liked the confident man who'd shown up at the house on Friday. She didn't like this accusing, angry man. She didn't like him, and she didn't think she'd ever trust him again.

CHAPTER EIGHTEEN

The only thing good about the long drive home was the lack of traffic. The tension in the car was palpable but dwarfed by that at the house when they'd left.

Harper had hugged and thanked Russell and Betts, who were kind and gracious, as always. Kitty was extra nice to her, inviting her to send along her resume if Harper decided to change jobs. She thanked her for the kindness but knew she never would. No chance any doctor or hospital would hire a nurse with a felony on her record. Keith was quiet, as usual, but grasped her hand and muttered, "It was nice to meet you."

Fortunately, Marjorie, Carter, and Constantine had still been upstairs when she and Derrick left, keeping the good-byes to a minimum.

As kind as the two couples were to them, tension hung over the group like the stench of bad fish as Derrick shook the men's hands and kissed the women's cheeks. Did everybody know about his conversation with Russell? About the poker game?

Only when they pulled into the circle drive in front of Red's house did Harper let herself begin to relax. She couldn't wait to get inside and away from Derrick. He put the car in park, and she reached for the door handle. He stopped her with a hand on her forearm. "Can we talk for a sec?"

"We've been in the car together for hours, and now you want to talk?"

"I'm sorry. I'm just... I don't know what to say."

She stepped out of the car. Derrick climbed out on the far side and popped the trunk. He snatched her suitcase, slid out the handle, but didn't let it go. "Five minutes."

"Okay."

He took a deep breath and looked at the house behind her a moment. "I'm sorry."

"I bet you are."

"Not for..." He hung his head. "Of all the stupid stuff I did this weekend, I'm most sorry about how I treated you."

She considered minimizing it, letting him off the hook. But she kept her mouth shut.

"I didn't pay enough attention to you," he said. "I knew Carter was hitting on you, but I was focused on Russell and Constantine, and I figured you could handle yourself."

"I can."

"I know, but you shouldn't have had to. I should have been there for you."

He was right. He should have. She acknowledged that with a nod.

"And I'm sorry for not telling you about the gambling. I just thought, when I met you... When I'm with you, I don't think of gambling. I thought I was over it. All those times I came to see you in Vegas, I didn't gamble once."

"Really?"

"I didn't think I needed to tell you because I thought it was managed."

"What happened?"

"You were home with Gramps when he was sick, and I

thought, just one night in Atlantic City... I thought it would be fine. But I got in over my head. Then, I kept going back, trying to fix it."

"Just making it worse," she guessed.

"I already owed this guy money, and now I'm in really deep."

"How deep?"

He blew out a long breath. "Couple hundred thousand."

"Whoa." She stepped back, caught her breath. "Are you kidding me?"

"I know, I know." He raked his fingers through his hair. "I've really messed up. The guy I owe is really pressing me for the money."

"So what are you going to do?"

He shrugged. "I'll figure it out." He stepped toward her and smiled. "It's not your problem, Harper. I know I should have told you, and I hope you can forgive me for that. I hope... I know you're probably plotting your escape as we speak." He smiled when he said the words, but she saw the flicker of worry in his eyes. "I just want to ask you... and I have no right to ask you for anything. I know that. But can you please give me some time to make all this right?" He stepped forward, so close she could feel his breath on her cheeks. "Don't give up on me yet, Harper. I need you."

She hadn't made up her mind about him, and while his apology helped, there was no guarantee he'd be able to do everything he'd promised. Her instinct was to break up with him. To distance herself. With her only serious boyfriends in the past, she'd told herself that she should have gotten out sooner. Depended on herself. If she cut bait now, she could save herself a lot of grief.

Frankly, she'd probably end things with Derrick. She should feel... what? Sad, depressed, let down? But she didn't. She cared about Derrick. She'd appreciated his kindness, his gifts, his concern when she lived in Vegas. But she'd fallen more for the idea of him—a successful man without all the baggage her previous boyfriends had hauled into the relationships.

She'd been wrong about that. Derrick had just hidden his baggage better.

Unless something monumental changed, she'd end things with him, but not today. Today, he'd been hurt enough. She'd hang in there a little longer. Maybe he'd surprise her, do everything he promised, and turn out to be her Prince Charming.

"Okay." She smiled at him and stepped back. "But from now on, you need to be honest with me."

He nodded, his eyes lighting up as if she'd just repaired his favorite toy. "Thank you."

"Are you going to hang around for a while?"

"I don't think so. I have some stuff I need to take care of before work tomorrow." Derrick carried her suitcase to the door and kissed her on the cheek.

As he walked back to his car, Harper had the feeling that more time wouldn't reveal Derrick as Prince Charming. Instead, she might only get a close-up glimpse of a frog.

CHAPTER NINETEEN

Harper carried her small bag upstairs to her bedroom, dropped it on the bed, and hurried back down in search of Red.

She found him in the wide backyard, standing in front of a rose bush, deadheading flowers.

She hurried out to meet him. "What are you doing?"

"Those gardeners don't know how to take care of Bebe's flowers." He snipped off an old bloom, dropped it in a plastic bag dangling from his wrist, and reached for another.

"What if you'd fallen?" Harper could imagine him struggling to stand back up on the uneven lawn.

He looked up, holding onto his fedora so it wouldn't fall, and surveyed the sky. "Sunny day. I'd have gotten a nice tan." He chuckled and continued with the roses.

"You're a stubborn old man, you know that?"

"I'm not old." He winked. "How was the beach? You got a whopper of a storm yesterday. I thought you might stay later today to soak up the sunshine."

"We were ready to get back."

Red dropped another spent rose in the plastic bag and peered at her with those sharp blue eyes. "Something happen?"

"No."

His lips closed while he studied her. "My grandson treat you well?"

She didn't want to lie to him but wasn't prepared to tell him the truth. "He spent a lot of time trying to drum up new accounts."

"Hmph." He inched around the bush.

She resisted the urge to suggest Red let the gardeners do it, or worse, assist him herself. He was in one of his I-don't-need-your-help moods, and offering would only irritate him.

Red cut another bloom and dropped it in the bag. "I love that boy, but sometimes I don't like him very much."

She'd gotten that impression before, but she'd never heard him say it. "Why is that?"

"He makes all the money he needs and more, but he spends it as fast as it comes in. Never has an extra dime."

"Maybe he'll learn to be wiser with it."

Another "hmph" told her what Red thought of that.

"His dad never did," Red said. "Died in serious debt. Mortgaged to the hilt. Used to gamble, that one." The words were delivered casually, but Red peered at her from beneath the rim of his hat and held her gaze.

"Oh... Well." It wasn't her place to tell Red about Derrick's gambling. She wasn't going to lie to the man, either. "That must have been hard for you."

"I like a risk." He turned his gaze back to the bright red blooms and continued snipping. "But I risked wisely. Risked in real estate. Only made safe bets. You buy a house, it's going to be worth something. It has intrinsic value. You work hard, keep it in good shape, do your best to keep renters in it while you make the payments, and the house goes up in value. If the market turns"—he shrugged—"you did your part. Maybe you lose a little here and there. But you don't lose everything. Gambling, though… That's not earning. That's trying to get something for nothing, and it never works."

She'd learned that lesson the hard way. She'd been sent to prison because her boyfriend and his friend had tried to take the easy way out, and they'd used her to help. She'd been ignorant of their schemes, but the judge hadn't believed her claim of innocence. All because Emmitt and Barry were too lazy to work and had already spent all the money she'd earned.

The memories didn't sit well. The comparison between Emmitt and Derrick turned in her stomach like a Tilt-A-Whirl.

"What happened to your son?"

Red maneuvered another foot around the bush until he was practically against the fence. "He and his wife were killed in a car accident. On their way home from Atlantic City. George had had too much to drink and swerved to miss a deer. Ended up driving into a tree."

"I'm so sorry."

"Long time ago." Red focused on the roses. "Derrick never told you?"

"Just that they passed away when he was eighteen. But he never told me how, and I never asked."

"Hard time for both of us." He pointed to a fading bloom out of his reach. "Get that one for me, would you?"

She took the pruners and cut off the bloom, then got a couple more she didn't think he could see from where he stood. While she worked, she thought of Derrick. She couldn't imagine the pain of burying both his parents at such a young age. Legally an adult, but not really. An age when he'd needed his father and mother. At least he'd had Red, who'd taken him in, sent him to college, and supported him all those years.

She handed Red the pruners.

"You don't have to stay out here with me, girl. I got this."

"I'm staying. Not because you need me"—not that he'd admit, anyway—"but because I missed you."

She had missed Red. He was kind and gentle and honest. And today he seemed as healthy as she'd ever seen him. His face was pink from the heat, but not frighteningly so. Another hour and he'd need to go inside, get out of the sun. But this morning, she figured the vitamin D was doing him good. His legs seemed strong. His smile was bright as he accomplished his task.

He probably didn't need her at all. But she stayed anyway, just in case. And because his peace, his kindness, were a balm to her raw nerves.

If she had any hope Derrick would turn out to be like Red, she'd stick it out with him through all the stuff—the gambling addiction, the debt. But Derrick wasn't like his grandfather. He was like his father. And look what a mess that man had left behind.

Derrick arrived for their date on Friday night bearing his suitcase and a handful of purple irises.

Harper glanced at the suitcase and took the bouquet. "You shouldn't have."

He kissed her on the cheek. "You deserve these and a million more."

She eyed the suitcase. "You're staying?"

"I thought I'd spend the weekend, if you don't mind."

"It's not up to me." The memory of the previous weekend, of Derrick in her bedroom, flashed through her mind. No. He wouldn't do that this weekend. He was trying to win her trust back. Besides, her bedroom in this house had a lock. "But I certainly don't mind."

His over-bright smile relaxed into one more natural. "Good. Tomorrow, you get the day off. I'll get up with Gramps, make sure he gets his meds, and you can sleep in."

Sleep in? She hadn't done that since she'd moved to Maryland. And hardly before that. But a morning off from work—she'd take that. "Sounds heavenly." She shooed him into the living room to visit with his grandfather. Then she put the flowers in a vase and ran upstairs to finish getting ready for their date.

She chose a red sundress he'd bought for her and added a pair of high-heeled sandals she'd picked up off the clearance rack. She added some lipstick and slid on a pair of earrings and a bracelet. She checked her reflection in the floor-length mirror in her private bath. Her outfit wasn't fancy, but it would be nice enough for wherever they went. Spending so much time in the garden with Red this week had given her a tan and lightened her hair. She looked summery, fancy-free. Maybe achieving the look would be a step toward achieving the feeling.

Downstairs, she went into the living room but found Red alone.

He whistled. "You look lovely."

She kissed his cheek. "Thank you."

"You mind Derrick spending the night?" Red asked.

"Not if you don't."

He nodded and turned his attention back to the TV.

A moment later, Derrick stepped into the room. "You ready?"

"Sure." To Red, she said, "Call me if you need me."

"I survived more'n eighty years without you, girl. I reckon I'll make it a couple of hours."

Harper settled into Derrick's car. "Can we stop at the store on the corner? I need to get some Gatorade."

"No problem." Derrick stopped, ran inside, and returned with a few bottles of yellow Gatorade. He tossed them in the backseat. "It's not like you to run out."

"Red worked in the yard all week. He was extra thirsty."

Derrick's eyes narrowed. "Should he be doing that?"

"He enjoys it. He's a grown man. It's not like I can tell him what to do. Besides, the sunshine was good for him, and I think the activity was, too."

"You're usually right about these things."

"Didn't he look good today? He's been so energetic all week."

Derrick exited the parking lot and headed toward the bay. "You've been good for him, Harper."

She shrugged. "I don't do much. I make sure he has his medication, make sure he eats, and encourage him to do his exercises."

Derrick glanced at her, then took her hand. "It's not what you do. It's who you are. You're a balm."

"Not really," she said, but her cheeks warmed with the compliment.

After a long wait with a crowd of tourists at the restaurant, they were seated on a covered patio overlooking a long dock and, beyond that, the sparkling waters of the bay. It was a warm night, but the breeze kept them cool. Every table was taken, and the buzz of conversation added to the gentle lapping of water and the caw of seagulls overhead.

Their conversation stayed on safe ground and far from the events of the previous weekend as they shared a delicious seafood dinner and chocolate dessert and sipped their drinks—sweet tea for Harper, a cold beer for Derrick. It was beautiful, the perfect night. And Derrick had been his old self. Sweet, generous, attentive. Maybe she could make things work with him. Maybe she'd made the right choice when she hadn't broken up with him the week before.

She glanced at him to see him not watching the view, but her.

He'd taken off his suit jacket and set it over the back of the chair when they'd sat. Now, he leaned over to reach something in the inside pocket. A moment later, he turned holding a thin rectangular box.

"Oh."

He smiled and handed it to her. "Open it."

Her hands trembled as she took the gift. She held it a long moment, trying to name the feeling that had her blood racing, her stomach flipping. It wasn't eagerness. It wasn't excitement or affection. Though she was eager to see the gift and thankful for it, something else caused her reaction.

Derrick was watching her, so she lifted the lid.

Inside, she saw a sapphire-and-diamond pendant on a slender gold chain.

She stared at the necklace, her hand covering her heart. She couldn't think of a word to say.

"The sapphire matches your eyes."

Sweet. Too much. She set the box down. "You didn't need to... You shouldn't have."

"I wanted to apologize for last weekend."

"You did apologize. On Sunday. And I forgave you."

"You're not one to hold a grudge." His smile faded. "Which is all the more reason I wanted to get you something."

"But..." She swallowed, put her hands in her lap, and ignored the jewels glimmering up at her from the tabletop. "You can't afford this, Derrick. You need every penny—"

"Don't do that." His lips flattened with the terse remark, turned white. "It's a gift. It's rude to refuse a gift."

"I'm not trying to be rude. I'm trying to... I don't understand why you would spend—"

"It's just a trinket."

"Oh." The satin-lined box looked fancy. But maybe it only *looked* expensive. Thank heavens. She blew out a breath. "It's not real. I'm glad, because—"

"Of course it's real." He sneered the last word. "You think I'd buy you some cheap, fake jewelry?"

Slowly, she replaced the lid and held the box out to him. "I think you're deeply in debt, and you can't afford to buy me anything."

He didn't take it. "Seriously? You're refusing it?"

She set the box on the table and turned toward the bay, thinking of what to say. A little crowd of seagulls had landed on the dock and were clawing and pecking at each other for a scrap of food.

Why did life have to be so hard?

She turned back to Derrick. "It was very sweet of you, and I love that you wanted to give me something."

His lips remained pressed closed, his eyes narrowed the tiniest bit.

"The thing is, if we remain together—"

"You say that like it's not likely." His words were harsh.

"Then we need to work as a team. People in a relationship should be on the same team, shouldn't they?"

His head angled just slightly to the side. "How is me giving you a gift showing that we're not on the same team?"

She shouldn't have started down this road. What did she know about sports? She'd never played a team sport in her life. But she knew how hard it was for people who weren't aiming toward the same goals to work together. She'd seen that tension at her first dancing job in Vegas. The showgirls had performed the same numbers while working toward their own selfish ambitions. Many had been cutthroat in their attempts to claw or sleep their way to the top. The only women who weren't that way had given up their dreams. They'd quit having any ambition at all. Together, the dancers had looked good on stage, but behind the scenes, the tension and drama had been cancerous. She'd hated it.

A relationship wasn't the same as a dance troupe, she knew. Or a sports team. But the analogy still worked.

"On a basketball team," she said, "everybody wants to win

the game. Sometimes, that means one player passes the ball to another instead of taking a shot, because the other player has the better chance of scoring. Maybe that first person didn't get the applause, but that's not the reason they play. They play to win the game."

His eyebrows lifted, and he almost smiled. "I didn't know you were such a fan."

"I'm not, I'm just saying—"

"What does basketball have to do with a gift?"

"When two people care about each other, they work together to achieve their goals. They're on the same page. If one is trying to do something, the other helps."

"And in this case...?" he prompted.

"You need to pay off a debt, and I know that. I want us to work together. Which means, you don't waste money. Not even on me. And I understand that and support you. I don't expect"—she indicated the restaurant, the remnants of their pricey dinners, and the jewelry box—"fancy meals or fancy gifts or flowers. I'd be just as happy grabbing takeout and eating on a park bench."

She expected him to be pleased with her words. To find relief from the pressure of spending money on her. Instead, he snatched the gift and shoved it back in his jacket. "Fine."

"Why are you mad?"

"I'm not mad. I'm just..." But he didn't finish. When the waitress walked by, he asked for the check. He paid it, and they walked out of the restaurant in silence.

After they got in the car—he didn't open the door for her like he'd done before—he pulled away from the parking space and headed toward Red's house.

"Can you please just talk to me?" she asked.

"What do you want me to say? I bought you a nice gift, and you threw it in my face, along with all my faults and failures. All

I wanted was to forget about my stupid crap for a little while. Is that so terrible?"

"If by 'forget' you mean you spend money you don't have, then maybe, yeah."

He took a deep breath. "I know what you're saying." The anger had drained from his voice. Now he just sounded defeated. "For the record, the necklace wasn't that expensive."

"For the record," she said, "it was beautiful."

He reached across the center console and took her hand. "I want to shower you with gifts."

"I don't need your gifts."

He lifted her fingers and kissed them gently. They were quiet until he pulled into Red's driveway. After Derrick slid the gear into Park and cut the engine, he took her hand again. "I hope, someday, you'll do more than just care for me."

She was forming an answer, but he continued.

"You're not there. I know. And I'm not pushing you. I'm just laying it out there. I know I said it the other night, but I was a little drunk and a little... Well, maybe not myself. So it was a lousy time to say it."

She knew what was coming and wished he wouldn't. But she'd already shut him down tonight with the necklace. She couldn't do it again.

"You're right about the team thing." He angled his shoulders to better face her. "I've never really been part of a team. What I do is dog-eat-dog. I played tennis in high school. Loved singles, hated doubles, because I hated having to depend on anyone else. I don't know how to be a teammate." He swallowed, looked beyond Harper. "Russell and Betts are a team. They're together in everything."

"They seem to be."

"It's beautiful. My parents weren't like that. They fought a lot." He focused on her again. "Anyway, it doesn't matter. I'm just saying, I want that someday. And not with just anybody." He leaned closer. "I love you, Harper. I hope someday you'll love me, too."

She didn't trust him nearly enough to consider anything deeper with him. But after he'd bared his soul, she couldn't very well say that. She placed her hand on his cheek and kissed him. "You're a kind man, Derrick Burns."

His chuckle was dark. "You might be the only person in the world who thinks so."

<h1 style="text-align:center">CHAPTER TWENTY-ONE</h1>

Harper finished reading her Bible before seven the next morning despite Derrick's suggestion that she sleep in. In her new life, she welcomed mornings. Nothing like her old, pre-prison life, which had thrived in darkness, drinking, and drugs.

She remembered one of the women who'd visited her in prison, a sweet Christian lady who ran the codependency group there. Whenever anyone would confess something particularly awful, she'd say, "Beautiful things only thrive in the light."

Harper was learning to thrive in the light.

It was Saturday, and again, clouds had moved in. She pitied all the folks who spent their weekdays trapped in office buildings, the people who yearned for sunny weekends. Based on her phone's weather app, they'd be disappointed today.

Since Derrick had promised to look after Red, Harper donned her running clothes and cheap tennis shoes, threw her hair into a ponytail, and stepped out of her room. She usually used the back staircase, which led straight to the kitchen, but she hoped to avoid Derrick and Red. There'd be plenty of time to visit later, and she didn't want to get pulled into a conversation that would keep her from her jog.

She shoved her phone in her shorts' pocket, just in case, and went down the stairs that led to the foyer. She was just about to open the door when she heard Derrick's voice in the kitchen.

What was he saying?

"Of course you wouldn't have to invest that much, but these stocks are supposed to go through the roof."

"And if they don't?" Red asked.

"It's what you've always told me. Make sure the investment is sound, do your homework. This company's numbers are good. They're making money. They're poised to take off. If they don't, it's not like you'll lose everything. You'll just have to wait it out."

"What kind of company is it again?" Red said.

"Tech. They build computer parts."

"Like Intel and Qualcomm?"

"Uh..." Derrick stumbled, obviously surprised to find Red so well informed. "Yeah, sort of."

What was going on? Derrick hadn't mentioned any investment to her. She'd heard nothing about it at the beach the previous weekend.

"How much do you need, son?" Red didn't sound eager or curious about the investment. Just tired.

"Whatever you want to invest." Derrick, on the other hand, sounded overly relaxed. Like it was all no big deal to him. He was good at that offhand tone. Very good. "But if I were you, I'd throw a couple hundred grand at it. I think the stock will double in the initial offering. Then, you can sell if you want, take your profit."

Harper looked at the front door, told herself she should go. What happened between Derrick and Red wasn't her business. Derrick was his grandson. She was just Red's nurse. And Derrick's girlfriend. Despite what she told herself, though, she tiptoed into the dining room, careful to stay out of sight.

Red blew out a long breath. "Let's cut the act. You're in over your head again, and you need me to bail you out."

"No, no," Derrick said. "It's not that. It's just this investment—"

"Where's the prospectus?"

"I forgot to bring it, but I can get you one."

"And you'd need me to make the check out to you?"

"Well..." Derrick cleared his throat. "I'm investing, and the more we put in, the better—"

"Listen, kid," Red said. "This ain't my first rodeo, and you're not the first desperate man who's tried to get money out of me. You forget, I was your father's father, and you're your father's son. I told you the last time I bailed you out I wasn't gonna do it again."

The chair scraped against the floor. Then she heard footsteps on the tile. "I'm not asking you to bail me out, Gramps. I'm trying to get you in on the investment of a lifetime."

"Hmph." Red was a lot sharper than Derrick gave him credit for. "Fortunately, I have all the money I need to last me until I leave this earth. So I'm going to skip your little investment."

"Fine."

Before she could react, footsteps stomped toward her. Derrick stepped into the dining room and froze when he saw her. His face was red, but the color faded as they stared at each other.

He continued past and bolted up the staircase.

Harper pasted on a smile and entered the kitchen. Red was seated at the table. The effects of his conversation with Derrick were etched on his face. "You on your way out?"

She glanced through the window at the cloudy day. "I was

going to, but it looks like rain. I think I'll just stay here with you."

He nodded, nibbled his breakfast. Seemed Derrick had gone all out. Red had eggs and toast, not to mention a little bowl of assorted berries she'd picked up a few days before. He opened his newspaper and focused on the stories there.

She poured herself a cup of coffee, doctored it up, and got a bowl of fruit before joining Red at the table.

They sat in silence. The sound of Derrick pacing in his room upstairs was a frantic background beat. She was halfway through her coffee before Red spoke.

"How deep is he in?"

It wasn't her place to get involved. But Red wasn't stupid. "It's bad."

He folded the newspaper and set it down. His fingers rapped on the table.

She ate a blueberry, then a blackberry. The sweet of one mixed with the tart of the other and created a nice combination in her mouth, but she could hardly enjoy it.

Overhead, Derrick pounded on something. Probably his bureau.

"He's mad at me," Red said.

"It's not your problem."

"I told him the last time I bailed him out that it would be the *last time*."

"Did he tell you it was an investment then, too?"

Red shook his head. "Just asked me for money. Twenty thousand. Not small potatoes, but this time... Two hundred? What did he do?"

Red didn't seem to want an answer, which was good, because Harper didn't have one.

"I did everything I could to help George." Red still didn't look at her. He was focused behind her, or maybe on events long past. "I bailed him out too many times before I said 'enough.' I thought if he knew I'd quit giving him money, he'd get his act together. They have those support groups, but he never went. Just blew every penny he had at the tables, and when I didn't help him, he mortgaged his house, his business. His wife was right there with him. She'd talk about how they needed to quit, but she was just as bad as he was. They'd gamble together, they'd win, all was well. They'd lose, and they'd fight." Red focused on Harper, his sharp blue eyes watery. "I knew better than to bail Derrick out. But the poor kid had lost his parents. He just had me, a grouchy old man. How do you do the tough-love thing in that situation? I got into the same stupid patterns with him. And now he's following the same path his father took."

"It's not your fault, Red. You know that, right?"

"Of course it's not my fault." His voice was sharp. "He didn't come to live with me until he was eighteen years old. The die had been cast long before that." He nibbled his toast, then set it down as if he was too drained to hold it up. "I sure wish I could've helped him, though."

The banging and pacing above quieted. She hated to think of how defeated Derrick must have felt. There'd be no easy way out of this situation for him.

Worse than that, she'd witnessed the whole thing. Witnessed him trying to swindle his own grandfather, this sweet, sweet man who'd done nothing but try to help him.

How desperate must Derrick be?

How low could a person fall?

She couldn't quantify the first and knew too much about the second.

They finished their breakfasts in silence. Red never glanced at the newspaper again. Poor man was worried. Heartbroken.

She knew how he felt.

Ten minutes later, Derrick's footsteps sounded on the stairs. She heard a thud, and then he stepped into the kitchen. "Something came up." He focused on his grandfather, avoiding Harper's gaze. "I'm headed back to the city."

Red nodded once. "Glad you came."

Derrick gave Red a pat on the shoulder.

He looked at Harper, and she stood and walked to the front door. She stopped beside Derrick's suitcase and turned to face him. Arms crossed.

He snatched the bag, opened the door, and stepped onto the stoop. She thought he was going to leave without a word, but instead, he held the door open. "Can we talk out here?"

She stepped into the muggy day.

He strode to his sedan, popping the trunk with his key fob halfway there. He tossed the suitcase in, then returned to the front step. He stopped a few feet from her and raked his fingers through his hair. "I don't know what to say."

"You're so desperate, you lied to your grandfather."

He crossed his arms. "You don't understand. I'm in trouble, Harper. These people—"

"How much is that car worth?"

"Not enough."

"It'd be a start, though."

"If I owned it, but I'm behind on my payments as it is."

"Could you refinance your condo?"

He swallowed. "I'll figure out something." He wore khakis and a golf shirt and looked like the successful young businessman she'd first thought he was. Nobody would ever know what he was capable of based on his looks. "I don't want this to come between us." Derrick stepped closer and reached for her hands.

She stepped back. "You're joking, right?"

His arms dropped. "Harper, I need you. And you need me."

"I just heard you try to con your grandfather out of two hundred thousand dollars."

His brown eyes lost their spirit, hardened until they looked like lifeless marbles. "It's not as if he doesn't have the money. He's loaded. He's got millions."

"Which he earned, Derrick. He spent a lifetime earning it."

"He got lucky in real estate." He stepped toward her again, and she backed up until she was pressed against the doorway. He was too close and too angry. "He gambled on real estate and won. But he looks down on me."

"Real estate and poker aren't the same."

"Whatever."

"Step back, Derrick."

"I need you. And you need me."

Was he crazy? "I don't need this."

He leaned closer, close enough to kiss her. She lifted her hands to block him, turned her head.

He didn't back up, just hovered, eyes hard.

She wanted to scream, to push him away.

A car door slammed down the street. The sound seemed to bring Derrick to his senses. He took a step back. Blinked. His eyes were black as tar. "You're dumping me, after all I've done for you?"

There it was. Because he'd gotten her this job, she owed him.

Except it had been Red who hired her. Red who paid her. And it was Red who could be trusted. Not Derrick.

Definitely not Derrick.

"I don't owe you anything."

"Great. So I've lost my biggest client and the potential for another client—because of you."

He was delusional, but she kept her mouth shut.

"I lost big in poker that night because you wouldn't let me stay with you."

As if she ought to have slept with him to keep him from being an idiot. All that would have done was made her an idiot, too.

"I've lost Gramps. And to top it all off, you're dumping me."

"You should try taking responsibility for your own mistakes, Derrick. You'd be surprised how much better your life is when you realize you're in control of your own decisions."

"Said the felon."

Hot rage made her hands tremble. "It's time for you to go."

"You can't order me away from my own grandfather's house."

She crossed her arms and stood her ground. She lived here. Derrick didn't. End of story.

He stared at her, seemed to be waiting for her to back down. Well, he'd be waiting a long, long time.

Spitting a curse word, he spun, ran to his car, and peeled out of the drive.

She watched the street until long after he'd disappeared.

That was not how she'd planned for this day to go. She waited for some twinge of regret or remorse. All she felt was relief.

CHAPTER TWENTY-TWO

Ever since Derrick had tried to swindle him out of money a few months before, Red hadn't been the same. His moods shifted faster than the autumn weather, and she walked on eggshells around him. Sometimes, he was the happy-go-lucky guy she'd first met. Other times, he seemed so depressed she worried for his health. Still other times, he was angry, lashing out at her and anyone else within earshot.

She missed the sweet old man he'd once been. But she understood. Broken hearts were painful.

She'd thought he was getting better, but the grouch was back. "We have to go." Harper stood by Red's recliner, arms crossed.

"Don't feel like it."

She took a deep breath to silence her initial reaction. "As you've made perfectly clear, Red, but you're going to the doctor."

He ignored her, his gaze on the TV.

Today was his check-up, and he wasn't missing it. "Come on." She leaned toward the lever that would lower his footrest. "I'll help you—"

He swatted her arm away. "Don't need your help." He glared at her, then focused on the TV again.

Usually, when he got like this, she let him have his way. But not today.

"Listen, old man."

The anger dropped from his expression, replaced by surprise.

"You're going to the doctor on your own, or I'll call 911 and have them come after you."

"You wouldn't dare."

"Don't tempt me."

He harrumphed, glared, and finally lowered the footrest of his recliner. "Fine. But you can't make me talk to him."

Stubborn old coot. She grabbed his jacket—the October chill had settled deep—and helped him to the car.

An hour later, a nurse escorted Red back to the doctor's office. Harper had already updated the nurse on how he'd been feeling—and behaving—so Red's refusal to talk to them shouldn't make a difference. And they'd fill Harper in. Red had made her his health care agent when she'd started working for him. He'd ensured she'd have full access to all his medical information so she could learn what the doctors discovered whether Red was in the mood to tell her or not.

Amazing what a difference a few months had made. Back in Vegas, she hadn't been trusted to do anything but feed the residents and clean up after them. Here, she'd been given the right to make medical decisions. She'd proved herself to Red and, even though she barely spoke to him anymore, to Derrick. She hadn't gone back to school, hadn't achieved any real level of success, but maybe if her parents heard what she had achieved, they'd accept her again. Maybe if she told them where she was and what she was doing, they'd be proud of her. Or, if not proud, less ashamed. She considered dialing her mother that moment, but now wasn't the time. No, she needed to think about it some more. Being estranged from her parents was awful. A second rejection might destroy her.

Her cell vibrated, and she pulled it out and glanced at the screen. She had two missed calls and three texts from Derrick. She ignored them, as usual. He'd been trying to reconcile with her ever since he'd left her on the front stoop that stormy Saturday morning. At first, she'd been firm but kind. Now, she didn't bother to respond. They spoke sometimes about his grandfather's health. But Derrick hadn't been to visit him once since that terrible morning, despite the fact that she'd told Derrick about the mood swings and how she believed they were a direct result of Derrick not visiting.

Was he still angry at Red for not giving him the money? Was this some sort of manipulation technique? Did he think that if he withheld his love long enough, Red would give in? Or was he too busy trying to dig himself out of trouble—or maybe gambling himself into more debt—to bother with Red? She had no idea what was going on in Derrick's life and wouldn't care if his absence hadn't been such a blow to Red.

It was thirty minutes before a nurse called Harper back and into an empty exam room. "He seems as healthy as he can be at his age."

"But what about his moods?"

The woman shrugged. "He didn't complain of depression or mood shifts. He said he's fine."

Harper sighed. "He's just different than he used to be. More forgetful. What could cause that?"

"Old age affects everyone differently. The forgetfulness—that could be signs of dementia, but we saw nothing to suggest that today. He was a bit crankier than usual."

He was definitely that.

By the time she returned to the waiting room, Red was there, seated in a chair, arms crossed. He looked exhausted.

All this effort and no diagnosis. Poor man. She hoped this wasn't his age catching up with him. Prayed he wasn't deteriorating. She couldn't lose him. Red was the closest thing to family she'd had in years. She wasn't sure she'd survive without him.

CHAPTER TWENTY-THREE

That afternoon, after Harper got Red settled in his recliner, she went to the kitchen to warm up something for dinner. Soup tonight. It rarely disagreed with him, and even a totally incompetent cook—which she was—could heat a can of soup.

While it warmed on the stove, she poured Red a glass of Gatorade, took it out to him, and set it on his end table beside the photograph of his late wife. He'd already dozed off in the recliner. She hated to wake him to eat, but she would. He needed to take his medication, and he'd be extra cranky if he didn't eat. She set his glass on the end table and returned to the kitchen.

Much as she dreaded it, she needed to call Derrick.

She stirred the soup and dialed his number.

"Harper," he said, nearly breathless. "Thank God you called me back."

"It's about your grandfather."

A short pause, then, "Is he all right?"

"He's depressed."

"Why?" Derrick said. "What's he got to be depressed about?"

She silenced the sarcastic response. "He misses you."

"How about you?" Derrick's voice softened. "Do you miss me? Because I miss you. I need you."

Irritation rose like an itchy rash. "This isn't about you and me, Derrick. It's about Red. He hasn't laid eyes on you since you took off that day. Since you tried to—"

"I know what happened, Harper. I was desperate, okay? Don't you think I feel bad enough?"

Nope. She didn't, but she didn't say that. "You're not making it better by staying away. It's been months. You're the only family he has left. He needs to see you."

There was a long pause. She heard street noises in the background and wondered where he was. "You're right. I know you're right. I'm just... I'm ashamed of myself."

"Then apologize. He'll forgive you."

"But will you? Will you ever forgive me?"

She sighed, stirred the soup. "It's not a matter of forgiveness. It's about trust. I care for you, and I want what's best for you. But after what I saw with your grandfather, I don't trust you."

"But that's all taken care of now. I've made arrangements, and the debt'll be paid off soon."

She was in the middle of pulling a bowl down from the cabinet when she froze. Two hundred thousand dollars, and just like that, it was paid? "How?"

"The details don't matter. The point is, it's going to be managed."

"Did you gamble your way out of it?"

His short chuckle was dark. "Hardly."

"Then how—?"

"It's not your problem, and pretty soon, it won't be my problem, either. I've got it handled. And I quit gambling. For good, cold turkey. I'm done with it."

"Really?" Could that be true? Could Derrick really have

done something so drastic, so quickly? "Are you going to meetings?"

"Don't need to. After I saw the way Gramps looked at me, and after you dumped me, I swore I'd never gamble again. And I haven't. Not since we went to the beach."

She was tempted, so tempted, to believe him. Because as certain as she'd been when she broke up with him that it was the right decision, she missed him. She missed the way he'd made her laugh, the way they'd dreamed of the future. She missed his attentiveness, the way he'd lavished her with tenderness. She missed the Derrick she'd met in Las Vegas. Maybe the real Derrick was the one she'd gotten to know at first. Maybe, without the gambling, he could be that man again.

"Give me another chance." His voice was quiet, pleading. "I need you."

There it was. His need. As if she could save him. As if his future were her responsibility. "I'm not ready for that yet. Maybe when your grandfather is himself again and you've been away from gambling longer, maybe then we can talk about it. Right now, let's just keep things as they are."

"As they are?" The tenderness had drained from his voice, and what replaced it confirmed her decision. "As in, we never see each other?"

"That's your choice, not mine. You know where to find me."

"Right. And I can visit you if I visit Gramps. But you don't want to date me. Or talk to me. You don't return my calls or my texts. You don't want anything to do with me."

She smelled something funny and realized the soup was bubbling in the pan. Crap. Only Harper could screw up soup. She yanked the pan off the burner and stirred. Bits of black came off the bottom.

"And now you're not even talking to me," Derrick said.

She dumped the soup and the scalding hot pan into the sink. Now what would they do for dinner?

"I guess I'll just hang up," he said.

Rage hotter than the soup rolled over her. "You know what, Derrick? Do whatever makes you happy. That's all you do anyway. Never mind your grandfather. Never mind that his heart is broken. You keep having your little hissy fit because he wouldn't give you his money and I dumped you. One of these days, you're going to be planning his funeral, and then maybe you'll realize what you missed."

The pause that followed was so long, she thought he'd hung up. She was about do the same when she heard, "You're right."

"So you'll come to see him?"

"Yeah," he said. "I'll try to get up there this weekend."

CHAPTER TWENTY-FOUR

Derrick didn't visit the following weekend. And he didn't visit the next, or the next. In fact, weeks went by, and they didn't hear from him.

Meanwhile, Red's moods didn't improve. They didn't get worse, either, so she decided to celebrate that.

The leaves changed, then dropped from the trees, but she and Red barely left the house to enjoy the cooler weather.

It was the first week of November, and Red was having a terrible day. He'd had a headache and been sick to his stomach all night. He'd skipped breakfast but had eaten a decent lunch. After he ate, he slept in his recliner all afternoon. Odd. She wondered if he was fighting a virus.

They were in the kitchen, Harper cleaning up from their dinner, when he slammed his glass on the table. "Bring me more Gatorade!"

She set down the dishrag, propped her hands on her hips, and glared at him. "I'm sorry. What did you say to me?"

"More"—he lifted his empty glass and shook it in her direction—"this stuff."

His words were slurred as if he were drunk.

And then he vomited all over his plate.

She rushed to his side, unbuttoned his soiled shirt, and slipped it off of him, leaving him shivering in the T-shirt beneath. She cleaned his hands and his mouth and helped him stand. "Come on. Let's get you into your recliner."

He could hardly get himself up. When he did, he swayed against his walker—a new addition he'd railed against when the doctor had suggested it. She steadied him and kept him from falling.

She managed to get him into his chair. He muttered something that sounded like thank-you.

She took his hands. "Squeeze my fingers."

He looked at her as if she were crazy but did as he was told. His grip was strong.

"Lift your hands above your head."

"What the devil—?"

"Just do it, please?"

He held his arms out horizontally, then lifted them up high. "Touchdown."

She chuckled politely. Hmm. His muscles were working fine. She lifted three fingers in front of his face. "How many?"

"Three." The word was strong and certain.

She snatched a pen off his end table. "Track it with your eyes." She moved in slowly in front of his face, and he followed it perfectly.

"What's my name?"

"Harper Cloud."

Right answer, but slightly slurred.

"Why am I here?"

"You're my nurse, though right now, I think you've gone a bit nuts."

"What's your favorite kind of nut?"

He narrowed his eyes, seemed to be formulating a wise crack, and then sighed. "Cashews."

Yup. The man ate them like candy. "What's your name?"

"Harold Carlock Burns. But everybody calls me Red."

She took his blood pressure. It was normal, if anything, a little low.

Perching in the chair beside him, she tried to think what could cause slurred speech. Aside from that, there were no signs of stroke.

"I'm thirsty," he said.

"You just threw up."

His eyes widened. "I did?"

He'd forgotten?

"I'm still thirsty."

She went into the kitchen, poured him a glass of Gatorade, and took it out to him.

He guzzled it.

"Slow down. You're going to be sick again."

But he ignored her and focused on the TV, the glass cradled in his hand.

If she didn't know better, she'd say he was drunk. She pulled a blanket over him and sat beside him until he fell asleep. It took him less than three minutes.

After she cleaned up the mess in the kitchen, she called the doctor's office and got a nurse on the phone. Harper described the symptoms, and the nurse confirmed that it was probably a virus. "If he continues to throw up or starts refusing to drink, you'll need to bring him in. Otherwise, let's just wait it out a couple of days."

Wait it out. That would be a good idea, except Harper couldn't silence the niggling thought that this was something serious.

Could his health fail this fast?

She'd seen it happen, of course. In the nursing home where she'd worked, she'd seen people go from relatively healthy to very sick to the grave in a matter of weeks, sometimes days. But there was always a reason. The flu or a virus could lead to pneumonia. A fall could result in a broken bone, which could be the first domino that ultimately led to death.

But in Red's case, what had been the catalyst? This virus couldn't be blamed. He'd only been sick a few days. But his health, his moods, his depression...

The only thing that had changed was Derrick's behavior. Could all this be the result of a broken heart?

Did Derrick care at all?

Yeah, Derrick cared. About the money Red hadn't given him. About his inheritance.

The thought shamed her. How could she think such a thing? Derrick loved his grandfather. He was angry Red hadn't given him money, but that didn't change the underlying love the two men had for each other. Derrick was just desperate, and desperate people did desperate things.

Which was why, the week after Derrick had tried to swindle Red out of money, Red had asked his lawyer and friend, Roger, to come by. They'd drawn up some sort of papers that would give Roger power of attorney in case something happened to him. The paperwork also protected Red's money, in case Derrick should try to swindle him again. Essentially, it gave Roger the right to appeal any large distributions of cash. She hadn't been in their meeting, of course, and didn't know the details, only that if Derrick came back with any tall tales that involved large sums of money, she was supposed to call Roger.

Red's money was safe. But Derrick hadn't come back.

So much for all his promises.

And now, Red was sick. She should call Derrick and tell him, but she knew where that would lead. Absolutely nowhere.

Besides, it was Thursday. Derrick wouldn't make the drive from Baltimore until the weekend unless there were an emergency. If things didn't change, she'd call him tomorrow.

From the living room, Red shouted, "Bring me a drink!"

She snatched his cup and poured the last of the yellow-green liquid into it. It only filled halfway, so she stepped into the garage where she kept the case of Gatorade she'd bought a few weeks before.

Red hollered again. "Thirsty!"

What in the world? This demanding tone was not like him. A virus couldn't make him mean, could it?

She returned to the kitchen and twisted the top of the Gatorade. It opened easily. Far too easily.

She lifted the bottle. It looked fine. It probably was fine. Did Gatorade go bad? Did it ferment?

No. Surely not.

But maybe that would explain the vomiting. Had the last bottle been easy to open? She couldn't remember.

Well, she wasn't taking any chances with Red's health. She returned to the garage, snatched another bottle from the case, and looked at the seal.

It was broken. The bottle had been opened. She twisted off the cap and sniffed it. It smelled like Gatorade. She looked at the yellow liquid. It looked like Gatorade. She took a sip. It tasted like Gatorade.

What in the world?

She hefted the other three bottles that remained in the case into the kitchen. All of them had been opened. Had they spoiled?

Sheesh. The store manager was going to get a piece of her mind when she went back. If that's what caused Red's illness, they were going to get a lot worse than that.

"I'm thirsty!" Red yelled.

She forced a deep, calming breath, then went into the living room. "We're out of Gatorade."

"There's a whole case out there."

"I think it went bad. I think that's why you're sick."

"Gatorade doesn't go bad." He winced, held his head. "My head is pounding."

She returned to the kitchen, grabbed two Tylenols and a glass of sweet tea, and took them to him."

"I want my Gatorade."

"We're out."

He snatched the pills, drank the tea, and scowled. "Don't like this stuff."

"I can get you water, if you'd prefer."

He started to say something, paused, and focused on the TV. "Sorry I've been so mean to you."

"Oh." She hadn't expected that. "You don't feel good."

When he focused on her again, she saw the sweet, gentle man who'd been there all along. "It scares me, you know?" His words were a little slurred. Again, she had the thought that if she didn't know better, she'd think he were drunk. "I'm afraid I'll never feel good again."

She set her hand on his bony shoulder. "You will. I'm sure you will."

He rested his head against the chair. "I'm gonna take a little nap. Will you get me more Gatorade?"

She considered it, but... "I don't want to leave you alone."

He patted the house phone, which was never very far. "Your phone number is programmed in here. Number three."

"That's right."

"I'll call you if anything happens. You can just run to the grocery store. You'll be gone, what, thirty minutes?" He closed his eyes. "What can happen in thirty minutes?"

She didn't want to leave him alone, but she needed him to

stay hydrated and knew he'd dig his heels in about Gatorade. "You promise you won't try to stand?"

He didn't even open his eyes when he answered. "Scouts honor."

Fine. She kissed his forehead. "I'll be right back."

CHAPTER TWENTY-FIVE

Harper snatched the keys to Red's Cadillac and headed out. She'd be happy to drive her Jetta, but Red and Derrick had both insisted that she use the Caddy as long as she was staying at the house. Which made sense—her Jetta was so old, it could die at any moment, and she needed a car she could rely on. So her old VW had been parked in the two-car garage for months.

The dark sedan that was so often parked in front of the house further down the street wasn't there. Even though she knew it was nothing to worry about, she was glad to see the spot empty. For some reason she never understood, that car made her skin crawl. Old habits. If nothing else, at least she was safe in Maryland. Eventually, her heart would believe it.

It was dark by the time she wheeled her grocery cart out of the store. She'd grabbed six bottles of Red's favorite flavor, lemon-lime. She checked her watch—she'd been gone twenty minutes already. She should have had the Gatorade delivered. She hadn't considered it until she'd stepped into the grocery store and seen the sign advertising home delivery. She'd never used it, relishing her trips away from the house, enjoying the change of scenery. Today, she hurried and told herself Red was fine. Asleep. And he'd still be asleep when she returned. Alive and snoring softly in his chair.

But her stomach filled with acid anyway.

And her skin crawled.

Paranoia, nothing more.

The parking lot was about a third full of cars but empty of shoppers and store employees at the moment. She stopped the cart beside the trunk of Red's Caddy, then walked to the door and pulled it open. She tossed her keys and purse onto the seat and popped the trunk.

"Harper?"

She whipped around, startled.

On the other side of the open door stood a man.

He wore a ski mask.

She opened her mouth to scream, but from behind her a hand clamped over her face, and an arm wrapped around her waist.

She struggled silently, uselessly.

The person holding her pulled her from behind the open door. He pressed her against his body.

The masked man slowly pushed her door closed. He wore dark jeans and a black wool jacket over a black turtleneck. It was too dark to see the color of his eyes or skin. His hair was completely covered. Only his lips showed through the hole in the mask.

He leaned in close. She thought he was going to say something, but he didn't speak. Just nuzzled his nose against her neck. His breath sent a shudder of terror through her, and she lifted her shoulder to block him from touching her. The man behind her yanked her head to the side.

The masked man inhaled her scent, then chuckled.

A deep, rumbly sound from the pit of hell.

He shifted, but she couldn't see what he was doing. The man behind her held her head too tightly. She heard a snap. Caught sight of a blade and squeezed her eyes closed. *Oh, God, help!*

The cold edge sliced across her neck. The cut burned, and a warm trickle dribbled toward her collarbone.

She was going to die. One more inch, and the blade would slice her jugular.

And then the blade was gone.

She opened her eyes, saw the man's face just inches from hers. His hot finger slid down her neck in a perversely gentle move. Again, she struggled away from his touch, and again, the man behind her held her still.

The man lifted his finger so she could see her blood, then wiped it on his jeans. Through that small opening for his mouth, she saw him smile.

Then he punched her in the stomach.

The breath whooshed out, and her legs buckled.

The other man lost his hold over her mouth, but it didn't matter. She couldn't get enough air to scream. He kept her upright, and the other man backhanded her in the face.

She crumpled to the ground, curled into the fetal position, and covered her head with her arms.

One of them grabbed her arm and yanked her back. Pain shot through her wrist, but still, she had no air to scream.

The other man grabbed one of her legs. They pulled until she was lying flat out and helpless on the asphalt.

They flipped her on her stomach.

She reached forward, desperate to crawl away, to slide beneath the car, to make it all stop. Her hand touched something, and she grabbed it, held on, before she realized it was one of the men's shoes. She recoiled as if she'd touched a rattlesnake.

One of them stomped a foot between her shoulder blades, and the little air she'd been getting was forced out.

The other dragged her in front of her car so she was hidden between hers and the one parked in front. She could feel him looking down at her, watching her.

She curled up, covered her head. Tried to pray but couldn't seem to form anything beyond, *please, please.*

She still couldn't get breath to scream.

She heard movement. Heard her trunk close. Heard the shopping cart being rolled away.

The man standing over her bent down, whispered in her ear, "Tell him we stopped by."

Then they were gone.

CHAPTER TWENTY-SIX

Harper worked to pull air into her lungs until her breathing was normal again.

They were gone. She was alone. Still, she didn't move.

Cold from the asphalt seeped through her jeans, soothed the pain in her right wrist. A shopping cart wheeled past. She told herself to rise but didn't. Because if the people walking by were good people, they'd call the police, who'd want her to answer a bunch of questions. She had no information to give them. No idea what the attackers had been driving or what they looked like. There was nothing the police could do for her. They'd just slow her down.

Red. She had to get back to Red.

When the noises faded, she sat up, took a deep breath.

The cold air revived her.

Using the front fender for help, she pulled herself to a standing position. Her back ached from where the man had stomped it, but she could move. It was only bruised, nothing worse.

She twisted her right wrist in every direction. Painful, but it wasn't broken. Just a sprain.

Tentatively, she touched her cheek and winced.

It hurt, but she was fine. She inhaled another deep breath of that sweet, sweet oxygen and made it to the driver's door.

She was fine. She'd be fine.

She grabbed her keys and purse from the seat, slid in, then slammed the door and locked it.

She was safe. For now.

Only then did she begin to tremble.

She glanced at the clock on the dash. Thirty minutes had passed since she'd walked out of the grocery store.

Two for the assault, twenty-eight for her to drag herself to her car. Not very good numbers.

She used to be so much tougher than that.

What if Red had woken, gotten confused? Her heart pounded a rapid-fire rhythm. She had one job—take care of Red. What if she'd blown it tonight? What if something happened to him while she was gone trying to help him?

All this for Gatorade.

She backed out of the spot and hurried to the mansion she'd had the gall to call home.

Ten minutes later, she pulled to a stop in the garage, hit the remote to close the garage door, and popped the trunk. Before she exited the car, she checked her reflection in the rearview mirror. She was pale, but no bruises had formed. She angled so she could see her neck. The cut was angry and red, and a trail of blood led to her golf shirt. She lifted the collar to hide it and pushed open the door.

She lifted one foot and set it on the concrete floor, then turned to get the other out. The motion sent a shot of pain through her upper back. She breathed through it, shifted until she was facing out, and stood.

So far, so good.

It seemed that if she kept her back straight, didn't twist or bend, it was fine. Walking as stiffly as possible, she made her way to the trunk. It was crazy to think her attackers had loaded the bottles for her, but something had been rolling around in there on the drive back.

She peeked inside, and there were the drink bottles.

What kind of attackers...?

The professional kind. The kind who attacked because it was their job, though that man's smile...

She shook it off, bent at the knees, and managed to pull out one bottle. She carried it into the house and set it on the counter. Then she moved as fast as she could into the living room.

Red woke with a start, glared at her. "Where's the fire?"

The anxiety she'd been holding whooshed out. She turned off the lamp on the table beside him, sat on the couch, and stared at the stupid game show on the screen. He was fine. Nothing had happened.

Not to him, anyway.

The room was dim, soothing with just the one small lamp on. Dim was good. Dim meant Red, with his failing eyesight, wouldn't be able to see her well.

His chair creaked, and the footrest on his recliner slid back beneath the seat. She turned to find him looking at her. His scowl was gone. Somehow, so was the strange behavior from earlier. He seemed normal. Like a drunk who sobered up in a crisis. "You okay?"

For the first time since the assault, tears filled her eyes. She sniffed, nodded. "I'm fine."

"What happened?"

"I... I slipped and fell in the parking lot at the grocery store." She pulled the collar up on her shirt, just in case. "Landed on my back."

He reached across the space and took her hand. The

strength of his grip always surprised her. "Should we go to the ER?"

"No, no. It's nothing. Just a bruise." She wiped the few tears, met the old man's eyes, saw kindness and concern there, which only made her want to cry more. She squeezed his hand. "I'm fine, really. I got your Gatorade."

He still watched her, his eyes piercing as if he could see through her lies. "You sure they aren't back?"

"They who?"

"Whoever..." The slur returned to his voice, and he waved his hands toward her. "Whatever it is puts that haunted look in your eyes. Makes you jumpy."

"Oh." He was more perceptive than she'd realized. "There's nobody. Just my own silly fears."

He studied her a minute more before he nodded. "Just sit with me and rest. Okay?"

She smiled and sat back in the chair.

A few minutes passed, and Red shifted his focus to Pat Sajak and Vanna White on the screen.

As much as she'd like to get lost in the puzzle on TV, Harper had a call to make.

"I'll be right back." She stood carefully, returned to the kitchen, and fixed him a glass of Gatorade. After she set it on the end table beside him, she returned to the kitchen and pulled her cell phone from her purse. She was still trembling.

Derrick answered after the second ring. "Hey." His voice was tentative. "Is Gramps all right?"

"I need you to come right away."

"Is he sick?"

She told herself not to analyze the tone of his voice, but the word *hopeful* sprang to mind. "He's fine, but we have an emergency. How soon can you be here?"

"This time of night... Probably forty-five minutes. I'm on my way."

After she hung up, she returned to the living room and watched TV with Red, careful of the sharp pains in her back. They were already better than they had been. After a night's sleep, she'd be good as new. Red was quiet, dozing. If not for the strange illness, he'd be studying her, trying to figure out what was going on with her. Even healthy, he'd never guess in a million years that she'd been assaulted. Funny how something so life-altering could be so easily hidden. Shoved to the back-burner. Forgotten. As if having her life threatened were nothing noteworthy. As if having strangers capture her, attack her, and leave her writhing in pain on the pavement were no big deal.

But she knew better. Knew the two minutes tonight in the parking lot would plague her for a long time.

Finally, a soft knock at the front door was followed by the sound of the key sliding into the lock. The door opened, and she walked through the formal dining room and met Derrick in the foyer. She stayed on the far side, crossed her arms. In the dim light, she saw the man she'd nearly fallen for. The brown hair with its widow's peak hairline, the kind hazel eyes and glasses that made him look geeky and kind. Everything about Derrick seemed normal, down-to-earth, gentle. She should have known better.

He looked at her, blinked, stepped closer. "What happened?"

"Quite a few things, actually."

He flipped on the chandelier. "Are you bleeding?"

She pulled her collar up to hide the cut. "Not anymore."

He reached toward her. "Let's go sit down. Is Gramps okay?"

She stepped back, out of his reach. "Go out to the Caddy and grab the Gatorade from the trunk. Please. Then we'll talk."

"Uh…"

She stepped into the half bath off the foyer, wet a tissue, and dabbed at the dried blood that had left a track along her skin. Thank God Red hadn't seen the cut. She added some antibacterial lotion and a bandage, then returned to the kitchen, where Derrick was setting down the bottles of Gatorade he'd carried in.

"It's not like you to run out of Gatorade. You want them in the garage?"

"Set them on the counter."

He did, then they both sat at the table. The light was brighter here than it had been in the foyer, and when he sat, he studied her. "Geez, Harper. What happened?" He reached out like he might touch her face, the red spot she'd barely glanced at in the bathroom. She leaned back, and he dropped his hand on the table.

"You're saying you don't know?"

"How would I?"

Based on the confusion on his face, he had no idea. But she'd quit believing anything Derrick said. He reached for her hand, and she jerked away.

Pain shot through her upper back, and she froze, breathed through it.

Derrick lowered his hand. "You're hurt. I need to take you—"

"You've done enough, I think."

His eyes narrowed. He leaned back just enough. "What are you talking about?"

"Have you had someone watching me?"

"Of course not. Why would I?"

Either he was the best liar in the world—and that was entirely possible—or he had no idea. Still…

"They told me to tell you they stopped by."

The color in his face faded. "Who?"

"The men who did this to me."

"Men?" He leaned toward her. "What men? Where were you?"

"This was about you."

"I don't know why someone would—"

"I assume they were trying to send you a message," she said. "Maybe if you'd let them know we broke up—"

"No, Harper. This wasn't... Whatever happened, it didn't have anything to do with me. I don't know what you're talking about."

"So you know nothing about the men who beat me up in the grocery store parking lot?"

He reached across the table. When she didn't take his hand, he left it there, palm up, an invitation she'd never accept. "Please, start at the beginning."

The memory of it had her rubbing her wrist. He caught the motion. "Here, let me—"

"No. You don't get to cause this and then comfort me. Whatever's going on with your goon friends, tell them we're not together anymore."

He stared at her with that fake innocence. She couldn't stand to look at him. "Go see Red. He misses you."

"I don't know what's going on."

"You still owe people money?"

His expression gave away nothing. After a moment, he nodded.

"I thought you said it was taken care of."

"I'm working on it."

"Apparently, it's time to renegotiate your payment plan."

His head dropped forward. He dug his fingers in his hair and kept his face hidden for a long time. When he looked up, his eyes were red, worried. "I'm sorry. I don't know what's going on.

I'll... I mean, if this had anything to do with me, then I'll see what I can do."

"Unless your grandfather is into shady business, Derrick, it has to be about you."

He swallowed, nodded. "You're probably..." Tears filled his eyes, but he didn't look away. "I would never hurt you. You have to know that."

But he had hurt her. A lot.

"I'm trying to fix it. I'm going to get it fixed. I still haven't gambled. And I haven't come by because I wanted to be able to tell you that it was all taken care of. I thought it would be, sooner than this. But things just... Nothing seems to work out for me."

Wow. She'd been assaulted tonight, and he had the nerve to feel sorry for himself. She couldn't even muster the anger he deserved.

"Go see your grandfather."

Derrick stood. "It's late. I'll visit this weekend."

She stared at this man she'd thought she might someday love. "I keep thinking you might surprise me. You might turn into the man I thought you were when I first met you." She stood. "Don't make promises you don't intend to keep."

"I never meant for you to get hurt. I love you, Harper." He wiped a few tears from his eyes.

The tears were authentic, but they weren't for her. He didn't love her. She wasn't sure what love was, but it wasn't this. It wasn't lies and manipulation and broken promises.

"I know I should have come sooner," he said. "It's just... It's hard to be here with us like"—he indicated the space between them—"like this."

She closed her eyes. "Just get out."

CHAPTER TWENTY-SEVEN

Somehow, Harper got through the rest of the evening. She'd been careful to keep her collar pulled up high to hide the bandage on her neck as she'd given Red his last round of medication. He drank his Gatorade and already seemed to feel better. After he finished his nighttime routine, she helped him into his room.

"I can put myself to bed, you know," he said. "I'm not a two-year-old."

She pulled the covers up to his neck. Normally, she'd lean down to kiss his forehead, but her back wouldn't like that. And if she leaned too much, he'd have a great view of her neck, and she didn't have the energy to deflect his questions right now. She patted his shoulder. "I want to tuck you in, you grouchy old coot."

He gripped her hand. "If your back's not better tomorrow, we're going to the doctor."

She didn't bother to argue. Sick as he was, he'd probably forget by morning.

After Harper closed his bedroom door, she checked all the doors and windows. Everything was locked.

Those goons had sent their message, and she'd passed it along. She was safe now.

Why was she always trying to convince herself of that?

All the events of the previous few hours came back, and her hands trembled again. She made it to her bedroom and locked the door. She kept the light off and peeked through the blinds out the window. The sedan that was parked in front of the neighbors' house so often was gone.

Had Derrick been watching her? It didn't make sense, but then, what did? The only people she knew in Maryland, the only people she knew on the East Coast, were Derrick, Red, Roger, Red's lawyer, the folks she'd met at the beach, and Red's many healthcare providers. So who would watch her?

And why?

All this time, she'd thought she was being paranoid, told herself the car was owned by the people who lived in that house. But she'd never seen anyone get in or out. She'd never seen it pull up to the house, either. It was almost always there after dark. From here, she'd never been able to see if anybody was inside the car. There'd just been that one time when she'd been sure she saw the glow of a cell phone.

She sighed and let go of the blinds. After tonight, she wasn't about to pass off her fear as paranoia. Tonight, her suspicion felt justified.

Red's illness had exhausted her. The attack... She didn't want to think about that. She didn't want to think about anything.

She went into her private bathroom and locked that door, too. She turned on the shower. While it warmed up, she undressed and looked at herself in the mirror. There'd be an ugly bruise on her cheek in the morning. She hoped makeup would cover it so Red wouldn't notice. They'd have to stay close to home the next few days until it faded. She removed the bandage and studied the cut on her neck again. It was ugly, but it wasn't deep. She could wear turtlenecks until it healed. Her stomach and ribs ached, but nobody could tell that from looking at her.

A bruise was forming on her wrist. Fortunately, it was cold enough for long sleeves.

She turned to look at her upper back but saw no shoe print there. As usual, the worst blows left no visible marks.

She had enough experience to know invisible scars could twinge for years.

She turned and met her gaze in the mirror. "You're fine. You've lived through worse."

She stepped into the shower, let the hot water wash away the memories, the feel of that man's hand over her mouth, the other man's breath on her neck.

Her tears fell, mingled with the water, left her feeling, if not clean, at least cleansed of the evil men she'd encountered that night. The attackers. And Derrick.

When the tears were spent, she breathed deeply of the humid air, let even her lungs be washed of memories so she could think straight.

If only she hadn't gone out for Gatorade. If only the Gatorade bottles hadn't already been opened. That a grocery store had let...

Wait. The case had been wrapped in plastic when she'd bought it. The bottles couldn't have been opened before that unless the person who'd opened them had had some way to rewrap them in plastic. But what would have been the point? It was just a handful of bottles. Worth, what, ten dollars? Why go to all that trouble?

Nobody would have done that. Which meant that the bottles had been opened after she'd gotten them home.

But who? Not Red. The only other person who had access to the house was Derrick, and he hadn't been there in months.

Or had he?

She'd kept the Gatorade in the garage. He wouldn't have even had to come in the house. He could have tampered with them out there, and nobody would have known. He could slip in and out without anybody knowing.

No. What was she saying?

It was insane.

And yet... Derrick was desperate.

She didn't want it to be true, but by the time the hot water faded to warm, by the time she turned off the spigot and dried off, she knew she needed to call the police. If those bottles had been tampered with, the police needed to know.

And she should report the attack as well. She'd been foolish not to.

Decision made, she dried off and was wrapping her wet hair in a towel when she heard a door slam.

Her heart pounded. It was probably just Red going to the bathroom. Based on the adrenaline rush to her veins, her heart wasn't convinced.

She slipped on her bathrobe, grabbed her can of mace out of her purse—her keychain with the knife was downstairs by the door—and stepped into the hallway outside her room. Red's bedroom was on the far end of the hall. His door was open. She peeked. He wasn't in bed. She looked into his attached bath. Empty.

She swallowed a rise of panic.

Normally, she'd call for him, but the memories of the evening were too close, whispering like ghosts in her ear. She tried to tamp down her fear as she stepped silently down the back staircase.

She made it to the kitchen, but Red wasn't there.

She transferred the pepper spray to her left hand, finger on the trigger, and grabbed a knife from the block on the counter.

Quietly, she crossed the tile and tiptoed into the living room.

Red was standing beside his recliner, one hand resting on the back of it, staring at the floor on the far side of the sofa. Sick as he was, how in the world had he gotten downstairs? Was he sleepwalking? What was he staring at?

She forced herself to speak calmly and said, "Red? Is everything okay?"

He looked at her, didn't seem to recognize her, and looked back at the floor.

What was that in his eyes? A look she'd never seen before on his face.

Terror.

She stepped closer and followed his gaze.

Two men were lying on the floor. She focused on one. Saw jeans and black turtleneck and black wool coat. There was a dark stain on the jeans. A bloodstain. Her blood. The ski mask was gone.

The other man... Her breath hitched. It was Kitty's husband, Keith Williams.

These were the men who'd attacked her.

She didn't have to take a pulse to know they were dead.

One look at their foreheads confirmed that. Bullet holes.

CHAPTER TWENTY-EIGHT

Harper couldn't make herself move.

This wasn't happening. This couldn't be happening.

Something gripped her arm, and she jumped and twisted. Pain shot up her back. She breathed through it while she stared at Red's bewildered gaze.

She slid the knife and pepper spray into the pocket of her bathrobe. Red wasn't holding a gun. Of course he wasn't. He couldn't have done this.

She gripped his upper arm. "Come on." She helped him into the kitchen, where she settled him in a chair. How had he gotten so far without his walker? Adrenaline. Fear could do that to people, give them strength they hadn't known they had. Eventually, the strength would run out, and they'd be left weaker, more vulnerable, than ever.

His face was pale, his hands trembling. She kneeled in front of him. "What happened?"

He only shook his head.

"Did you see anything? Was someone here?"

His gaze flicked to her. Behind his eyes, she saw nothing but confusion. This time of night, considering how sick he'd been all day, considering what he'd just seen... He'd checked out. He probably wouldn't remember any of this in the morning. It was one of the reasons Derrick had insisted he needed a private nurse—these sporadic moments of forgetfulness.

He'd be no help.

She checked the doors. The one leading to the garage was still dead-bolted, as was the front door. The door that led to the back patio wasn't fully closed, even though she knew she'd bolted it earlier. She didn't touch it. Maybe there'd be finger-prints or something.

She should call the police.

She turned, saw the bodies again. Keith. Kitty's husband. A loan shark's goon. Also, a detective. A cop. Dead in the house where she'd been living.

She had to force herself to take deep breaths, to think.

She returned to the kitchen, where Red was staring at the wall, half asleep but safe. For now.

Who'd killed those men? And why leave them here?

Was someone trying to frame her? With her record, she'd be the perfect person to frame for murder. But for what purpose? What threat did she pose to anyone? All she did was care for...

The bottles of Gatorade she'd just bought caught her eye.

If her suspicions were right, then somebody was trying to kill Red. Maybe that same someone wanted her out of the way to get to Red's money. The most obvious person who'd benefit from Red's death was Derrick. Would he have killed these men?

She couldn't imagine. The man she'd known would never be capable of such violence, of such evil. On the other hand, the man she'd known had never truly existed.

But to frame her? Why would he do that, when he'd been trying to get her back for weeks? Just today, he'd told her he loved her. Was that all a lie? For what purpose?

And why leave the bodies here?

Was it a threat? Were she and Red in danger?

Obviously they were. A murderer had left two bodies in this house. And Harper didn't know why.

A murderer. In her house.

Fear skittered down her back, and she looked around. She patted Red on the hand and began to search. She was sure the murderer was gone. But what if he wasn't?

She made sure the door to the garage was dead-bolted. Then she pulled her mace and the knife she'd grabbed earlier from the pockets of her bathrobe. Her hands trembled as she held her weapons in front of her and crept through the house, a scream trying to claw its way up her throat. The pantry, the half-bath, the front closet, Red's office—all empty. In the living room, she kept her gaze away from the dead men and looked behind the sofa. She crept upstairs, searched Derrick's room—his since his parents had died—the guest room, and Red's room. Then her own room, just in case.

She grabbed her cell phone. An intelligent person would've called the police immediately. Or just jumped in the car and run.

She wasn't making very logical decisions.

She returned to the kitchen, certain the house was empty of bad guys. For now. Red was dozing in the hard-backed kitchen chair.

She sat beside him and returned to the question she'd been mulling before the sudden search. Who else would benefit from Red's death?

The people Derrick owed money to. If Derrick inherited Red's estate, he'd be able to pay them back. Was that how this kind of thing worked?

It didn't make sense.

And until she understood why the men had been murdered and left there, how could she call the police? She'd be in jail before the sun came up. And then where would Red go? To a nursing home? Or would the police hand him over to Derrick? Derrick, who may be trying to kill him.

Could Red's attorney get involved? Would he believe her if she told him Derrick had been poisoning Red? How could she trust Roger when she barely knew him?

And how could she trust the police to protect Red? She'd trusted the police before, and she'd paid for that decision with two years in a state penitentiary.

With a dead cop thrown into the mix... They'd be ruled by emotions, not logic. They wouldn't care about some sick old man. They'd only care about finding the killer. And they'd look at her first. With Red's dementia, they wouldn't trust his accounting of her whereabouts tonight. Red wouldn't be able to tell them what time she'd gone to bed. He wouldn't be able to convince them she'd been home all evening. And she hadn't been. She'd gone out for Gatorade. Would they use that against her?

The only person who could corroborate her alibi wouldn't be fit to testify.

Her reason for going out wouldn't make sense to anyone. Why buy more bottles of what you already had?

But she could explain. She could prove it—show them the bottles of Gatorade. She rushed to the garage to grab one of the bottles, to keep it for evidence.

But the Gatorade that had been there, the Gatorade she'd thought poisoned, was gone.

Derrick must have taken them. Which proved her theory—he'd poisoned his grandfather.

Prison. She'd end up back in prison.

She returned to the kitchen, collapsed into a chair, and squeezed her eyes closed. She'd survived prison before. She could survive again. But Red...

Somebody had planted the bodies there for a reason, and Harper had no idea what that reason was. A threat? An attempt to frame her? Something else?

All she knew was that she didn't know anything. She certainly didn't know whom she could trust. Not the police. Not Derrick. Not anybody.

Just herself.

She had to keep Red safe. That was her first priority. And then she had to figure out what was going on. Maybe if the police found the bodies, they'd investigate and discover who the real killers were. Or maybe, if she had enough time, she could do some research, figure it out herself. Then, she could come back.

But right now, she and Red had to go.

CHAPTER TWENTY-NINE

arper left Red in the kitchen and rushed upstairs. She snatched his suitcase from his walk-in closet and filled it with his favorite clothes and a spare pair of shoes. After she tossed in all his toiletries and medications, she rushed into her room. Her suitcase was falling apart, but she'd make it work. She grabbed all the clothes and toiletries she could fit into it. Warm things, comfortable things. The gifts Derrick had given her—clothes, shoes, jewelry—she left.

Careful of her back, she carried the suitcases downstairs and hefted them into the trunk of her beat-up VW Jetta. The Caddy was better in every way except one: its navigation software would make her far too easy to track. The Jetta would blend in and keep them safe.

She had no money. Derrick didn't have access to Red's accounts, but Red's lawyer did. He could help Derrick—or the police—track her.

She'd have to get as much cash as she could as fast as possible. Once they settled somewhere, she wouldn't be able to access Red's accounts.

What choice did she have, though? She'd figure something out.

Back inside, she checked on Red. His head lolled forward in the kitchen chair. She grabbed the bottles of Gatorade she'd purchased earlier and set them in the trunk. One less thing she'd have to buy.

She rushed up the stairs and grabbed his walker. She looked around at his room. What was she forgetting? She couldn't think straight. After another moment of concentration, she shook it off. As long as she had his medications, they should be able to replace everything else.

In the kitchen, she set the walker in front of Red and shook his shoulder gently. "We need to go."

He was confused, but he didn't argue as she helped him stand and walked him to her car. He didn't even complain that they weren't taking the Cadillac.

She got her purse, took one last look around the house, and then returned to the car and sat behind the wheel. She pressed the button to open the garage door and backed into the driveway.

The dark sedan was parked in front of the neighbors' house again. That creepy feeling of being watched followed her right now, but was that a surprise?

She had been watched. She'd been followed to the grocery store.

She was being watched right now.

At the street, she turned toward the highway. Red's house, the house she'd called home for months, faded in the rearview mirror.

Had it been so wrong to wish for a home? For a family? Maybe Red wasn't her grandfather, but she loved him. Being estranged from her own parents and brothers had left her adrift.

Red had given her a safe place, a solid foundation. Now, even that was gone.

Her security was gone.

Her dream of reconciling with her own family was gone.

If she wasn't careful, her freedom would be gone, too. Evaporate like mist and leave her shackled and alone.

She didn't know where they would go or what they would do. All she knew was that, one way or another, she'd keep Red safe. As long as he was safe, she could take whatever consequences came her way.

II

BEAUTY IN HIDING

To Ray Patchen
Korean War veteran
Father-in-law extraordinaire
And inspiration for Harold "Red" Burns

CHAPTER ONE

Of course it was raining.

And not merely raining. Harper had been whiteknuckling the steering wheel of her used VW Jetta through an absolute deluge since Rhode Island. Visibility had been practically nonexistent on the interstate. After she'd exited onto the state highway that brought her to Nutfield, thanks to the lack of street lights, visibility had been no farther than a few feet in front of her car.

The constant swish-swish of the wipers was the only sound as she stopped at a T in the road. The area was deserted. Maybe that was normal in a little town for a Monday night at eightthirty. She had no idea. She'd never lived anywhere this far off the beaten path.

She consulted her phone to check the map, but her navigation software was trying—and failing—to figure out where she was. Shocking that a fifty-dollar pay-as-you-go phone from the convenience store didn't work properly.

Fortunately, she'd studied the map enough at the last stop that she sort of knew where she was going. Sort of.

She glanced at Red, the elderly man in her care. His eyes

were wide with worry, and she didn't blame him. He'd had a very difficult few days. Both of them had, but they'd survived this long. She'd keep Red safe even if it killed her.

Which it very well might.

She turned left and picked up speed. The car hit a puddle that had looked manageable, but water splashed against the windshield, momentarily blinding her. The wheels slid, and she hit the brake.

"Be careful!" Red shouted.

By the time she got the car under control, her heart had wedged in her throat.

She pulled into the breakdown lane, stopped, and rested her head against her hands on the steering wheel. They were okay. She hadn't careened off the side of this dark road and landed in a ditch. They were almost there.

If she remembered correctly, the street they were looking for wasn't far. She glanced in the rearview, which revealed no headlights, and maneuvered back into the lane, driving slowly to peer at the street signs.

And there it was. Thank God. She turned onto a street barely wide enough for two cars. The house they wanted was supposed to be the first on the left, but there were no houses anywhere. She'd driven about two hundred yards and was about to give up when she saw a driveway.

Harper checked the address on her phone, peered through the downpour at the mailbox, and focused on the house beyond. She could barely make out the shape of it in the rain. It was completely dark.

"Where in the blazes are we now, girl?"

Harper stretched her face into what she hoped would look like a smile and turned to the old man in the passenger seat. "We're home."

Red peered through the pouring rain. "This isn't home. This isn't anywhere near home."

She patted his leg. "It will be, soon enough."

He harrumphed, a reaction that had become familiar to her in recent days. Thanks to the traffic, the rain that had battered them all day, and Red's frequent need for stops, what should've been a five-hour drive from the hotel in Newark had become eight. Every bone in her body ached with exhaustion. She couldn't imagine how he felt.

She maneuvered the car beside the mailbox, pulled it open, and snatched the keys, but not fast enough to keep the rain from soaking the arm of her sweatshirt. It'd been a long time since she'd lived anywhere safe enough to leave keys in a mailbox. Maybe it was a good sign the landlord left them there. Maybe those keys meant that coming here wasn't the stupidest, rashest thing she'd ever done.

Not that she'd had a lot of choices.

She backed into the driveway so Red would be closer to the front door.

Gramps. Gramps. She had to get used to calling him Gramps.

"Let me unlock the house, then I'll come back for you."

"Don't you leave me out here." His words were gruff, but they didn't conceal the fear beneath them. As if she'd ever do anything to harm him. As if she hadn't risked everything to protect him.

But he didn't know that. He didn't know what she'd discovered about his grandson, Derrick, and he didn't remember the bodies he'd discovered in the living room of his home.

"I'll be right back. I promise." After she snatched her raincoat from the backseat and slipped it on, she pulled the hood over her head, and pushed open the door. Cold rain splattered against her jeans as she hurried around the car and up the steps.

The wind whipped, blowing the hood of her jacket against her face and making it hard to see while she tried to shove the key in the lock. Finally, she opened the door.

Inside, she lowered her hood and took in the space. There were hardwood floors that needed to be refinished and off-white walls that looked freshly painted. A sofa and a recliner were separated by a side table, and a narrow coffee table stretched in front of the sofa. The furniture seemed, if not new, then only gently used. A fireplace was tucked into the wall on her right. What she wouldn't give for a blaze in there right now. An old TV stand stood empty against the wall beside her.

She crossed the living area into the kitchen. Small and functional. The cabinets were worn but clean—on the outside anyway. She opened the refrigerator door. Clean, and cold inside, so the landlord had made good on his promise to turn it on. A small round kitchen table had four chairs surrounding it.

Harper headed down the hallway toward the bedrooms. Just like the landlord had said, each had a bed and dresser. No bedding, but she'd taken care of that. The only bathroom was just before the smaller bedroom.

This would work.

She stared at the bed in the smaller room, her room, and fantasized about falling into it for a nap. She and Gramps had been in New Jersey by the time the sun rose Friday morning. They'd spent the weekend in a hotel near Newark. On Friday, she'd treated Red for antifreeze poisoning after doing extensive research on what could have been slipped into his Gatorade based on his symptoms. Everything matched, and lucky for her, antifreeze could be flushed from the body with alcohol. Lucky for her, but not for Red. She'd given him multiple doses of his *medicine*—straight vodka—for twenty-four hours. Once the hangover faded, he seemed weaker than when she'd begun. His dementia had been worse than ever, though that might have been in part due to the unfamiliar surroundings. But the effects of the poison had worn off.

Maybe she'd saved him. The cure was awful, but alcohol wouldn't kill him. Antifreeze would.

Using Gramps's debit card, she'd taken the daily limit out of his checking account every day, done some shopping, and searched for a place to live. She figured Derrick would assume she'd headed southwest, since that's the direction she'd come from, so she'd searched northeast and found this place in rural New Hampshire. The price was right, the location so random, nobody would think to look for them here. Now that they were settled, she couldn't use the debit card again. Too easy to track.

Now, she was in a rental home in New Hampshire. Nobody would find her here. But could she discover what had happened back in Maryland? Until she did, she and Red would have to stay hidden. Gramps. She and *Gramps* would have to stay hidden.

She pulled her hood up again and rushed through the rain to the car, where she took Gramps's walker out of the trunk and unfolded it. Then she opened his door.

"Took you long enough." He was staring at the house, his voice raised to be heard over the rain. "What are we doing here?"

"This is our new home."

He crossed his arms. "I want to go back to my house. I don't like this one."

"I know," she said. "Let's just go inside and check it out. You've got to be tired of this car."

He stared at the house, then at her, then at the house again. Finally, he blew out an angry breath. "I'm not gonna like it."

"That's the spirit." She stood back, left the walker close by, and helped him turn so his feet were on the driveway. The events of the previous few days—the poison, the treatment, and seeing those dead men, not to mention running for their lives and staying in a shady hotel—had left him weaker than she'd ever seen him. "Come on out, Gramps."

"Why you keep calling me that?"

She'd explained it to him, but he'd forgotten her desire for people to believe they were related. Now wasn't the time to go over it again, so she ignored the question while he tried to stand. Couldn't seem to make it. She moved the walker out of his way. "Let me help."

"Don't need your help." But he gripped her forearms like he might a lifesaver in the ocean. She hid the pain his grip caused. The bruise on that arm wasn't his fault. He didn't even know it was there.

She eased him out, then steadied him on his feet and adjusted his fedora. At least his head would stay dry. He leaned on the door while she got his walker into position.

"Can you just—?"

"I got it," he snapped.

Shuffling, they made their way through the rain to the front porch steps. Just three. Should be no trouble, considering at home he navigated an entire flight of stairs every day.

She lifted the walker to the landing, positioned herself on one side while he gripped the wrought-iron handrail on the other. He got his grips right, but when he tried to step up, he couldn't quite make it and rocked back down.

"Let's try that—"

"I don't need your help."

But he didn't move.

He'd been sitting too long. After the poisoning and the antidote, his legs were too weak to make this work. And he was embarrassed.

She forced a deep breath, wiped rainwater out of her eyes, and said as brightly as she could, "Let's give it another shot."

He put his stronger leg on the step, rocked forward. She helped as much as she could and cursed the sprain in her wrist. If not for that, this would be easy. As it was, pain shot up her arm as she took his weight.

He made it to the first step.

Then stopped.

"Two more."

"I can count."

She waited for him to catch his breath. When the rain had thoroughly soaked through her sneakers, she said, "You ready?"

He lifted his foot, rocked forward, and tried. She could feel his effort. Tears filled her eyes from the ache in her arm. Normally, getting up three steps would be no problem. He strained, she strained, and they made it to the second step.

A car splashed by on the street behind them. She didn't turn to see. It wasn't as if it would be a friend. She didn't have any of those, not in this town. Not anywhere.

After a moment's rest, Gramps lifted his foot to the landing, took a deep breath, and rocked forward.

His hand slipped on the rail, and he fell forward. Instinct had her grabbing him. Pain shot up her arm, and gravity pulled him down. He banged his shoulder against the railing and barely got his hand down in time to keep himself from landing face-first on the concrete. He turned, sat on the step, and stared at the wooded front yard.

She sat beside him and buried her face in her hands. Hot tears joined the cold rain. Neither spoke.

What was she doing? How could she protect this man when she couldn't even get him into the house?

Father, help.

She'd begged God for help all weekend. Begged him to make Red better. And He had. Red had woken up today looking better than he had in a week. His bright eyes and the color in his face, the concern in his expression and the joy in his smile had been a blessing. This morning, feeling both grateful and helpless, Harper had decided to embrace the God Gramps and her friend Estelle trusted so completely. She'd been trying, trusting, failing, and trying again for months. That morning, her decision made, she'd felt able to conquer the world. There was a God, and He loved her.

She'd been sure of it.

Now, the world was dark and gray and closing in on her.

A real Christian would know how to pray. Harper didn't know anything about God except what Red and Estelle had told her and what little she'd understood from reading her Bible. If she was wrong about God, then she was lost.

Maybe she was lost anyway.

"Can I help?"

She looked up and wiped her eyes as a man jogged down the driveway. He wore a jacket, jeans, work boots, and a baseball cap. A pickup was parked on the road in front of the house. A total stranger. A man.

"Who are you?"

He stopped at the bottom of the steps and smiled up at them as if conversing in a storm were the most normal thing in the world. "Jack Rossi."

Jack Rossi. This was their new landlord? They'd only corresponded through email, but for some reason, she'd pictured a middle-aged, gray-haired man. She'd been very wrong.

"I presume you're Harper Cloud."

She wiped moisture from her eyes and attempted a smile. "We were just admiring the view."

The man's grin only got wider as he focused on Red... Gramps... who was watching him through narrowed eyes. "Let's do formal introductions inside, shall we?"

Gramps nodded once, turned, and reached for the railing to

pull himself up. She started to position herself on his other side, but Jack stopped her with a touch on her shoulder. He said nothing, just lifted his eyebrows and nodded toward the old man. *May I?*

She wanted to cry all over again, though she wasn't sure why. Because she didn't want to need help? Because she did need it? Because somehow, God had actually answered her prayer?

She opened the door while Jack put Gramps's arm over his shoulder and helped him up. They maneuvered into the house in no time.

Thank God for Jack Rossi.

CHAPTER TWO

The old man's teeth were chattering, and he seemed too worn out to speak. Jack helped him shuffle through the living room and ease into the recliner.

The woman stood in the doorway dripping rainwater from her coat and a hood that obscured her face. Jack asked, "The rest of your stuff is in the car?"

"I can get it."

"There's a quilt in the closet in the master. Why don't you grab that?" He cut his gaze toward the old man.

She paused a moment, nodded to the keys she'd tossed on the coffee table, and headed down the hall.

Jack snagged the car keys, ducked through the rain, and popped her trunk. He lifted a large fancy suitcase, a smaller beat-up suitcase, and a giant department store sack. He returned to drop the things inside before running back out. Seemed the woman had loaded up on groceries. He hooked the bags over his arm and grabbed a case of Gatorade and took them to the kitchen. Back outside, he checked the trunk one more time before opening the rear door. A box containing a brand new flat-screen TV was positioned on the backseat. A purse and a small duffel bag were on the floor behind the passenger seat. He hooked the purse and duffel around his arm and then pulled out the TV. It was a decent size with a handle on the top of the box to make it easy to carry. He slammed the car door with his hip and hurried inside to keep the box from getting too wet.

In the living room, he set the TV box in front of the stand and the purse and duffel on the sofa.

Harper's back was to him as she helped the man out of his wet jacket. She was still wearing hers. Probably too chilled to take it off.

He should take his off, too. Not that he hadn't already dripped all over the living room and kitchen. And he hadn't exactly been invited to stay. "What can I do?"

"We got it," she said, not bothering to turn. "Thanks."

She got the old man's jacket off, set it beside the hat on the hearth, then tucked the quilt around him. "You warming up?"

"It's colder than a witch's—"

"Gramps..."

The man's words died as Harper backed away, shed her own jacket, and turned toward Jack. "Thanks for your help."

"Uh..." Whatever he'd been about to say died on his lips. Holy cow, she was beautiful. Straight blond, shoulder-length hair, blue eyes, Hollywood cheekbones. And a body that made him congratulate himself for noticing she had a face.

Her eyebrows lifted as if she knew what he was thinking.

"Right," he said. "No problem. Good thing I happened along when I did."

"We'd have made it." She crossed her arms and attempted a smile, though the effort looked painful. "We just needed a little rest."

He let the comment pass and turned to the man. "I'm Jack."

"I'm not deaf," he said. "Heard you outside." The gruff words were barely out before he broke into a smile. "Harold Burns. But everybody calls me Red, on account of my luxurious red hair." He ran a hand over his head, which was bare as a dog's belly.

Jack shook the man's hand. His fingers were ice. "Great to meet you, Mr. Burns."

"Didn't you hear me, boy? It's Red."

"Okay, Red." He turned to Harper, who was staring at the bags on the floor. She looked like she wanted to cry. He was pretty sure, based on the red in her eyes, that the moisture on her face when he'd found them was from more than rain. "Why don't I take those back to the bedrooms for you. Which ones go where?"

"I can do it," she said.

He swallowed his sarcastic answer. "I bet you've had a heckuva day. Let me help."

He was sure she was going to argue. Then, her shoulders slumped. "Yeah, okay. Thanks. The bigger suitcase goes in the bigger room, the smaller one and the duffel in my room."

He glanced at the smaller suitcase, which was fastened closed with duct tape. "Nice luggage." He'd meant the words to be teasing, but added "no offense" when her back stiffened.

"It broke."

"I see that." He grabbed the things before she could change her mind and order him out of his own house.

His house, except he'd rented it to them. He had no right to be there. So far his plan to make his way in real estate was working out swimmingly.

Despite Harper's defensiveness, Jack was glad he'd seen them when he'd driven by. He'd been keeping an eye out for his new tenants all day, so he hadn't been surprised at the car in the driveway. He *had* been surprised to see two figures struggling up the steps.

He set the bags where she'd directed and returned to the living room. Red was staring at the box on the floor. In the kitchen, Harper had opened cabinets and was staring inside. They were all clean, lined with fresh liner, and, of course, empty.

"You looking for something?" he asked.

She pulled a cell phone from her jeans' pocket, peered at it, and tossed it on the countertop. "Piece of crap."

"No service?"

"Can't even order a pizza. I guess it's cold sandwiches."

He cut his gaze to the shopping bags. Clearly, she was too tired to cook.

"I have a phone you can borrow," he said. "Better yet, why don't I run home and grab some dinner? I made a pot of chili tonight, and there's plenty to share. You guys like chili?"

"I don't—"

"We love chili," Red shouted.

She lowered her voice. "He loves it, but spicy food doesn't agree with him."

"Still not deaf," Red yelled.

She closed her eyes, dropped her head.

Jack had the sudden urge to laugh, which he was smart enough to stifle. "I have some chicken and gnocchi soup in the freezer. I can defrost it and be back in a flash."

She turned again to the empty cabinets, opened the empty drawers. "I don't know why I thought *furnished* meant there'd be dishes."

Ah. She had nothing to cook with or eat on.

"It's not a timeshare," he said.

"I know that. I just…"

When she didn't finish, he said, "Why don't you sit?"

She stared at the table, didn't move. "Been sitting for twelve hours."

"And you look like you're about to drop." He stepped out of the doorway and gestured to the sofa. "Have a seat. I'll take care of dinner, and after you've eaten, you can regroup. Okay?"

She seemed to be formulating an argument, so he walked away. There was another quilt still in the house, a castoff from the previous owners. He'd thought to take the handmade blankets home with him, maybe try to sell them like he planned to do with the rest of the stuff the previous owners had left. Most of that was still in his garage collecting dust. But the quilts were too nice to leave out there, and his house was always in some stage of reconstruction. He'd forgotten about them until tonight. He snatched the quilt from the closet in Harper's room intending to use it to entice her to sit, but when he returned, he found her half sitting, half lying across the sofa. He draped it over her, and she smiled.

Oh, man. That was the kind of smile that could compel a man to wrestle giants.

"Thanks," she said. "You're right. I'm so tired, I can't think."

"Been there."

She glanced past him to the TV box, and he debated. Entertainment or food? Maybe a little escape from reality would do them both good.

"Don't just stand there, boy," Red said. "Set it up. Let's see if there's anything on."

"Okey-doke. I'll see what I can find." He removed the packaging, got the TV out, and plugged it in. It went through its start-up sequence, finally finding a few channels. Not a lot, but without cable or satellite, it was all they'd get. "Looks like we have news, cartoons, or *Frasier* reruns."

"*Frasier*." Red left no room for arguing, and Harper didn't seem to care.

"I'll be back in a little bit." He focused on Harper. "For now, just rest. Okay?"

"I don't need…" But her argument was cut-off by a yawn.

"I'll take that as a yes." He walked out before she could stop him.

CHAPTER THREE

Derrick Burns had stayed home all weekend, certain with every noise and slamming door on the street outside his Baltimore condo that the police were coming to arrest him. There would be no evidence against him. After Harper had confronted him the other night, Derrick had snuck in the side door of the garage and retrieved the contaminated Gatorade bottles. Then, he'd taken them to a fast-food restaurant along I-95, dumped the contents into the bathroom sink, and rinsed the bottles before he'd stuffed them in the trash can. By now, those bottles were in a landfill somewhere.

The police wouldn't be able to prove a thing.

Assuming Harper had figured it out. He didn't think she had. There'd just been a bunch of open bottles. But he couldn't be too safe. Or maybe paranoia was closing in.

Derrick went to work on Monday as if everything were normal. He had a good day, made some money for his clients—and for himself. He landed a few new clients, too. It had been months since he'd lost Russell Caldworth's business—lost it thanks to Harper. Since then, Derrick had built his clientele up again, so now he had more clients and managed more accounts than ever.

Screw Russell. Screw Russell's rich friend, Constantine. Screw Harper. He didn't need them. He didn't need anybody.

He did need two hundred thousand dollars.

And fast.

The thought of the money he owed brought back the image of Harper's bruised cheek, the cut on her neck he'd seen Thursday night. At the time, he'd felt terrible, but the further he got from that day, the clearer he saw it. It was her fault he didn't have the money to get out of debt. If she'd supported him at the beach house last summer instead of working against him all weekend, he'd have kept Russell's business and landed Constantine's, too. If she'd just given in and let him stay with her, he wouldn't have lost that night's poker game to Carter. He'd had to pay the snake almost all that had remained in his checking account. A few thousand dollars, but he'd needed it to make a good-faith payment to Quentin.

Quentin Gray, the scariest moneylender in Vegas, was after Derrick. And it was Harper's fault.

And she was going to fix it.

After work that Monday, he drove straight to Gramps's house, pounding his steering wheel and directing more than a few curse words at the other drivers slowing him down. Morons, all of them.

He had two goals for this visit. To get back into Gramps's good graces—he should have done that months before—and to make up with Harper. He needed her on his side. He needed her to help him convince Gramps to loan him the money. And it would be a loan. Derrick could make it back, no problem. He'd get on a payment plan with Gramps. He just needed a few more clients, and he'd have the extra cash he needed to keep Gramps off his back. As if the old man needed it.

The rich cheapskate, gripping his money in his old, wrinkled fists.

Derrick had to get Gramps to loosen that grip, or Gramps's supposedly beloved grandson would be the next one with the bruises. And Quentin's goons wouldn't be as gentle with Derrick as they had been with Harper.

He rubbed his knee instinctively.

He'd heard of broken kneecaps, crushed feet. Nothing bad enough to keep a guy from working, but a lesson he'd never forget.

He parked in the circular drive in front of the house, glanced at his image in the rearview mirror, and practiced his humble smile.

He could do this. He had to do this.

When nobody came to the door at his knock, he used his key and let himself in. "Harper? Gramps?"

The house was silent. The TV wasn't even on.

He started in the kitchen. Empty. The living room was empty, too. He crossed to the back door and reached for the deadbolt, but it was already unlocked. Odd. Maybe they were out back, but a quick look proved the yard was empty.

He ran up the steps. Nobody in Gramps's room. He opened Harper's door, stepped into the sacred space.

Sacred because she'd never let him in.

As if she were so pure. He knew better.

Her room was empty, too. He was tempted to go inside, look around, touch her things, just because he could. Because she'd kept so much of herself from him.

Because she owed him.

But they'd probably just gone to get something for dinner. They'd be home any minute.

So he closed the door and went to the kitchen, where he poured himself a glass of ice water.

And he waited.

But an hour passed, and they still weren't home.

He dialed her phone number. It went straight to voice mail. "I'm at the house," Derrick said. "I wanted to check on Gramps, see how he was feeling. Where are you guys?"

He figured he'd get a call back, but ten minutes passed, fifteen.

Weird.

He checked the fridge, but there was nothing worth eating in there. He'd check the garage freezer, maybe find a frozen meal he could heat up. He opened the door and froze.

The Caddy was gone—he'd expected that.

But Harper's car was gone, too.

That made no sense at all. Gramps didn't drive anymore. How could both cars be gone?

Where were they?

He forgot about eating and returned to the kitchen and dialed her phone again.

Voice mail again.

Something wasn't right.

He sat, skimmed through his phone, and checked his email. Got one from his bank and clicked on it, but the link seemed broken. Everything was messed up today. Didn't matter. He knew what his bank was going to tell him. He was out of cash.

And without Harper and Red, he was out of luck.

CHAPTER FOUR

Harper forced her eyes open. Thanks to her wet jeans and socks, her legs were freezing.

She heard a man's voice, a low chuckle, and clanging dishes.

The TV was on but muted.

Red's chair was empty.

She sat up, fought a wave of pain and dizziness, and stood. "Gramps?"

"Don't get your knickers in a knot," he called. "I'm fine."

His voice came from the direction of the kitchen behind her, so she stepped that way and froze.

Red...Gramps...was seated at the kitchen table sipping from a steaming mug.

Jack smiled over his shoulder as he stirred a steaming pot of something that smelled of chicken and some heavenly spice she couldn't identify. "Have a nice nap?"

"How'd you get in?" That was a stupid question, though. Had she even locked the door?

One eyebrow lifted. "You always wake up so cheerful?"

She tried to come up with a good retort but was silenced by a shudder. She should've changed out of her wet clothes before she'd fallen asleep. She crossed her arms and eyed the steamy mug in Gramps's hand.

"Go change into something warm and cozy," Jack said. "I'll have a cup of tea waiting when you get back."

She stared at him. This man, this total stranger, was going to make her tea?

She squinted at him. What was his angle? Why was he there acting like a neighbor, a friend? She nodded toward the mug Gramps held. "That better be caffeine-free, or he'll be up all night."

Jack's smile stayed in place, maybe even got a little wider as if he found her amusing.

His response made her want to growl at him, but he'd probably break into raucous laughter.

Jack tapped the side of his head with his fingertips. "Actually thought of that." He looked at Gramps and added, "When you got a face as pretty as this"—he circled an invisible outline of his face with his free hand—"they think you must have all the brains of a sweet potato."

Gramps lifted his cup in a sort of salute. "Happens to me all the time, son. All the time."

The men chuckled at their brilliance.

She maybe did growl a little as she turned toward her bedroom. Just what she needed, some man to give Gramps more material.

When she reached her room, she froze. Her bed was made with the cheap bedding she'd bought on sale. The suitcase had been left on the bed.

Gramps couldn't have maneuvered around it with his bad hips and back. And he'd been too tired to do anything.

Which meant Jack, a total stranger, had found her sheets and stretched them across the bed. He'd pulled the comforter on, made sure it draped evenly over both sides.

He'd stuffed her pillowcase with the pillow on which she'd lay her head.

Even as she marveled at the kindness, the image of his hands on her bedding made her shudder again.

She tore the duct tape from her luggage and dug through it looking for something warm.

A total stranger had come into her house, had made her bed, and was now fixing her tea. And her dinner. What kind of weird dimension had she and Gramps landed in? Because nothing in her experience had ever led her to believe that men like Jack existed outside of romance novels. He might have been joking about the pretty face, but he hadn't been wrong. The man was good-looking in a rugged, flannel-shirt-and-work-boots kind of way. Though he may have looked different from the men in her past, she'd learned the hard way that no matter what a man wore—suits and ties, joggers and sweatshirts, or jeans and flannel—men were not to be trusted.

She found a clean pair of jeans and a sweatshirt. Then she pulled something else out of the bag. Her fleece pajamas. Baggy, fluffy, ugly, pink fleece pajamas.

He'd said to slip into something warm and cozy. These fit the bill.

She peeled off her still-wet clothes, careful with her wrist, which was more tender after the debacle on the porch steps, and climbed into the fuzzy warmth. With a cup of something hot, she just might warm up before spring.

She touched the cut on her neck. It was healing. Hopefully, Jack wouldn't notice it.

What did he want from her? If he was like every other man she'd ever known, at least every one who wasn't so old he needed a little blue pill and an hour's notice, she could guess exactly what he wanted.

She pulled on a pair of dry socks and slipped her feet into her furry slippers.

Nothing said no-way-not-gonna-happen like furry yellow slippers.

She shuffled back to the kitchen and leaned against the doorframe. Now that the sleepy haze had worn off, she noticed all the changes since she'd first seen the room. Stuff...everywhere.

"I hope you don't mind." Jack adjusted the heat on the stove and turned to face her. He started to say something, stopped, and said, "Nice jammies."

"They're warm."

Their eyes met and held for a second before he cleared his throat and turned back to the stove. If she wasn't mistaken, a flush of pink climbed up his neck as he poured water from a saucepan into another mug, added a tea bag, and handed it to her.

"Thank you." She heated her hands on the warm cup and inhaled the scent. Smelled like cinnamon and something heavenly she didn't recognize. "This is perfect."

"Some kind of herbal something," Jack said. "I thought it would warm you up and help you relax." He stirred the soup. "When I bought this house, it was filled with... Well, it seemed like junk. All that stuff was still in my garage, and I remembered..." He turned to the counter, pointed at an old microwave and a toaster. Behind the toaster...was that a coffee maker? "No idea if they work."

She eyed the appliances, thought of what they represented. Coffee and food. Glorious—and easy—food. Her eyes tingled. Seriously, what was wrong with her? "That's... Thank you so much."

"We cleaned them up," Jack said. "The microwave was... well, it's clean now."

Gramps added, "It looked like someone had nuked a rat in there."

"Nice visual." She couldn't help smiling.

"Smelled like it, too," Gramps added. "But we got it clean."

"You helped?"

"Not like you were gonna do it," the old man said, "snoring and drooling on the sofa out there."

"I was not!"

She glared at Gramps, whose eyes crinkled with his smile. Proud of himself, the old codger.

Jack opened the cabinet, though not before she saw the corners of his lips twitch in an almost grin.

She was stifling her amusement when she caught sight of what was in the cabinet. Plates, bowls, cups.

"What did you...? Where did all that stuff come from?"

"Oh," Jack said. "I had some extras. Didn't have much silverware, but I grabbed a box of plastic ware at the store. Should hold you over 'til you go shopping. There's a little convenience store in Nutfield for essentials, but you'd be better off starting at the Walmart in Epping. Cheaper than our local store."

Cheap was good. Cheap was necessary.

She spied a sack on the floor beside Gramps. Snatching it up, she asked, "How long was I asleep?"

"Couple hours, if you drifted right off," Jack said.

"Hours? I can't have!" That would mean it was nearly nine o'clock. She sat at the table and looked around for a clock, but there was none. Her phone...she'd tossed it somewhere earlier.

"Girl, you haven't slept in days," Gramps said. "I'm just glad you got us here without snoozing at the wheel and killing us both."

"I would never..." She glanced at Jack, who'd gone back to

stirring the concoction on the stove. "I was wide awake when I was driving. Just... I guess..."

Jack grabbed bowls from the cabinet. "Tired, obviously."

"She works too hard," Gramps said.

"Works?" Jack ladled some soup into a bowl, shooting her a glance over his shoulder. "All I've seen her do is sleep."

"Trust me, son. She works like a dog. Doesn't get enough rest."

She cleared her throat. "I'd prefer you didn't talk about me as if I weren't in the room."

"Well, go on, then. Get out." Gramps waved his hand toward the hallway, then laughed at his joke. "It sure was easier when you were sleeping."

She ignored the remark and looked in the grocery sack. She found a box of plastic forks, spoons, and knives.

Jack slid a bowl of soup in front of her. "Red had only nice things to say about you."

There was that kindness again. What was she supposed to do with that?

But what had Red...Gramps said? The man was more lucid tonight than he normally was at this hour, amazing considering the day they'd had. It figured that the one night she needed his dementia to flare up, he'd be clear-thinking.

Had he exposed her? She glanced at the old man, who winked at her. When she turned toward Jack, he was setting another bowl of soup on the table, and he seemed content, guileless, and utterly without suspicion. How long could that last?

She opened the package of plastic ware and handed a spoon to Gramps.

He grunted his thanks.

Jack slid into the chair beside them.

"No soup?" she asked.

"I ate chili earlier. Go ahead."

She lifted her spoon, then set it down when she caught Gramps's pointed look. Apparently, even though Jack was there, even though this was the most surreal experience in the world, Gramps would still pray.

He set both of his old, wrinkled hands on the table. She took one. After a moment's pause, Jack took his other. Gramps eyed them both until she and Jack closed the circle with their joined hands.

While Gramps prayed, she tried not to think about the warmth and strength of Jack's grip.

Men often seemed that way at first, didn't they? But they always had a reason behind their kindness.

Considering all Jack had done for them already, she had little doubt about what he was after.

CHAPTER FIVE

Derrick's phone alarm woke him at five a.m. It took him a minute to remember… He'd spent the night at Gramps's house. He figured he'd hear them when they got home from wherever they'd been, and he'd left his door open to be sure.

But nothing had awakened him all night long.

He pulled on the pants he'd worn the day before and walked down the hallway. Gramps's door was open, and the bed was empty. He looked in Harper's room and found the same thing.

They hadn't come home, and they hadn't called.

Where were they? Where would she go?

He would stay to confront her when she got back, but he had to work. So he left a note on the kitchen table—*Where are you guys? I'm worried. Please call as soon as you see this.* And he left for the long drive back to Baltimore. He'd be lucky to get home and showered and to work on time.

Another thing he could blame on Harper Cloud.

Despite her pretty face and gorgeous body, she was more trouble than she was worth. After all he'd done for her, she'd betrayed him again and again.

Because if Gramps were in the hospital, Harper would have called. If he were sick, she would have called. She hadn't called, and she wasn't home.

When he found her, she'd be sorry she ever crossed him.

<h1 style="text-align:center">CHAPTER SIX</h1>

The deluge that began on Saturday continued into Tuesday morning. The leaves had changed and fallen weeks before, and the snow wouldn't start for another month. The tourists stayed home in November, giving Jack more time than usual to work on his real estate business.

The house he lived in and the one next door had come as a package deal, a great deal, but they both needed a lot of work. He'd decided to live in this one while he fixed it up and rent the other to offset some of the costs.

Which was how he'd come to meet Harper and Red.

How had their night gone? With no phone, they had to feel cut off from civilization. He'd tried to help, which had earned gratitude from Red and suspicion from Harper.

In his experience, people who didn't trust others often couldn't be trusted themselves. What was Harper hiding behind that pretty face?

So much of what he'd seen the night before had felt incongruous. The old man's suitcase was high-dollar, but hers had been falling apart. Her jeans had looked several steps above what a person could find on a Target clearance rack, not that he was any kind of expert on fashion. Even soaking wet, they'd sure looked good on her. The Volkswagen was beat up, but both Red's jacket and hers were good brands. He might not know jeans, but he knew L.L. Bean.

And then there was the address she'd put on the rental application. Call him paranoid, but renting to someone he'd never met before had made him nervous, especially when it all happened in a matter of days. He'd put the house up for rent on Friday, she'd contacted him on Saturday, and they'd arrived on Monday. Who relocates to another state that fast? Of course he'd done a credit check. Harper Cloud didn't have much in the way of credit history, but there was nothing that struck him as unusual.

He'd also checked out her current residence. The address she listed was located in Maryland and worth over a million dollars. The property in Maryland was owned by Harold Burns. Red.

Why were they living in a dumpy rental when he owned a million-dollar home?

Incongruous.

Jack finished sanding the baseboards and stood to admire his work. Dust hovered in the air and landed on his plastic-covered furniture and TV, which he'd pushed to the middle of the room before starting the project. After he painted the baseboards in the entire house, he'd refinish the hardwood floors until they gleamed. He'd already replaced all the windows and painted all the walls. Next, he'd tackle the bathrooms and the kitchen.

He stared out the new bay window at the front yard. The rain was tapering off, the sun trying to peek through the thick clouds and trees that surrounded his property. As usual, the street out front was quiet. There was only a handful of houses on this narrow side road.

He showered, dressed, and debated what to do. He couldn't

stop thinking about his new neighbors. Finally, he walked the hundred yards or so between their houses before he could talk himself out of it.

The Jetta was in the same spot where she'd parked it the night before.

At the front porch, he stopped. Of course they hadn't left. Red couldn't navigate the steps.

Jack quickly calculated the cost of adding a ramp and groaned. He had to do it, little though he wanted to.

He made it to the front door and was about to knock when he heard a crash inside.

Then a roar of anger. "Why are you doing this to me?" Red screamed.

"Gramps, stop—"

"Stop calling me that." His voice rumbled and shook. "I don't know you."

Jack knocked on the door. "Everything okay?"

Harper said, "Now's not a good—"

"Help!" Red's shout sounded terrified. "Help me!"

Jack tried the knob, but the door was locked. "Harper, open the door."

"Help!" The man's cries continued. "Help, help, help! She's gonna kill me. Help!"

Jack pounded on the door. "Open up, or I'll break it down."

He barely heard Harper over the old man's screams. "I'm coming. Hold—"

Another crash sounded through the door.

Jack yanked his keys from his pocket and fished for the right one.

The door opened.

Harper stood on the other side, tears streaming down her cheeks, an angry gash on her forehead near her hairline. A small drop of blood was making its way into her eyebrow. Before he had time to react, she turned and crossed to Red, who was standing in front of the recliner.

"Help me!" He looked like a different person from the one Jack had met the night before. His skin was mottled and red, his eyes were wild. His hands were fisted, trembling.

"Gramps, sit down." Harper stood in front of him, reached for his arms, but he slapped her hands away.

"Get away from me!"

"Please. I know it's—"

"Don't touch me!" Red looked past her at Jack. "You've got to help me. She kidnapped me!"

Jack focused on Harper again. "What happened?"

"He didn't sleep well, and he doesn't remember—"

"She's a liar, a liar. I have no idea who that woman is. You have to get me out of here."

"Okay, okay." Jack didn't know what else to say as he crossed the room. He glanced at Harper. "Why don't you go in the other room?"

"You don't know how to handle him."

Gramps screamed. "I want to go home! Somebody take me home!"

"All right." Jack ignored Harper and focused on Red. "You need to sit down and tell me about your home, okay? Can you do that?"

"I have to go." But the old man seemed to be losing steam.

"You will," Jack said. "Soon. But first, I need to get my truck. And I need to know where we're going. Just..." He gently took the man's upper arms in his hands. "Let's just sit and make a plan, okay?"

He could feel Harper behind him but didn't chance a glance. He'd heard of this, dementia patients getting angry and aggressive. He'd never witnessed it and had no idea how to handle it. By the looks of things, Harper hadn't done such a bang-up job on her own.

Red settled into the chair with a harrumph. "Take me home."

"Where is your home, Red?"

The man blinked at the use of his name. "Do I know you?"

"I'm Jack. We met last night."

The man seemed to accept that without question. "My house is in Maryland. Maryland."

"I bet it's nice."

"Yes. In Maryland. This isn't Maryland." The man nodded, his lower lip trembling. The fight was gone. Red's voice was high-pitched, nearly a sob. "I want to go home."

"I know."

Behind Jack, the TV came on. A game show, by the sound of it. The volume went up, and Red focused on the screen.

Jack sat back on his heels and turned to see Harper. She settled on the arm of the couch and watched Red. They stayed like that for a few minutes—her watching Red, Jack watching them both. He didn't know if the tirade was over or if Red would start again. Tears streamed down Harper's cheeks. The wound on her forehead was dripping, and she dabbed at it with the sleeve of her sweatshirt.

Red seemed to have forgotten the whole incident.

Jack stood and faced Harper. "Can we talk in the kitchen, please?"

Her gaze flicked to Red, to the TV, to him. She stepped into the adjacent room, where she settled into a chair, propped her elbows on the table, and dropped her face into her hands.

"What happened?"

She sighed, didn't look up. "He's done this before. Never that bad, though."

"He's under a doctor's care?"

Her head jerked up. Her glare was filled with malice. Or was that defensiveness? "Of course he is."

Jack started to speak, stopped at the sight of the blood dripping into her eyebrow. He scanned the counter, found the roll of paper towels he'd left the day before, and snagged one. He moistened it in the sink and kneeled in front of her chair. "That looks like it hurts."

She touched the cut with her ring finger and winced. "He didn't mean to do it."

Jack dabbed at the cut with the paper towel. It was bleeding badly. He pressed the towel against it, assessed her face for other wounds.

She met his gaze and leaned away. "I can hold it."

Their fingers touched as she took the paper towel, and she flinched.

Okay, then.

He rocked back on his heels, stood, and peeked into the other room. Red was focused on the game show, eyes vacant.

He turned back to Harper. "Why are you here?"

"We live here." Her voice was tired, as if she'd fought a war's worth of battles since he'd seen her last. "I have the paperwork to prove it."

"That's not what I mean."

"Why are *you* here?"

"I came to see if you needed anything."

"We're fine."

"Right. You had it well in hand when I arrived."

He waited for biting words, but her shoulders slumped. Her voice was barely a whisper when she said, "You have no idea."

When she said nothing else, Jack returned to the living room. Red was staring at the game show. Pieces of a broken coffee cup were scattered against the hearth beside his chair.

Jack picked them up, saw blood on the jagged edge of what had been the cup's handle.

In the kitchen, he grabbed one of the plastic bags he'd brought in the night before and a couple of paper towels. He collected the broken shards of the cup, then wiped up the little bit of coffee that had spilled. Good thing the cup hadn't been full of hot coffee.

Once he had the mess cleaned, he returned to the kitchen and shoved the smaller plastic bag into the trash bag that lay crumpled on the floor beside the counter. He made a mental note to bring them a can—he was sure there was an extra in his garage—and sat at the table across from her. He kept his voice low and tried for kind. "I'm guessing he smashed the cup against the fireplace, then swung at you with the handle still in his hand."

"He wasn't trying to hurt me."

"I'm not judging. Just trying to understand."

She met his gaze, her eyes narrowed, her lips closed tight.

"That bruise on your arm. Did he—?"

"No!" She yanked down the sleeve of her sweatshirt, then the other one. She'd been careful to keep it covered the night before. He'd glimpsed it when she'd been sleeping. "Gramps didn't... I just... It's not important."

He studied her face. Was there a trace of a bruise on her cheek, too?

She turned away. "Gramps would never hurt me." She lifted the paper towel, looked at the red stain, and returned it to the wound. "It was an accident."

"The other bruises—"

"How is it any of your business?"

Good question. It didn't take him long to find a good answer. "Neighbors have to look out for each other. It seems you two could use a friend."

Her eyes widened, filled, and she dropped her face into her hand.

What was going on with these two? Where had her bruises come from? If that sweet old man was hurting her, what could Jack do about that?

How was he supposed to navigate this minefield?

And why couldn't he just leave them alone?

CHAPTER SEVEN

W hy wouldn't Jack leave them alone? He was likable, handsome. Surely he had better things to do on a Tuesday than hang around her house. What was he after? Harper couldn't get the question out of her mind as she drove home from the store that afternoon. She was grateful that Jack had offered to hang out with Gramps so she could shop without dragging him along. Considering how tired Gramps was, Harper was happy to leave him at the house. The question remained, though—why was Jack Rossi being so nice to them?

She'd have to find a way to repay his kindness before he came up with his own plan.

The problem was, she had nothing to offer. Hardly any skills, barely enough cash to get by—and less of that after the trip to Walmart. No job, no prospects, no plans. She had no friends, no influence, no talent. She couldn't even afford to pick up a pizza to share for lunch.

She hated owing people.

One rash decision and her whole life was a big tangle of sticky threads she'd never straighten out. And that was okay. She'd known that going in, known she'd never be able to undo this decision, and she'd likely never recover from it. She could live with that after all Gramps had done for her. But the memory of their terrible morning, Gramps's fear, then anger, then aggression. The dementia had never been this bad before. Sure, he'd been forgetful at times. When Derrick quit coming around, Gramps had fallen into a funk, which kept him from doing the activities he enjoyed—gardening, walks. He hadn't even been attending church as regularly. And now, Harper had ripped him away from everything he knew, everything familiar. Away from the home where he'd spent most of his life, from the memories, from the photographs and souvenirs of a life well lived.

Had there been another choice? She went over the facts again and couldn't see one. Anyway, what was done was done.

If only she'd remembered to bring that picture of Gramps's wife he always had with him. Of all the things to forget, she had to forget the one thing they couldn't replace.

She pulled up to the house. The night before, in the pouring rain, it had seemed creepy, but today the word *charming* came to mind. Sure, it needed a paint job and a lot of work on the inside, but nestled beneath the towering trees, the blue sky beyond the bare branches, the house seemed cozy and safe.

Please, let it be safe.

As she opened the car door, Jack stepped out of the house. "Can I help?"

"Sure."

She popped the trunk and grabbed a couple of the lighter sacks. Her wrist felt better, but she was careful with it. She needed it to be back to normal as soon as possible.

Jack somehow managed to wrangle the rest into his arms and slammed the trunk. "After you."

They dumped her purchases on the kitchen table. She

peeked in the living room and checked on Gramps, who was sound asleep in the chair.

"He fell asleep half an hour ago," Jack said.

"He's had a rough couple of days."

Jack leaned against the door jamb.

She tried to ignore him as she put away her purchases—cheap plates, silverware, pots and pans and bowls. If only she could use Gramps's debit card. There was plenty of money in his account. But that would lead Derrick—and the police and whoever else was looking—right to her.

And then she'd miscalculated what was in her own account. She'd had to refuse some of the items, going through the sacks and pulling out things they could live without while the checkout girl and a guy in line behind her watched, sharing looks and checking their watches. Her face burned with shame and fear at the memory. She hadn't planned well enough. She and Gramps barely had enough food to last a week. She had a little cash left, and that wouldn't last long. And then what would she do?

She thought about the small package of turkey in the refrigerator. She had to offer to feed Jack. It was well past lunchtime, and Jack had fed them dinner the night before. She sent up a quick prayer, thinking of the Bible story about loaves and fishes. "Can I make you a sandwich?"

He flashed a smile, but his eyes didn't seem on board with his mouth. "I had a big breakfast."

"Okay." She turned away so he wouldn't see her relief. "I appreciate your help. You don't have to stay. I've got it from here."

When she got no response, she glanced at him. He hadn't moved except to cross his arms.

"What?"

"Did you get a job in Nutfield?"

"I need to find one." Soon. She opened the package of flatware and tossed the items in the sink to wash. A glance at Jack showed his eyes had narrowed to accusing slits. Or maybe she was only seeing a reflection of her own opinion, because she was a fool. An idiot and a fool who was in way too deep.

"So if you didn't move here for a job," Jack said, "why did you?"

"It's a very long story."

"Have you been here before?"

The container of oatmeal blurred as she remembered all those summers when she was a child. The cabin, the boat, the lake. The joy she'd always experienced. "My family used to vacation in a town like this."

"This is a vacation community. Not a lot of jobs this time of year."

She hadn't thought of that. She hadn't thought of much except *run, run, run*.

She tossed more silverware in the sink, the sound clanking and loud, and forced a bright smile. "I'll find something."

"What kind of work are you looking for?"

"Anything right now. Just—"

"And what will Red do while you're at work?"

If only she could hide until Jack went away. Because he was asking all the right questions, and she had no answers.

Run, run, run.

That was all she knew.

Her smile felt as fragile as thin glass. "It'll be fine. We'll figure it out. We have enough to get by."

He didn't speak, and she couldn't hold eye contact. She finished with the flatware, gathered the empty plastic bags, shoved them all in one, and stowed the bundle beneath the kitchen sink.

"Look," Jack said. "I have no idea what's going on with you or why you're here, but—"

"You don't have to worry about Gramps and me. We'll be fine. I've got it all worked out."

His eyebrows lifted, and he rocked back a shade before he recovered. "Right. Well, I'm sure that's true. There's a great little food pantry—"

"We don't need—"

"If you'd let me finish."

She tossed out a *go-ahead* wave, all the while thinking, *food pantry*. A food pantry. As much as she'd been about to argue with Jack, because, hey, the guy didn't need to know his renters were destitute, the words *food pantry* felt like a lifeline. Maybe they wouldn't starve this month.

Maybe.

"It's only open one day a week to customers, but they've just built a room on where a lot of older folks hang out. It's a recreation center for old people, and it's open Monday through Friday. They help with the pantry when they can. They like to be involved, but most of the time, they just watch TV, play cards, and talk. I was going to suggest that you see if Red likes hanging out with them. Maybe that'd be an option for when you're working."

"That sounds..." But words failed her, because, maybe, here was a solution. Maybe, here was a way out of the hole she'd dug for herself.

"Anyway," Jack said, "the pantry's open tomorrow at ten, if you want to go. You'll want to talk to the lady who runs it, Vanessa Baker. In fact, she might be able to hook you up with a job, too."

"Oh." Harper turned away, this time to hide the tears that seemed so close to the surface these days. She swallowed, sniffed, tried to rein in the emotions. Waited for Jack to say something.

When he didn't, she peeked back toward the door, but he wasn't there.

She wiped her eyes and saw Jack beside the couch watching the soap opera Gramps was missing thanks to his nap.

She took a deep breath and stood beside him. "You've been very kind to us. Thank you."

He turned to her, lowered his chin. "Happy to help." He headed for the door. "I'm going to get some supplies. I'll start building a ramp this afternoon. God willing, I'll have it finished by the time you guys need to leave tomorrow."

"You don't have to do that."

Jack raised his eyebrows and nodded toward Gramps.

"He can handle stairs," she said. "He was just tired."

Gramps's gruff voice cut off whatever Jack had been about to say. "Don't you guys talk about me as if I'm not in the room."

Harper turned and smiled at the old man. "I was just telling him how good you usually are on stairs. Right?"

His bushy gray eyebrows lowered over his tired eyes. "Most of the time."

Jack's smirk told her what he thought of that answer. "'Most of the time' doesn't cut it." Harper started to speak, but he cut her off. "And I don't want to hear how I don't have to, okay? I'm not having one of my tenants fall and break a bone because I was too cheap or lazy to offer a solution."

"But, it's—"

"I'll be back and forth, so if you see me outside, just ignore me. I'll have to take some measurements."

He was gone before she could argue.

CHAPTER EIGHT

I t had been an exhausting day by the time Jack stepped into his house that night. Exhausting, but productive. It had taken until sundown, but he'd completed the ramp so Red could get in and out of the house without risk.

Now all he wanted to do was heat up some leftover chili and collapse into bed.

But the ramp wasn't all his new neighbors needed.

Not that any of it was his business, as he kept reminding himself. Harper and Red had issues, but they'd had issues long before he happened along. They'd brought those issues with them to Nutfield, and it was not Jack's job to fix them.

He shouldn't get involved. He had plenty to keep him busy, and he didn't need additional drama in his life. If he wanted to get his real estate business up and running this winter, he needed to stay focused.

But no matter how many times he told himself that, no matter how many times he berated himself for worrying about them, he couldn't get his neighbors off his mind.

So, fine. He'd do what he could. Then maybe he'd be able to drag his focus back to his own problems.

He grabbed his keys and headed to the food bank in town. He knocked on the back door. A moment later, Vanessa Baker pulled it open.

"I figured you'd still be here," he said.

Behind the woman, a little girl yelled, "Who is it, Mommy?"

Vanessa opened the door wider and stepped into the storage area. "Come on in." Even with those three words, her accent was discernible. She spoke English well, but no one would mistake her for a native. Where she was from, Jack had no idea. Vanessa wasn't one to talk about her past and didn't seem open to questions.

As reticent as Vanessa was, her daughter was an open book—probably a fairy tale featuring wood nymphs and magic spells. The little girl had certainly cast a spell on him.

"Jack, Jack, Jack." Five-year-old Katarina barreled into him and wrapped her arms around his legs.

He lifted his hand to high-five her, feeling her mother's watchful eyes as he did. Had this been one of his nieces, he'd have lifted her up and hugged her, but Vanessa had rules about her daughter. No man was allowed to hug the girl. Even the old men who hung out in the rec center had to be careful.

More than once Jack had wondered what lay in Vanessa's past that caused her to be so cautious. Right now, he had another woman's problems to deal with.

He focused on the girl. "And how are you this fine evening, little kitten."

"I'm not a kitten." The girl's smile told him she liked his game.

"You're Kat, and little cats are kittens, right?"

She giggled. "I wanna show you something." And with that, she bolted through the doorway into the rec center.

He looked around the warehouse. It looked well-stocked for the clients who'd come the following day. In the morning, more groceries would be delivered, perishables picked up from nearby grocery stores. He didn't know how all that worked, but he'd been here often enough to marvel at the operation when the pickup trucks came in.

"You need something?" Vanessa asked.

"A favor."

She shifted to her back foot, narrowed her eyes.

Another defensive woman, as if he hadn't dealt with enough of that the last couple of days. "My new tenants," he said. "The old man looks like he needs some looking after, and his grand-daughter needs to get a job. I wondered if it would be okay if the man hung out here."

"You know our policy. If he can't volunteer, then she has to if she wants to bring him."

"What if I volunteer in her stead?"

Vanessa flashed a rare smile. "You already volunteer many hours. Without your work, there wouldn't be a rec center."

He started to answer but stopped when Kat ran back into the room. "Look, look!" She waved a piece of paper up toward him.

He took it and gazed at the drawing. A cat and a kitten. He met Vanessa's eyes and lifted his brows before focusing on the girl. "You didn't draw this all by yourself, did you?"

"Mommy got me a book to teach me how to draw animals, and I copied it."

"Wow. This is really good. And all the fur, you did that, too?"

"Uh-huh. And the eyes. They were the hardest. In the book, I was just supposed to color them all in one color, but cats' eyes are pretty, so I wanted to make them look like real eyes."

They weren't perfect, but they had slit pupils and a little variation in the color. "You did a great job." He handed the paper back to the little girl and focused on Vanessa. "She's very talented."

"Yes." Vanessa looked at her daughter with affection before focusing on him again. "You think your tenant needs our services, food, anything else?"

"She claimed they were fine, but..." He thought of the sparse groceries, the state of her car, and the few items they'd brought with them. "If you tell her she has to be a client to leave Red here, then she'll be *forced* to get some groceries, which I think she needs."

Vanessa studied him, eyes narrowed and lips pursed, before she nodded once. "Da. Yes, bring her tomorrow, and we will work it out."

"Thank you. Her name is Harper Cloud." He turned to Kat. "And thank you for showing me your beautiful picture. You're a very talented young lady."

"I'm only five."

He chuckled. "You sure? You seem so much more mature than that."

"I am." She looked at her mother. "Right, Mommy?"

"Yes, *ceri*."

Jack focused on the little girl. "What is '*ceri*'?"

Vanessa answered. "It means daughter in Serbian."

"Is that where you're from?"

"Da." She grabbed the doorknob. "You need anything else?"

Jack took the hint. "Nope. Thanks so much for your help. I'll send them over tomorrow. I'll be here, too, to install the crown molding."

Vanessa nodded. "Thank you. I will help your new tenants if I can."

CHAPTER NINE

Harper parked in the lot at the address Jack had given her. The food bank was a block off Crystal Avenue, Nutfield's main drag, and located in a small warehouse-type building. Though the tan metal sides weren't attractive, the area around the glass doors had been landscaped with evergreen shrubs so that even in November it looked inviting. Other vehicles were parked in the small lot, many clunkers like hers. Beyond a chain-link fence, she saw newer, fancier cars, pickups, and SUVs. Maybe that was where the workers parked.

"What are we doing here?" Gramps asked.

She couldn't very well tell him she was looking for elderly day care. "I'm going to see somebody about a job."

"You got a job. Taking care of me is your job."

"A little extra money never hurt."

"Let me call Roger and have him wire us some cash. You don't need to be working."

If only. But Roger Canfield, Gramps's attorney, would demand to know where they were and why they'd left. Could he be trusted? Were the police looking for her? The thought left her hands trembling as she stared at the doors. She couldn't go in there. They'd ask for ID, and what would happen then? Would her name be put in some online system? Would it trigger an alert? Would the local cops realize they had a fugitive, an ex-con, in their sleepy little town?

They'd call Derrick. Derrick, who'd been poisoning his own grandfather.

She couldn't risk it.

She'd reached for the gear shift to reverse out of the spot when a knock startled her. She turned to see Jack leaning beside Gramps's window, smiling. She slid the gear back into park, stepped out of the car, and spoke to him over the top. "What are you doing here?"

"Working inside. Saw your car and thought I'd see if you two need help."

"We're okay. I was just thinking..."

But he'd quit listening. He opened Gramps's door, and the two greeted each other like old friends.

It seemed Harper didn't have a choice. And really, had she ever? She couldn't let Gramps starve to death, and without a job —or at least this food bank—that was likely. So, whatever. If she got arrested, she got arrested. She'd survived prison once.

And Gramps? She'd have to trust God to manage him, to manage all of this, because she was out of options.

She pushed the fear aside and grabbed Gramps's walker from the trunk. By the time she had it unfolded, Gramps was standing beside the car. She set the walker in front of him, and they shuffled across the parking lot.

Jack opened the glass door, and she and Gramps stepped onto linoleum floors. There was a reception desk to her right. Beyond that stood fabric-sided cubicles. In one, two people were holding hands across a desk, heads bowed.

In front of her, people of all sorts sat in chairs set in neat rows. Some of the men and women were wrinkled and worn.

Others were young and had children in tow. Some were dressed nicely, while others looked as if they'd shopped at Goodwill on a bad day. There was an older couple taking turns with a toddler, who kept crawling from one lap to the other.

"I'll get Red settled," Jack said. "You go check in."

Harper watched while Jack walked with Gramps to one of the few free chairs before she turned to the desk. Behind it, a woman with long blond hair was typing and staring at a screen. She looked up and regarded Harper with the greenest eyes she'd ever seen. The woman looked young, mid-twenties at most. She was beautiful, but she had a don't-mess-with-me look Harper wished she could perfect. Would that she could be that strong.

"Hi," Harper said. "I heard you have some kind of elderly recreation center."

The woman narrowed her eyes. "You are Jack's renter?"

The question surprised her. "Uh…"

"He told me to expect you." The woman spoke with a slight accent as she handed Harper a clipboard with paperwork. "After you fill this out, bring it back, and I will get you in the system."

The system.

Harper swallowed her apprehension and reached for the clipboard. The instant she had it, the woman focused on the screen again. Harper sat next to Gramps, who'd struck up a conversation with the elderly gentleman beside him. Jack was chatting with a woman behind them while he played peek-a-boo with the toddler in her lap. Harper focused on the paperwork.

Name, address, number of people in her household and their ages, income amount, and source. The income part was easy. Zero. She had to work to keep her hands steady enough to fill out the information. Surely this place wasn't connected to some law enforcement database, right? She squeezed her eyes shut. *Please, God. Please, God. Please protect us. Protect us, heal us, direct us.* Was she asking too much? Was there a limit to what God could—or would—do?

She had to trust. Gramps had been trying to teach her to trust God for months. She was trying, despite everything.

She returned the clipboard to the woman behind the counter, who took the paperwork with hardly a glance. "Have a seat. Someone will call you back in a minute."

When Harper returned to the chairs, Jack stood. "I'm going to get to work. Red, don't cause too much trouble."

"No promises."

Jack turned that smile on her. As if she didn't feel vulnerable enough. "Good luck. I hope she has some ideas for you."

"You've gone above and beyond," Harper said. "Thank you."

"What are neighbors for?" He walked down a long hallway and disappeared through a door.

She fretted and Gramps chatted with other clients while people disappeared into the cubicles, then continued down the hallway, where they grabbed grocery carts that were lined against the wall. Harper didn't see what happened after that, but she imagined there was a room back there filled with food. Glorious, free food.

With Jack here, she should refuse it. Her landlord didn't need to know the level of her desperation. But her pride was overshadowed by her need. The first month's rent was paid for, and all the utilities were included in the rent. If she could get food, they could survive until she had a paycheck coming in. Maybe, just maybe, she could build a life here in Nutfield. Maybe with her and Gramps out of the way, Derrick would take what he wanted and leave her alone. Maybe nobody would connect her to the two bodies.

No, she couldn't think about that.

The chairs were empty except for her and Gramps when,

finally, the blonde came around from the front desk, flipped a sign on the front door to closed, and approached. "You will come with me now." She looked at Gramps. "Sir, do you mind waiting here?"

"Not a bit. Gotta read about my Redskins. Maybe this'll be the year." Gramps focused on the sports page. He wouldn't actually read it—he hadn't done much reading since his memory started to slide. But he'd find a way to keep busy, so Harper stood and followed the woman. They stepped into an empty cubicle, and the woman took a seat behind a desk, where she tapped on a keyboard and focused on the screen. She waved toward a clipboard on the desk. "If you'll sign in."

Harper filled out her name and address and signed it. When she looked up, the woman was watching her with calculating eyes.

"I am Vanessa Baker. I'm the manager here."

"Nice to meet you."

The woman's expression didn't shift from... what was that? Caution? Suspicion? "What brings you to Nutfield?"

"We just needed a change."

"Bah. I don't think so." She waved Harper's words away like an unwelcome smell. "But you don't have to tell me. And your grandfather, he is well?"

Harper was reeling from the woman's words but forced herself to focus. "Usually. He has dementia, which has been getting worse lately. Today is a good day, so far. He also has a bad back that makes it hard for him walk."

"He is in pain, no?"

"He never complains."

"On painkillers?"

"He doesn't like to take them, but sometimes, he has to. When the pain is unbearable."

The woman regarded her with narrowed eyes, mouth

pinched. After a moment, she nodded once, said, "Okay," and typed on her computer. "You are looking for a job?"

"Yes. I'll take anything. But Gramps... It would be better if I didn't have to leave him at home alone."

"You have no other family who could take care of him?"

"No. None."

The woman wrote something on a yellow sticky note and handed it across the desk. "Go there, tell Bonnie I sent you. She is looking for someone reliable. You can be reliable?"

"Definitely." Harper looked at the note. *McNeal's, 102 Crystal Ave.* She'd seen the place driving in this morning, a restaurant just a few blocks from here.

Before she could ask, Vanessa said, "Your grandfather can stay in the rec center during the day when you work. If you work evenings or early mornings, you'll get someone else to help. Maybe Jack."

"Oh, I couldn't ask—"

"You don't have many options, Miss Cloud."

"Harper."

The woman nodded. "Harper, you should also know that your grandfather will be allowed to stay in the rec center because Jack volunteers for us. Usually, it's just for volunteers and their family members."

More favors. More to owe the man. "That's not necessary. I can volunteer, if that's what it takes."

"Very kind but not necessary. Jack has already agreed, so you can focus on getting a job and caring for your grandfather."

"But, I mean..."

For the first time, Vanessa's green eyes filled with warmth. "I understand this fear you carry. None of us wants to owe another person. Especially a man." Her eyebrows lifted, waited.

"Right." How did this woman see so easily into her heart? "It's not easy."

"They are not all..." She waved toward the air, as if words were floating about, waiting to be snatched. "Some are... many are not trustworthy. I have met many of these kinds of men. You have, too, no?"

This woman knew exactly what she was thinking. "Yeah."

"I do not know him well, but from what I do know, Jack Rossi is a nice man, a kind man. So I think it will be okay. If he has any expectations beyond a thank-you"—she pierced Harper with a knowing look—"you tell me, and I'll take care of it. We have to stick together, no?"

Harper let out a surprised laugh. "We do, don't we?"

The woman smiled, and her expression lit the room. Beyond the tough exterior resided a woman Harper would love to know better. But she doubted she ever would. Because to get Vanessa to open up, she'd have to do the same. And there was no way Vanessa or Jack or anybody could know the truth about Harper Cloud.

Derrick checked his watch again, then compared it with the time on his cell phone. Sure enough, the watch was two minutes behind. Seven thousand dollars for this state-of-the-art timepiece—bought used, though nobody needed to know that—and the piece of crap didn't keep good time.

He needed to sell it. He needed to sell everything he owned, and even that wouldn't be enough.

He glared at the receptionist, whose focus was on her computer screen. She didn't care that Derrick had a job to do. She couldn't care less that his entire life hung from a very thin thread, that if he didn't find his grandfather—fast—he'd lose everything.

Derrick stood, paced across the small room, his gaze hitting and bouncing off all the so-called artwork. Pretty pictures with pretty lies, quotes from a Bible only the most foolish believed. *Trust in the Lord with all your heart...* Right. Like, if only he believed in some invisible God, everything would work out just fine. Derrick knew better. He was the only one who cared about his life and his future. He was the only one willing to fight for it.

The receptionist's phone dinged, and he spun to stare as she answered. A moment later, she set the phone on its cradle. "Go on in. He's ready for you."

"It's about time." Derrick yanked on the ends of his shirt sleeves, smoothed his jacket, and pulled open the door.

Roger Canfield stood behind his huge desk. He wore a dark gray cable-knit sweater and slacks, a far cry from the attire Derrick expected of an attorney. Apparently, when you were still working in your seventies, you could dress however you wanted. Roger extended his hand. "Derrick. Glad you could come in."

Derrick shook his hand and stifled the complaint about the wait. "Thanks for seeing me."

Roger gestured toward the two leather chairs that faced the desk. "Tell me what's going on."

Derrick unbuttoned his suit coat and dropped into the chair. "Harper Cloud, the nurse I hired to take care of Gramps—"

"And your girlfriend, if I remember correctly." Roger settled himself in the huge chair on the other side of the desk, knees creaking with the effort. The desk itself was clear except a telephone, a cell phone, a legal-sized notepad, and a pen. "I met her. She's a lovely person. Devoted to your grandfather."

"She *was* devoted to him, and she *was* my girlfriend. I guess when I broke up with her, she took it harder than I realized."

"What happened?"

"She took him. I went over there Monday, and they were gone. Checked again yesterday. No sign of them."

"So you explained on the phone," Roger said. "And you're sure they didn't take a trip and forget to tell you?"

"She's not answering her phone. And Gramps was sick last week. They're gone, Roger."

"You called the police?"

"Of course." Derrick had had a long conversation with a police officer the day before, asking that a Silver Alert be put out on his grandfather. "Since he's never been diagnosed with dementia or Alzheimer's, they won't do anything."

"Your grandfather is an adult. He has the right to come and go as he pleases."

"But she took him! He would never leave without telling me."

The old man looked past Derrick and nodded slowly. After a moment, he focused his sharp eyes on Derrick again. "Why would she do that? It would be one thing to take off, but why take your grandfather with her?"

"I don't know!" Derrick threw up his hands to emphasize the point. "To get back at me, I guess. To punish me for dumping her."

Roger settled back in his chair, tented his fingers, and waited.

The scrutiny burned, but Derrick forced himself to meet the man's gaze. After a moment, he shifted, adjusted his glasses, and cleared his throat. "I have no idea what's going on in her mind, Roger. But..." He blew out a breath, considered his next words very carefully. "After I started dating her, after I...well, I fell for her. Hard. And then I learned about her past. She's an ex-con." He looked at the floor, tried to school his face with regret, and looked back up. "If I'd known that, I would never have hired her to care for Gramps. That's why I broke up with her. I mean, I probably could have forgiven it, but she lied about it. She didn't tell me until we'd been together for almost a year. I felt betrayed."

"Did you try to convince your grandfather to fire her when you learned about her past?"

Here's where it got tricky. "I should have. I mean, if I'd known before, I'd never have brought her here. But she was so good with Gramps. I didn't want him to let her go until I found somebody else just as good. I should have waited to break up with her, but it seemed wrong to pretend. I tried to be honest with her, aboveboard." He shook his head, filled his voice with despair. "This is all my fault. I handled it all wrong. And now..." Derrick waited for Roger's response. At this point, the man should tell him it wasn't his fault and offer to help. That's what most people would do.

But Roger Canfield wasn't most people. And no doubt Gramps had told his attorney all about Derrick's life and problems.

"You want me to report the debit card stolen?" Roger asked. "I'm sure you don't want her to have access to his cash."

"No, no. Just keep an eye on it, let me know if she uses it and where. At least that'll be a clue."

Roger nodded. "What do you think she's after?"

"Money, of course. I think she'll call you, beg you to help her. She'll probably have some sorry story. Or..." He paused as if this idea had just occurred to him. "Oh, my God, you don't think she'll make a ransom demand? She has to know what Gramps is worth."

"If she did, would you want to pay it?"

"Of course! I'll do anything to get Gramps back."

Roger made a note on the sheet in front of him. "How much would you be willing to pay?"

"Me?" He feared his true reaction had come through. As if he'd pay a dime for the old man's return. "I don't have the kind of money she'll want, but Gramps's estate could cover it."

"I see." Another notation on the sheet. This one took more time.

What was the man writing? Derrick tried to read the words upside down, but the scrawl was illegible. Roger set the pen down, and Derrick snapped his gaze up.

"If I hear from her," Roger said, "or if there's any activity on the account, I'll certainly let you know." Roger stood. "I trust you'll do the same."

Derrick stood as well. "Of course. In the meantime, I'm hoping to hire a private investigator to help me find them."

"Excellent idea. Do you need some recommendations? I'm sure one of my associates—"

"I've been in contact with someone who comes highly recommended." He adjusted his glasses again, buttoned his jacket. "I will need some help with the retainer, of course."

Roger's smile was tighter than his grip on Gramps's money. "Of course. Have him send me the bill, and I'll take care of it."

"This guy's not with a big firm. It would be faster if you just gave me—"

"I would need your grandfather's go-ahead to transfer the money to you. I have the leeway to pay necessary expenses, but not to give cash payouts."

"Under the circumstances, you could make an exception."

The man's smile was Splenda-sweet, but his eyes were shrewd. "No need. Just have your investigator send me a bill, and I'll be happy to pay it."

Derrick stifled his reaction. "Excellent, then. That'll work. Thank you for your help."

They shook hands, and Derrick left, seething. It was time to cash in a favor.

Harper followed Vanessa back to the waiting area, where Gramps still sat, alone. He looked up, smiled his most charming smile, and set the newspaper beside him. "Did you get yourself a job?"

"Not yet," Harper said, "but I have a prospect."

"No idea why you want to work," he said, "but it's your life." He looked beyond Harper to Vanessa and struggled to his feet.

Harper had to squeeze her hands into fists to keep from helping him, because he'd certainly bat her arm away. In the six months she'd been caring for Gramps, she'd learned his moods. This was his happy I-don't-need-you mood. Offering to help would offend him.

He made it to his feet and held out his hand to Vanessa. "Harold Burns, but everybody calls me Red, on account of my luxurious red hair."

Vanessa shook his hand. "It is a pleasure."

"Nice accent. You're not from around here, eh?"

"I am from Serbia."

"Never been there. Spent some time in Korea way back.

Once I hit American soil, I swore I'd never leave the good old US of A again."

"I can understand," Vanessa said. "I love this country. I hope I will be allowed to stay forever."

"You're not a citizen?"

"I am not, but I'm working on it."

"Well, good for you. Good for you." He focused on Harper again. "Where we going now, girl?"

"Actually," Vanessa said, "I hoped you'd let me introduce you to some of my friends. Can you come with me?" Vanessa turned and started slowly toward the door in the back, the one where Jack had disappeared.

Gramps looked at Harper with narrowed eyes. "You know what's going on?"

Harper shrugged and set the walker in front of him. "Let's find out."

They followed Vanessa down the hall and through the door. On the other side, they found a huge warehouse to their left where people were working and chatting. It was chilly, thanks to the open garage-style door in the back. In the center of the room was a walk-in freezer, if the stainless steel exterior was any indication. A wall stood to their right with a single door and, beyond that, a set of double doors. Harper could see through a glass window into the first, an office.

Vanessa led them to the double doors. These, too, had glass windows, so Harper got a glimpse inside. It seemed like a living room. They stopped just outside the entrance. "Mr. Burns—"

"Red," he corrected with a smile.

Vanessa nodded slightly. "Red, your neighbor Jack has been kind enough to build this room for us. It's a place where our volunteers and their families congregate. I think you'll enjoy it because a lot of our volunteers are near your age. They play cards, watch TV, and generally try to stay out of trouble."

Gramps's charming smile slid off, and he focused on Harper. "What's going on?"

She shrugged as if this were all perfectly normal. "Jack just thought you might like to meet some people."

Before Gramps could argue, Jack appeared in the doorway. "Red. So glad you're here."

Gramps's suspicious expression didn't fall away entirely, but it did slip a little. "You again."

"I'm everywhere."

Gramps peered from Harper to Jack and back as if he were trying to solve a riddle.

"Come on in," Jack said. "I want to introduce you to my friends."

"Well, all right." His frown stayed in place. "If you really want to."

Harper started to follow, but Vanessa stopped her with a hand on her arm. "You give me your cell phone number, and we will call you if there's a problem. They'll keep him entertained until you get back."

"Okay." She touched Gramps on his elbow. "I'll be back in a few minutes."

He nodded and focused on the room. It was designed like a living room. It was warm in here. Six recliners faced a TV mounted on the wall. Two were occupied with gray-headed women. Behind the La-Z-Boys, a game table was surrounded by six padded chairs, and three old men were engrossed in a loud conversation and playing cards. Windows along one wall filled the room with natural light. A few lengths of molding leaned against the wall beside a step ladder. That must have been where Jack was working. Jack would take care of Gramps if he needed anything.

Harper followed Vanessa back into the warehouse, pulled her cell from her purse, and sighed. Two bars here in town. Not great, but at least she had service. She'd had service at the house all day the day before and that morning, too. Maybe it had just been bad on Monday because of the storm. She hoped so. She couldn't afford another phone.

She focused on Vanessa. "If you have a piece of paper—"

"Program my number in your phone. Then, if you need me, you can call."

"Uh... okay." She typed in the phone number as Vanessa rattled it off, then she texted the number with her name. A phone dinged from Vanessa's pocket.

"Good," Vanessa said. "We're set then."

Harper knew it was time to go, but she couldn't quite figure this woman out. "You give all the clients your phone number?"

"Almost none. But you... I think I have been where you are, at least on some level. If not for the kindness of strangers, I do not know where I would be. So, I will be a kind stranger to you."

Oh. Harper had no idea what to say to that.

Vanessa waved her toward the back door of the warehouse. "Go out that way and walk around. The front door is locked. I will take Red to get some food and have it ready when you return. Do either of you have food restrictions or allergies?"

Food. She'd totally forgotten about food. She wanted to hug Vanessa for thinking of it. "He can't eat anything too spicy. And don't let him get all junk food."

"Don't worry. I've done this before." She nodded toward the door. "Good luck with Bonnie." Vanessa stepped into the rec center, where voices and laughter floated out.

Harper headed toward the door. There were people between here and there, volunteers loading shopping bags into waiting cars, others stacking food or sorting produce. This was a big operation for such a small community. She weaved among the people, trading smiles and how-are-yous until she got outside.

Five minutes later, she stepped into McNeal's. The scents of coffee and bacon enticed her. The place had a hometown feel to it, with walls painted sage green and decorated with sports paraphernalia and posters. She grinned at all the Patriots, Red Sox, Celtics, and Bruins stuff and looked more closely at the few framed newspaper articles and banners bragging about the Nutfield Squirrels, apparently the local high school's team, that hung from the wall behind the hostess station. There were TVs in every corner and a very large one on the back wall.

The dark hardwood of the floor matched the long bar. The walls were lined with booths, and round tables filled the center of the space. Many of the tables were empty, but a few were occupied by folks drinking coffee and enjoying a late breakfast.

A woman came through the door beside the bar that had to lead to the kitchen. She called, "Be right with ya, hon," as she carried plates to the couple seated by the front window.

Harper glanced at a menu. McNeal's served a full breakfast until eleven, then switched to the lunch and dinner menu. Lots of Irish fare—corned beef and cabbage, Reuben sandwiches, shepherd's pie. There were multiple hamburger options, a few steak dinners, chicken—grilled, baked, or fried. They served salads, though not for the health-conscious, if the toppings were any indication.

Comfort food, comfortable surroundings. Harper could see herself working here. It wasn't ideal, but it would keep her bills paid and food on the table.

The waitress headed her way. She was maybe five-foot-two and certainly not in bathing-suit shape. She had short curly brown hair and wore a name tag that read *Bonnie*. "Table for one, hon?"

"Actually, Vanessa sent me. She thought you might have a job for me."

The woman stopped at the hostess station and eyed Harper

head to toe. Her lips pinched. The well-worn wrinkles told Harper she'd made that expression before. "You don't look the waitress type."

Harper pushed her hair behind her ears. "What type would that be?"

The woman shrugged. "No offense. It's not like people are banging down the door to work here."

So far, this wasn't going as Harper had imagined. "Is it that bad?"

"Nah. People are just lazy. It's a great job if you know how to work." She gave Harper another once-over. "You look a little bit like a princess, tell you the truth."

"Then think of me as Cinderella before the prince."

The woman cracked a smile, and her whole face changed. "I like the wit. I'm Bonnie Wells." She thrust out her hand, and Harper shook it.

"Harper Cloud."

"Good to meet you. Come on in, and let's have a chat."

Harper followed Bonnie to the back of the room, where Bonnie indicated a chair at the bar. "Sit. I'll be right back." She disappeared into the back, returned with an application and a pen. "Fill this out." After Bonnie rushed away, Harper sat on the wooden barstool and filled out the application. She stopped when she got to the question that would keep her from getting hired.

Have you ever been convicted of a felony?

Her hand hovered over the honest answer, but she didn't check the box.

How could she? If she didn't get a job, she and Gramps would be lost.

She ignored her conscience, shot up a quick *forgive me*, and checked *No*.

As Harper was completing her employment history, Bonnie returned. "You done?"

Harper looked up and smiled. "Just a few more jobs to add."

"Any waitressing experience?"

"Yeah. I worked a cocktail lounge in Vegas." She hadn't done a lot of waiting tables, but she'd done enough for it to qualify. She didn't figure Bonnie would care about her kitchen duty in prison.

"Other jobs you're adding—are they waitressing?"

"No. When I was in high school—"

"We're good then." Bonnie snatched the application and looked it over. "You're a nurse?"

"Used to be."

"So why not get a job doing that?"

"I really need something close by, and fast."

The woman eyed her a moment, and Harper braced for more questions. But all Bonnie said was, "What hours can you work?"

"The lunch shift would be ideal. I care for my grandfather, and he'll need more attention in the evenings and mornings."

"I can't guarantee you'll only get lunch shifts, but we can try. If I can't, can you make arrangements for your grandfather?"

Harper swallowed, smiled. "Sure. I'll work something out."

Bonnie looked over the application, and her eyebrows lifted. "Dancer? What kind of dancer?"

Of course she'd pick up on that one. "The kind you're imagining."

Bonnie leaned back almost imperceptibly. But Harper noticed. Keep your distance from the stripper. She might be diseased.

She imagined how Bonnie would react if she knew the whole truth.

"I don't do that anymore," Harper said. "Believe me, I could make a lot more money if I did."

Bonnie's lips pinched again as she regarded Harper. "I bet you could." She tsked, paused, tsked again. "Lots of women would lie. I appreciate your honesty."

Harper couldn't speak for the sawdust wedged in her throat. Honesty. If she were truly honest, nobody would ever hire her for anything.

But Bonnie didn't pick up on the guilt that felt as solid as the seat beneath her. "Can you start tomorrow?"

CHAPTER TWELVE

J ack finished caulking around the crown molding and returned the ladder to the warehouse. The food bank's clients were gone, and only a few volunteers remained, their keys jingling from fingertips as they finished up conversations.

Vanessa was in her office. Just outside her door stood a shopping cart loaded with food. That must have been what they'd collected for Red and Harper.

Jack returned to the rec center for his tools. Red was seated at the game table with Steve, the father of one of the board members. Ever since Steve had been coming here instead of rattling around his big house alone all day, his health and memory had improved. Amazing what a little companionship could do.

As a member of the board, Jack had been happy to volunteer his services to build this room. His own folks were still going strong, but one day he hoped they'd have somewhere like this to spend time.

"Jack, come over here," Red called from the table. "I need you to prove me right."

"Fat chance, old man." Steve's eyes narrowed as Jack approached. "You know the movie with Marilyn Monroe and Jack Lemmon?"

"Can't say that I do," Jack said.

"Come on, boy." Red shook his head as if he'd never heard anything so preposterous. "It's called *Some Like it Hot.* 'Course you've seen it."

"That's not the name of it," Steve said. "That was that other movie with Marilyn and Jane Russell."

"No, that's..." Red paused, seemed to be digging through very dusty file cabinets in his mind. "Don't tell me. It'll come to me."

Jack pulled out his cell. "I can figure it out."

The men continued to argue while Jack typed on his keyboard. He got the answer and looked up. "Sorry, Steve. *Some Like it Hot* has Marilyn, Jack Lemmon, and—"

"Tony Curtis," Steve said. "Just like I told you."

Red's eyes bulged. "You said that was that other movie." He snapped his fingers. "*Gentlemen Prefer Blondes.*"

Steve shook his head, though his eyes twinkled. "That's the one with Jane Russell."

"That's what I...!" Red looked at Jack for backup, but Jack just lifted his hands and stepped away. "Not my circus, not my monkeys."

"You just call me a monkey, boy?" Steve said.

"More like an elephant with those ears," Red said.

Steve cupped his dinner-plate sized ear. "What'd you say?"

Red started to repeat himself, then laughed. He banged the table beside him with age-spotted hands. "Sit down, son. Want to join us for a game of cards?"

Jack pulled out the chair and sat. "You guys play without me."

"In my day, a man wouldn't turn down a game of cards." Steve shuffled and shook his head.

Red turned his sharp gaze on Jack. "So, you're in real estate."

"Just dabbling right now, but—"

"Why you dabbling?" Red asked. "Jump in. Real estate's a great investment."

"I know, but there's only so much time. And money."

Red waved off the words. "You don't risk your own money. You gotta find investors, look for houses you can assign to come up with the cash."

Jack rubbed the back of his neck. "Not sure what you mean by that."

Red shot a look at Steve, who was still shuffling cards. "You believe this guy?"

Steve straightened the cards against the table. "You find a property that's going for cheap, get a contract, then turn around and sell it for a little more, a couple thousand. You did the legwork finding the place, so your buyer's happy for the deal. They know you're making money, but if they do it right, they will too. Everybody wins."

Jack's gaze went from one man to the other. "Were you both in real estate?"

"Just a little," Steve said. "I never got into assigning properties, but I always wanted to. Just too busy with the day job. I bought a few multi-families in Manchester back in the eighties. Held on to them, too. In my day, we didn't do all that house flipping like you young people do."

"You said it," Red said. "How'd those buildings work out?"

"Had to weather some storms," Steve said, "but I held onto them. Just sold them a few years back when I retired. The hassle, you know?"

Red nodded. "I still own a few of my properties, but I have a management company taking care of them. It's rough. I have to trust them." He turned his gaze back to Jack. "That's the biggest thing, son. Knowing who you can trust. It's not like it was in my day. Back then, a handshake meant something. People kept their word. These days, most folks'll sell you out for a couple bucks. And not just strangers, either." The light in his eyes dimmed at that, and he focused on the table.

After a beat, Jack said, "Maybe you guys could teach me some stuff. I can use all the help I can get."

Red's gaze snapped up. "Happy to, son. I'll tell you everything I know."

Steve snorted. "Five minutes later, you can come find me."

The men were laughing when the door swung open and Harper stepped in.

Steve whistled. "Who's the looker?"

Harper blushed and focused on her grandfather.

"Did you get the job?" Red asked.

Her smile lit the room as if someone had flipped a switch. "I start tomorrow."

"Well, then." Red pounded the table. "I'm proud of you, girl. And that'll be perfect, 'cause I can come back here and hang out while you're at work."

Harper's glance flicked to Jack.

"Sounds like a good plan," he said. "Let me grab those groceries for you. Did you park out back?"

Ten minutes later, he'd loaded the groceries in Harper's trunk and helped Red to the car. He promised to stop by soon and closed the door. Harper was standing beside the trunk, so he joined her there. "Congratulations on the new job."

"Thanks." She swallowed, seemed to want to say more, so he kept quiet. "Jack, it's been a long time since..." Her voice faded, and she forced a smile, though the tremble he saw on her lower lip told him there was a lot going on behind those beautiful blue eyes. "Your kindness has meant the world to me. I can't even begin to..." She swallowed again.

"All I did was—"

"Bring us dinner, build a ramp, tell us about this place, get them to let Red hang out, help me find a job. Not to mention yesterday, when Gramps was..."

When she didn't finish, he reached out, rested his palm against her arm. Even through her thick jacket, the touch sent a zing all the way to his toes. He pulled his hand away. "It was my pleasure. Truly."

"It's been a long time since anybody's gone out of the way to help me."

He couldn't imagine that. She was sweet and caring and, frankly, drop-dead gorgeous. He figured people would fall all over themselves to help her.

The emotion behind her eyes told a very different story.

"I was happy to do it. And your grandfather promised to teach me about real estate, so I might be hanging around more than you want."

Her eyes lit, and another zing coursed through. Yikes, this woman had an effect on him.

"Gramps invested his savings from his government job and made himself a very wealthy man." As soon as the words were out of her mouth, her face paled. "Of course, that was a long time ago. He doesn't invest anymore."

Except Red had just told Jack he still owned properties—rentals and the big million-dollar home in Maryland.

"Anyway," Harper said, "thanks again. I'd better get home and feed him lunch. He doesn't do well when he's hungry."

Jack watched as Harper pulled away, taking the rest of her story with her.

CHAPTER THIRTEEN

Knowing there was food in the fridge and a job to go to today had been good medicine for Harper. Answered prayers made for a restful night. She felt safe here, safer than she'd felt in a long time. That icky paranoia that had followed her off and on since she'd been released from prison was gone. For now.

While coffee brewed, she showered and tried not to worry about all the things that could go wrong today. Gramps would have to be lucid, willing to take his meds, and eager to go back to the rec center. She'd have to pack him a lunch so he'd have something to eat while she worked, and then he'd have to remember to eat it. Meanwhile, she'd have to learn a new job and get done before the rec center closed at three.

It should work. She'd been told she'd be working ten-thirty to two. But if she had a table that didn't want to leave or if her replacement didn't show up or if Bonnie decided she needed her to stay longer...

She squeezed her eyes shut and rinsed her hair. *You'll have to handle all those ifs, Lord.*

She waited for some reassurance that her day would be as

smooth as Gramps's bald head. None came, and she wasn't surprised. It seemed God didn't give a lot of details. She could use a few concrete answers right now. And not just about her day.

Since the storm had passed, her phone had had decent reception at the house. The internet was slow, but it worked. She'd spent the previous afternoon trying to find out what the police knew about those two dead bodies she'd discovered in the living room back in Maryland. One had been Keith Williams, a Baltimore detective. She'd known that already. She'd called 911 from a pay phone right after she and Red had left the house Thursday night, but *The Baltimore Sun* had no information, nor did their little local paper. If the bodies had been discovered in the city, no news might make sense. But two murdered men— one a cop—found in the living room of a mansion near the bay? Surely somebody would pick up that story.

Harper had even checked the TV stations' websites for something, anything. She'd turned up no information whatsoever, no mention of bodies being found, and no mention of missing men.

A week had passed, and there'd been no news.

Obviously, the police were keeping the information secret. But why?

And weren't murders public information? If so, how would they be able to keep a lid on the story?

She'd counted on learning enough to figure out what had happened, who'd killed those men, why they'd been left for her to find, and who they'd worked for. If nothing else, she wanted to know if she was a suspect in their murders.

Instead, she was left in the dark.

After she dried off, brushed out her wet hair, and dressed, she returned to the kitchen, poured herself a cup of coffee, and opened the Bible she'd picked up at Walmart. She wished she'd thought to grab the journal and Bible she kept in her nightstand at Red's house. She'd been keeping a list of thoughts and questions, things to pray about, things to think about. God might not have spoken to her about the circumstances she'd face today, and God might not have given her the information about those two dead bodies, but He'd made her a lot of promises in this book, and she'd chosen to put her life in His hands. That meant she had to hold onto those promises. God knew she hadn't murdered anybody and would never, ever hurt Gramps. God would vindicate her. She just hoped He'd do it before she landed back in prison.

She'd finished her daily reading when Gramps pushed his walker down the hallway and settled in the chair across from her. "How about some coffee?"

She poured him a cup, watching to see which of his personalities she'd have to deal with today. Happy would be ideal, grumpy she could handle, but confused... that would ruin everything. "What would you like for breakfast?"

He sipped from his mug and set it down slowly. He looked up, met her eyes. She wasn't sure how to interpret the look she saw there. "What are we doing here?"

Crap. "Having breakfast. Eggs and toast, or..."

He pointed his arthritic finger at her. "Not in the kitchen. In this house. Why are we here?"

She still wasn't sure which Gramps had graced her this morning, but at least he seemed lucid. The problem was, he didn't remember the bodies and had no idea what Derrick had been up to. She wasn't about to tell him. It was all so murky. If she told him what she did know, she had no idea how he'd react. But she couldn't afford for him to demand to go home and straighten it out. He trusted law enforcement. She'd tried that once and paid dearly for her mistake. She wouldn't let Gramps get pulled into that minefield.

She sat and leaned across the table toward him. "Remember I told you we had to get away."

"I don't remember why."

She'd told him an elaborate lie, which he'd bought because he trusted her. She took a deep breath, let the lie come back. "There are people after me, and I had to run. People from my old life. You remember, I told you about my old life."

"I remember."

"I couldn't bear to be away from you, so you decided to come with me."

"Decided?" He narrowed his eyes, met her gaze, and held it. "Don't remember being given a choice."

He'd been so out of it that night, he didn't remember anything.

"I'm sorry, Gramps."

"And that's another thing. Why do you call me that?"

"We decided it would be easier if everybody thought we were related. That way, if you have any health issues, people will naturally come to me."

"You're my nurse. Surely you brought that paper that gives you authority over my healthcare, right? Of course they'd come to you."

"I brought it, but it's so much simpler if everyone thinks we're family. We are family, aren't we?"

He harrumphed. "You're better than that grandson of mine. What did Derrick think of you taking me away?"

She stood and pulled the bread from the drawer. "Oh, Derrick was okay with it. He knows how close you and I have become."

"And you two aren't going to get back together?"

"Definitely not." She turned to meet Gramps's eyes. "But that doesn't change my relationship with you. You know that, right? You're the only real family I've got, and I'll do anything for you."

They held each other's gazes for a long time. She worried he was seeing all the lies in her eyes, but after a moment, he nodded. "If this is what you need to do to be safe, then I'm with you."

She released a breath. "Thank you."

"Just wish I had a picture of my Bebe."

Of all the things to have forgotten. "I'm so sorry."

"Maybe Roger could mail us a copy. He's got a key to the house, and he won't tell anyone where we are."

"That's an idea." One she wouldn't use.

Red sipped his coffee. "I would like to talk to Derrick, though. Can we call him now?"

She busied herself at the fridge, trying to avoid eye contact. "It's awfully early."

"We gotta catch him off guard."

"Probably true." She went to her bedroom, grabbed her phone, and returned to the kitchen, where she checked the service. Three bars. She shook her head sadly. "We don't have service again. We're going to have to get a better cell phone plan."

Gramps shook his head. "Not safe to be without a phone. Why don't we call the phone company, get the kind that plugs into the wall instead of that thing?"

"Good idea. I'll make the call today." And probably discover it was way too expensive, but if it got Gramps's mind off Derrick...

"We'll try him later," Gramps said. "And I'll call Roger, too. Have him wire us some cash. I don't understand why you think you have to get a job."

Gramps wanted to make calls. She hated to pray for memory loss, but he really needed to forget those ideas. She popped two pieces of toast in the toaster. "I don't mind working."

"I guess you don't want to spend all your days with a grouchy old man."

She turned again, shook her head. "Don't say that about yourself. You're not old."

When he got her joke, he laughed. "Ornery girl. Make me some eggs, would ya?"

One crisis had been averted, *thank You, God*, but it was barely seven a.m. She prayed the rest of the day would go as well.

With ten thousand things to remember, she'd never keep them all straight. Harper had thought studying to be a nurse was hard, but that had nothing on waitressing at McNeal's.

When she smiled at the cook, he only scowled at her. The middle-aged man had hardly said two words to her since she'd been there. Now, she set two orders on an oversize tray and headed for the dining room, stopping at the table in front of the windows. "Baked potato soup for you"—she slid the bowl in front of the pretty woman—"and a steak for you."

The man nodded.

"Thanks so much." The woman had a Southern accent with the manners to match. "You new here?"

"My first day," Harper said.

"New in town, too?"

"Just moved here."

"Welcome." The woman's smile was wide. "This town'll make you feel like you're home. Sure did me, anyway."

It had been so long since Harper felt at home, she didn't

know if she'd recognize the sensation. "So far, it's been wonderful."

"Don't let Bonnie give you any flack," the man said with a wink. His accent was Southern, too, though not the same as his wife's. More Texas and less twang. "That woman's got all the charm of a rattlesnake."

"I heard that."

Harper jumped at Bonnie's voice just inches behind her.

"Don't listen to Eric," Bonnie said. "That man lies like a dog. I don't know how Kelsey puts up with him."

Harper smiled at the couple and headed back to the kitchen. So far, the customers had been nice, patient with her when she'd made mistakes. And Bonnie was tough, no doubt, but also kind. A good teacher. Harper could do this job. Based on the tips she'd already collected, she might even be able to support herself and Gramps with it.

Maybe.

It was nearly two when Jack walked in and scanned the restaurant. She was about to head toward him, but he waved her off and crossed the dining room, where he sat across from a gorgeous brunette at one of Bonnie's tables.

Harper tried to shake off the sadness that settled on her shoulders. What in the world did she have to feel sad about? Jack was only a friend, and that was all he could ever be. Apparently, some foolish corner of her heart had hoped for more.

She checked on her tables, refilled a few glasses, and returned to the kitchen for her last party's food, all while trying to push away the image of Jack with the brunette.

Wow, she was a fool. When would she learn not to give her heart away? Every single man she'd cared for had burned her, badly. One had landed her in prison. And Derrick? It was thanks to him she was in hiding. Yet the first guy who showed her a little kindness, and she was falling for him.

Idiot.

Idiot, idiot, idiot.

"Whatcha doing, just standing there?"

She jumped at her boss's voice. "Making sure I didn't forget anything."

"You're doing a good job. Get those meals delivered, and you might even get out of here on time."

Harper returned to the dining room. She served the meals, ran a credit card for a party of four, and was giving the check to another table when she glanced at Jack. He waved her over.

She pasted on a smile and joined him. "Good to see you," she said.

"Harper, I'd like you to meet my real estate agent, Ginny Lamont."

Harper turned to the woman. Yup, she was gorgeous. Dark brown hair, bright blue eyes, wide smile. She held out her hand. "You're the new tenant?"

Harper shook her hand. "Just moved here."

"Welcome."

Jack said, "I saw Red this morning, and he seemed to be having a good time. Steve's there, of course."

"That's good news," Harper said. "I've been worried. Did you have more work to do there?"

"I was in the neighborhood and thought I'd check on him."

Jack had done that just because? What was with this guy?

"I was hoping to grill him about his real estate business," Jack continued. "Ginny's looking for more rentals for me, but Red suggested something else yesterday, and I hoped I'd get more information."

"I'm sure he gave you an earful," she said.

"Nope. He was too engrossed in his poker game."

"Please tell me he wasn't gambling."

"Just pennies, which somebody else supplied. I thought maybe you'd let me bring you guys dinner tonight."

Harper couldn't help the way her gaze darted to Ginny. The woman's smile was still there, tight as a fitted sheet over her gritted teeth. Harper glanced back at Jack, who seemed utterly clueless.

Maybe he didn't care.

Or maybe he liked making her jealous.

"Red said it was fine," Jack said, "but I figured I'd better tell you so you don't fix something. You'll be exhausted after your day."

"Uh..."

"I'll be there about five with lasagna. Your grandfather says it's his favorite."

"It is, but—"

"Excuse me." A customer from another table was waving her over.

Harper just nodded and turned away. She had to focus on work right now. Later, she'd worry about Jack and his suspicious kindness... and Ms. Realtor's angry eyes.

CHAPTER FOURTEEN

Derrick leaned against a wall in his old friend's shabby office. The furniture was generic, the beige walls bare, the carpet one step up from indoor-outdoor and stained in multiple places. The room smelled like stale cigarette smoke along with the bathroom odors from the hall right outside the door.

To say this wasn't the best part of Baltimore would be an understatement. This guy was way outside the circles Derrick usually traveled in. The other businesses in this building included an attorney who specialized in DUI cases, a bail bondsman, and a woman who read tarot cards.

"Seriously," Tank said. "Could you sit? I'm trying to work." Tim *Tank* Anker eyed him from the faux-leather chair behind his worn desk, which was piled high with files and papers and pens and who knew what else. He grabbed his head with his sausage-link fingers, turned it to the side, and cracked his thick neck. Apparently, being a professional private investigator hadn't changed the man too much.

"Check again," Derrick said. "See if he's paid."

Tank blew out a loud breath. "When I get an email, it dings. You hear a ding?"

"Just check."

Tank clicked, looked at his screen. "Nothing. Just let me call you when it comes in."

Derrick wasn't leaving Tank until he had the money. He couldn't. He'd called the night before and explained what he needed. After a long and tense discussion, Tank had sent the invoice to Roger, but by the time he had, Roger had left the office for the day.

Last night at his condo, Derrick had gotten a visit from two of Quentin's goons. Not Keith and his sadistic buddy, which surprised him, but two new guys. They'd given him twenty-four hours to produce "a substantial portion" of what Derrick owed him.

With his checking account having dwindled to pennies, he didn't have enough to pay his electric bill, much less *a substantial portion* of two hundred thousand dollars.

He was in deep trouble this time. He'd called in to work that morning, feigning the flu, so he could find Harper and his grandfather. His boss, a man who saw everything in the same shade of green as a dollar bill, hadn't been pleased. Join the club. Derrick couldn't afford to be away and didn't want to think about all the money he was losing by handing his clients off to another broker. What was that expression? The tyranny of the urgent? In this case, it was the tyranny of the tyrants. If Derrick didn't get his hands on some cash, fast, he would lose everything —including his life.

So here he was, first thing Thursday morning. Who cared that the office was shabby? With Tank he was safe. There weren't a lot of guys willing to take on a man like him. This wasn't college anymore, and Tank wasn't the starting fullback on the football team. And sure, what once had been nothing but muscles born of steroids and hours in the gym was now shrouded in fat and encased in an oversize suit and tie. Still, only a half-wit would take Tank on.

And the guys watching Derrick weren't half-wits.

"I'll wait."

Tank stood and grabbed a Mr. Pibb from the mini-fridge behind his desk. "Want one?"

"You still drink that swill?"

"You used to love it."

"I'm not in college anymore."

Tank popped the top, downed half the soda, and set it on his desk. "When did you get to be such a snob?"

Derrick ignored the question. He and Tank had gone their separate ways after their senior year. After the incident they never talked about.

He leaned against the wall and pulled out his cell, then navigated to his email and answered the latest ones.

Tank lowered himself into his chair, which responded to his weight with a high-pitched gasp. He pointed to the chair across from his desk. "If you're gonna stay in here, you gotta sit. You're making me nuts."

Derrick swallowed his retort, slid his phone back into his jacket pocket, and sat.

Tank steepled his fat fingers. "Tell me what's going on."

"My grandfather's missing. His nurse took him."

"That much you said, and so did that lawyer when we talked this morning. Any ideas where they might be?"

So Roger had called Tank to check on Derrick's story. He shouldn't have been surprised. "I have a couple."

"But you don't want me to find them."

"I can find them. I just need cash."

Tank looked at his computer screen. When he trained his gaze on Derrick again, his eyes were narrowed. "Lotta cash."

"It's none of your business."

Tank leaned back, sat straighter. "Heck it isn't. You call me demanding I make like your PI to funnel cash to you—that makes it my business. And if you really wanna find them, just let me do my job. I'm good at it."

Derrick made a show of looking around the shabby office. "I can see how successful you've been."

Tank dropped his hands to the desk and pressed. His knuckles turned white.

Derrick swallowed hard as he leaned against the back of his chair. He'd seen Tank lose his temper before, and he didn't need to be on the receiving end of that. He started to backpedal, but Tank spoke first.

"Don't jump to a bunch of conclusions, old *friend*." He took a deep breath, and, surprisingly, seemed to rein in his temper. Tank must have picked up a new skill in the years since college. "I like my office. The rent is cheap, and unlike you, I'm not trying to impress anybody. I don't need to. You know why? 'Cause I'm good at what I do. I got a wife now and two kids. So my money goes to support them, not to impress stuck-up suits."

"Okay, okay." Derrick lifted his hands in surrender. "I'm just saying, this isn't the most impressive place to entertain clients."

"I don't meet my clients here. I either go to them or meet 'em at the coffee shop on the corner. You're the one who insisted we meet here, remember?"

Derrick had needed privacy, and to be away from his normal routine. He pushed his glasses up the bridge of his nose. "I'm sorry. It's been stressful with my grandfather missing."

Tank didn't look a bit moved. "I can find him faster than you can."

Derrick didn't know if that was true, and he wasn't about to find out. He didn't want anyone to find them before he did. Not

PIs, not lawyers, and not cops. He'd called them in a panic, but he'd been relieved to learn they wouldn't search for Gramps. Better if they stayed far away.

If only Harper had just kept feeding Gramps the Gatorade. Gramps would be out of his misery, reunited with Gram, and Derrick would have the money he needed. Then, if Harper had been lucky, Derrick might have taken her back, given her a second chance. But after this stunt, no way.

"Dude, what do you think?" Tank said. "Just lemme—"

"If I can't locate them in a few days, I'll bring you in. But I have some leads."

Tank drummed his fingers on the desk. He didn't look happy.

The computer dinged. "He sent it."

A twinge of relief settled in Derrick's stomach. "Good. Excellent."

"I'm gonna have to pay tax on this money, man."

"Tax?" Derrick stood, rested his hands on the desk, and leaned forward. "Imagine what you'd have paid back in college if not for me."

Tank stood, too. "I know what you did for me. I don't even know..." He shook his head, stared out the window to the dingy street beyond. "Sometimes I think it would have been better if I'd just done my time, you know?"

"And gone to prison? That what you wanted? To be an ex-con? 'Cause I know a few of those, and life isn't easy after prison."

"I'm not saying that." Tank sat again and stared at the desk. Finally, he looked up. For the first time in...ever, Derrick saw genuine regret in the man's eyes. "What I did to her...it was awful. I shoulda gone to jail for it. That night haunts me. And 'cause you lied for me, I can't ever come clean. Can't tell Emily the truth. Can't tell anybody the truth. I just gotta live this...this lie."

Derrick made a show of taking out his phone. "I can fix that for you right now. Emily? That's your wife? Give me her number, and I'll tell her all the gory details. I'll tell her how you followed your girlfriend out of our apartment that night. How you offered to walk her home, to 'keep her safe.'" He made air quotes around the words. "And how, when you got to her apartment, you forced your way inside, ripped off her clothes, and—"

"Stop!" Tank hid his face behind his hands.

"What? You don't think Emily wants to hear it from me? That's fine. I'll just call the newspapers. Maybe nobody can throw you in jail for it now—you made that fine deal—but the press can destroy your business. I'll tell them how you threatened me, made me lie for you."

"That's a lie. I never asked—"

"*After witness tells all, former fullback finally fesses up.* I like the alliteration, don't you?"

Tank dropped his hands, glared. "You made your point."

"What, you don't want the world to know?" Derrick paced to the back wall and leaned against it. "I thought the guilt was killing you."

"Just..." He waved his Frisbee-sized hand toward the chair.

Satisfied, Derrick sat again.

Tank focused on his computer, tapped a few buttons, and turned to Derrick. "Here's what's gonna happen. You and me, we're gonna go to the bank. I'm gonna get you the cash, and then you're gonna walk away. What we're doing here, it's illegal, and you're just as involved as I am. This ever comes back to bite me, and I'll tell 'em everything. Now, I got something on you, and you got something on me. Got it?"

"As long as our friendship's still intact."

The expletive-laden retort suggested the friendship was off.

CHAPTER FIFTEEN

With a grocery sack hanging from his wrist, Jack carried the pan of lasagna next door. His stomach rumbled with the scents of tomatoes and garlic and sausage as steam rose and mixed with the cold November air.

He had no idea why he was here.

What in the world had prompted him to offer to bring dinner to Harper and Red tonight? Sure, he wanted to talk to Red about real estate. The man seemed to know his stuff. But Jack could easily have stopped by earlier to do that. Besides, he'd had better things to do than spend an hour in the kitchen putting this meal together.

He climbed the ramp and knocked on the door with his foot.

Harper greeted him with a smile. "That smells delicious." She stepped out of his way, and he headed for the kitchen.

"Hey, Red."

The old man lifted his hand in greeting without taking his eyes off the TV.

Harper folded a dishtowel and rested it in the middle of the kitchen table. "Just set it there."

He did and took the foil off the top. "We'd better let it cool before we dig in."

She eyed the concoction with lifted eyebrows. She'd changed out of her jeans and now wore yoga pants and a sweatshirt the way a runway model would wear yoga pants and a sweatshirt. He flashed back to the sight of her in those ridiculous pajamas, and his cheeks warmed. Did this woman ever not look gorgeous?

"You *made* this?"

He laughed at the awe in her voice. "Surprised?"

"When you said lasagna, I just assumed you'd warm up one of those frozen ones. But that's not a disposable pan."

"We Rossis know Italian food."

She inhaled slowly. "I should say so." She turned, pulled three plates from the cabinet, and set them on the table. "You like to cook?"

Jack slid the plates to their spots in front of the chairs. "It's a hobby. Unfortunately, I rarely have anybody to cook for."

Harper opened the silverware drawer. "I bet Ginny would love to sample your masterpieces."

"My real estate agent?" He grabbed some napkins, folded them, and set them beside the plates.

Harper turned, lifted her eyebrows.

"Our relationship is nothing like that."

She turned back to the drawer and took her time pulling out the utensils. "If you say so."

"Besides, she's not my type."

Harper set the forks and knives on the table. "What type is she?"

"I don't know. She's a great real estate agent. But she's from California, and she has some weird ideas." He grabbed the sack he'd carried in, grateful for something to do besides explain to this beautiful woman why another beautiful woman didn't appeal to him. "Salad. Just Caesar. You have a bowl, or should we just serve ourselves from the bag?"

"The bag works." She crossed her arms. "So, tell me about poor Ginny and why being from California is a turnoff."

He shrugged. "Today she suggested that I should spend time every day visualizing the future I desire and the types of properties I want to buy. She said if I did that, then the universe"—he put air quotes around the word—"would work with me to get me what I wanted."

"Wow." Harper laughed, shook her head. "So have you tried it?"

Behind Jack, Gramps said, "That's just New Age mumbo jumbo."

Jack stepped out of his way. "I agree."

Gramps shuffled through the kitchen behind his walker and sat. "The universe. Pfft. You need something, you ask God. You start making requests of *the universe*, and who the heck knows who's gonna answer." He eyed the pan on the table. "Well, we gonna eat or what?"

"Give me a sec, Gramps." Harper focused on Jack. "I have sweet tea, water, or coffee."

"Sweet tea, huh? Y'all aren't from around here, are you?"

Harper rewarded his fake Southern accent with a laugh. "You want to try it?"

"Why not."

She poured two glasses of iced tea and refilled Red's Gatorade before she settled between him and Red.

Red set his hands palms-up on the table. Harper slid her hand into his and glanced at Jack. He grabbed the old man's hand before taking Harper's. That's when he realized why he'd made the lasagna for them.

An hour of work just to hold a pretty girl's hand. He'd think about how pathetic that was later. Right now, he had to focus on

Red's prayer and not on the delicate fingers resting snugly against his palm.

He must've failed, because Harper's amen startled him. Reluctantly, he let her go.

He forced himself to drink the tea, though it was sweeter than rock candy, while he watched Harper and Red savor the meal. What wasn't to like? Homemade spaghetti sauce, hot Italian sausage, three kinds of cheese. But it was Harper's little moans of pleasure that brought him the most joy. And maybe some other emotions he chose not to name.

"You cooked this, boy?"

Jack set his fork on the plate. "My mother's recipe."

"Your mother's a genius." Red forked another bite. "A veritable genius."

"I'll tell her you approve."

Harper set her tea down. "Your folks live around here?"

"I grew up about an hour from here, in Nashua. They still live in the same house."

"What brought you to Nutfield?" Harper asked.

"After college, I got a job working for a real estate management company here. I figured I'd just stay a year or so, get some experience. But I like it here. Nothing wrong with Nashua, but the traffic, the busyness—it's just not me. I prefer small-town life."

Red said, "I like it here, all these trees, all this quiet. Makes a man feel close to God."

The look Harper gave her grandfather was filled with such affection, Jack felt like an intruder. She reached across the table, rested her delicate hand on his gnarled one. "I'm so glad you like it."

He harrumphed and forked another bite of lasagna.

Whatever was going on with these two—and Jack was sure something wasn't right—it was clear they loved each other. And for a woman to do all Harper was doing to take care of her grandfather—that kind of love covered a multitude of sins.

After the meal, Harper gathered their dirty dishes and turned to the sink.

Jack focused on Red. "You said something about assigning properties yesterday. I looked it up online, so I know a little about it. Can you tell me more?"

Red's crinkly eyes narrowed, and he regarded Jack like he might a poisonous snake. "What are you talking about?"

"Uh..." He glanced at Harper, but her focus was on the dishes. "At the rec center yesterday, you mentioned that you used to assign real estate to protect your own money. Right?"

"Don't know what you're on about, boy!"

At the sound of Red's raised voice, Harper turned, eyes wide.

Jack leaned back, lifted his hands in surrender. "I'm sorry. I must have misunderstood."

Red looked at Harper. "What is he talking about?"

She turned off the water, dried her hands on a towel, and walked to the table. "It's okay. Jack's a friend. He brought us this lovely dinner."

Red eyed the pan of lasagna in the center of the table, seemed to study the pasta still there, the empty place where they'd cut away their slices, the sauce and cheese and sausage that had oozed into that empty place. "I don't like lasagna."

Harper glanced at Jack, then took Red's hand. "That's okay. You already ate anyway. You want to watch some TV?"

Red glanced at her, glared at Jack, and nodded once. "Don't know what I'm doing at this table, anyway. Is Wheel of Fortune on yet? I never miss Wheel of Fortune."

Harper pulled his walker close and helped him stand. Together, they shuffled into the living room while Jack sat at the table uselessly.

A moment later, Harper returned. "Sorry about that. Considering the day he had, the week we've had, I'm amazed he was lucid as long as he was today."

"I didn't mean to upset him."

"It wasn't your fault."

She returned her focus to the dishes.

He wrapped the aluminum foil back over the lasagna and slid it into the fridge.

When he closed the door, he caught her watching him over her shoulder. "You aren't leaving that, are you?"

"You guys can have it. I made a second pan for myself and put it in my freezer to enjoy later."

She turned back to the sink, her head shaking. "Wish I could cook."

"You don't?"

"I can make eggs. I can bake a can of biscuits without burning them. I've perfected the art of tomato soup and grilled cheese."

"How do you survive?"

She set the last plate on the towel she'd laid out and turned to him. "I just told you. Eggs, canned biscuits, tomato soup, and grilled cheese. And... let's see. There's boxed macaroni and cheese, and I can fry those hamburgers you buy in bulk."

"Please tell me you don't mean those frozen things that come already made into perfectly round patties."

She shrugged. "Ground beef is gross. I'm not touching it to make patties."

He shook his head and laughed. "What else?"

"Spaghetti."

"With jarred sauce?"

"It works. Doesn't taste like that, though." She gestured to the fridge and the lasagna he'd stowed there.

"You're killing me."

Her smile made his full stomach do a flip.

She grabbed the sponge to wipe the table.

"Did your mom or dad cook?"

"Mom did," Harper said. "She was a great cook."

"Was? Is she—?"

"Oh, I'm sure she's still a great cook."

Harper turned to wipe down the counters, which were already perfectly clean, while he let her words process. The way she'd answered made him wonder...

"When was the last time you saw her?" he asked.

Harper scrubbed the already clean surface. "It's been a while."

"Is she Red's daughter?"

She turned, looked confused. "Oh. Uh, no. Gramps is on the other side of the family." She tossed the sponge into the sink, passed Jack, and poked her head into the living room. He could just make out Red's soft snores over the sound of the TV.

She returned. "Well, I'd better start getting him ready for bed."

Bed? It was just after six.

She leaned against the door jamb and crossed her arms. "He's had a long day, and so have I. Thanks for dinner."

A not-so-subtle hint even Jack could pick up on. He walked to the front door. "Thanks for the hospitality."

She barely cracked a smile. "Sure. Anytime."

If *anytime* meant *never again*, he might believe her.

On the short walk home, he thought about what had just happened. Everything had been going just fine until he'd asked about her family. Then, her countenance had snapped shut like a trap door.

He couldn't help but wonder what was beyond that door.

CHAPTER SIXTEEN

Harper couldn't believe the crowd. For some reason, she'd thought Monday would be slow at McNeal's. One more thing she'd been wrong about.

She'd really blown the *keep her head down* portion of her plan the week before. What had she been thinking, asking Jack about his family? Of course he'd reciprocate and ask about hers. She couldn't tell him the truth. And she was a lousy liar. What choice had she had but to send him away before he asked more questions?

His expression still haunted her. She'd insulted him. Apparently, she'd insulted him a lot, because she hadn't seen him since. In fact, if she weren't mistaken, he'd gone out of his way to avoid her. When she and Gramps had returned to the house on Friday afternoon, she'd seen that Jack had been there to rake up the last of the leaves in the front yard. She could picture him now, watching from his house next door until their car drove away, then rushing over to get it done while they were gone.

That's how rude she'd been Thursday night.

She'd thought surely she'd see him over the weekend, be able to offer her thanks, maybe even an apology. It was probably better she hadn't, because an apology might lead to more questions she couldn't answer. It would be better if she kept her distance from Jack and Bonnie and everybody else she had contact with. If they knew the truth, they'd reject her.

Except Gramps, who knew everything and loved her anyway.

Everything she was doing, all she'd lost—it would all be worth it if she could only keep Gramps safe.

She managed to finish her shift in time—barely. The rec center would close in ten minutes, so she hung up her apron, waved to Bonnie, and headed for her car. On her way, she checked her phone and discovered she'd missed a phone call.

She swiped it on, looked again to make sure she wasn't crazy. She'd missed four phone calls.

Crap, crap, crap.

While she drove toward the food bank, she listened to the first message. Vanessa's voice, her no-nonsense tone and Serbian accent. "Your grandfather is very confused, and he is getting agitated. Please call us immediately."

In the food bank's lot, she jammed the car into *Park* and ran in the back door. The warehouse was empty.

Steve, the older man she'd met the other day, was just coming out of the rec center.

He saw her, shook his head. "Your grandfather isn't here."

Her shock must've shown on her face, because he patted her arm with his age-spotted hand. "He's okay. He got confused and—"

"I called you."

Harper turned to see Vanessa coming from her office.

"I'm sorry. My phone has terrible reception. Where is Gramps?"

"He was not able to be calmed," Vanessa said.

"He was ticked off," Steve added.

Harper turned back to Vanessa, who said, "I called Jack. He took him home."

Jack. She closed her eyes, felt the tears burning. Poor Gramps. He must have been terrified. And she'd had no idea.

A hand squeezed her shoulder. She opened her eyes and smiled at Steve, who patted her arm awkwardly. "It'll be okay."

"You need a new phone," Vanessa said.

"Yes. I'll... It won't happen again."

Vanessa nodded once, spun, and returned to her office.

Steve let his arm drop and tilted his head toward the door where Vanessa had just disappeared. "She was worried. I don't know her very well. Nobody does, to tell you the truth. But from what I can tell, she masks every emotion with irritation."

Harper focused on the old man. "If you say so."

"She'll get over it."

She'd better, because without this place, Harper wouldn't be able to keep her job. And then what would she and Gramps do?

CHAPTER SEVENTEEN

Jack settled on the sofa in Red's house and exhaled a long breath.

Vanessa had called him when she couldn't get in touch with Harper. He'd left the work he was doing at one of the cabins he managed and rushed into town. He'd thought to stop at McNeal's to tell Harper what was going on, but he figured he'd better check on Red first.

Once he had Red in his pickup, there was no leaving him alone. The old man beside him bore no resemblance to the Red that Jack had come to know. He was angry, aggressive, and irrational. This was the man who'd caused that gash on Harper's temple almost a week earlier. It took all of Jack's focus to keep him from diving out of the pickup and hurting himself.

Jack had considered taking Red home with him, but Red had never been to his house, and Jack hoped maybe the familiarity of his own living room might help calm him down. So he'd used his spare key, let himself into Red and Harper's house, and then cajoled the angry old man up the ramp and into his chair.

Red had complained and yelled and fought him every step.

It wasn't until Jack turned on the TV and found a soap

opera that Red settled down. Jack made him a sandwich, encouraged him to eat it, and managed to get him to drink half a glass of Gatorade. He had no idea if food or hydration would help, but they couldn't hurt.

Jack was way out of his league here.

He'd planned to call the restaurant and ask for Harper as soon as he had a free moment. But by the time he got Red calmed down enough to do so, he was so angry, he couldn't think straight. Why hadn't she answered Vanessa's calls? Did she really intend to leave her grandfather for others to care for? She hadn't seemed that type of woman, but after Thursday... Well, clearly he had no idea what type of woman she was.

Rude, no doubt about that. Secretive. And, if Thursday night's conversation could be believed, estranged from her family. A family that could have helped her with Red. Seemed to Jack that if she really cared about the old man, she'd mend whatever fences she'd torn down with them.

After Red had finished the sandwich, he'd focused on the TV. Now, he was snoring softly, his head lolling to the side.

Finally, he heard a car in the driveway. A moment later, Harper burst through the front door. She looked at the old man and grabbed the door jamb. "Thank God."

Jack's anger slipped a few notches. With a nod toward the kitchen, he whispered, "Come on."

She collapsed on a chair and dropped her head into her hands. "I'm so sorry. My phone... I don't know what happened."

Tears dripped between her fingers and landed on her lap.

He'd seen her phone. It looked like a cheapie one might buy in a convenience store. No wonder it didn't work. He leaned against the counter and crossed his arms. "You need to replace that phone."

She reached for a napkin, wiped her eyes, took a deep breath. "As soon as I get my first paycheck." More tears dripped, and she wiped them away, focusing on her lap. "Why didn't Vanessa call me at McNeal's?"

He'd wondered the same thing. "Maybe because she knows it's your first week there. Maybe she didn't want to jeopardize your job. And she figures we're friends."

Her gaze snapped up and met his. She swallowed, blinked away fresh tears. "I'm sorry I was so rude last week. I just... My family is a hard topic."

"I gathered."

She straightened her shoulders, took another deep breath, seemed to be steeling herself. "What happened with Gramps?"

"According to Steve, he was fine. And then he wasn't. I figure it was sort of like what happened the other night. Except nobody there knew how to handle it."

"Sometimes I can't handle it, either. You saw him last week."

"Do you think it's Alzheimer's?"

She shrugged. "It's just been in the last month or so that he's gotten aggressive." She paused, took a breath. "To be honest, he's actually better than he was a few weeks back. His memory was failing a little, yes, but for a while, he was angry and confused much more than he has been here." She turned toward the doorway and her sleeping grandfather.

Jack surveyed the kitchen, the dingy house he'd rented them. He weighed his next words carefully, figured he was about to get thrown out again. But it had to be said. "Wouldn't he do better in his own home?"

She deflated like a balloon with a fast leak. "You don't understand."

"Explain it to me."

She pressed her hands together, stared at the cabinets.

He lowered his voice, tried to sound gentle. "If you took him home to your family, would they take care of him?"

She didn't answer, but fresh tears dripped down her cheeks.

"You don't think your father, Red's own son, would help you?"

"You don't understand."

"So you said."

She stood, opened the fridge, pulled out a package of American cheese. Well, those nasty individually-wrapped orange squares people tried to pass off as cheese. She unwrapped it, nibbled the edge like a frightened mouse.

"Have you eaten?" he asked.

She shook her head, focused on the floor.

He edged by her, opened the fridge again, and pulled out the pan of lasagna. Only one serving remained. "How about I warm this up for you?"

"I can feed myself."

He just lifted his eyebrows and waited.

She took the pan from him, cut the small portion in half, and put it on a plate. "You want some?"

"There's barely enough for one."

She glanced at the portion she'd dished herself. "I won't eat more than that."

He'd had a sandwich with Red, but the lasagna looked good. When he said nothing else, she took the rest, put it on a second plate.

While the food heated in the microwave, she washed the empty pan and set it on the table. Then she got them both glasses.

"Water for me," he said.

She filled two glasses and grabbed their meals.

They ate with only the sound of the soap opera in the other room and their forks against the dishes for noise.

When he finished, he stood with his empty plate. "You about to kick me out again?"

"I didn't kick you out. I just…"

When she didn't finish, he turned to the sink to rinse the empty dish.

"Just leave it."

"And go," he added, figuring that's what she wanted.

She gestured toward the other chair. "Unless you need to go. You probably have work to do or something. I'm sure we messed up your day."

He sat. "I'm good."

Her plate was still half-full when she pushed it away. "I don't have a relationship with my parents. I want to. Maybe someday I'll have the nerve to go home, but not yet."

"Why?"

"Why what?"

It was like trying to question a hostile witness. He'd have made a terrible lawyer. "Why don't you have a relationship with them?"

"They were good parents. Raised me with love. Taught me right from wrong. I chose wrong."

Vague, but getting somewhere. "How so?"

She sipped her water, set it down. Folded her hands. They were trembling. "After I graduated from high school, I took off. Decided I wanted to be an actress."

"They didn't like that idea?"

"They were very supportive. I got a job in Hollywood as a barista, auditioned for every role I could. At one of them, I met this guy. He offered me a job dancing in a show in Vegas. It wasn't Hollywood, but it was a paying job. I was thrilled."

Her wry smile told him the thrill had worn off quickly.

"The job was fine. The guy and I started dating. And then we had a falling out." The way her lip ticked up at the corner, a look of pure disgust, made him wonder. "He kicked me out of his apartment, and I got fired from the job."

"Because you dumped him?" A rush of anger had the words out before he could stop them.

"Apparently, sleeping with him was one of my job requirements. I hadn't realized..."

The lasagna turned in his stomach. "I'm sorry."

"I should have gone home. But I'd made this big deal about how I was going to make it in show business, not just to my family but to everyone. To old friends who'd gone off to college and gotten real jobs. I was embarrassed." She sipped her water. "I knew people. I had work experience. I thought I could get another job."

Her gaze darted around the room as if collecting words, trying to put them together. "But that guy, the one from before... He'd introduced me to drugs." She swallowed. "I had a hard time... I thought if I could just make enough money, then it would all be okay. I just had to work. I was sure I'd figure everything out."

More tears. The woman leaked more than bad plumbing. And everything in him wanted to fix it for her. Because beyond the beauty, beyond the walls she'd put up, lay a woman he was drawn to. A woman he wanted to know. A woman in pain.

She wiped her eyes. "I got a job dancing again."

Why didn't that sound like good news?

She raised her hand, made air quotes. "Dancing."

It took him a second. Then he realized what she meant.

"It wasn't a... Vegas is..." She swallowed. "I always wore something. It was barely anything, but—"

"You don't have to—"

"I'm just saying."

"Okay."

She was quiet a moment while he tried very hard not to picture what she'd described. Tried very hard to push away the anger, the disgust. Not at her, but at every person who'd seen her, every person who'd taken advantage of her desperation.

Finally, she continued. "You start doing that for a living, and the last thing you want is to have a *better* grip on reality. I used more drugs, drank more, partied more. Anything to forget."

He couldn't imagine. Didn't want to.

"I met a guy. He was... I didn't realize how much he was like the first guy. I mean, not in all the ways you can see. The first guy was rich, this one was poor. The first guy was classy and sophisticated, this one was down to earth and funny. But they were alike in the ways that mattered. I chose not to see it, because I so desperately needed somebody to... to love me, I guess."

He kept his mouth shut. On his lap, his hands were clenched so tightly they hurt.

"Money was always an issue," she said. "I made it, he spent it. Then..." Her gaze started darting again. Here, there. Anywhere but at him. "He got arrested. Sent to prison."

He hadn't expected that. "What did you do?"

There was a long pause. "This and that. And then I ended up with Gramps."

This and that. What did that mean? Not that it was any of his business. She hadn't had to tell him all of that. She hadn't had to tell him any of it. So why had she? And why had she stopped?

And what did *this and that* mean?

"You still haven't gone home?"

"How can I, after...?"

He thought of his own parents. The love they'd always shown him. He knew all parents weren't like his, though. "Are you afraid they'll reject you?"

"Wouldn't you?"

He unclenched his fists and rested his hand on hers. Tried

to ignore the electricity that zinged through him. "No. I wouldn't."

She met his gaze, blinked, looked down.

"What if they didn't reject you, Harper?" At the sound of her name, she met his eyes. "What if they greeted you with open arms? What if they hugged you and held you and told you how much they loved you?"

More tears. "What if they didn't?"

"What would you have lost?"

When she didn't answer, he pulled his hand back. At least now he understood the haunted look in her eyes, the reason she chose to be alone rather than with family.

But there were those bruises. And there was Red.

"Did your grandfather have a falling out with them, too?"

She blinked. Twice. "Uh. He hasn't had a relationship with them in a long time."

"Why not?"

She shrugged and carried her plate to the trash, where she dumped what she hadn't eaten. "I don't know the story. Don't ask him about it, though. He doesn't like to talk about it."

Amazing how fast the woman could shift from truth to lies. After all she'd told him, what in the world could she be hiding?

CHAPTER EIGHTEEN

Derrick stepped out of the shower in his Las Vegas hotel room Tuesday morning and dripped on the fancy tile while he dried off. This had been an utterly useless trip. He'd been so sure he'd be able to locate Harper. Where else would she go except back to the crappy life she'd left?

All day Friday and then all weekend, he'd looked for her. But nobody at the nursing home where she'd been working had seen her since she'd moved away. He'd even offered money for information on her whereabouts. Zip, zero, nada.

Derrick had visited her old apartment building and canvassed the residents, but they all claimed not to remember her. Those people were probably lucky to remember their names half the time. Bunch of bums. Even those fools at the grocery store where Harper had worked for chump change had come up with squat. Trying to grease their palms had gotten him nothing.

Unfortunately, it was Vegas, and without Harper to distract him, the poker tables had beckoned.

When he'd first met Harper, he'd believed she would be his angel. Once he'd turned his focus to her, his desire to gamble had waned. It had gone from a pounding need to a dull ache easily ignored. But when she'd blown him off over the summer because Gramps was sick, that ache had grown, and, with nothing else to do, he'd gone to Atlantic City.

The money he'd lost—her fault. All her fault.

And he was back here in Vegas because of her. He'd lost more money because of her.

So now he was tapped out, and not just financially. He'd been winning all night. At one point, he'd had thousands of dollars' worth of chips stacked in front of him. He'd been so sure this would be the moment of his big score. The solution to all his problems. But by the time the sun rose over the distant mountains, he'd lost every penny.

Derrick scoffed at his reflection in the foggy mirror. His angel. Right. Thanks to Harper, he was pretty sure he'd soon get a visit from the angel of death.

Why couldn't she have just been on his side?

Didn't she understand what he'd done for her? Rescuing her from the low-class life she'd lived here, when she'd had to work two jobs just to get by. Derrick had given her a place to live and a job—a job nobody else would hire an ex-con to do. He'd showered her with gifts, given her everything she needed. He'd loved her.

And she'd betrayed him.

He dressed in a fresh suit and tie and checked his image in the mirror, smiling at his reflection despite the fury filling his gut. He still looked like the kind of guy you could trust with your money. And people could trust him. At least he'd kept that part of his life unsullied.

He slipped on his glasses, packed his small roller bag, and headed for the elevator.

He'd never be back. Never. Not to Las Vegas, not to Atlantic City, not to any of the other casinos that had popped up all over the country like zits on a teenager. After last night, he was done with gambling forever.

He meant it this time.

Thank God he'd put most of the cash he'd gotten from Tank into his savings account, an account not accessible by ATM and not attached to his checking account. No matter how much he'd wanted to dig into it the night before, he hadn't been able to. So he'd only lost the money he'd had on him.

Only. Like a thousand dollars was chump change.

Except it was, compared to what he owed. And now he had less cash to use for finding Harper and Gramps.

As he pushed the button to summon the elevator, he cursed the cards that had turned against him, his own stupidity, and Harper.

Someone approached from behind.

A man stood to his right, another behind him. Too close. He turned to nod, felt his automatic smile freeze.

He didn't recognize them, but he didn't need to. Their sneers told Derrick all he needed to know. He faced them head-on. The shorter one snatched Derrick's suitcase. The one shaped like Rambo gripped Derrick's arm as if he were in the mood for juice and Derrick was the orange.

"Let's take a walk," Rambo said.

Fighting would only get him hurt. Yelling for help would probably get him knocked out cold. He walked with the men to the room next door to the one he'd occupied. How long had they been watching?

They knocked, and a man on the inside opened the door.

This one, Derrick recognized. Quentin Gray. Medium height, medium build, medium red hair, medium brown eyes. Freckles all over his face. Didn't look a day over twenty-five, but Derrick guessed he was at least in his thirties. He passed himself off as a tech millionaire, and maybe he was. He'd developed some obscure program for some obscure industry. But that program didn't account for the bulk of his income. That came from other, more lucrative, sources.

One of which was the reason Derrick was face-to-face with him now.

The goons pushed Derrick into the room and followed. The door closed with a thud.

Quentin crossed to a small desk and sat in the chair behind it. "You've been avoiding me."

Derrick shrugged off Rambo and forced himself not to rub his aching arm. He straightened his suit coat, pushed up his glasses, and stepped closer to Quentin, mostly to distance himself from the guys behind him. "I didn't know you were in Las Vegas."

"When I heard you were in town, I thought I'd fly in, say hello."

Derrick was smart enough not to ask how he'd heard. "I'm trying to get your money."

Quentin took his phone, pressed the screen, then lifted it so Derrick could see the image there.

Photos of him at the poker table the night before. The first photo showed a stack of chips in front of him. He wore a stupid smile. Quentin swiped so Derrick could look at the next photo. Fewer chips, smaller smile. Then he saw the next, and the next, until finally, no chips remained in front of him. Derrick stared at the image of his own face, the shock he saw there, as if any idiot couldn't have seen that coming. As if the same thing hadn't happened every single time.

Derrick looked past the phone to the man. "I'm back on the wagon today."

"Figured you'd turn your paltry cash into the two hundred grand you owe me?"

Derrick tried his most charming smile. "Worth a try."

Quentin pocketed his phone and shook his head slowly. "I don't know what we're going to do with you. We tried talking sense into you—"

"I've got a—"

"I was sure," Quentin said, "after we had that little chat with your girlfriend, you'd come to your senses."

Derrick tried to blink away the images that reminder brought. Harper, black-and-blue and terrified after the attack. She'd known it was his fault. What she hadn't grasped was that it was her fault, too. If she'd worked with him instead of against him, he'd have gotten the money from Gramps months ago.

"I'm doing everything I can," Derrick said. "And that little stunt of yours just made it harder."

"Stunt, huh?" Quentin looked beyond Derrick to the goons behind him. "Can you believe this guy?"

Rambo and his sidekick remained silent.

Derrick pushed his glasses up. "Look, I've got a plan. I'll get your money, every penny."

Quentin's gaze was hard. "Money isn't the only issue."

"What does that mean?"

"My guys in Baltimore, they're missing. You know anything about that?"

Derrick's mind raced. Guys in Baltimore? Who could he...? "You mean Keith and his goon friend?"

Behind him, Rambo grunted. Maybe *goon* hadn't been the best word choice.

"I had two men on the payroll, and you were one of their jobs. They reported their chit-chat with your girlfriend, and I haven't heard from them since."

Rambo approached from behind. Derrick didn't turn, but he could feel the man's heat on his back, his breath on his neck.

"My employees get nervous when fellow employees go missing."

"I don't know anything about that," Derrick said.

Rambo dropped a huge hand on Derrick's shoulder, squeezed the trapezius muscle hard.

Derrick was on his knees almost before the pain registered. "I swear, I know nothing." His voice was high-pitched, but he couldn't lower it. "Harper and my grandfather disappeared that weekend. Maybe she did something to them."

Behind him, the goon removed his hand, and Derrick had to fight to keep from collapsing in a heap. He rubbed the sore spot, swallowed hard, and stood.

"If we learn you came against my men"—Quentin's words were slow and measured and deadly serious—"you'll want to do yourself in before one of us gets to you."

He lifted his hands, palms out. "I have no idea what happened. I never saw them that weekend."

Quentin nodded and tapped the table in front of him with a pen. "If you can't come up with the cash, I can think of some other ways to get what's owed me. I have an associate who might be interested in a trade, and that girlfriend of yours... I've done a little digging. Seems she might be able to earn back—"

"I'll get you the money." At this point, Harper didn't deserve better than what Quentin was suggesting, but Derrick couldn't stomach any other man's hands on her. She was his. Until he was done with her, she belonged to him.

Quentin dropped the pen on the desk and stood. "I've given you extension after extension, listened to your promises over and over. No more lies, no more promises. And there'll be no payment plans. I expect the entire balance in one week."

A week? Even if he found Gramps and did him in, he wouldn't get his inheritance in a week. "That's not enough time." He'd tried to keep his voice measured but failed, and the words had come out squeaky and scared.

A smile spread across Quentin's features. "Between your

wealthy grandfather and your, shall we say, talented girlfriend, I'm sort of hoping you don't make your deadline. Seems I might be able to find a way to get back my investment with interest. And I won't need you at all. Of course, once I no longer need you..." He shrugged. "Nobody gets away with not paying me back."

Derrick swallowed a huge lump in his throat.

Quentin laughed, looked past Derrick. "You should see his face. White as a corpse."

That elicited a chuckle from one of the goons.

Derrick tried to act nonchalant, act as if he received death threats all the time. He glanced at his watch. "I have a flight."

Quentin stood, gestured toward the door. "Don't let us keep you."

Derrick started to turn, but Quentin held him in place with a lifted palm. He looked past Derrick again. "Doesn't seem fair that his girlfriend got beat up and he walked away without a scrape."

Behind him, one of them gripped his upper arms.

"We don't want to do anything that'll keep him from paying me back." He gave Derrick a quick assessment. "He seems a bit delicate."

Derrick's arms ached from the man's meaty grip, but he tried to look tough and unconcerned.

Quentin said, "Just pop one of his eyes out and send him on his way."

Before he could react, the goon flipped him off his feet. Derrick landed on his back, lost his breath.

Rambo straddled him and pressed his arms into the floor.

The smaller goon leaned over Derrick's head. He used one hand to hold his eye open. In the other, Derrick saw the glint of a knife.

It closed in.

He had no breath to scream. No energy to fight. All he could do was lie there and watch as the knife neared his face. The little goon smiled.

An eternity passed before Quentin laughed. "All right, all right. Let him keep the eye for now."

The goons let him go and stood, relaxed, as if this were the most normal situation in the world.

The whole thing had happened so fast, Derrick still didn't have his breath back.

Then, Rambo kicked him in the side.

Derrick rolled in to the fetal position and waited for more blows.

"Look at me," Quentin said.

Derrick forced himself to shift, though his ribs protested the movement. He sat up and did as he was told.

Quentin's lips pressed together as he shook his head. "I don't know why I keep giving you chances to betray me. But hey, I guess I'm just a good guy. Trusting, you know? So here you are. One. Last. Chance. You blow it, you're dead, and I'll get what I need from your grandfather and that girlfriend of yours."

Derrick struggled to stand, tried to get air into his lungs.

The sidekick opened the door and looked up and down the hall. Then Rambo pushed Derrick out of the room. He stumbled and crashed against the opposite door and fell in a heap.

One of them tossed his suitcase on top of him. The door slammed, leaving Derrick alone.

He couldn't move, couldn't think.

Finally he got a deep breath, touched his eyes to reassure himself they were both there. His ribs throbbed. Broken, bruised? Should he go to the emergency room?

He didn't know. Couldn't think.

His shoulder ached.

He pressed a hand to his head where it had hit the door. A knot was already forming.

Slowly, muscles protesting and lungs tight, he used the door knob to pull himself up and hobbled to the elevator, dragging his suitcase behind him.

Every minute waiting for the elevator was torture. He needed to be around people, somewhere Quentin and his goons couldn't hurt him again. He'd take the stairs but feared he might pass out.

Finally, the elevator came, and he stepped in beside a mother with two kids. She took one look at him and pulled her kids behind her.

In the lobby, Derrick made his way toward the front door to get a taxi to the airport. Those few minutes in Quentin's hotel room had been terrifying, but they could have ended so much worse.

Derrick was walking away.

He would get Quentin's money. He just had to get his hands on Gramps and Harper and figure out a way to get Gramps to hand over two hundred grand. If Derrick had to hurt them... Well, the old man shouldn't have been so stingy.

And Harper shouldn't have betrayed him.

They both had it coming.

CHAPTER NINETEEN

Tuesday turned out to be a beautiful day. The sky was bright blue, and the temperature was predicted to hit a very unseasonable sixty-five. Jack had worked double-time to finish the projects he'd started the day before. He caught up by lunchtime and was on his way to look at a multi-unit property in the next town when Ginny called to reschedule.

"Let's do it tomorrow," she said. "Meanwhile, you keep visualizing the kind of property you want to find."

He rolled his eyes and swallowed his retort. "I'll pray about it, too."

"Right," she said. "Well, then..."

They made an appointment for the following day, and he turned the truck around too fast, causing it to slide on the gravely road. He'd really been looking forward to seeing the place. He should go home, get some painting done. Except the weather was so beautiful.

And he couldn't stop thinking about Red and Harper, his confusion and her bruises. They'd faded now, but after Red's aggression the day before...

He was traveling through downtown Nutfield when he

turned on a whim and parked at the food bank. He let himself in the back door.

It wasn't a client day, so the warehouse was empty of people. Voices came from the rec center, but he passed the entrance and knocked on the door to Vanessa's office.

On the other side of the door, he heard the scrape of a chair, then Vanessa's voice. "Come in."

He opened the door to find a man standing in front of her desk. Her eyebrows were lifted. "We are finished here."

"Look," the man said, "I'm just trying to—"

"I have it under control." Vanessa regarded him with a cool look. "But I thank you for your concern."

"For your clients," the man said.

In the awkward silence that followed, Jack said, "I'm sorry, I didn't mean..."

The man turned. He was a little taller than Jack, maybe a little older, and right now, his jaw was clenched tight. "Not your fault. The woman's stubborn streak is wider than the Atlantic."

He brushed past Jack, who turned to Vanessa with raised eyebrows. "You okay?"

She waved off his comment and the man who'd just stormed off. "He had some ideas, which I said I would think about. He calls me stubborn. He has all the patience of a newborn with a ... a bottom rash."

"Diaper rash?"

She waved that off, too. "What do you need?"

He nodded toward the chair across from her desk. "Do you mind?"

"One moment." She tapped on her keyboard before she pushed it away and turned to him.

Jack sat. "I wanted to talk to you about Harper and Red."

"Harper apologized. Apparently her phone does not work well."

"So she said."

"She told me to call McNeal's if something else happens, and I said I would do that."

"Yeah, I figured."

"You know everything. Why are you here?"

He tried to stop the smile but failed. Some people found her abrasive, but he knew better. Vanessa had built a wall around herself, this facade of anger. But he'd known her long enough to see the big heart underneath.

Maybe whatever had caused her to build her wall had enabled her to see beyond Harper's. "I'm worried about them. When they first moved in, Harper had some bruises."

"I saw the one on her cheek," she said. "There were others?"

"A big one on her arm. And maybe a sprained wrist. Seemed like she was favoring it. I was just wondering if you think... I don't know what to do. Red's such a nice guy, but you saw him yesterday. I wonder if, when he has those episodes—"

"You think he did that to her?"

"Not on purpose. I don't know what to think."

Vanessa looked past him, her bottom lip caught between her teeth. Finally, she said, "I do not think so. I think she is here because of those bruises, no?"

"Oh." That made sense. "You're saying she came to Nutfield—"

"Because some man showed his displeasure with his fists. Do you not think so?"

"I hadn't—"

"And if her grandfather had given her those bruises, then why would she have brought the problem with her?"

"That's a good point. But..." He told her about the cut to Harper's forehead.

"What did she say about it?"

"That he didn't mean to do it."

"Then you must believe her. If she wants to confide in you, she will. But do not be surprised if she doesn't. Women in her situation do not trust men easily."

The image of the man who'd just stormed out flashed in Jack's mind. Vanessa didn't trust men so easily, either. Jack knew that well enough. She'd treated him just as coolly when he'd first started volunteering. He wasn't sure she trusted him now.

Jack stood. "Thanks for your advice. If she tells you anything you feel like I need to know..."

Her eyebrows rose.

"I mean, as her landlord and neighbor, I want to make sure she's safe."

"We will have to trust Harper to share what she wants to share with whom she wants to share it."

Jack walked out of Vanessa's office feeling not at all reassured. How could he keep Harper safe if he had no idea who he was trying to protect her from?

He decided not to examine why he felt it was his responsibility.

It wouldn't hurt to check on Red, make sure everything was okay after the episode the day before. Maybe Red would be lucid enough to tell him about his real estate business. And maybe he'd give Jack some insight about what was going on with them.

He stepped into the rec center. A couple of women were sitting on the couches facing the TV. Red and Steve, as usual, were seated at the game table with playing cards spread in front of them.

Red pushed himself to his feet when Jack walked in. "Good to see you, son. It's been a while. Where you been?"

Jack gripped his outstretched hand and glanced at Steve,

who was shaking his head slightly. Seemed Red had no memory of the day before.

"Keeping busy," Jack said. "How about you?"

He lowered himself into the chair. "Just beating Steve at gin."

"You wish, old man." Steve's oversize ears wiggled with his smile.

Jack sat between them. "Don't let me stop you."

The men resumed their game, and Jack watched for a few minutes. They both seemed sharp and aware.

"I was hoping you'd tell me about your real estate business, Red," Jack said.

Red picked up a card, studied it, and set it on the discard pile. "What do you wanna know?"

Jack shrugged. "Whatever you want to tell me, I guess. I'm trying to learn all I can."

For the next hour, Red and Steve regaled Jack with stories of their real estate ventures. It didn't take long for the men to start one-upping each other, though it was clear that while Steve had only dabbled, Red had built a solid enterprise.

"At one point," Red said, "I owned over five hundred rental units. Most of them were small apartment buildings or multi-family homes."

"Lot of work," Jack said.

"Sure, sure. But it wasn't like I managed them."

Jack was the manager for a lot of local investors, so he understood the importance of that part of the business. He hoped to be able to farm out the management of his properties one day, too.

"But you sold most of them?" Jack asked.

Red picked up the deck of cards, which by then had been sitting, forgotten, on the table for some time. He shuffled it a few times.

Something in the man's eyes kept both Jack and Steve quiet. Was that regret? For what?

Finally, Red tapped the edge of the cards on the table and set the deck down. "I sold almost all of them, put the money in a trust for my grandson." He blinked. "Grandkids, I mean."

Jack didn't miss the slip. What did it mean? "Why'd you get out?"

"Too much work for an old man. Got to where I'd look at the numbers, and I just couldn't... They didn't make sense to me like they used to."

Jack wrestled with something to say. He ended up with, "Well, that sucks."

Red chuckled. "Gettin' old ain't for sissies, kid, lemme tell you."

"You said it." Steve slammed his hand on the table.

The white-haired woman looked up from her needlepoint and shushed them.

Red and Steve chuckled. "The librarian's mad at us," Red whispered.

Jack's question must've shown on his face, because Steve tipped his head toward the women. "Forty years she worked as a school librarian. Never seen her with a book, but lemme tell you, she doesn't put up with loud pupils."

Jack chuckled, focused on Red again. "The other day, you said you still owned some properties."

"I haven't been able to part with my earliest investments. They're single-family homes, and they got me started. Helped me believe I could do it. They have sentimental value. And the renters have been there forever. When the renters move out, I'll sell."

Jack pulled out his cell and navigated to the link his Realtor had sent him. "I'm thinking about buying this place." He showed Red the property.

The old man peered through his glasses with narrowed eyes. "How much per unit."

Jack told him, then went on to explain what he knew about the place. "Most of the units have been updated, and the plumbing is—"

"All that stuff'll break," Red said. "Figure everything in the house will eventually need to be replaced or repaired over the life of the loan."

Jack nodded slowly while the man's words penetrated. "I'd never thought of it that way."

"If you're in this for the long haul, you have to. That's how people screw this up. They look at income and expenses, but they forget that, over thirty years, there'll be a lot of repairs. So you have to plan on that, put away money to cover new furnaces and roofs and water heaters, and—"

"Floors and paint and appliances," Steve said. "And everybody wants air conditioning now. In my day, we could handle a little heat, but nowadays people think it's inhumane if every room isn't kept at seventy degrees."

Their suggestions spun in Jack's mind. What the men were saying made sense. But that would definitely affect his numbers. "Looks like I've got some work to do."

Red squeezed his shoulder. "You'll get there."

An idea crossed his mind. "Hey, do you want to go for a ride with me, drive by the place? It's only about fifteen minutes away."

"I been staring at Steve's ears long enough. I'd love to."

Jack turned to Steve. "How about you? Would you be able—?"

"Elizabeth's picking me up. I'll wait for her."

Jack started to stand, then glanced at his watch and sat back down. "Actually, I probably need to check with Harper, make sure she doesn't mind."

Red waved him off. "Use that phone you got there and give her a ring. She won't care."

Jack stepped out of the rec center and was dialing when Harper walked in the back door. She froze when she saw him. Was that a blush that rose to her cheeks?

He hoped not. He certainly hoped she wasn't embarrassed about all she'd told him the day before. His problem wasn't what she *had* told him but what she *hadn't*. And he knew there had been plenty left unsaid.

He took a few steps toward her. "I was just about to call you."

She approached as if he were a hostile animal. "It was slow, so Bonnie let me go early." She stopped a few feet from him. "Is Gramps okay?"

He hoped his smile would relax her. "He's fine. I was going to ask if you'd mind if I took him for a ride. Now that you're here, you can join us."

"A ride where?"

"I'm looking at a property, and I thought your grandfather might be able to give me some advice."

Her eyes narrowed. "He's not strong enough to be traipsing all over—"

"We were just going to drive by. It's a nice day. I figured he might like to get out in the sunshine."

She bit her bottom lip. Her gaze flicked to the door to the rec center. "He wants to go with you?"

"Said he did."

She swallowed. "I guess that's okay."

"Good," Jack said. "You can leave your car here and go with us. I'll drive."

"I'll go on home. You two don't need me."

That was true. They didn't. But now that she was here, he

craved her company. "I thought we'd look at the house, then maybe drive over to the beach and get some ice cream."

Her lips twitched. "It's not *that* warm outside."

"In New Hampshire, sunshine means ice cream. The temperature is irrelevant."

He could practically see her gears moving, trying to decide what to do.

"It's really good ice cream," he added.

Finally, she smiled for real. "You talked me into it."

CHAPTER TWENTY

Harper watched the world slide by from the backseat of Jack's pickup. The evergreens shone greener against the backdrop of the sapphire blue sky. The forest on either side of the road called to her, deep and inviting. This land of trees and trees and more trees was so different from where she'd grown up in Kansas. When she was a kid, she'd loved those wide-open spaces, the skies that burst in color every morning and night. There was a little rise not far from her house in Wichita where she used to ride her bike. From the very crest, she'd have sworn she could see all the way to Canada. She used to imagine some little girl looking south toward her, wearing a heavy jacket and a knit cap and waving. The years since had taught Harper her vision wasn't nearly as good as she'd once believed.

Nowadays, she could barely see her next step.

What had Gramps told her? God's word was a lamp unto her feet? She wished it were more like a street lamp and less like a cheap flashlight with a dying bulb.

When she'd been young, all those open spaces had made her feel very small in the universe. Small, but she'd always known she was loved. Now, as Harper peered at the tops of trees that made the ones back home look like oversize bushes, she felt that smallness again. Small, insignificant, and lost.

Up front, Jack and Gramps talked real estate. She couldn't keep up with their conversation and didn't care to. All she could think about—all she'd thought about since Jack had left her house the previous day—were the confessions she'd made to him.

As if he were her priest, not her landlord.

She needed more than a drive in the country and some ice cream. She needed a brain transplant.

Seriously. Had Jack needed to know all her ugly history? Now that he knew, he could never un-know. To him, she'd forever be a former exotic dancer.

Fine, then. Who cared what he thought? As long as he didn't assume she'd give him a private show, they were fine. Maybe now he'd stop asking her questions, stop trying to dig into her life.

She swiped her stupid tears. Her heart didn't understand what her head knew. That, as desperately as she wanted a friend, she couldn't have one. Eventually, everyone would ask questions she couldn't answer, questions that would only get her in trouble. She and Gramps couldn't run again. Gramps wouldn't survive. And the only way to stay here was to fly under the radar.

Keep her head down and her mouth shut.

So what in the world was she doing in the backseat of Jack Rossi's pickup truck?

Definitely time for that brain transplant.

But Gramps was with them. She was safe from spitting out all her secrets as long as she didn't end up alone with Jack. That was when her mind got muddled and confused.

The truck slowed, and Jack turned into a parking lot that served three white buildings.

"All of them?" Gramps asked.

Jack nodded and peered through the windshield at the two-story structures. The buildings were square and so close together they were practically joined at the corners like spaces on a checkerboard. The parking lot sat in front of them. Jack was thinking of buying this? What must it be like to have that kind of freedom, that kind of optimism?

"Each one has eight apartments," Jack said. "Four downstairs, four up."

Gramps was nodding slowly. "Twenty-four apartments, but only three roofs. Only one parking lot to maintain. Only a handful of walkways that need to be cleared of snow and ice. Something to be said for that."

Jack focused on him. "Am I crazy to take on such a huge project? All I have under my belt is your house and mine."

"And years of management experience," Gramps said.

Harper studied the old man as he focused on the buildings. His mind seemed to be churning, considering. She loved watching him work. She'd seen so little of that since Derrick had tried to con him out of money this summer. Between his worsening dementia, the viruses he'd battled, and the antifreeze—not to mention his broken heart after what Derrick had done—it had been a long time since Gramps had been interested in anything but the TV. Today, he seemed one hundred percent the real estate investor he'd been for thirty years.

Gramps turned to Jack. "You need to pull together those numbers we talked about. Bring them by when you're ready, and we'll talk through it."

Jack took one last look at the building. "I'll do that. I can't tell you how much I appreciate your help."

"Glad somebody values me. That idiot grandkid of mine..."

Harper patted Gramps's shoulder.

He glanced at her, mouth pinched shut.

After a pause, Jack shifted into drive. "Let's go get that ice cream."

Gramps wasn't in the habit of talking about Derrick with strangers, mostly because there was very little good he could say. But he was coming to trust Jack. As long as he didn't let the truth slip, they should be all right.

But what if he did? She'd need a story, a plausible story to explain her dishonesty. And she'd need to improve her skills at lying.

Please, God. Tell me how to handle this.

There was no answer. She envied those people who seemed so close to God, they heard His voice. Right now, there was nothing she could do but stay on this ride and hope it would come to a soft landing.

Jack weaved through some of the prettiest little villages Harper had ever seen. Bright white churches and lovely town commons with gleaming monuments and colorful parks. They passed old farmhouses, some just a few feet from the road, with pretty barns and lush bushes and towering trees. Finally, they turned a corner and crested a hill, and she got her first glimpse of the rocky New England coast.

"Wow." Her word was barely a whisper.

Jack glanced at her in the rearview mirror. "I thought you'd like it."

"It's breathtaking."

They turned onto the road that hugged the shoreline. She was mesmerized by the waves as they crashed against the boulders below. On the other side of the street, mansions of every shape and style overlooked the raging waters. Many had platforms standing above the roofs.

"I bet those are good for sunbathing," she said.

Jack glanced at one particularly huge house. "Those are widows' walks."

"Back in the day," Gramps said, "women would watch for ships, waiting for their husbands and sons and fathers to return."

She could imagine it, the women's fears, the prayers they'd lift up from their perches above the sea, prayers for a glimpse of the ships that would bring their loved ones home. Harper's perch was her floor and her knees, and her prayers were for a glimpse of freedom from this crazy situation she'd found herself in. A hope for a future.

They stopped at a little white building with a sign shaped like an ice cream cone. A few folks were sitting at the outdoor picnic benches enjoying their treats.

Jack parked and opened her door.

She slid out. "Thanks."

He grabbed Gramps's walker from the bed of his pickup and hurried to help him out.

A cold breeze blew in from the ocean, and she shivered. Slowly, they walked toward the window on the side of the building.

"What's your poison?" Jack said.

"Hot chocolate?" she suggested.

He chuckled and shifted them toward a door. "We can eat inside."

They stepped into the tiny—and blessedly heated—dining room. Two of the six tables were occupied, one with an older couple, the other with two teenage girls. The girls seemed to be focused more on the long-haired boy behind the counter than on their cones.

Harper studied the board and settled on strawberry.

Jack shook his head as if he'd never been more disappointed. "I pegged you for a mint chocolate chip girl."

"So far off, you're not even on the radar."

Jack turned to Gramps. "How about you?"

"Cookies-and-cream for me," he said.

"Good choice." Jack placed their order. When Harper reached for her wallet, he stopped her with a hand on her arm. "My treat."

She considered arguing, then decided against it. She couldn't afford it, and Jack knew that.

This place was shifting her mood. Yes, her life was falling apart. Yes, she was tangled in a web of deception she might never escape. But the ocean, the blue skies, this charming ice cream parlor... There was something to be said for not being at work or at home, taking a break from the worries that weighed her down.

Jack handed her the ice cream cone, gave Gramps his double scoop of cookies-and-cream, and then sat with his own.

"What'd you get?" she asked.

"Peanut butter chocolate chip."

She regarded his cone. "Looks yummy."

He leaned it toward her. "Try it."

"Oh, well..."

"Go on," he said. "It won't kill you."

She licked a tiny spot, and he scoffed. "You can do better than that."

She took a bigger bite, tasted the salty peanut butter and sweet chocolate. "You're right. That's good."

"Now you'll know for next time."

Next time.

Wouldn't that be nice?

Gramps settled against the wall and stared out the window and across the street at the long stone jetty that reached into the ocean. "Sure is pretty here."

"Is it much different from the coastline where you're from?" Jack's question was aimed at her.

"Uh..." She'd only seen Rehoboth Beach in Delaware. "It's rockier." She turned to Red. "What do you think?"

He shrugged. "Much colder."

Jack chuckled, gaze on Harper again. "I've only ever been to beaches in New England."

Harper swallowed a bite of ice cream. She didn't have much information to compare. But if she were Gramps's granddaughter... "We didn't go to the beach a lot."

"We didn't go to the beach a lot when I was a kid, either," Jack said. "Our vacations were usually in the mountains."

She focused on her ice cream, had to keep quiet. Keep all her secrets. If she started talking, they'd slip out.

Gramps wiped a dribble of ice cream off his chin. "What did you do in the mountains?"

"In the winter," Jack said, "we skied. You guys ski?"

Harper said, "No," at the same time Gramps said, "Used to."

Jack looked between them again, focused on Harper. "You should give it a try. I love it. What kinds of vacations did you go on?"

She thought of their summers spent in Eureka Springs, Arkansas. "We used to camp near a lake. We'd go swimming and boating. Sometimes, my parents rented jet skis." She loved the speed, the feel of the spray on her skin, the feeling of weightlessness when she got thrown off. Nutfield reminded her of that little lake town.

"I bet you're a boss on a jet ski," Jack said.

She nodded. "Pretty much."

He smiled and turned back to Gramps. "In the summer, we'd rent a place on a lake. My sisters and my mom would sleep in, shop, swim, and work on their tans."

"You?" Gramps asked.

"Dad and I would go hunting," Jack said.

"Hunting." Gramps grunted. "Never could stand it, sitting there in the freezing cold, staring at empty woods."

"I was up for doing whatever Dad wanted. And hunting was the only time he relaxed."

Gramps said, "Good guy, your dad?"

"The best." Jack worked on his cone, then glanced at her.

"So," she said to steer him away from questions about her past. "Besides hunting, what else did you and your dad do together?"

Jack's chuckle seemed filled with memories. "My dad worked a lot. He was the kind of guy who could never keep still."

"Kind of like you?" She'd observed that same boundless energy in Jack.

"Huh." Jack's gaze went to the ceiling before it settled on her. "You think?"

"Based on what I know of you."

He nodded slowly, seemed to be letting the idea settle. "Nobody I'd rather be compared to than my dad." He licked his ice cream.

She said, "You were about to tell us—"

"Right. So he worked a lot. We didn't see him much during the week. On the weekends, he was always doing something. The house we lived in was old, and Dad was forever fixing it up. Refinishing the hardwood, replacing tile, repairing plumbing. He could do everything. Install new light fixtures, build furniture, hang drywall. When I was in middle school, he built an addition to the house."

"Guy like that," Gramps said, "worth his weight in gold."

Jack aimed what was left of his ice cream cone toward Gramps. "You said it. And not just because he's handy. He wasn't a Christian back then, but he raised us right. When he did become a Christian, most of the family went right along with him."

A frown crossed his face like a shifting shadow, gone almost before she'd seen it. She suspected it had something to do with that remark—*most* of the family. Jack recovered before she could ask. "Anyway," he said, "I used to follow Dad around, and he'd teach me what he was doing. Sometimes, it would be so boring sitting there watching him work, but I loved being with him. And sometimes, Dad would realize how bored I was and stop for no reason except just because, and he'd take me for ice cream."

"Good memories," Gramps said.

Harper thought of her own father, of the times they'd spent together. She hadn't appreciated him when she was a kid. He was a good man, but she'd been too busy with her friends and social life and dreams to value her own father. Maybe if she'd shadowed him, everything would have been different.

They finished their ice cream. Gramps set down his dirty napkin and nodded toward the jetty. "Folks walking on that."

"You want to go?" Jack asked.

Harper gave him a look intended to say, *With his walker? Are you nuts?*

But Gramps only chuckled. "I wouldn't make it up the first steps. But you two should go."

Harper said, "I'm okay."

"We wouldn't want to abandon you," Jack added.

Gramps looked back and forth between them, his sharp eyes missing nothing. "You two think I'm too old, too feeble, to sit here by myself a few minutes?"

"Of course not," Harper said.

Jack focused on her. "He's trying to goad us into taking a walk."

Gramps glared at her. "I promise I won't wander off or break a hip while you're gone."

She gathered the trash from the table. "I'm really not comfortable—"

"Ten minutes alone, girl," Gramps said. "Ten minutes to stare out at the sea and remember my Bebe. She'd have loved it here." He inhaled a long breath, shook his head, and blew it out. "Is that too much to ask?"

She looked to Jack for help. He gently took the trash she was squeezing in her fist, dropped it in the can, and held his hand out to her. "Come on. He'll be fine."

Defeated, she leaned down, kissed Gramps on the cheek. "You sure?"

He patted her arm. "I'll be right here when you get back."

Just what she needed—to be alone with Jack. His hand was still reaching toward her. What else could she do but slip hers into it. Together, they stepped into the sunny day.

CHAPTER TWENTY-ONE

Jack was having a hard time focusing. The day was beautiful, the sun was shining, the waves were crashing against the rocks across the street, but his mind was on the soft, chilled hand wrapped in his and the woman beside him.

They reached the edge of the road, and Harper looked behind them. "You sure he'll be okay?"

Jack looked, too. Folks were congregated at the tables around the ice cream parlor soaking up the sun. "How far can he go?"

"What if he gets sick or something?"

Jack squeezed her hand. "He wanted to be alone."

"I know." She sighed and turned toward the street. At a break in traffic, they darted to the far side.

He climbed the rocks of the jetty before helping her up. When she was steady, they turned toward the sea and walked. She kept her hand in his.

The rocks on top were mostly flat, but Jack and Harper still had to be careful not to slip.

The wind whipped Harper's hair, and she pushed it out of her face. He glimpsed the tiny cut on her forehead that she'd gotten a week earlier. It seemed to be healing well. Her bruises had faded completely.

He wanted to ask her about them, but Vanessa's words reverberated in his ears. She didn't trust him enough to tell him. Questioning her wouldn't make that better.

They made it to the end of the jetty, where she stared out at the blue waves, at the rocky coastline to the north dotted with little cabins and giant mansions and hotels and ice cream stands and restaurants. To the south lay Hampton Beach and the boardwalk with its tourist shops and arcades and hotels and rental cabins.

"It's so beautiful," she said.

He forced his gaze away from her face to see what she was seeing. "It is."

For a moment, she seemed as carefree as the seagulls cawing overhead.

She turned his direction and met his gaze. "I say this a lot."

"What's that?"

"Thank you." She gestured to the scene surrounding them. "I needed this today."

He shrugged. "Sure."

"You've been a good friend to us." She met his gaze, her blue eyes watery and sincere, her cheeks pink in the chilly wind, her hair blowing behind her like some sort of sea goddess. She seemed lost, alone in the world except for an old man who needed her. She was lonely, frightened, needy, and everything in him wanted to help. To give her everything she needed, everything he had.

"I'm sorry I'm so..." She looked back out to sea. "I should be a better friend. It's been a hard transition."

He stared at her silhouette and fought the urge to pull her to his chest, to hold her and tell her she could trust him. Waves of protectiveness and sheer desire washed over him. They lingered like salt after a dip in the ocean, seasoning his every thought. He swallowed, licked his lips. Touched her chin and urged her gaze back to his. Those eyes. He could dive into those eyes and stay forever.

They narrowed, and her head tilted to the side.

Right. She'd said something. He thought back, remembered. Something about the transition. "You're doing a wonderful job."

Her lips parted like she might speak, but she said nothing.

Hair blew across her face. He wanted to push it back, to feel the silky strands between his fingers.

She turned toward the shore and let go of his hand. "We should…"

No. He didn't want to go back. He liked the glimpse of the true Harper, the girl behind the mask. But the connection was broken. The memory of it wouldn't fade that quickly. If ever. "Okay."

They started back. He searched his brain for something to say, something innocuous, something that wouldn't push her away. Finally, what felt like a safe question entered his mind. "Where'd you grow up?"

She looked at him, eyes wide as if he'd just caught her stealing from the till.

Crap. Were there no fields that didn't contain land mines where this woman's past was concerned? "I figured it wasn't Maryland. I mean, since you don't ski and didn't have much to say about the coast. Maybe you visited as a kid. You and your grandfather have a good relationship." He was babbling. It seemed to be working as the shock in her expression faded.

They reached a gap in the rocks, and she focused on her steps. "Wichita, Kansas."

It sounded true. "I don't think I've ever met anybody from Kansas."

"Never been there?"

"Never been that far west. What's it like?"

"Flat. Skies as wide as…" She looked around, and her lips quirked in an almost smile. "As wide as this, actually. Except instead of ocean, we have grassland."

"And tornadoes?"

"I've never been swept away, so you can keep the Dorothy jokes to yourself."

"Dog named Toto?"

"Not even close." She walked a few steps and added, "Dog was named Lassie."

"All sorts of American film references going on."

She giggled. An actual joyful, troubles-abandoned, I-trust-you-at-least-for-this-second giggle. The sound made his heart race, his palms sweat in the cold breeze. That giggle did something to his insides, something he'd better not name. Something he'd better figure out how to undo and fast.

But she looked at him, those blue eyes sparkling like the water beneath him, and he knew there was no undoing it.

"Lassie was not named after Lassie."

He tried to make sense of that. "Okay."

"He was named after Bobbie Douglass, former KU quarterback. Played most of his NFL career for the Bears. How Douglass became Lassie, I have no idea."

It was Jack's turn to laugh. "I'm sure you'll be shocked to know that I've never heard of him."

She shrugged. "He's before our time."

"Is your mom a big KU fan?"

"Both my parents are."

"Huh." He tried to fit those pieces into the puzzle. "How'd your dad become such a KU fan if he's from Maryland?"

"Oh." She looked forward, swallowed.

Another landmine tripped.

"He went to college there," she said.

"That makes sense." And it would have, if she were a better liar.

Truth was, none of it made sense.

She switched from truth to lies so fast. But the fact that she was so bad at it told him something. Told him her entire life wasn't built on lies. For whatever reason, she felt she needed them right now. And that wasn't okay.

Yet, somehow, her lies didn't push him away. Because he'd known this woman just over a week. He'd seen her tender care for her grandfather. He'd watched her labor to provide for them both. Whatever was going on with her, he couldn't suspect her of wrongdoing.

And no matter how little he wanted to admit it, he was falling for her.

CHAPTER TWENTY-TWO

The next morning, at the start of her shift, Harper stared at the schedule posted in the kitchen at McNeal's.

The door behind her swished open, and she glanced at Bonnie as the woman beelined toward her.

Harper tapped her finger against her name scrawled beside the evening hours. "I have nobody to stay with Gramps."

The older woman took a deep breath. "I know you don't want to work evenings, but my grandson's in a recital, and I'm not gonna miss it. Nobody else can do it."

"*I* can't do it."

Bonnie crossed her arms. "You're doing a great job here, Harper. You fit right in, and the customers love you."

"Thank—"

"But I gotta have employees who can be flexible. If you can't, then maybe we need to rethink this."

The words settled in her gut like ice. She couldn't lose this job. She was barely getting by as it was.

Bonnie patted her on the shoulder. "You can take tomorrow off. I can get someone to—"

"No." She swallowed, shook her head. "No. I need all the

306

hours I can get." She focused again on the schedule. "Maybe I can bring Gramps with me."

"Ask Vanessa. I bet she'll know somebody who can keep an eye on him for you."

Harper turned, forced a smile. "Yeah. I'll do that. Thanks."

Vanessa probably would know somebody. Maybe one of Gramps's friends at the rec center would let him come hang out. Except evenings were his worst time. He did best when he was home, when he was in a familiar setting with familiar people. When he could fall in and out of sleep for a few hours in his chair before going straight to bed.

She had no idea what to do, but staring at the schedule wasn't going to help.

She tied her apron strings, grabbed her order pad, and headed into the dining room.

As she worked, the answer, the obvious answer, dogged her like a pesky fly.

Hadn't he already done enough for her?

How could she ask more of him?

As if conjured by her thoughts, the man in question arrived after the lunch crowd and was seated in one of her booths.

With a gaze at the ceiling, she thought, *Fine. I'll ask him.*

Jack saw her approaching and smiled as if she were the best thing he'd seen all day.

Wow. That smile.

How could she ask one more favor of this man? So far he hadn't acted as if he expected anything from her. But hadn't every man in her past fooled her?

"Hey," he said. "What's wrong?"

"Oh." She shook off her warring thoughts. "Sorry. Distracted. You know what you want?"

"I'll wait and order when Ginny gets here."

Ginny again. Right.

"I looked at those apartments this morning. I'm going to make an offer today."

"Oh. Good."

He shrugged. "I stopped by the rec center a little while ago, and your grandfather and I went over the numbers. I think it's a good deal, if I can get it for the right price."

"Then I hope you do."

His gaze held hers, and she couldn't seem to shake it off. He tilted his head to the side. "Is something wrong?"

"Oh, no. It's nothing." Her stomach churned as if she were standing up for an audition, not asking a neighbor for a favor. "I just... Bonnie had to schedule me for tonight, so I'm trying to figure out what to do with Gramps. I thought maybe—"

"No problem. What time?"

"I... Oh." The relief was so strong, she nearly had to sit down. "Thank you. I feel like I'm always needing something from you, and—"

"Sorry I'm late."

Harper turned as Jack's real estate agent slid into the seat across from him. She met Harper's eyes. "Haley, right?"

"Harper," Jack said.

"Oh. Sorry." She shook her head, smiled too widely. "I'm usually good at names." She closed her eyes, said, "Harper, like harpoon." The eyes popped open. "If I just visualize you harpooning a whale, I'll never forget again."

"Ahoy, matey," Harper said.

Ginny laughed. "It's a good trick. You should try it."

Harper closed her eyes, opened them, and said, "If I visualize you with a straw and a lime twist, I'll remember yours, too."

Ginny's smile faded just a bit. "Right. Well, then. I'll have a Sprite."

Harper turned to Jack, whose lips were fighting a smile. "Water for me."

Trying very hard not to look like Captain Ahab, Harper turned to fetch their drinks.

She kept an eye on them, delivering their lunches and refilling their drinks, as Jack and Ginny pored over paperwork spread across the table. They hardly spared her a glance when she asked if they needed anything else.

And if she caught Ginny looking at Jack with longing, at least she never saw the look returned.

Harper had cashed out all her customers but Jack by the time Ginny paid her bill and left. Harper approached the table. "Well?"

"She's going to fax the offer right now."

"Wow," she said. "This could really happen."

He pulled out his wallet, counted out some cash, and dropped the bills on the table. "I gotta run. What time tonight?"

"I need to be here at five."

"Aye-aye, captain." He winked. "I'll be over at four-thirty."

CHAPTER TWENTY-THREE

Derrick was parked a few houses down from Harper's childhood home in Wichita. He'd flown in from Vegas the day before, rented a car, and come straight here, and he'd been watching the house off and on ever since.

She had to be here.

Where else would she have gone? She'd always told him how much she wanted to reconcile with her family. She had little money and an old man to take care of. According to Roger, she hadn't used Gramp's debit card since the previous weekend. Seemed she and Gramps had been holed up in a hotel in Newark. But then she'd disappeared.

If she hadn't returned to Vegas, she must have come here.

But there'd been no sign of her. And except to use the bathroom and buy food, Derrick had hardly left this spot. He'd parked about a block down from her parents' house in the shade of an oak tree that kept dropping leaves and acorns on his rental.

He still couldn't get over the neighborhood. He knew she hadn't grown up poor, but still. The homes here were huge, and each sat on at least two acres of beautifully landscaped property. The house Harper had grown up in was one of the largest on the street, a two-story brick home with a three-car garage. The front porch was decorated with straw bales and potted mums. After the Thanksgiving holiday, he'd bet his last dollar those would be replaced with Christmas decorations.

How had a girl from this neighborhood ended up as a stripper in Vegas? Harper had told him the stories, but seeing her childhood home in person brought into perspective just how far she'd fallen.

Dreams of show business had lured her away.

Promises from lying men had kept her from coming home.

Derrick had never intended to be one of those lying men. He'd wanted to save Harper. Believed they could save each other. And they could have, if only she'd supported him.

There'd been a time when he'd hoped he and Harper could still make their relationship work. If she apologized, if she promised to be true to him... But with his arms, his back, and his pride all wounded after the showdown with Quentin, Derrick was well past caring a whit about Harper. He needed to find her because he needed Gramps's money. Gramps wouldn't turn over his money to Derrick voluntarily, but Harper could talk him into it. If she refused, then he'd use Gramps's love for her— love that should have been Derrick's—to get the cash.

It was still early in the day, but Derrick couldn't stand it any longer. He drove to the house, parked, and strode to the front steps. He'd seen her father leave for work an hour earlier, and he hadn't seen any sign of her brothers. According to Harper, the older was married, the younger college-aged. Her mother would be home alone.

Derrick knocked. A minute later, the door swung open.

The woman was a more mature version of Harper. Tall and slender with blond hair and blue eyes. "Can I help you?"

Derrick offered his most charming smile. "I hope so, ma'am. Are you Mrs. Cloud?"

"I am."

"My name is Derrick Burns. I'm a friend of your daughter."

The woman's eyes widened, and her jaw dropped a shade. "Oh." She blinked twice. Then her eyes narrowed. "Has something happened?"

Derrick let his smile fade. "Not that I know of, but I'm worried about her safety." He let that hang in the air for a moment before he added, "Can I come in?"

The woman blinked, glanced beyond him, then behind her. "Are you with the police or something?"

"No, ma'am. Like I said, I'm a friend."

"Why are you worried about her?"

He dropped his gaze to the porch, left it there a moment before he looked back up. Going for embarrassed and nervous. "I'm in love with your daughter. I must've scared her off when I asked her..." He shrugged. "I know she wanted to reconcile with you guys. I thought maybe..." He swallowed, added another shrug for good measure. "I guess if you've never heard of me, then she must not be here. I'd like to think she'd have mentioned me. So I guess I'll just..." He turned away.

"Wait!"

He forced the triumphant smile into hiding and turned back.

"Please, come in." She stepped aside, and he entered the two-story foyer, let his gaze wander up the curving staircase in front of him. "We can talk in the kitchen."

He followed her down a tiled hallway and into the great room. She indicated a stool at the long bar that separated the kitchen from the family room, and he slid onto it.

"Can I get you something? Coffee, tea?"

"Did Harper learn to make her sweet tea from you?"

The woman's eyes filled, and she blinked the emotion away. "She likes it sweeter than I do."

"I've gotten used to it." Derrick let his polite smile fade as the woman watched. "I'm worried something's happened to her."

"Oh, no." Mrs. Cloud's tears dripped down her cheeks. "If only she'd come home."

Crap. Obviously, the woman was telling the truth. This trip had been a waste of time and money, unless Mrs. Cloud could give him a hint as to where Harper might've gone.

"I'm sorry." She wiped her tears, filled two glasses with ice, added some tea, and slid one across to him. "I just miss her. I wish she'd come home."

He sipped it, said, "Thanks," and set it on the granite countertop.

"We haven't heard from Harper since...in a while." Her voice faded.

"Since she was incarcerated?"

"You know about that." The woman's tense shoulders relaxed just a bit. "When she called and told us what happened, my husband answered the phone. He was so angry with her that he refused to help her. He told her..." She swallowed, shook her head. "He told her never to call here again. Of course, he's regretted that ever since. I finally convinced him we should go see her. We drove to Nevada, went to the prison."

They'd gone to see her? Harper hadn't said that.

"We should have gone sooner. Right away, but my husband... Anyway, she'd been released before we got there. Paroled." The woman's voice caught. "She didn't even call. We had no idea how to find her. All she had to do was come home. That's all we wanted."

"She thinks you hate her," Derrick said.

"How could I hate my own child?" With tears streaming down her face, she looked both older and more vulnerable than she had just moments before. "Where was she...? I mean, are you from Nevada, or—"

"She and I met in Vegas, and we fell in love. She moved with me to Baltimore last spring."

The woman swallowed, whispered, "Maryland." She pulled a paper towel from a rack near the stovetop and wiped her eyes. "I'm sorry."

"Don't apologize. I miss her too. I'm worried about her. I asked her to marry me, and she just... She didn't say no, but she didn't say yes, either. Just said she needed time. That was a week ago, and I haven't heard from her since. I thought she'd come here, figured she wanted to reconcile with you guys and tell you the good news. Can you think of anyplace else she might have gone?"

Mrs. Cloud shook her head. "I'm sorry. I have no idea. She hasn't lived at home since she was eighteen. I'm sure there are a lot of things in her past we don't know anything about. She lived in LA for a while, and you know about Vegas."

"Maybe other family members?"

"If she'd gone to any of their houses, they'd have told us. Everyone in the family knows how desperate we are to see her again."

A dead end. Derrick let his head loll forward before he looked up again. "I'm sorry I bothered you. I didn't mean to dredge up bad memories."

The woman sniffed. "Not at all. You seem like... I mean, we know her last boyfriend wasn't exactly..." Her words trailed off again.

Derrick ducked his head, smiled slightly. "I hope I'm a better choice. I think that's what scared her away. She's afraid to trust me."

"She's not a great judge of character, especially of men."

"I understand the kind of guys she's been with before. But

I'm... Not that I'm a catch or anything. But I have a good job. I don't break the law. I was hoping she and I could buy a house and..." He pursed his lips. "I can't think about that, not until I find her."

"What can I do to help?" Mrs. Cloud asked. "We could hire a PI or something. We've talked about it before, but my husband thought, if she wanted to come home, she'd contact us. But if you think she might be in danger—"

"I don't know that we should assume that yet." Derrick thought about the words Mrs. Cloud hadn't said, the words she'd implied. *We have money.* That might come in handy. First, he had to win their trust, and he figured Harper's dad wouldn't be nearly as easy to win over as her mom had been. "I think she must've just gone somewhere to think things through. Maybe an old vacation spot or something?"

The woman looked toward the ceiling before she met his eyes again. "We used to vacation in Eureka Springs. She loved it there."

Derrick pulled out his cell phone and tapped on an app to take notes. "Where is that?"

"Arkansas. We always rented a cabin on Beaver Lake."

"Do you remember the name of the resort?"

Her slight laugh died fast. "More of a campground than resort. I can't remember the name off the top of my head, but my husband will know."

They exchanged cell phone numbers, and Mrs. Cloud promised to call him with the name of the campground after she'd spoken to her husband.

"And you promise to call us when you find her?" she said.

"Yes, ma'am. As soon as I know she's safe."

"Promise me you'll tell her..." The woman's eyes filled with tears, but she didn't bother to swipe them away. "Tell her how much we miss her. How badly we want her back."

"I promise."

Derrick left the house with the woman's image in his mind. He would find Harper, and he might even tell her what her mother had said. But only after Harper helped him get the money. Otherwise, the woman would have to visit her daughter in the cemetery.

CHAPTER TWENTY-FOUR

Jack transferred the steaks to a platter and covered them with foil.

"Something sure smells good," Red said.

Jack turned as the man shuffled in from the living room and sat at the table. "Steak *au poivre*."

Red's eyes narrowed. "Sounds froufrou."

"Doesn't smell froufrou, though," Jack said.

"Smells like heaven in a frying pan."

Jack had to agree as he added cream and pepper to the skillet and stirred. While that simmered, he checked the potatoes and vegetables in the oven. It was fun to have someone to cook for. Someone to appreciate him. He'd been cooking for one for too long.

Not that Red was the dinner companion of his dreams. He'd had a few girlfriends in college, but nothing serious. When he'd moved to Nutfield, he'd figured he'd eventually meet the right woman. Until then, he'd focus on saving his pennies and building his real estate business.

Now, it looked like he was well on his way with the business. What about the woman?

He imagined Harper, those beautiful eyes, the way she smiled when she let her guard down. He'd love nothing more than to see that smile every single day of his life.

It was too soon to start thinking of her like that. Way too soon.

Ten minutes later, he prepared two plates and carried them to the table.

Red leaned over his, pulled in a long breath, and said, "I'll give you ten thousand dollars to teach Harper to cook."

Jack laughed as he sat beside him. "You're a tough negotiator, old man."

After they said grace, Jack watched Red cut a small bite, dredge it in the creamy gravy, and pop it in his mouth. His eyes closed as he savored the meat. When they opened again, he said, "Okay, twenty thousand, but that's my final offer."

Twenty thousand dollars to spend time with the woman he was falling for?

His amusement faded as the truth of it settled in his belly with the steak. Yes, he was falling for Harper Cloud. Falling hard. And he couldn't seem to keep his heart in line no matter how many times he told himself he was crazy to even consider getting involved with her.

And it was crazy. The woman had kept as much from him as she'd told him, and he didn't know how much of what she'd told him was the truth. She seemed shrouded in mystery, and not the good kind. The trouble kind.

He knew women like that. Had a sister like that. A sister who couldn't seem to pick the right guys or the right friends or the right jobs. Angel had been arrested so many times, Jack had lost count. A couple of times for drug possession, but she wasn't an addict. Just an idiot. Most of her arrests were for shoplifting. The latest one had been thanks to a check-cashing scheme, and that stunt had landed her in prison. He thought she was still there, but his parents had quit updating him on Angel's latest dramas. He didn't want to hear about it. He prayed for her every day, but that was as much as he intended to be involved in her life. It was sad, and it was wrong, but Jack had very little hope that his baby sister would ever get her life together.

Jack had told himself he'd never become involved with a woman like that.

Did Harper love the rush of life on the edge? Did she thrive on drama like Angel did? She must to some degree. Moving to LA, dancing in Vegas. How else would she have ended up as an entertainer at a strip club? She'd told him the story, and it made sense. But a rational person didn't end up like that.

Rational people grew up and got jobs and reconciled with their families. Or skipped the falling-outs all together.

Which meant there was something off about Harper. And if that were the case, what was he doing letting her into his life?

Was Harper like Angel, though? She seemed down to earth, devoted to her grandfather. She worked hard. She was reliable. Jack couldn't say any of those things about Angel, who'd only ever been devoted to herself and hadn't held down a real job more than a few months at a time.

Maybe Harper wanted normalcy. Maybe, despite the lies and half-truths, she was trying to get her life together. Jack could feel differently about a woman who'd learned from her mistakes, couldn't he?

After the meal, Jack cleaned the kitchen, left a plate of dinner in the fridge for Harper, and joined Red in the living room. He opened a paper bag he'd carried in earlier and pulled out a DVD player.

"What are we gonna do with that?"

"Watch movies," Jack said.

"Don't have any movies."

Jack reached into the bag and grabbed the two DVDs he'd ordered online, which he handed to the old man.

His face broke into a wrinkly smile. "Marilyn Monroe."

"Those are the ones you and Steve were talking about the other day, right?"

"*Gentlemen Prefer Blondes* is my favorite."

"Then we'll watch that first." Jack hunkered down behind the TV with cords.

"Bebe loved Marilyn."

Jack connected the HDMI cord. "Bebe was your wife?"

"Yeah." Red's voice softened. "Lost her eight years ago. Cancer."

"I'm sorry." Jack peeked out from behind the TV. "Must have been rough."

"The worst. At the end, I just wanted to crawl into that hospital bed and go with her."

Jack plugged in the DVD player, scooted out from behind the TV, and sat back on his heels. Seemed Red was in the mood to talk. "I can't imagine."

"I'd thought burying our only child was the worst pain a man could live through. And it had been." Red's eyes filled, but he hardly seemed to notice.

Jack couldn't imagine what had brought on the maudlin mood, but now wasn't the time for a comedy film.

Something didn't make sense though. Their only child? But Harper's father...

"It was a car accident," Red said. "Took him and his wife. Left Derrick." Red's lips pinched closed. Based on the look on the old man's face, Derrick must have been the "idiot grandkid" Red had referenced the day before.

"How old was he when his parents died?" Jack asked.

"College student. Dumb kid had everything he needed, but he took after his dad."

Apparently, that wasn't good.

"Don't get me wrong," Red added. "George was a great guy, a hard worker, decent husband and father. But he had a weakness for the tables."

"Gambling?"

"Died in debt up to his eyeballs. I paid it all off, paid for the rest of Derrick's college, tried to give the kid everything he needed."

Jack had a feeling Derrick hadn't made his grandfather proud.

"He's just like his father," Red said. "Great job, makes all the money he should ever need, and loses it as fast as he can make it." He shook his head. "I thought he'd changed. Thought Harper was having a good influence on him. When I hired her to be my nurse, he started coming around more."

Whoa. Red had *hired* her? Red continued before Jack could fully form the questions materializing in his mind.

"I thought he moved her in to take care of me because he cared about me." He shook his head sadly. "I'm just a stupid old man. I believed him. I wanted to believe him. He's my grandson, you know? I love the kid. And then, he tried to con me out of money. 'To invest,' he told me. Right. I'd raised George, knew all the tricks. I can smell a liar a mile away. Especially when there's money involved. At least George was smart enough to keep all his loans on the up-and-up. Mortgaged to the hilt, but banks don't break your kneecaps."

Jack rubbed his knee. "Surely it wasn't that bad."

Red shrugged. "Harper doesn't know this, but I called him once this summer after I'd refused to give him the money, just to find out the truth. He admitted he was in debt and desperate. Tried to convince me that if he didn't come up with the money, they'd kill him." He harrumphed like only an old man could.

"I'm not stupid. If they killed him, they'd get nothing. I told Derrick a broken knee would serve him right."

"Tough love."

"Love. Not sure you could call it that. Fact is, I worked hard for my money. It's not like I can go make more. He's gonna get most of it when I die anyway. He'll probably gamble it away in a year."

"Maybe he'll surprise you."

Red continued as if Jack hadn't spoken. "That's why I wrote Harper into the will. She won't fritter it away. She'll be able to finish college or do whatever she wants with it."

Jack was reeling from all the information. But one thing seemed abundantly clear. "She's not your granddaughter."

Red blinked twice. Narrowed his eyes. Then he smiled for the first time since dinner. "Don't tell anybody. We're supposed to keep that quiet."

"Why?"

"She figured it'd be easier for her to take care of me if people thought we were related. If I need medical attention or something, she can make decisions for me."

"Right," Jack said. But his steak turned over in his stomach. He shifted to a more comfortable position on the floor, took a deep breath, and threw out the next question. Maybe the old man would give him an honest answer. "Why are you two here? Why did you leave Baltimore?"

Red's mouth flattened. "Don't think I'm supposed to say."

"You've told me everything else."

"You got a trustworthy face."

Jack forced a smile. "Gee, thanks."

"You won't hold it against her?"

His stomach tightened even more. Maybe he didn't want to know. But the words "I promise" popped out before he could think it through.

"I don't remember everything that happened, but..." His voice faded, and his eyes narrowed. A moment later, he shook his head. "Anyway, something happened. There's someone from her past she's scared of. I figure it's an old boyfriend. You know about her past. Lotsa checkered fellows back there."

Jack didn't let on how little he knew.

"She told me she had to leave and begged me to go with her."

"Why didn't she just hire you a different nurse?"

"It would have been easier on me. But I couldn't stand the idea of her taking off all by herself. Nobody to look after her. Harper might not be family, but she's the closest thing I got, considering Derrick hasn't come around in months. I was worried about her. I saw some bruises."

Those bruises... An old boyfriend had done that to her? What horrors had Harper suffered at the hands of men? It was no wonder she was suspicious, no wonder she fought to protect herself.

Despite all Jack had learned tonight, a wave of affection rose. An irrational, ridiculous urge to show Harper that not all men were like the ones she'd known before. That a man could love her the way God intended. If only he could help her learn to trust, to be loved...

Whoa. What was he thinking? She'd done nothing but lie to him.

Red stared at the black TV screen a moment. "Someone hurt her. And something happened..."

Red's words faded away, and he stared beyond Jack. The color in his cheeks paled. He swallowed, rubbed his eyes.

Jack stood. "You okay?"

"Something just... I feel like something else happened, something... but I can't remember." He shook his head and focused on Jack. "My brain..." He tapped the side of his head three times. "I used to be able to rely on it. It's turning against me. Now, I never know if I can trust what I remember. All I know is, I don't remember enough." He took a deep breath. "But I trust Harper. She said she had to go, so here we are."

Jack tried to process all Red had told him, tried to reconcile the information with the stories Harper had told him. Who was after her? The ex who'd gone to prison? The big-shot dance club owner who'd had her fired? Or was this problem related to the *this and that* she'd neglected to tell him about? "So you guys just took off? What did your grandson think about that?"

Red's scoff told Jack as much as his words. "All he cares about is my money." Red sighed and sat back in his recliner. "Seems unbelievable, I know, but I miss that idiot grandson of mine."

"He's your only connection to your son. He's your family."

"That's right." Red nodded a few times. His eyes filled again. "Haven't talked to him in weeks. Harper keeps saying we'll call him, but he never answers his phone." Red nodded to the TV. "We gonna watch that movie or what?"

Jack finished connecting the DVD player while he mulled over all he'd learned. One thing still didn't make sense.

He kept his focus on the TV. "You have money, right? You didn't give it to Derrick."

"Of course I didn't. I just told you that." He huffed a long breath. "And they say I have memory issues."

Jack slid in the DVD, waited for it to load.

"I started forgetting stuff," Red said. "Least that's what Harper told me. So I turned over power of attorney to my lawyer, an old friend of mine. That way Derrick couldn't swindle it out of me."

Jack had witnessed the dementia, so he knew that part of the story was real. He turned on the TV, pressed the button to bring up the video, and tried to sound casual. "So how come Harper has to work so hard to pay the bills?"

When Red didn't answer, Jack turned to face him. The man's eyes were scrunched up like he was thinking. "You know what, son? I don't rightly know."

CHAPTER TWENTY-FIVE

It was after ten when Harper got home. She pushed open the door to find Jack seated on the sofa, staring at the TV. Gramps's chair was empty.

"How was your night?" she asked.

He didn't return her smile. "Interesting."

What did that mean? She closed the door behind her and crossed to the kitchen. "Was Gramps okay?"

"He's tucked in bed."

"Sorry I'm late."

Jack clicked off the TV and joined her. "You're right on time." Still no smile. Maybe he got grouchy when he was sleepy.

"Thanks for staying with him." She opened the refrigerator, saw a plate covered with plastic wrap. Was that...? "You made steak?"

"Yup." He leaned against the door jamb and crossed his arms.

She pulled out the plate, took the plastic wrap off, and inhaled the scent. "That smells divine. You mind if I eat in front of you?"

"I ate."

She paused halfway to the microwave and turned. "What's wrong?"

"Red and I had a long chat tonight."

Uh-oh. She set the plate on the table, her appetite quickly fading. "About what?"

"This and that. Like how you're not really his grand-daughter."

She lowered herself into a chair.

Jack didn't move.

"I just..." She forced herself to make eye contact, but it wasn't easy the way Jack was glowering at her. "I'm his nurse, and he's given me... I can get out the paper that gives me the right to make medical decisions for him. But it's easier—"

"Why are you here?"

Her empty stomach filled with acid. Could she trust Jack with this? Would he believe her?

She nodded to the chair beside her. "Can you sit down please?"

He eyed the chair.

She pushed away the cold plate, clasped her shaking hands together in her lap.

"Derrick—"

"Your boyfriend."

"Ex." She said it too fast, as if it mattered. As if Jack would care, which, after this, he obviously wouldn't. Not about her, not that way. "He's been my ex for a while. He has a problem."

"Gambling."

What *hadn't* Gramps told him? "He owes a lot of money."

"To loan sharks," Jack said. "They want their money, and Red wouldn't bail Derrick out."

She nodded, prayed for wisdom. Would he believe her, or would he turn her in?

She met his eyes, saw the determination there. And the anger. "Gramps doesn't know everything," she said.

His eyebrows lifted. "He thinks he does."

"I didn't tell him the truth."

Jack crossed his arms. "At least I'm not the only one. You've lied to me about everything. You lied to 'Gramps'"—his air quotes told her what he thought about that—"so why should I believe you now?"

A wave of irritation—or was it fear?—had her pushing back in her chair. "What makes you think you deserve the truth from me? You're my landlord. I don't have to tell you anything."

He blinked. "I've done nothing but—"

"Yeah, I know. You've helped and helped." Here it came, what she'd been waiting for. His demands for repayment. Tell him everything, and then he'd have even more of a hold over her. Then he'd be able to use it all against her. She stood, backed away until she bumped into the countertop. "And now it's time to pay up? Because that's what every other man I've ever known has told me. How much I owe them for their kindness." Her voice cracked. *Stupid, stupid Harper.* She'd known this would happen.

She'd thought Jack was different.

"Harper, I would never—"

"Kindness is never free. Never."

His hands lifted, palms out. "I didn't—"

"I'll come up with the money to pay you back for...for whatever you think I owe you. Your time, your energy, that ramp outside. Whatever. But I won't... I can't..." She waved at the air, at the expectations she knew he had.

"What do you think I'm asking for?"

"More than I can give."

"Just the truth."

"And then you'll know everything. And then what will you want? What will you demand?"

"Nothing."

Right. Like she could believe that. "We'll be gone in the morning."

"What?" He stepped back, hands still lifted. "No. Wait. You don't have to—"

"We're paid through the end of the month. You can take what I owe you out of that. If you think there's more—"

"You don't owe me money. You don't owe me anything."

Tears burned her eyes, and she looked away. She couldn't tell him the truth. She couldn't trust him. She couldn't trust anybody. "Just go."

"Harper, I'm not trying—"

"What's going on here?" Red's shout had them both turning.

The old man stood in the doorway. His pajamas were wrinkled, his eyes bloodshot and rimmed in dark circles. He leaned heavily on his walker with one hand and pointed a gnarly finger at Jack with the other. "What did you do?"

Jack's hands were still up. "I was just asking her—"

"You hurt that girl"—Red shook his finger—"I'll take you out."

"I would never..." Jack's eyes were wide, his mouth open.

Harper looked back at Gramps. The color had drained from his face, making his red eyes look even worse. "We're okay," she said. "Everything's fine. We were just talking."

"Talking loud enough to wake the dead." He glared at Jack.

"We're okay." She crossed toward the old man. Jack had to step out of the way so she could pass. She was careful to leave plenty of space between them. "I'm sorry we woke you."

Another moment passed before he jerked his walker back toward the hallway. "Had to use the bathroom anyway."

She followed him into the hall and waited outside the bathroom door, then escorted him back to his bedroom and got him settled. He seemed hardly awake as he rested his head on his pillow.

"Are you all right?" she asked.

"I heard yelling. I thought... I thought..."

"You thought I was in trouble. I understand. You were protecting me." She patted his shoulder. "And I love you for it." She reached for the lamp, but he stopped her with a hand on her arm.

"Did he hurt you?"

She shook her head. Of course Jack was frustrated with her. She'd lied to him. A lot. And now she'd overreacted. Accused him of... Shame burned her cheeks. What was wrong with her?

"I told Jack stuff tonight," Gramps said.

"I figured that out."

"I didn't mean to make trouble for you. But I think we should trust him." His lids drifted shut. When he said nothing else, she switched the light off and left him to sleep.

She found Jack pulling a plate from the microwave. The room was filled with the scent of meat and pepper and roasted vegetables. He set the plate on the table. "I think you need to eat."

She tried to come up with a witty response, but her stomach spoke for her with a growl.

Jack's lips twitched. "*Hangry* much?"

She snatched a fork and knife from the drawer and sat. The first bite of steak melted in her mouth. She couldn't help the "Mmm" as she cut the second.

Jack slid a glass of water onto the table, then stood behind his chair and curled his hands over the top.

She swallowed her third bite while she tried to figure out what to say. What to do.

She couldn't trust this man.

She couldn't *not* trust him, either. Because despite her big pronouncement earlier, they had nowhere to go and no money to get there.

"You might as well sit," she said.

"Your... Red... is pretty angry with me. Maybe I should go."

"He won't remember any of this tomorrow."

Jack blew out a long breath. "You don't owe me anything. My kindness doesn't come with a price tag."

"Gramps..." She took a deep breath, started again. "Red doesn't believe in debt. Did he tell you that?"

Jack didn't respond. Didn't sit. Just studied her as if he were trying to solve a puzzle. Eyes hooded, mouth closed, fists clenched over the chair.

"He doesn't believe in consumer debt, anyway," she said. "He'll take out a loan to buy a property but nothing else."

She met his gaze, waited for a response. Finally, he said, "Okay."

"He does believe there's something we should all owe."

"Which is?" Jack asked.

She nodded to the chair again. "Sit down, and I'll tell you."

He sat, back straight, hands clasped together on the table.

"He says, 'The only thing you should ever owe is love.'"

Jack blinked, tilted his head to the side.

She shrugged, ate another bite of her dinner, sipped her water. "I guess it's from the Bible."

"'Owe no man anything, but to love one another,'" Jack said. "It's in Romans."

Jack knew the reference? If that wasn't confirmation that she should trust him, she didn't know what was. "So I do owe you something, don't I?"

"You really—"

"I don't think it's possible to..." She faltered, looked away.

"It's impossible to love your neighbor..." There, that sounded non-romantic, right? She met his eyes again. "When you're telling so many lies."

He nearly smiled. "Good point."

"I'm not good at trusting people."

"Not even Red, apparently."

"What? No. I trust him completely."

"You just said he doesn't know the whole story. So you must not."

"Oh. That." She took a deep breath, speared a bite of potato. It was delicious, but she'd already eaten more than she should this late at night. She pushed the plate to the center of the table and sipped from the water Jack had given her.

He glanced at the plate. "You're not done already, are you?"

"It's a lot."

He eyed the steak, and she couldn't help but chuckle. "Go on. You know you want to."

"I'm not proud." He pulled it toward him and cut a piece for himself.

"Typical man."

His amusement faded. "I hope what you think is 'typical' for a man isn't true of me."

She felt her cheeks burn. The last thing she wanted was to return to this conversation. "I just meant..."

When she didn't finish, he said, "Yeah, I know."

He finished off her dinner in about five minutes, then pushed back in his chair.

She stood before he could, grabbed the dirty dish, and set it in the sink.

"You don't have to tell me anything," he said. "You're right. It's none of my business, and you don't owe me anything."

She wanted to tell him. But what if he didn't believe her? There was too much to lose. Not just the tenuous life they'd made here in Nutfield, but the connection she and Jack had forged. She didn't want to lose that. She didn't want to lose Jack.

He stood, pushed in his chair. He glanced at the doorway, then focused on her again.

Their gazes met, though neither spoke.

The air between them pulsed.

Neither moved. She knew she should look away, but she couldn't seem to force herself to. Here was a man who'd done nothing but help her. Who'd been kind to her and Gramps. Here was a man who cooked for her and served her. How could she not want to be with a man like him?

He crossed the room toward her. She should step back, out of his reach, but her feet weren't cooperating. Or maybe they were listening to her heart, not her head, because there was something reassuring in his movements.

He took her hands in his. When he met her eyes, he was so close, she could feel his breath in her hair.

She had to stop this, now. Before it went too far. But she didn't have the strength.

She'd never had the strength.

He bent his head, his gaze flitting from her eyes to her lips. He was going to kiss her. A kiss was supposed to mark the beginning of something good.

But for her, every kiss had been the beginning of a downward spiral that led to her destruction.

A descent into drugs.

A prison sentence.

A horrifying assault in a parking lot.

And now, this.

But Jack didn't know any of that. His lips brushed hers.

She told herself not to, but as always, her body refused to obey. She kissed him back, feeling his hunger, his need. Every cell in her body responded to that need.

Her arms slid around his neck, her mouth opened, and her self-control disappeared.

This kiss was more powerful than any she'd experienced before. Which meant the fallout would be devastating.

She pushed him away.

He stepped back, eyes wide. "I shouldn't have—"

"You need to go."

He blinked, and his gaze filled with sadness, worry, regret.

She understood that last one. She'd live to regret that kiss. This time, she might never recover.

"I'm sorry," he said. "You don't owe me anything."

Her laugh was short and joyless. "Right."

"I promise. I'm not—"

"Go. Now."

He watched her, his eyes pleading, begging. For what, she wished she didn't know. But she did know what he wanted, and she knew exactly what it would cost to give it to him.

"I'm sorry." He turned, walked toward the front door. She didn't move, couldn't bring herself to watch him leave.

The door opened, then closed with a soft click.

CHAPTER TWENTY-SIX

Jack set his egg-and-sausage burrito on the kitchen table beside his coffee and opened his laptop.

He'd run a credit check on Harper before he'd rented her the house, and he'd found nothing that bothered him. He'd called her previous landlord in Las Vegas, who'd confirmed that she'd always paid her rent on time and never caused any trouble. What else had he needed to know?

Nothing then. And nothing now.

Because her life was none of his business. She'd made that very clear the night before when she'd ordered him out of the house.

He swallowed a sip of coffee and tried not to think about that kiss.

It was just a kiss. And he shouldn't have done it. He'd known it was a mistake even as he'd crossed the room.

What an idiot. Red and Harper meant so much to him, but when he stripped away his emotions and looked at the core of the situation, he remembered that they were renters. His first renters, and he'd totally blown it. What if Harper reported him for sexual harassment or something?

The thought didn't take root. Even after everything, he didn't think she was the type. Not vindictive. Not vengeful.

Just suspicious.

And people who were suspicious of others were often the ones others needed to be suspicious of.

If that even made sense.

He opened a browser window, clicked in the search bar.

Hesitated.

Bit into the burrito. The spicy pork sausage and salty cheddar cheese were the perfect accompaniment to the eggs. He had another bite.

Finished the whole thing.

Sipped his coffee while he glanced at the news on his home-page. Typical political junk. Why couldn't people just get along? Be nice, for crying out loud? Be honest?

Harper had been anything but honest.

She was absolutely not the type of woman he should fall for.

Should have fallen for, he amended, because he was already careening toward a crash landing. And there wasn't a thing he could do about it.

All the lies, all the deception, all the suspicion didn't change who she was beneath that hard shell.

He'd felt the truth in her kiss. In the way her arms had slid around his neck. The way her lips had parted, soft and eager and—

Not going there.

Right.

This was ridiculous.

He found a website that would do a national background check for thirty bucks. Paid the money and typed her name.

He hit enter before he could talk himself out of it.

He watched the progress bar inch to the right, his slow internet practically huffing with the effort. Only a handful of results were returned. It just took a second to find the listing for his Harper.

His Harper. Like that was ever going to happen.

He clicked, watched the progress bar again. Sipped his coffee. Hated himself.

What kind of man did a background check on the woman he...

Nope. He had to shut his stupid brain up.

And then, results.

He set down the coffee and stared at the screen.

His hands trembled. It couldn't be.

More clicks, more searches. He read the stories. A man had been killed in a liquor store robbery.

Three people had gone to prison for the murder.

Harper Cloud was a convicted felon.

T*his and that.*

The words kept running through Jack's mind as he showered and prepared for his day. The words Harper had used to describe the time between when her boyfriend had been sent to prison and the time she'd moved to Maryland.

This and that.

Jack couldn't get the situation, or the woman, out of his mind.

Because *this and that* referred to prison.

She'd been in prison.

That sweet, beautiful woman had been an accessory to murder?

It couldn't be. Surely she'd been wrongfully convicted.

He couldn't wrap his mind around it. So he focused on something else.

After some back-and-forth negotiating the day before, the sellers had accepted his offer on the twenty-four-unit complex, and he needed to sign the paperwork. He and Ginny had planned to meet at McNeal's—his idea. A very bad one, in retrospect.

He called Ginny and asked if they could meet at her office instead. Because Harper would be at McNeal's, and he couldn't see her right now.

He didn't want to.

Or at least, he didn't want to want to. Which wasn't exactly the same thing, but nobody was splitting hairs.

He arrived at the Realtor's office and was ushered to a large conference room, where he took a seat on the far side of the long table.

Ginny came in a moment later carrying a thin file. "Congratulations!" She held out her hand, and he shook it.

"Thanks."

By the look on her face, he hadn't exhibited the enthusiasm she'd anticipated. He tried to muster it up. "I'm looking forward to making it mine."

She sat beside him, opened the file, and slid the contract around for him to see. "Trouble in paradise?"

He looked up. "I'm sorry?"

She looked at him with raised eyebrows. "You and your whaler girlfriend." She grinned. "You know. Harpoon. Harper..." She watched his face, and the grin faded. "Sorry. Just kidding."

"She's not my girlfriend."

Ginny put back on her professional face. "Right. If you'll just sign here"—she pointed to a line—"and here."

He signed those two and the other places she indicated, then set the pen down. "I really appreciate—"

"Look, I'm—"

They'd spoken at the same time, then stopped. He nodded to her.

She swallowed, took a deep breath. "Your love life is none of my business. I'm trying..." Her voice faded, and then she forced the corners of her mouth up, though nobody would call it a smile. "I haven't lived in Nutfield very long, and I don't know very many people."

When she trailed off, he said, "I'm sorry. That must be hard."

"I moved to Nutfield because my sister lives here. She's married, has kids. My dad died, and Mom's not exactly... Well, my sister's the only family I've got. But they're busy. And I'm just..." She dropped her head into her hands and sighed. Then she looked back up with a plastic smile. "I'm trying to make this work. I'm trying to make friends. That's all that was—me trying to be friendly. But what I said was inappropriate."

Jack was so shocked by Ginny's gush of honesty that he couldn't think of a word to say. He considered taking her hand, because he understood loneliness. He understood that deep, aching need to be seen, to be touched. To have contact with another human being, one who cared. He'd lived it. Was living it. The couple of weeks he'd spent with Red and Harper were an aberration in his otherwise solitary life.

He didn't take her hand, though. Instead, he patted it, then sat back. Safe, friendly. Nothing else. "You aren't wrong about Harper and me. At least, I wouldn't have thought you were wrong yesterday."

Her eyes narrowed the tiniest bit as she studied him. "You care for her."

"I do. If nothing else, she's a friend."

A look passed over her face, and he realized what he'd said. "You're a friend, too, Ginny. I'm just a guy, so I don't talk about my feelings and stuff." He smiled, shrugged. "But I'd like to think we're friends."

Her face brightened, and if he wasn't mistaken, he thought he saw tears fill her eyes.

Sheesh, he had to get out of there.

Because as pretty as Ginny was—and she was quite attractive—she held nothing on the damaged, lonely, frightened woman who'd stolen his heart.

And been involved in a man's murder.

Ginny composed herself, gathered the papers. "Well. Okay, then." She stood and held the papers against her chest like a shield. "So, you'll let me know when you get the inspection scheduled? I'd like to be there."

He pushed back his chair and stood as well. "Definitely. And about the other thing—"

"It's fine," she said. "I'll make friends. These things take time."

He left her office with his copies of the contract and considered the odd conversation he'd just had. Ginny was a woman with a college degree and a real estate license. She had coworkers and clients and family. And yet, she was struggling to make her way in a new town.

How could somebody like Harper, somebody with no degree, little work experience, and a felony on her record, ever make it?

Why was she here?

That was the question that plagued him. Why would she bring Red, not even a relative, and leave the comfort and familiarity of his Maryland home to barely scrape by living in a shack in New Hampshire?

It made no sense.

And when he added the felony conviction to the list of

things he knew about her, suddenly her being in New Hampshire felt sinister.

What was Harper Cloud doing?

Why was she hiding?

Who was she hiding from?

CHAPTER TWENTY-SEVEN

Derrick paced at his gate at the Charlotte, NC, airport. He'd arrived in Eureka Springs the day before, trolled the campground Harper's family had visited as a child.

No sign of her. Not at the campground, not at the nearest grocery store, not anywhere.

People didn't forget a face like Harper's. A beautiful woman with an old man? If she'd been there, surely someone would have remembered her. Unless she'd rented a house from a private owner.

She could be less than a mile away or anywhere in the US.

Derrick didn't think she was in Arkansas. Even if she were, he'd never be able to find her on his own. So he was on his way back to Baltimore. His best chance was to go back to Tank and hire him to track her down. And then hope Tank cooperated when he found her. Derrick couldn't have Gramps's attorney— or the cops—knowing Derrick had located the two of them.

Over the loudspeaker, the gate agent began pre-boarding his flight. He was itching to get on the plane. This entire trip had been a waste of time, time Harper'd undoubtedly been using to make herself invisible.

His cell rang, and he glanced at the screen. He didn't recognize the number or the area code. "Derrick Burns."

"Son? Is that you?"

He gripped the phone as if it might escape. "Gramps?"

"Aha! I knew Harper was dialing the wrong number. How are you, son?"

Derrick took a deep breath. He had to tread very carefully here. "I'm doing well. Missing you guys, though. When do you think you'll be home?"

"Not anytime soon, I'm sorry to say. Not that I don't like it here."

"Sure. Of course." *Think, Derrick.* What would she have told him? Surely Gramps didn't know he wasn't supposed to call. "What's the name of the town again?"

"Uh... I don't remember. Something funny."

"Oh. Which state are you in?"

"We're up north."

That didn't exactly narrow it down. The gate agent made another announcement, and Derrick paced toward a quieter space on the far side of the corridor.

"It's cold here," Gramps continued. "We went to the coast the other day. Friend of ours drove us. Pretty coastline. Real rugged. Your grandmother would've loved it."

"A friend? Does Harper know people there?"

"Don't think she did 'til we got here."

So she'd just chosen some random spot? He doubted that. "Must be hard being all alone. I wish you two would come home. What made you decide to leave?"

"I thought she told you all this."

"She wasn't really speaking to me."

There was a long pause, then, "Hold on a sec. Lemme get somewhere private."

Derrick heard the man's heavy breathing, the rattle of the walker, the slam of a door.

"Where are you, Gramps?"

"The rec center. I was playing cards with Steve, and he got a call on his cell, and I thought, I'm gonna borrow his phone and try calling Derrick myself. I remembered a long time ago you gave me one of your business cards, and I put it in my wallet. I looked, and there it was."

Steve. A rec center. A little house somewhere up north in a town with a funny name. "I'm glad you found it. I've been worried about you two. I've tried to call, but Harper's phone always goes to voice mail."

"That so? She's always got it on her. But it doesn't work real well."

"Any chance you know her phone number?"

"Someone here probably has it. Want me to ask?"

That didn't seem like a good idea. Somebody could tip her off. And then she'd run again, taking his grandfather with her. Rage rolled over him like a Las Vegas wind.

"Anyway." Gramps lowered his voice. "Some guy roughed her up pretty bad."

Not as badly as Derrick would once he got ahold of her. His ribs still throbbed after his meeting with Quentin. Her fault. All her fault. "I knew about the bruises. But why did that make her want to leave?"

"She was afraid whoever did it would come back, finish her off. And I didn't want her to be all alone."

He'd never known Harper to be a liar, but she'd worked that one out pretty fast.

"There was something else, too," Gramps said. "Something... But I don't remember exactly. Something bad."

What? When Derrick had left her that night at Gramps's house, he'd had no reason to believe she'd run away. And then, they'd been gone. Why? What had changed?

A memory filtered back. Quentin's remark about the goons who'd beat Harper up going missing. Derrick had suggested that maybe she'd done something to them, but that had only been a defense mechanism. He'd never considered it could have been true. Sweet Harper couldn't hurt anyone. But now... What if she'd killed them?

How could she have? Keith wouldn't have shown his face. Probably neither had the other guy. She wouldn't have known how to find them, even if she did have it in her to kill somebody. Which she didn't, he was sure, despite the felony conviction.

Maybe Keith and the other goon had gone to the house.

When he'd been there Monday, had anything been out of place?

He thought back. He'd been so focused on talking to her, but he hadn't seen anything that raised alarms.

Except... The deadbolt on the back door had been unlocked. Odd, but not too much so. He hadn't worried they'd been kidnapped, not with the cars gone. He'd thought it an oversight.

"You still there, son?" Gramps asked.

"She must have been terrified to take off the way she did."

"She was," Gramps said. "I had to come with her. You understand, right? You don't come around very much, so I figured you wouldn't miss me—"

"I do miss you, though. I miss you a lot."

"That's mighty kind of you to say, son. I miss you, too."

Derrick remembered his plan from earlier that week. Mend fences with Gramps. Get in his good graces again. He forced himself to add, "And I'm sorry about what happened this summer. About the investment and... all that."

After a moment, Gramps said, "I'm proud of you for saying that. And of course I forgive you."

Derrick barely kept himself from scoffing. Forgiveness. If Gramps cared a whit about him, he'd have given him the money, and they wouldn't be in this situation now. "Thank you. That means a lot."

"You get all that mess worked out?" Gramps asked.

Right. Like two hundred grand had just dropped into his lap. "Yeah. Thanks for asking."

"Good. Good to hear it." He didn't sound convinced, but at least he didn't push it. "And anyway, I don't blame you for not coming around more. You've got a life. Friends and work. Harper... She hasn't got anybody. I didn't want her to be alone. So I offered to come with her until all this stuff was cleared up."

"How's that going?"

Gramps was quiet. Derrick paced to the windows and stared out at the airplanes on the tarmac, forcing himself not to speak. Finally, Gramps huffed out a breath. "She's always on that danged phone looking at websites. But I don't know exactly what she's looking for. Whatever it is, I don't think she's found it."

What could she possibly have been hoping to find? "I miss you guys. I'd like to come see you."

"I'm not giving you any money, son."

"I know." Derrick forced a smile into his voice. "I don't need it. I just want to make sure you two are okay."

"I guess that'd be all right."

"But I need to know where you are exactly, and I don't have Harper's phone number. Do you think you could get your address for me and call me back?"

"Sure. Of course."

But then he'd have to wait, and who knew when—or if— Gramps would call back. And of course he'd tell Harper they'd talked.

"Better yet," he said, "can I ask a favor?"

Another long pause. Derrick interrupted this one with, "I promise, I'm not asking for money."

"What is it then?"

"Are you on an iPhone?"

"How in the blazes should I know?"

Derrick took a deep breath. "Can you put me on speaker? Look at the phone. And press the button that says speaker."

Seconds ticked by while Gramps muttered. A moment later, he said, "Did it."

"Great. Now, I want you to go to the messages app. It looks like a little dialog balloon. You know what I mean? Like in comics?"

"I'm not that old," Gramps said. "Done."

"Start a new text to me." Derrick recited his phone number as he walked the corridor to the bank of screens that displayed departures and arrivals.

"Done," Gramps said.

Derrick led his grandfather through the process of sending his current location. It took forever, lots of starts and stops, but finally, it worked.

Derrick studied the map on the cell phone. They were in Nutfield, New Hampshire.

"Got it." He looked up at the screens with all the flight information. And there it was. A direct flight to Manchester. He could be there in a few hours.

He looked around, spotted an airline service counter, and started in that direction.

Derrick's heart pounded. He had her. Now, he had to make sure she wouldn't get away before he could get there. "One more thing. Please, don't tell Harper we talked. I want to surprise her. And... Well, I think you know this already. I'm in love with her, Gramps, but I blew it."

Gramps harrumphed like only an old man could. "I'm sorry

to say, son, but I think you did." He was quiet again. The man was never in a hurry. Must be nice. Derrick made eye contact with the woman behind the counter. She stood waiting for him, so he gestured to his phone, rolled his eyes, and mouthed an apology. Never hurt to be charming.

"I almost lost your grandmother once," Gramps said. "We were dating, and I acted like a jerk. She swore she was finished with me. But I wooed her back. Brought my old guitar and sat outside her folks' house and serenaded her." His laugh was somehow both happy and sad. "Sang *Earth Angel* at her window until she opened it up."

"I didn't know you could sing."

He chuckled. "Can't sing, and I was terrible on that guitar. I always wondered if she just came outside to shut me up before the neighbors started throwing stuff."

Derrick couldn't imagine his grandparents young and in love, though they'd definitely been *old* and in love until Gram died.

"I want to do something like that. I want to surprise her with a big, romantic gesture."

"Then I won't warn her you're coming. But on winning her back...you might have some competition."

Derrick's heart pounded a war beat. "What do you mean?"

"She's got a fellow up here. Not sure they're an item yet, but they seem to like each other."

Derrick swallowed his anger and said, "Uh-oh. What his name?"

"Jack."

Jack. Derrick would remember that. "Well then," he said, "I guess I'd better bring my A-game."

He ended the call, approached the counter, and smiled at the woman behind it. "My grandfather. Never in a hurry."

"I got one just like that," she said. "What can I do for you?"

"I have to change my flight. I was headed to Baltimore, but there's a family emergency, and I need to get to Manchester right away."

She clicked away on her keyboard, looked up, and smiled. "That flight leaves in forty-five minutes, and there are seats available. Seems like it's your lucky day."

CHAPTER TWENTY-EIGHT

Harper hadn't spoken to Jack all day Thursday.

She kept waiting for him to come by, kept thinking she'd run into him at McNeal's, but he'd kept his distance.

What did that mean? Had he lost interest in her? Or was he trying to learn more about her past?

She thought of little else all day Thursday and into Friday. It was nearly noon when Harper saw the two uniformed police officers on the sidewalk outside the window at work. Cops came into McNeal's all the time. She'd gotten used to them. But after Wednesday night, after the conversation with Jack... She was a fool for still being here. Red had told Jack too much. And her behavior could only have fueled his suspicions. Jack would do some research on her, and then he'd know just enough to think she was up to no good.

The police officers came in. One made eye contact with her. She'd never seen this one before. Not a regular. He was here for her. He recognized her. Why else would he be watching her so closely? He smiled, his eyes crinkling at the corners. What did that mean? Happy he'd found her? Big collar for the day?

His smile faded, and his eyes narrowed.

Bonnie walked past her, brushing her shoulder and whispering a vehement, "Get to work." Then, she focused on the men at the door. "Sit anywhere, guys. The usual?"

The cops chose a table.

Harper spun and headed for the kitchen.

At a table against the far wall, a woman lifted her hand to get Harper's attention. She wanted nothing more than to bolt, but she had to act normally, so she beelined in that direction.

The woman was sitting alone. She had long brown hair and kind eyes. "I'm going to order for myself and my husband. He's running a little late."

Harper took out her order pad. "Okay. What can I get you?"

The woman rattled off the orders. When she was finished, she cocked her head to the side. "You look a little pale today."

Harper had served this woman before many times. She'd always been kind, and she'd never been nosy. Of course today would be the day she'd pry. "I think I've caught a bug or something."

"Oh, dear." The woman smiled. "I'm Samantha, by the way. Most people call me Sam." She held out her hand.

The restaurant door opened. Harper cut her gaze that way. She didn't see a face, just the height of a man who carried himself like a cop. She had to get out of there.

She shook Sam's hand. "Harper Cloud." The tall man approached, and Harper cringed, waited for a hand to clamp down on her shoulder, a set of cuffs to be fastened on her wrists.

Samantha's gaze shifted from friendly to concerned as she glanced from the man to Harper.

Behind her, the man said, "Pardon me."

Harper jumped, stepped out of the way.

"I didn't meant to startle you." The man smiled down at her, then slid into the booth across from Sam.

Right. This was the husband. Another cop. He had to be, the way he carried himself. They were everywhere.

She nodded, spun, and bolted into the kitchen.

She was leaning against the counter, trying to slow her heart rate, when Bonnie walked in. "What is wrong with you today?"

"I just..." She shook her head, tried to think.

"First, the uniforms in the door, then you jump out of your skin at the sight of Garrison, who's in here three, four times a week. What is your problem?"

"Garrison startled me. And the other one, the cop in the doorway, looked familiar. I was trying to place him." Her excuses sounded feeble, and Bonnie was too smart to fall for them. Harper gave the cook the orders she's just gotten from Samantha.

The older woman let out a snort. "You aren't supposed to place 'em. You're supposed to seat 'em and serve 'em. That's your job."

"I know. I'm—"

"You been in another world for two days. I shoulda got someone else for your shift. I think I worked you too hard this week."

"I'm sorry. I'll try harder." The cook slid one plate across the stainless counter. Harper waited for the second in the order while Bonnie watched her through narrowed eyes.

Now Bonnie was suspicious, too. Harper used to think she was a good actor. Apparently not, since everyone could see right through her to the terror she was trying so hard to hide. Suspicion was mounting on all sides. There was no more time to waste. She had to get Red and leave town. Now.

"Actually," Harper said. "I don't feel well. Do you mind if I take off early?"

CHAPTER TWENTY-NINE

J ack had kept his distance from Harper and Red, but his mind was never far from them. He didn't know much, but he did know Harper was in trouble. And as much as he'd tried to help, he'd probably only made everything worse.

The conversation from Wednesday night plagued him as he drove toward the lake. He'd planned to work on one of the rentals today, thinking the manual labor would do him good. He needed to get Harper out of his mind.

He'd kissed her. He shouldn't have done that. But the kiss wasn't what bothered him right now. She'd told him more than she'd planned to, thanks to Red opening up. She'd let her guard down and had been almost honest with him. And then she'd erected those walls again and ordered him out.

Would she suspect he'd dig into her background? If she knew, what would she do?

The answer to that question had him making a quick U-turn and heading toward Nutfield. Because he suddenly had the very strong suspicion he knew exactly what she'd do.

She'd run.

Jack would go straight to the house, except Harper was

probably working. He'd check McNeal's first, see if she was there. He had to talk to her, to... he didn't know what. Keep her from leaving, promise to help her with whatever it was she was running from.

How had he gotten himself into this, anyway? Whatever *this* was?

He screeched to a stop outside McNeal's and rushed inside. He scanned the restaurant, saw Bonnie on the far side. The tables were almost all occupied, people eating and drinking and laughing and chatting. Everything seemed normal.

Harper wasn't there.

She could be in the back, though. Maybe.

Bonnie disappeared into the kitchen.

He spotted Samantha Kopp, who waved from a table against the far wall. Sam was one of the property owners he worked for, someone he'd known for years. He walked toward her, noticed her husband Garrison, and gave them both a quick nod.

"Want to join us?" Sam asked.

"No. I'm just..." He glanced toward the kitchen. Where was Harper?

"Too distracted to finish sentences," Garrison suggested.

Jack glanced at the man.

Garrison wore a wry smile. "You're looking for the pretty waitress?"

"Harper," Sam said. "She went in the back a couple of minutes ago." She slid over on the bench seat and patted it. "Join us until she comes back out."

Well, that was a better option than standing there. He slid into the booth.

"What's her story?" Garrison asked. "I've seen her before, and she's always seemed shy, but today she jumped out of her skin when I walked up."

"She said she didn't feel well," Sam said. "She was white as a sheet." She focused on Jack. "Has she been sick?"

Before he could answer, Garrison said, "She didn't seem sick. She seemed scared."

"You think?" Sam tilted her head to the side. "It was right after those two uniformed police officers came in."

Garrison leveled his gaze on Jack's. "What do you know about her?"

"Nothing, really. She's my tenant."

Garrison's eyes narrowed. Jack had always found the man to be kind and funny, but right now, he was every bit his former-FBI self. "You're a terrible liar. How long have you known her?"

"About ten days."

"Has she done something wrong?" Garrison asked.

Jack was afraid to look away and afraid not to. And more than a little irritated that he couldn't answer that question with a definitive *no*.

When Jack didn't answer, Garrison said, "What's her name?"

"Harper," Jack said.

"Last name?"

"I don't—"

"Cloud." Sam said the last name, then shrugged. "She just told me. It's unusual, isn't it? Where's she from?"

Garrison seemed to be waiting for an answer to that question, too. When Jack said nothing, Garrison pulled out his cell phone and typed into it. "I love a unique name. So easy to look up."

"Don't do that," Jack said. "She hasn't done anything wrong."

"Call me eternally curious," Garrison said. "Her actions and your evasiveness suggest something different."

"I'm not being evasive."

"That's what every evasive suspect says."

"I don't know anything." Jack tried to keep his voice level, but worry laced his words.

Garrison said, "They all say that, too."

"She's a tenant." Jack threw that out as nonchalantly as possible. "A pretty one, so yeah, maybe I came here to see her, but nothing else."

Garrison didn't look up from his phone. "I don't even have to see your eyes to know you're lying. Seriously, don't ever try to run a con."

He had no idea how to answer that. How had this conversation gotten out of control so fast? "I think I'm just going to catch up—"

"Hey, Jack." Bonnie approached the table and set plates down in front of Garrison and Sam. The scents of corned beef and french fries filled his nostrils and made his stomach churn. "You here to eat or to stalk my waitress?" She smiled as she said it, but Jack couldn't return the gesture.

Garrison hadn't looked up from his phone at her approach.

Sam was watching her husband with a tilted head and narrowed eyes.

"Is she here?" Jack asked Bonnie.

"Took off a few minutes ago. She said she didn't feel well. There's something off about that girl. She's been distracted for days."

Garrison slid out of the booth, causing Bonnie to sidestep out of his way. He looked down at Jack. All business.

"Don't go anywhere." Garrison marched through the room and out the front door.

Bonnie watched him leave before turning back to them. "The whole town's taking crazy pills today. You need something?"

Jack swallowed rising nausea. Something was really wrong. "No, thanks."

She walked away, shaking her head.

Jack slid out of the booth and stood, but Sam stopped him with a hand on his wrist. "Garrison said not to leave."

"Am I required to do as he says?"

She glanced toward the front door. "He must have a reason."

"I need to go."

He started toward the front door just as Garrison stepped inside, phone still pressed against his ear.

Jack felt like a teenager who'd been caught sneaking out the window. Which was ridiculous. He hadn't done anything wrong.

Garrison approached, pointed at the bench seat across from his wife, and lifted his eyebrows. There was something commanding about the man, and he was already suspicious. If Jack took off, Garrison would be more convinced something nefarious was going on.

Jack slid into the seat.

Garrison said, "Right. C-L-O-U-D." A moment passed, and then, "For how long?" He waited, then said, "Sure, I'll hold." He glanced at his wife and pointed at the food. "Get that to go, would you?"

She flagged Bonnie down.

Garrison spoke into the phone. "I'm here." He wandered toward the door and continued his conversation.

As Bonnie boxed the meals and Sam paid the bill, Jack pulled out his cell and dialed Harper. No answer. He texted her. *Where are you? I need to talk to you.* No answer. He set his phone on the table.

He didn't know what was happening or what he was

expected to do. He wanted to leave and find Harper, but he also wanted to know what Garrison had learned.

Was that so wrong, to want to know the woman he was falling for?

Harper would think so. Would that even matter? Because if he guessed right, Harper was preparing to leave town right now.

He decided to stay another five minutes and shot up a quick prayer. *Don't let her leave before I get there.*

When Bonnie walked away, Sam asked, "What's Harper like?"

Such a loaded question. Wednesday, he'd have had a thousand good things to say about her. Beautiful, kind, genuine, sweet. And a great caretaker. The way she tended Red, the way she loved that old man she wasn't even related to—that told him so much. Harper had a heart made to love, made to care. Two days before, he'd have sworn she'd go out of her way to save a spider's life. But that was then. Today, all the things he'd believed about her seemed wrong. Because she was an ex-con. A liar. A felon.

And even as he told himself that, he didn't believe it.

"I thought I knew her. But apparently..."

When he didn't finish, Sam said, "People change, you know."

He thought of his sister. She'd been a mess all her life, and as far as he knew, she still was. Because some problems couldn't be fixed, not by people. Some problems went soul-deep. With all his heart, Jack believed God could change his sister. He'd held on to faith that God was working on Angel, even though he'd seen no evidence of it.

But what about Harper? She was open to God. She believed, even if her faith was shallow. Right?

Or had she fooled him completely?

He had no idea, but the longer Garrison talked on the

phone, the worse Jack felt about this whole thing. Had it been five minutes yet? "I should go." But he didn't move. Because more than he wanted to go, he wanted to know what Garrison had learned.

"Let's just wait another minute."

"What if it's terrible? What if she's running for her life, and your husband has just told the bad guys—"

"Garrison's not talking to bad guys. He's talking to cops. Probably friends at the FBI. Most cops are good people trying to protect the weak. You can trust them."

Sure. He'd always believed that, but Harper didn't believe it. She couldn't, or she wouldn't be in hiding.

Assuming she was.

Wow, Jack's imagination was out of control.

Garrison started toward them, phone still at his ear. He was an imposing man when he wore that serious expression. He spoke into the phone. "Yeah, I'll get back to you."

That didn't sound good.

Garrison ended the call and slid into the seat beside his wife. He folded his hands on the table and met Jack's eyes. "She's a person of interest in a double homicide."

Jack's heart landed on the tile floor. "She didn't do it."

Garrison's smile was weak. "How can you be so sure?"

Jack looked at Sam, then back at Garrison. "Would you believe Sam capable of murder?"

"Sam's not a convicted felon."

Sam's eyebrows rose while her jaw dropped.

Jack said, "Harper did her time."

"You knew about that." Garrison blew out a long breath and leaned back. He held Jack's gaze, and Jack forced himself not to look away, though he was squirming under the man's scrutiny. Because he had no idea what kind of person Harper was. Because though he'd spent time with her and kissed her and—

God help him—fallen for her, this ex-cop knew more about her right now than Jack did.

"I don't know you very well," Garrison said, "but you seem like a sharp enough guy. You really think, after everything you learned and after what I just told you, that Harper is on the up and up?"

"Yes." He made the word strong and sure. "If she did anything wrong—and I don't think she did—then she did it in self-defense."

"The murders weren't self-defense, not according to the detective."

"You don't know her."

"Neither do you," Garrison said. Before Jack could argue, he added, "And ten days doesn't count."

"Look, Garrison, I don't know why you think this is any of your business, but—"

"A person acts strangely around law enforcement, it makes a cop wonder. I had a feeling, and I checked it out."

"You need a new hobby."

"I tried knitting once, but it didn't work. Fat fingers." Garrison lifted his gigantic hands. "My lack of hobbies aside, your girlfriend—"

"She's not my girlfriend. She's my tenant."

"—is wanted for murder."

"Let's keep our voices down." Sam leaned forward and focused on Jack. "Garrison has good instincts. He had a feeling. Now, he knows, and what's done is done."

Yeah. What Garrison had done was alert every law enforcement agency on the eastern seaboard of Harper's whereabouts. With a previous conviction, would she be treated fairly? "What evidence do they have?"

Garrison looked at his wife, and they had one of those silent conversations only married couples had. The kind that drove single people crazy. He wanted to demand they say what they were thinking, but before he could, Garrison spoke.

"No offense, but it's not really your business," he said. "We need to talk to Harper."

Not *his* business? "It's not *your* business. I'm her friend."

Garrison snatched Jack's cell off the table, stood, and pocketed it. "Where is she now?"

"Give me that back."

"Look, I'm not a cop anymore, okay? But the law's still important to me. Now, you can tell me where she is, or I'll call Chief Thomas and alert him there's a wanted woman in his town. He's a good guy, but he's by-the-book. I had a hunch, and now I'm in it. And we're going to deal with it." Jack glared at the man, but Garrison only smiled. "Forget I asked. I'm sure Bonnie has her address."

"She lives next door to me." Jack rattled off the address.

Sam and Jack stood.

Garrison placed his hand on Sam's shoulder. "I want you to stay here." He looked at Jack. "You stay, too. I'll keep you two in the loop."

Sam ducked out from his hand. "I'm going with you."

Garrison shook his head. "She could be dangerous."

"I'm going," she said. "If I'm there, maybe she'll open up. You'll just scare her to death."

Garrison said, "Well, she's a criminal, so—"

"I'm going," Sam said.

"She's not a criminal." But neither Garrison nor Sam was listening to Jack.

Garrison studied his wife's face, then turned toward the door. "Stubborn, pig-headed…" Garrison was still muttering as he marched away.

Sam patted Jack's shoulder. "You should come. It'll be easier for her if you're there."

This was all his fault, though. If he hadn't gone to McNeal's, Garrison wouldn't have looked her up. "If he gets her thrown in prison..."

"Garrison will hear her out. Trust me, okay?"

He leaned away from her hand. He still didn't know what was going on, and taking a cop with him to find out wasn't the right course of action.

Harper would never forgive him.

Jack would have called to warn her if Garrison hadn't taken his phone. Which was, of course, why Garrison had taken his phone. So instead of warning her, he bolted out the door and took off in his pickup before Sam had climbed into Garrison's Camry.

Maybe Jack could give her a moment's warning, anyway.

But Garrison caught up with him within minutes. Of course. Because Garrison was a former cop and Jack was just a fix-it guy who'd blown everything out of proportion. Who'd thought it was a good idea to run a background check on a woman he cared about. Then he'd somehow brought in a straight-arrow guy like Garrison Kopp to make everything ten times worse.

He was pretty sure he'd spend the rest of his life regretting the previous few minutes.

When he pulled up to the house, Harper was dragging Red's suitcase to the car.

Part of Jack wished they'd wasted more time, given her a chance to get away. Jack would never have seen her again, but at least she might have remembered him with fondness.

She turned toward him. Her face held curiosity as he parked on the narrow street.

The look shifted to suspicion, then fear, as Garrison pulled in the driveway and parked a foot behind the little VW Jetta.

Jack jumped out of his truck and ran across the spotty grass toward her. "Harper, I'm so sorry."

She glanced at him, said nothing, and focused on the others.

Garrison and Sam stepped out of the car and started toward her.

She looked behind her. Jack couldn't blame her. Garrison was six-four, broad-shouldered, and carried himself like a cop. She had to be terrified.

Sam rushed around the car and approached Harper. "We met at the restaurant, remember?"

Harper just stared.

"I'm Samantha Kopp." She stopped a foot from Harper.

Harper turned to Jack, who'd stopped about five feet from her. "What's going on?"

"I'm so sorry. I tried to call earlier—"

"Harper Cloud?" Garrison stepped beside his wife. "I'm Garrison Kopp, a friend of Jack's."

"Friend's a strong word," Jack said, "all things considered."

Garrison ignored him. "Can we go inside? I'd like to talk to you."

Harper looked at Jack. "What did you do?"

"I didn't do this. I mean, not on purpose. I never meant—"

"If you wouldn't mind," Garrison said.

She left the suitcase beside the car, swiveled, and marched up the steps.

Garrison and Sam followed. Jack came in and closed the door behind him. The living room was empty. He hadn't realized before how Harper and Red had filled the place. Red's newspaper was usually folded on the little table between the sofa and the recliner. There was almost always a glass of Gatorade or a cup of coffee there, too. In the afternoons, there'd be a small bowl of some snack. Cashews, peanuts, those gross little soy nuts. Harper's cell phone often rested on the coffee table alongside a novel with a bookmark sticking out.

All that was gone. Jack continued into the kitchen, where Garrison and Sam pulled out chairs and sat at the table. Harper was leaning against the counter, arms folded, staring at the floor.

"Where's Red?" Jack asked.

She didn't look at him when she said, "I was going to pick him up on the way."

"To where?"

She shrugged.

He stepped closer and reached for her shoulder, but she backed away. "Don't."

"I'm sorry."

She didn't acknowledge the words.

Garrison cleared his throat. "Just for the sake of full disclosure," he said, "you should know I'm a former FBI agent. But I'm not a cop right now, and I'm not here in any official capacity." He paused, but nobody spoke. "You acted strangely at the restaurant when I walked up beside you, and then Jack showed up, and he seemed unduly concerned about telling me anything about you. I got suspicious and looked you up, then made a few phone calls. I learned some things that are really troubling."

Still, Harper said nothing.

"The fact that you're packing up and leaving doesn't look good."

She glared at the man. "Am I under arrest?"

Garrison smiled. "I've never actually done one of those citizen's arrests things. Feels very Barney Fife. Of course, he was a cop, wasn't he?"

He watched Harper, and she stared back. Finally, she said, "I don't know who that is."

"What?" He eyed Sam, then Jack. "Kids these days, am I right?"

When nobody answered, Sam said, "I don't think you're putting her at ease."

"This is some of my best stuff," Garrison said.

Sam chuckled and focused on Harper. "Forgive my husband. He's trying to be funny."

Harper narrowed her eyes. "What do you want?"

Garrison blew out a long breath. "Can you please sit down and tell us what's going on?"

"Do I have a choice?"

He shrugged. "The problem is, I know just enough to cause you a lot of trouble. But your friend here"—he nodded toward Jack, who glared at him—"seems convinced you haven't done anything wrong. So I'm willing to give you the benefit of the doubt."

Very slowly, Harper turned to face Jack. "I think you need to go."

"I have no idea how this happened. I just went to McNeal's to see if you were okay."

"It's not his fault you're wanted," Garrison said.

"Wanted?" Harper yanked out a chair and sat heavily.

Garrison's amusement faded. "In connection with a murder."

CHAPTER THIRTY

All Harper's searching for information had led to nothing. No news about her on the internet. No news about the two murdered men. Yet, in no time at all, this total stranger had found the information she'd sought. And now, she'd be arrested. Maybe she wouldn't go to prison. The police couldn't have any evidence against her. She hadn't done it.

But she hadn't committed the last crime, either. And she'd spent two years behind bars for that.

And that wasn't the worst of it. No, the worst had to do with the man in the doorway and the fact that she'd hoped, deep down, that maybe this time would be different. Maybe this man could be different.

She'd been a fool.

Despite the fact that she'd ordered him out, Jack was still there, eyes pleading. And what did that mean? That he cared about her? Fat chance.

Maybe it was like when a person watched a horror flick and wanted to see how it ended. *Would Harper be led away in handcuffs? Would a judge toss her in prison and throw away the key? Stay tuned...*

"What I found concerned me," the ex-cop, Garrison, continued. "Seems you're wanted in connection with a homicide."

Her hands rose as if on their own, palms out. "I swear, I didn't kill those men. I couldn't... I don't even own a gun."

"If you didn't do it"—the man's words were casual, measured—"then how do you know there was more than one victim? And how do you know they'd been shot? And how do you know they were both men?"

Stupid. She was so stupid.

She should ask for an attorney. This guy wasn't a cop, but still...

"Maybe just start at the beginning," the cop said.

Former cop. No, former FBI agent, who'd introduced himself as Garrison. And brought his wife. Which was weird if they were going to haul her off to jail. Who took his wife for that kind of deed? Pregnant wife, if Harper weren't mistaken.

The woman reached out, settled her hand over Harper's. "I think you're going to have to trust somebody."

"And it should be you two? Why?" And how? How to trust anybody when everybody she'd cared about had betrayed her. Everybody but the old man she'd done all this for.

She'd thought Jack might be the exception.

She should order him out, and this time, make sure he left. Because somehow, he'd gotten these people involved. He acted like it was an accident, but that made no sense at all. So maybe Jack had called them... Except she'd seen these two at the restaurant earlier.

Oh, she had no idea. And she couldn't order Jack out, because when she was in custody, she'd need him to take care of Red for her. So he needed to know what was going on.

Fine. She nodded to the fourth chair.

"You sure?" he asked.

"You wouldn't want to miss the best part."

He sat beside her and reached for her hand. She yanked it back. "Don't touch me."

She didn't miss the hurt in his eyes and didn't feel the least bit sorry.

With her focus on the table in front of her, she let the truth settle. This was *her* fault. Her fault for trusting Derrick. Her fault for believing things could be better. Her fault for running when she should have stayed to face the music.

Except... she still didn't know how she could have turned herself in and protected Red.

Garrison cleared his throat. "You were living in Maryland?"

She took a deep breath and met the man's eyes. He had kind eyes. His wife seemed tenderhearted. She'd always been nice to Harper at the restaurant. Anyway, Harper had no choice. "I was working in Las Vegas and met a guy. Derrick Burns. We started dating, sort of. Talking on the phone a lot. He lived in Baltimore, but he came out to see me sometimes. I was working at a nursing home, and he asked me to move to Maryland to take care of his grandfather. I had nothing else going on, so I agreed."

"Let's back up a little," Garrison said. "You were in prison, right?"

Heat filled her cheeks. She didn't want to look at Jack, but as if his presence were magnetized, she glanced his way. That wasn't shock on his face. So he'd already known.

"Years ago, my boyfriend and his friend robbed a liquor store. Emmitt, my boyfriend, was carrying a gun. The owner of the liquor store reached for a shotgun, and Emmitt shot him. Killed him. I was driving the car."

"But you turned yourself in the next day," Garrison said.

She asked, "How did you—?"

"Talked to the detective who arrested you. He said you didn't know about the robbery."

"I didn't. I had no idea. When I saw the news the next day, I realized what had happened. I went to the police and told them the truth. But I wasn't smart enough to get a lawyer, and I believed them when they told me I wouldn't be charged if I told them everything. They arrested Emmitt and Barry, and we all went to prison."

"You just went for two years," Garrison said.

"Which is still ridiculous." Jack's words were vehement. "She didn't do anything."

Garrison glanced at him and nodded. "I agree. The detective does, too. The ADA was trying to make a name for himself, and"—he focused on Harper—"you didn't have a good lawyer to protect you. You got railroaded."

Yes. She closed her eyes, thanked God this guy believed her.

Maybe God had brought her somebody who could help.

Maybe God really did love her. Even her. Even after everything.

"You got out," Garrison prompted, "and then met Derrick and moved to Baltimore."

"Not Baltimore, but Maryland, yes. I wasn't going to, but I had this stalker back in Vegas. I think. I wasn't sure, but then one night..." Her words trailed off. "None of that matters. The point is, I took Derrick's offer because it was a better offer than anything else an ex-con could get, and I was afraid. Probably just paranoid." She scoffed and shook her head. "I thought I'd be safer in Maryland."

"Go on," Garrison said.

"I moved in the spring. Stayed with Red." The thought of him had her glancing at her watch. She looked at Jack. "He needs to be picked up by three."

Jack reached into his pockets, then glared at Garrison. "Can I have my phone?"

"Right." Garrison pulled it from his pocket and handed it over.

What was that about?

As if he'd read her mind, Jack said, "He didn't want me warning you." He offered a half smile, then stepped into the living room and dialed.

She listened while he spoke to someone. She kept her gaze on the table. Garrison and Sam didn't say anything. The kitchen was thick with tension, but nobody tried to cut it.

A moment later, Jack stepped back in. "Steve's daughter is going to take them both back to her house. He'll be fine."

"Thank you." Harper focused on Garrison again. "Derrick, my newer ex-boyfriend, is a gambling addict. Because I have terrible taste in men." She resisted the urge to glance at Jack. "I didn't know about the addiction. If I had, I would never have gotten involved with him. I found out this summer that he owes a lot of money. We were at a party, and a guy who was there, Keith Williams..."

She waited for a reaction from Garrison to the name, but his face was unreadable.

"Anyway, Keith was leaning on Derrick pretty hard. I didn't know what about—I just saw them arguing. But later, Derrick told me Keith was working for his loan shark."

Garrison nodded. Jack started to speak, but Garrison shut him down with a look.

"A week later," she continued, "I overheard Derrick trying to swindle Red out of money. He was asking for two hundred thousand dollars. Red saw right through him and refused."

"Good for him," Jack said.

Neither Garrison nor Sam responded.

"We didn't see Derrick again. He kept his distance, and he and I only talked when I had something to tell him about his grandfather. A month or so ago, Red started really going downhill. Forgetting things, getting angry. Then, it got worse. Headaches, throwing up. Almost as if he'd been drinking. He doesn't drink, so it wasn't that. I called the doctor, and they said it sounded like a virus. I was willing to accept that, but the slurred words, the swaying… I started to fear he'd had a stroke, but nothing else indicated that. I went to get him a fresh bottle of Gatorade one afternoon, and I realized the top had already been opened. I stored them in the garage, and I knew Red wouldn't have gone out there and opened them. I started to get suspicious."

Jack said, "But what does this have to do—?"

"Let her finish." Garrison nodded to her.

She forced a fortifying breath. "I didn't know what it meant, but at that moment, I was more worried about Red than anything else. I decided to run to the grocery store real quick and get him more Gatorade, because he balks if he has to drink anything else, and he needed to stay hydrated. I went to the store." Her voice started to shake with the memories. She wiped sweaty hands on her jeans. "When I got back to my car…" She swallowed. The fear had her voice rising. She couldn't stop the emotions. She couldn't stop the trembling as she remembered that moment.

Jack took her hand, and she met his eyes. She saw kindness there. Tenderness. Trust.

Maybe.

Maybe not.

She held on anyway. "There were two men. One was behind me, so I didn't see him. He held me still. The other wore a mask. He had a knife." She rubbed the healed cut on her neck automatically. "They hurt me." Tears streamed from her eyes as she related the incident. Somehow, she found herself leaning into Jack. His hand gripped her shoulder, her cheek pressed to his chest. She inhaled his rugged scent. If only… But the thought died when Garrison spoke.

"You're saying they walked away?"

She pushed away from Jack and sat up straight. Sam pulled a tissue from her purse, which Harper grabbed to wipe her eyes. "They loaded the Gatorade in the trunk and then walked away."

"Did you call the police?" Garrison asked.

She shook her head. "I had to get back to Red. I'd been gone too long, and he was so sick. What were the police going to do? I didn't see the men's faces. I didn't know what kind of car they drove. I had no information, no evidence."

"A cut on your neck, bruises all over your body." Garrison's eyebrows rose. "Seems evidence enough."

"If I'd known... I didn't know what was going to happen. I didn't see the point. I just had to get back to Red."

The kindness she'd seen in Garrison's face morphed to suspicion. "The point would have been to find the guys who'd beaten you up."

She glared at the man. "I'm a felon. An ex-con. Why would the cops care?"

His suspicion didn't fade a bit. "So you just walked away? That was it?"

"I hid the bruises and took care of Red. I did my job. At that moment, I was more worried about him than anything. I called Derrick, and he came up. I told him what happened and the message they'd given me for him."

"'Tell him we stopped by,'" Garrison clarified from the story she'd just told.

"Right."

"And then what happened?"

"Derrick left. I got Red to bed and took a shower. When I got out, I heard something."

Garrison said, "Define 'something.'"

"It sounded like a door closing. So I went to investigate. And

I found..." She swallowed the bile in her throat. "I found two men dead on the floor in the living room."

Garrison sat up straighter. "Just like that? They were there?"

She nodded, unsure what to say next.

"How'd they die?" Garrison asked.

"They'd been shot."

"The old man was in bed?"

"No. He'd heard the noise. He was standing there, staring at them."

Garrison tilted his head to the side. "You don't think he—"

"Absolutely not. There was no gun. And he might've been able to get off one round, but how would he have shot them both? And anyway, there was no blood on the floor. They hadn't been shot there. They'd been left there."

"Why would somebody do that?" Garrison asked.

"To frame me. I mean, that's the only thing that makes sense."

"But why?"

"I don't know. I don't know anything!" She stopped, forced a few deep breaths. Her voice was hysterical, and the higher the pitch, the less credible she sounded.

Jack pulled Harper's hand into his again. Sam patted her shoulder.

"So you left them there?" Garrison's eyebrows were hiked to his hairline.

"After I got Red in the car, I found a payphone and called 911 and told them that I'd seen a disturbance. I called as if I were a neighbor. I left the back door unlocked so the police could get in and find the bodies. I mean, one of the guys was Keith. I'd met him." She swiped at the tears, tried to speak calmly. "I was friends with his wife. Kitty. They have children. I couldn't believe he'd hurt me."

"Wait." Garrison held up his hand, looked toward the ceiling as if he were trying to solve a puzzle, then focused on her again. "How do you know these were the men who assaulted you? You said they'd worn masks."

"I recognized the one's clothes. Not Keith—he'd been the one holding me. I mean, I assume it was him. Oh, and when the guy cut me, he wiped my blood on his jeans. There was a bloodstain there."

Garrison huffed out a short breath. "So the DNA will lead to you."

"I assumed that was the evidence they had against me."

"Doubt it," Garrison said. "Most states' labs are behind. It usually takes months to get DNA evidence back. Must be something else."

"You don't know what, though?"

He shook his head. "All I know is that you're wanted for questioning." Garrison pressed his lips together. "So you were in the house. You found two bodies on the floor. Then what did you do?"

"Red was out of his mind. I didn't think he'd remember any of it, but I had to take care of him. I had to protect him."

"What made you think he was in danger?"

"Oh." She hadn't told them that part. "When I was in the shower, I thought about the Gatorade bottles. I'd bought a case, and they'd come wrapped in plastic. It didn't make sense that they'd been opened before I got them home. Which meant somebody had tampered with them."

Garrison's eyes narrowed. "Go on."

"I think Derrick was trying to kill him."

"Oh, God." Jack breathed the words like a plea, a prayer. "His own grandson?"

"Who else?" Harper turned to face him. "Derrick was desperate for money. Red wouldn't give him any. But when Red dies, he stands to inherit everything. It would have solved all of Derrick's problems."

"But murder?" Jack said. "That's pretty extreme."

She thought about how, way back in Vegas, Emmitt had tried to pin the liquor store owner's death on Barry. How he'd sworn Barry had pulled the trigger. And Barry had sworn Emmitt had done it. Best friends, turned against each other. And since she'd turned him in, Emmitt had turned against her. "Desperate men do desperate things."

"So you took him to the hospital?" By the look on Garrison's face, he already knew the answer to that.

"I couldn't. I was afraid."

"Afraid you'd get arrested," Garrison said. "Afraid you'd go back to prison."

"Yes. No!" She pushed back in her chair and stood. "Not afraid for me. Afraid because nobody would have believed me. I'd have been thrown in jail, and Red would have been turned over to the man who'd tried to kill him."

"But if you had the Gatorade bottles—"

She paced across the kitchen floor. "I didn't realize until after my shower that Red was being poisoned. I'd called Derrick before that. Because I'd been in so much pain after the attack, I'd asked him to get the Gatorade from the trunk for me. So he had to have known I'd figured something out. When I went to grab one of the opened bottles in the garage, they were gone."

Garrison blew out a long breath and ran his hand over his cropped haircut. "Okay. Fine. So there was no evidence. You were scared. You didn't think you could go to the hospital. Except he'd been poisoned. So I guess, what, you just hoped for the best?"

"I'm a nurse, remember? Maybe I'll never be a registered nurse like I wanted, but I understand medical things. I figured out that Derrick had poisoned him with antifreeze." She met

Garrison's eyes. "The poor man's antidote is liquor. It's not pretty, but it works."

Garrison's eyebrows hiked again. "So you plied an old man with alcohol to"—he made air quotes with his fingers—"help him."

"Why don't you give her a break," Jack said.

Garrison ignored him. "Where did you go?"

"To a hotel in Newark."

"Harper." Garrison managed to fill the word with incredulity. "Come on. You're missing a step."

"I swear. That's all that happened. And then we came here."

"You need to tell me everything," Garrison said.

"It sounds like she did." Jack stood and wrapped his arm around her back, but she stepped away. She couldn't get close to him or anybody, not right now, not while she fought irritation and fear and the itch to bolt out the back door.

Garrison didn't believe her. She could see the suspicion in his eyes. She took another step away and glanced at the door.

As if he'd read her mind, Garrison stood and walked, calmly, to stand between her and freedom. "What did you do with the bodies, Harper?"

CHAPTER THIRTY-ONE

J ack watched her face. The way her eyes narrowed, the way her mouth formed a little O. The way her skin paled until she looked almost sick. Her blue eyes stood out in bright contrast, rimmed in red. Her hands—her whole body—shook.

Garrison's question hung in the air like the scent of burned dinner.

"I didn't do anything with the bodies." Harper's voice was a whisper. "I left them there."

"I can understand what happened." Garrison's tone was placating, but Jack wasn't buying it. He hoped Harper wasn't either. "You panicked. You had to hide them."

"I swear, I didn't—"

"I just can't figure out how you got them in the car. Did someone help you? Did Red—?"

"He's an old man, Garrison." Jack's voice was too loud. He tried to tamp down his anger. "He uses a walker. And he was sick. Red couldn't possibly have helped anybody move bodies."

"Someone else, then." Garrison stepped forward.

Sam stood and laid a hand on her husband's arm. "Don't jump to conclusions."

Garrison ignored his wife, kept watching Harper.

"I swear," Harper said, "I didn't do anything with them. I... I... I left them right there. I called..." She swallowed, glanced at Jack. "I called 911. I reported a disturbance at the house. Like I told you before. You can check that, right?"

Jack would do anything right now to get her out of this mess. Anything. If only he could figure out how. But even if he could keep Garrison from following if she bolted out the door, Jack wouldn't be able to hold him off long enough for her to get away. If she did disappear into the woods, eventually she'd be found.

She was trapped.

"Call," she said. "Find out if a call came in, if anybody went out to the house."

"I can check, Harper," Garrison said, "but there's no reason to, because the bodies weren't found at the house. They were found stuffed in the trunk of a Cadillac in a parking garage in a little town off I-70."

"No." Her head shook violently. "No, that makes no sense. I left them in the living room." She looked at Jack. "I didn't touch them. How could I touch them?" Her eyes filled with tears and terror. He wrapped an arm around her, and this time, she didn't push him away.

Jack glared at Garrison over her head. "How do you think this tiny woman moved two grown men, two dead bodies, into a car?"

"An accomplice, I assume," Garrison said.

She sobbed into Jack's chest. He held her tighter. Held her for all he was worth. Because she was the victim here. Everything she'd said convinced him of that. How could Garrison not see it?

"This is ridiculous," Jack said. "Where would she have gotten a Cadillac?"

At that, Harper sniffed and turned to Garrison. "Red's car,

right?" She looked at Jack. "It was Red's car. I left it... It was in the garage when I left."

"I'm sorry, but the story doesn't work," Garrison said. "Who would leave two bodies in the house for you to find, then remove them after you left?"

"I don't know! I don't..." She took a deep breath, then another. She swallowed, stepped away, and focused on Jack. "You have to take care of Red for me. Don't let Derrick get his hands on him. Derrick can't be trusted."

"It's going to be okay," Jack said, though he had no idea how.

"No. It's not." Her gaze darted around the room—Garrison, Sam, Jack. Her eyes were wide, her lower lip trembling. "It's not going to be okay."

Garrison said, "Harper, why don't you—?"

"Promise me." She held Jack's gaze. "Whatever happens, promise me you won't let Derrick have Red. He'll kill him. If you care about him at all, if you ever cared about me—"

"I never meant..." He stepped toward her, but she backed up, bumped into the counter.

"Don't. Just, please... Red doesn't know anything. He doesn't remember the bodies. He doesn't know about the antifreeze. I didn't want to hurt him."

Jack wanted to reach for her, but everything in her stance told him not to. So he nodded. "I'll take care of him. And I'll get you a good lawyer—"

"That's enough." Garrison's raised voice had them both turning to face him. "Sit down. Both of you. Now." He looked at his wife. "You, too."

Sam's eyebrows hiked, but she slid back into her seat.

After Harper perched on the edge of her chair, Jack sat beside her.

Garrison remained standing. He took a deep breath and ran his hand over his head. "Okay." But then he said nothing else.

Jack rested his hand palm-up on the table between him and Harper. She glanced at it. Then slid her hand into it. He lifted it to his lips and kissed her knuckles.

Tears slid down her cheeks. Her mouth was pinched at the corners, her lips white and pressed together.

This was too much. He still didn't understand any of it. Garrison seemed to be wrestling, too.

"Let's say you're telling the truth," Garrison said.

Harper wiped her tears. "I swear, I would never—"

He held up his hand to silence her. "I'm not saying I believe you. I'm just throwing it out there as a possibility. Maybe Derrick did it."

She sniffed. "That's what I thought at first, because he was the only one who knew about the attack. And maybe he was trying to frame me, to discredit me, in case I told anybody about the poison."

Garrison's eyes narrowed. "You thought that *at first*? What changed?"

"I just can't imagine it. I keep seeing it in my head, and I can't..."

"He's the nicest guy," Garrison said. "Kept to himself."

"Said the neighbors of every serial killer ever," Jack supplied.

"I know." Her eyes squeezed closed, unable to face the obvious truth. "I couldn't imagine Emmitt killing anybody, either. But he did."

Sam, who'd been nearly silent for the entire conversation, tapped on the table. "What I don't understand is why somebody would break in, leave the bodies, and then take them after you left. That doesn't make sense."

"I agree," Garrison said. "If Derrick did it, and if he was trying to frame you, why not leave the bodies there?"

"But that doesn't make sense, either," Jack said. "If he were trying to frame her, leaving two bodies in her living room doesn't work. I mean"—he focused on Harper—"they weren't shot there, right? That's what you said."

"There was no blood on the floor. And I would have heard gunshots."

Garrison paced, seemed to be talking to himself. "If somebody wanted to frame you... We're assuming the bodies were found in the old man's car. But why would they...?"

Jack waited for Garrison to explain what he'd just said. Instead, the other man paced and muttered incoherently. Then, he froze and faced Harper. "You're saying Red owned a Caddy, right?" When she nodded, he considered that. "The Cadillac at the airport had no plates, and the VIN numbers had been filed off. So whoever left it didn't want it traced back to you or Red."

"If they're trying to frame her, then why do that?" Jack asked.

"My first thought"—Garrison focused on Harper—"is that somebody did it to protect you. Or *you* did it to protect you."

"I swear—"

"I heard your story," Garrison said. "I'm not saying I believe it. I'm just trying to work it out. It doesn't make sense."

The four of them were silent. Jack tried to fit all the details he'd heard in the last hour into the larger puzzle. There was a big piece missing. He didn't know what it was, and a glance at Harper's confused expression told him she didn't either.

Nothing had been solved. But Jack was convinced of one thing. Harper wasn't a murderer. She was a sweet, caring, innocent woman trying to protect an old man who was no relation to her, but whom she loved.

He'd stand by her forever. No matter what happened next.

CHAPTER THIRTY-TWO

Derrick shifted on his rental car's cheap fabric seats and glanced at the giant fountain soda he'd picked up at the corner store. His throat was parched, but he needed to empty his bladder, and he dared not leave this spot. The rear entrance to the building where Gramps had called from the previous day was quiet right now. Derrick had seen people coming and going from the back—the main door on the side hadn't opened—since he'd arrived that morning. Lots of elderly people, a few younger ones. Based on the sign in front of the building, this was a food bank, but it was only open on Wednesdays. Seemed the rec center Gramps had told him about was open daily.

If Gramps was in there, Derrick hadn't been here in time to see him arrive. He'd come by the night before, but the building had been deserted. So he'd rented a hotel room in Manchester, overslept, and gotten here by eleven. He'd been watching the building ever since. What if Gramps wasn't here? What if he'd told Harper they'd talked? The two of them could be miles away by now.

Impatience had him tapping the steering wheel. He'd

parked behind an adjacent building, where he could see both the side and the rear door through a chain-link fence that separated the two parking lots. He'd keep watching until Gramps came out or someone locked those doors. He had no other leads.

What would he do if they'd run again? He'd have to go into hiding himself. Which meant he'd lose his job, his car, his condo. Without Gramps's money, there was no way Derrick could pay Quentin what he owed him. He'd lose everything. His life, his future.

No.

The very thought had his blood simmering. Gramps had money to spare. Gramps would give it to him, one way or another. He couldn't lose everything he'd worked for. He wouldn't.

Now, it was nearing two o'clock, and activity picked up. Cars came. People went inside. They returned with old folks, climbed into their cars, and left. Three cars, four cars. No sign of Gramps.

A red sedan parked beside the back door, and a middle-aged blond woman went inside. A few minutes later, she came back with two old men, one of whom was leaning heavily on a walker. Was that...? Derrick leaned forward for a better look.

It was Gramps.

Where was Harper, though? Who were these people?

Gramps climbed into the backseat, the other man sat in front, and the woman drove away.

Derrick followed.

Ten minutes later, the car pulled into a driveway in front of a two-story Colonial-style house surrounded by trees. Derrick continued on the road, parked fifty yards or so beyond the driveway, and hurried back. He watched as Gramps hobbled to the door, then slowly made his way up the steps and into the house.

Was this where they'd been staying?

Where was Harper?

The woman came out of the house a few minutes later and drove away.

Derrick jogged back to his car, pulled on his jacket and gloves, then locked the doors. He was emptying his bladder in the woods outside the house when he heard what sounded like a screen door slam. Were they out back?

He crept among the trees, thankful for the dark color of his jacket and jeans, and made it to the backyard. Sure enough, he spied Gramps and the other man sitting in a glass-enclosed sunroom that had been added to the back of the house. They sipped drinks and munched on something while they talked. He could hear them through the glass, though the words themselves were lost. Otherwise, the sunny afternoon was quiet. The leaves rustled in a slight breeze. The birds twittered in the trees.

Derrick was chilled to the bone by the time the other old man went inside the sliding doors. After a few minutes, Derrick darted from the woods to the side of the house to get a closer look. He peered around the corner and into the sunroom. Gramps was sound asleep in a recliner.

The other man was nowhere to be seen.

This was his chance. Nobody knew he was in New Hampshire. Nobody'd seen him in Nutfield. He could creep inside, suffocate the old man, and be gone before anybody saw his face.

He only regretted that when he did this, he wouldn't get his hands on Harper. But killing Gramps would hurt her dearly.

It wasn't the solution he'd hoped for, but for now, it would have to be enough repayment for all the ways she'd hurt him.

He crept to the door. The knob turned, and the door opened silently.

Gramps was snoring softly. Beside him, there was a small,

rickety table that held a lamp, a bowl of small orange crackers, and a glass of water.

The sound of a TV drifted from inside the house. Derrick peered through the slider that led to the kitchen. The room was empty.

The other man must've gone in to watch TV when Gramps drifted off. He was probably sleeping, too.

Derrick could do this. He had to do this.

He grabbed a throw pillow covered with bright yellow flowers from an adjacent sofa and stood over his grandfather.

The old man looked good. Healthy, even. Peaceful.

Derrick closed his eyes, took a deep breath. He thought of Quentin and Keith and broken knees and popped-out eyeballs and losing everything.

He opened his eyes and squeezed the pillow in his fists.

Gramps's eyes opened. "Derrick?"

He jumped at the single word. "Hey, Gramps."

The old man blinked. "What are you...? Did Harper tell you where to find me?"

Derrick glanced into the house. No sign of the other guy.

"Nope. She wouldn't have, either. She was hiding from me."

Gramps tilted his head to the side. "From you? Why?"

"You should have given me the money."

Gramps's eyes widened, and his jaw fell.

Derrick pressed the pillow over his face.

Tears streamed from Derrick's eyes as Gramps gripped his wrists, tried to push him off.

He wanted to stop. He wanted to run away. How could he kill this man who'd loved him, who'd protected him after Mom and Dad died? How had Derrick fallen this far?

This was crazy. He wasn't a killer. If he ran now, Gramps might think it had all been a dream. A weird, crazy dream. He hesitated. Let up on the pressure just a tad.

No. He had to do this.

Gramps's arms flailed wildly, and he knocked over the lamp.

The crash reverberated in the room.

A shout came from the house. "Red?"

Derrick dropped the pillow, met Gramp's wide, terrified eyes.

And bolted.

CHAPTER THIRTY-THREE

Harper sat as still as she could and watched Garrison, who was still standing and staring at nothing.

The silence would kill her. Not Derrick, not prison. Waiting while Garrison processed all she'd told him—that would be the death of her.

Jack squeezed her hand and offered a slight smile. Part of her wanted to hate him for getting these people involved. But another part of her was glad he had. Because now, whatever happened, at least the running was over. She could tell her side of the story. As long as Gramps was safe, she could take whatever was coming.

What laws had she broken?

She hadn't stolen anything or hurt anyone. Red was an adult, and he'd come with her willingly. All along, she'd tried to do the right thing. For her sake. For Red's sake.

But would anybody believe her?

Harper glanced at Sam, who gave her a slight smile as if this were a perfectly normal situation.

Garrison stared beyond her.

Jack pushed back in his chair. "Look—"

"Just let me think," Garrison said.

Jack met her eyes, shrugged.

"Honey," Sam said, "do you think you could let us know what you're thinking?"

He blew out a long breath and met Harper's eyes. "Your story is strange. If I'd heard it from anyone else, I'd have dismissed it out of hand because it doesn't make sense."

Harper couldn't seem to form words, but Jack said, "You said 'if.' Does that mean you believe her?"

"I do," Garrison said. "I'm good at telling if people are lying, and I don't think you are."

"I'm not," she said. "I swear I'm not."

Garrison's mouth flattened into a smirk. "And I hope that if you'd made up a story, it would've been a little better than what you've told me. Made-up stories make sense. Usually."

Harper swallowed, nodded.

"None of that changes the fact that you're wanted in connection with two murders. You need to turn yourself in."

She stared at the table. She could do that, but what would she do with Red? Would he go with her back to Maryland? Could she have Roger hire him another nurse while she dealt with this? Would anybody be able to protect him from Derrick? Would anybody believe he was trying to kill his grandfather?

"I'll call the detectives investigating the murders," Garrison said. "I'll give them a heads-up, tell them you're here and you had no idea you were wanted. I'll try to pave the way, but I can't promise anything."

"I didn't do it."

Garrison held her gaze. "I believe you." He stood, grabbed his cell phone, and went out the front door.

"I didn't get them involved on purpose," Jack said. "It's important to me that you understand that. I was worried. It all just got out of hand."

"That's the truth." Sam's voice was kind. "My husband can be like a dog with a bone sometimes. He got suspicious. He misses being a cop."

Harper just shrugged.

"I think," Jack continued, "maybe this is better than you running away again. Maybe it's better if you deal with it."

Jack was probably right.

"I believe you, too," Sam said. "And I'll be praying. God can handle this." Her smile was kind, gentle. "Do you mind if I use your restroom?"

"Help yourself."

After Sam walked away, Jack squeezed Harper's hand. "I never doubted you for a minute."

Right. She looked at him, raised her eyebrows.

"I was afraid you were in trouble," he said. "I never thought..." He swallowed, glanced away, then met her eyes. "Okay, I doubted you, a little. Can you forgive me?"

Had he done anything wrong? "I've lied to you about everything, and I was about to take off without a word."

"None of it was my business."

"Maybe," Harper said. "What's going to happen now?"

"I have no idea. I don't know Garrison well enough to guess, and the guy's sort of an enigma. Scary intimidating cop who tells stupid dad jokes."

Harper nearly smiled. "My dad tells stupid dad jokes, too."

"They all do. I probably will someday, too. If I'm ever lucky enough to..." He turned his chair toward Harper, then turned her chair so they were facing each other. He took her hands and met her eyes. "I'm with you in this. Whatever happens now, whatever you need me to do. I'm on your side. I'll make sure Red is taken care of, protected from Derrick. I'll do whatever you need me to do."

A flood of emotions filled her, almost too big to name. His

kindness, his quick understanding, his generosity. How could she refuse him anything?

How could she draw him into her nightmare?

"Don't." His voice was intense, and he leaned closer. "You're so easy to read. Don't push me away. Not now. Please."

"Maybe after I get this all—"

"No. Not after. Circumstances are never going to be perfect, Harper."

"But none of this is your problem."

"It is, though. It is my problem, because it's your problem. And I care for you."

She leaned away, wanted to stand, to put distance between them so she could think. "You don't even know me."

"I know you risked your own life and freedom to protect an old man who's not even related to you. I know you've been through hell, and all along, you've just been trying to take care of him. No thought for your own comfort, your own needs."

"You make me sound so noble."

"Noble." He nodded. "That's the right word."

She looked away. "It's not. You don't know."

And even if he did, even if he really did care about her, could she trust him?

"I want to be here for you."

Harper pushed back her chair and stood.

Jack stood, too. Her plan to get farther from him so she could think was not working. Because there he was, tall, broad, beautiful, and just inches away.

Sam stepped out of the bathroom. Surely Jack would back up now, put more space between them. But he didn't move.

Sam disappeared into the living room. A moment later, the front door opened and closed.

They were alone.

"I'm not..." She swallowed, shook her head. Tried to think.

"I can't be who you want me to be. I don't know you. I don't trust... easily."

"I've given you plenty of reasons not to trust me."

No, that wasn't true. "You've been nothing but kind to me. And you didn't have any reason to trust me."

"I've seen how you've taken care of Red. How you've been breaking your back to provide for a man who, by all accounts, is very wealthy. How devoted you are to him. I was afraid for you. I certainly didn't intend for this to happen."

None of that changed the truth, though. Of course Jack wasn't trying to hurt her, not yet. But her history was too long to be discarded that easily. "Every man who's ever found me attractive has lied to me, hurt me, treated me like..." But she couldn't finish the sentence. Because the men in her past had treated her exactly the way she'd acted. She'd never deserved better because she'd never behaved better.

She didn't know if she could now.

And she didn't want to reduce either one of them to the kinds of relationships that littered her past.

"Not all guys are like the yahoos you've fallen for," he said. "Is your father like that?"

Her father had his issues, but he was a good man. He'd treated her mother with respect. "No."

"How about Red. Is he like that?"

"Of course not." She thought of the men from her past. Then all the men at the strip club, men with handfuls of dollar bills and opened mouths and lust in their eyes. "Because of how I look, men don't see me, the real me. They want things from me because I'm..." She didn't know how to finish that statement.

"Beautiful?"

Her cheeks warmed, and she didn't respond.

His eyes crinkled at the corner. "Well, then, you can trust me. Because I think you're a dog."

The way he was looking at her belied his words. Every cell in her body responded to him. It was as if her entire being were leaning toward him, needing him.

He lowered his gaze to her lips. "Woof, woof."

She shouldn't kiss him again. If she did, she'd fall for him completely. And then she'd be lost.

But maybe Jack really was different. Maybe this was a man she could trust.

Anyway, she didn't have the strength to resist.

His lips brushed hers. He paused and waited for her to step back. Which she probably should have. But she'd lost all control when it came to Jack Rossi.

She leaned in, kissed him back, and surrendered her heart.

CHAPTER THIRTY-FOUR

Jack's cell phone rang, and Harper jumped as if they'd been caught doing something wrong. But kissing Harper wasn't wrong. Nothing had ever felt so right.

Though she leaned away, he didn't release her. He wanted to ignore the call, to ignore the outside world and stay locked in an embrace with Harper forever.

But the moment was over.

"You should get that," Harper said.

He reluctantly pulled his cell from his pocket. "Hello?"

"Jack? It's Elizabeth."

Oh, no. "Is Red okay?"

"I don't know. Dad called, said he thinks maybe he had a heart attack, but he wasn't sure. Just said he was clutching his chest and talking gibberish. Dad called 911."

Jack met Harper's eyes. "What hospital?"

He got the details and hung up.

Harper's face was white as death. "Please tell me he's all right."

"They're not sure what happened, but to be on the safe side, they took him to the hospital." Not exactly what Elizabeth had said, but it would keep Harper from panicking. He took her hand and headed for the front door. She snatched her purse from the counter on the way. Harper started for her car but pulled up when she saw Garrison's car parked right behind hers.

Jack said, "I'll drive."

Sam was seated in Garrison's Camry. Garrison was on the phone, pacing in the yard. He saw them, then spoke into the phone. "Hold on a sec." He covered the phone and met Jack's eyes. "What's up?"

"We have to go." Harper's words were frantic, terrified.

"Red's on his way to the hospital," Jack said.

Garrison headed toward his car. "We'll follow you."

Harper stared forward silently throughout the drive to Manchester. Jack tried to engage her in conversation a couple of times, but she barely seemed to register his words. Finally, Jack parked at the doors to the ER, and Harper rushed inside.

Jack parked and hurried to meet her. Harper was nowhere to be seen. He approached the nurse behind the desk. "My friend just came in looking for Harold Burns."

"She's back there with him. You'll need to take a seat."

He started to argue, but the woman cut him off. "Are you family?"

He blew out a long breath. "Just a friend."

"Then have a seat."

He turned, surveyed the room, and saw Steve in a chair on the far side. He crossed to him and sat. "What happened?"

Steve shook his head. "He fell asleep in the sunroom while we were talking, so I went inside to watch TV." He lifted his trembling hand to rub his nose. "I mighta drifted off myself. I heard a crash. I got up, and when I got into the sunroom, Red was in the chair. His skin was gray. His eyes were terrified. And he was talking about someone trying to kill him."

Jack had witnessed that fear in the old man's eyes when he had one of his dementia moments. "What did he say?"

"Something about someone named Derrick. Said he was trying to smother him."

Jack's stomach dropped. He looked around the emergency room, but Derrick could be anywhere. Jack had no idea what the man looked like.

"Don't know who Derrick is," Steve said. "Figured he was doing like he did that day at the rec center. But the color of his skin, the way he was clutching his chest... I called an ambulance."

"You did the right thing," Jack said.

"Yeah." Steve nodded, then shook his head. "You know what's weird, though?" He paused, seemed to be thinking back. "Elizabeth put these throw pillows on the couch out there. Nobody ever touches them. And the sofa was a good five feet away from Red. But when I went out there, one of those pillows was on the floor by the back door."

Derrick.

It didn't make sense. And it was the only thing that did make sense. "What caused the crash?"

"The lamp. He must've knocked it over."

Or Derrick had. Or he had been trying to get away from Derrick.

"Be right back." He left Steve in his seat and rushed to meet Garrison as he and Sam walked in. "Derrick's here."

Garrison froze. "What do you mean?"

Quickly, Jack told Garrison everything Steve had said. "Red didn't know his grandson had been trying to kill him. So why would he say that? Derrick must be here."

Garrison stared beyond him at nothing for a moment, then nodded once and turned. He was already dialing his phone by the time he stepped back into the cold November afternoon.

CHAPTER THIRTY-FIVE

Harper sat by Gramp's side in the ER. Now that the truth was out, she could go back to calling him Red, even if she thought of him as family. The door was closed to their little space. Outside the room, the rest of the hospital buzzed with activity. Footsteps, voices, ringing phones. Inside the room, the only sounds came from Red's quiet snoring and the hum of machines monitoring his health. And the smells. After working in a nursing home, the hospital smells shouldn't bother her, but right now, her stomach churned.

It seemed like hours had passed, though it had probably been no more than one. Occasionally, the nurse came in and checked his vitals. Once, she'd drawn blood, probably looking for troponin, the protein in the blood that rises in response to heart damage. So far, nobody'd felt the need to tell Harper any of their findings.

A woman had wheeled in a computer to ask about Red's health insurance and medical history. Now that Harper had been found by the authorities, she could share his insurance information. She'd need to call Red's lawyer and let him know what was going on. And she'd need to stay with Red to make sure Derrick didn't get to him.

She watched the monitors but saw nothing to worry about. His heartbeat was steady. His pulse was normal. His blood pressure was a little high, but nothing to be concerned about.

She took his cold hand and closed her eyes. *Dear God. Please save him. Whatever happens to me, please protect him.* She prayed for his health, for his life. And then she prayed for herself. That God would show her what to do now that her story had fallen apart. That He would protect them both. That the truth would be brought to light, and that she would be free of the charges that were no doubt coming.

And she prayed for Jack. *Lord, You know how I feel about him. Protect him from this mess I've made. Make a way for us to be together. If that's not what You want, then please, help me not to care for him.*

Finally, an Asian woman stepped into the room. She was petite with short black hair and wore a white coat over scrubs. "I am Dr. Pham."

Harper stood and shook her hand. "Harper Cloud."

The woman peeked at Red, who was still sleeping. She lowered her voice. "You are his granddaughter?"

"I'm his caretaker, his nurse. I have legal documentation, if you need to see it."

"Do you have it with you?"

Harper dug into her small purse and pulled out the paperwork. The doctor read it over and handed it back. "The ECG showed that Mr. Burns suffered a minor heart attack." She kept her voice low, and Red didn't stir. "The blood tests confirmed that. Right now, his vitals are steady. Nevertheless, we will keep him here for a few days. He will be transferred to a room, and I will hand over his care to a cardiac specialist."

Harper took all the information in, tried to think of something intelligent to say but came up with nothing. "Thank you so much."

She smiled. "They will take good care of him upstairs." With that, the doctor left, and Harper sat beside him. A few minutes later, his eyes opened.

Harper took his hand. "Hey, sleepyhead. How you feeling?"

He squeezed her hand and looked around the drab room, his eyes settling on the monitors beside him before he focused on her again. "I'm alive, I guess."

She let out a short laugh. "That you are, thank God."

He started to smile, but the look faded. His eyes widened, and he held her hand tighter. "Derrick. He was there."

Uh-oh. He was awake but not as lucid as he'd first seemed. "We're still in New Hampshire. What would Derrick be doing here?"

"He was there. He found me."

"That's imposs—"

"Listen to me."

She quieted at the urgency in his voice.

"I called him yesterday from Steve's phone."

No, no, no. Harper covered her mouth with her palm.

"I showed him where I was with that pin-thing." Red's voice quivered. "He told me how." Tears filled the old man's eyes. "He told me not to tell you. Said he wanted to surprise you." His grip loosened. "I'm just a foolish old man. I believed him."

"It's okay." Harper worked to keep her voice steady, to keep him calm. She glanced at the monitor, saw his heart rate had increased. "It's fine. It's okay that he's here."

Tears filled the old man's eyes as he looked away. "He almost killed me. Put a pillow over my face. Tried to smother me."

She sat heavily in the chair. "I should have... I tried to—"

Red met her gaze. "Tried to what? Did you know he might...?" His voice was filled not with accusation but surprise.

She took his hand. "I didn't want you to know."

"You need to tell me what you're talking about."

"Remember how sick you got those last few days before we left?"

He nodded, eyes narrowed.

"He was poisoning your Gatorade. That's why I made you drink that whole weekend, to get the poison out of your system."

His eyes narrowed. "It was vodka, wasn't it? You kept calling it medicine, but—"

"It's an antidote to ethylene glycol. Antifreeze. Not the best one, certainly not the easiest one. I didn't want to take you to a hospital." She hoped he wouldn't ask why, because after the scare he'd had, the last thing he needed was to be reminded of the bodies in his living room.

"You were trying to protect Derrick. And trying to protect me from knowing the truth."

She nodded and swallowed the half-truth. Mostly she'd been trying to protect herself and Red from whoever had killed those men.

"You took good care of me." He looked away. "My own grandson..."

She didn't know what to say. Didn't know how to soften the blow for this kind, gentle man. "He's just... He's in too deep."

They were silent for a few minutes. His heart rate returned to normal. He kept his gaze away from her when he said, "I guess I should have just given him the money."

"None of this is your fault."

"I'll keep telling myself that."

She squeezed his hand. "Look at me."

Slowly, his head turned toward her. She leaned a little closer. "You've been nothing but good to him. He got himself into a terrible mess, and now he doesn't know how to get out of it."

He stared at the ceiling. "He couldn't go through with it. All of a sudden, I couldn't see. Couldn't breathe. Couldn't fight. I thought I was a goner. And then, he just let up."

"Thank God." At least Derrick had a sliver of decency left in him.

"I was ready to go see my Bebe. I was ready." He met her eyes again. "If anything happens to me, I want you to know, whenever the Lord wants to take me home, I'm ready."

"Don't say—"

"I'm glad, though." He took a breath. "Glad he didn't do it. Glad he doesn't have to live with that on top of everything else."

"Me, too," Harper said. Not for Derrick's sake. Derrick deserved whatever he got. But she couldn't imagine losing Red. Not now. Not yet. *Please, God, not by murder.*

There was a soft knock. Harper waited for a nurse to walk in. When none did, she stood and opened the door. Jack and Garrison stood outside. Jack said, "How is he?"

"Come on in."

She stepped aside, and Jack came into the room, bringing his steady presence with him. "Hey, Red. How you feeling?"

While Red answered, Garrison gripped Harper's arm. "We need to talk."

Jack pulled up a chair. He sent her a quick nod, then focused on Red.

She didn't want to walk away, but they weren't giving her much choice. "Be right back."

Red waved her out, and she followed Garrison down a corridor and into a room not much larger than the exam room she'd just left. It was like a waiting room. Lining the walls were chairs interspersed with a table here and there.

Inside were two men. She recognized them both—regulars at McNeal's. She'd heard one called Chief. The other was the guy with the drawl she'd served her first day at work. They stood when she walked in, straight and solid. Were they going to arrest her right here?

She turned to Garrison. "Please, don't let them—"

"Don't worry," Garrison said. "I'm on your side."

Right. She'd heard that before. The cops in Vegas had told her to trust them, too. She wasn't stupid enough to get herself into the same mess twice. Jack had promised to take care of Red. She'd tell whoever these people were everything, but not alone. "I want a lawyer."

Garrison sighed. "You're not in custody. We're not here to question you or arrest you. We're trying to protect you and Red. We think Derrick is here."

"Oh." The icy backbone she'd pretended melted away, and she collapsed into a chair. "Yes. Red said the same thing."

Garrison stepped inside. "These are friends of mine. Brady Thomas."

The taller and older of the two, the one they called Chief, stepped forward and shook her hand.

"And this is Eric Nolan." The younger one did the same, and then they both sat.

"Brady's the Nutfield Chief of Police, and Eric's a detective."

"You work at McNeal's, right?" the chief asked.

"Uh-huh. You're here because of what Red said?"

Chief Thomas nodded once. "Seems the other older gentleman, Steve, thought Mr. Burns was hallucinating, but based on what we learned from Garrison and your friend"— he glanced at a small notebook—"Jack Rossi, it seems it's possible this Derrick person may have tried to kill his grandfather."

She nodded, swallowed. "Red said he tried to smother him, but then... I guess he couldn't go through with it."

"But he's tried before?" the chief clarified.

"I can't prove it, but he put antifreeze in Red's drinks."

"You should have called the police right away."

She chuckled, though she felt anything but amused. "Things got a little out of hand."

Chief Thomas glanced at Garrison, who said, "That's a long story. It's not relevant to this discussion."

The chief stared at Garrison another moment, then said, "You'll tell me later," and turned back to Harper. "I'll contact the Manchester PD, and I'll have all the surrounding departments on the lookout for Burns. I've already spoken to hospital security, and they have his photo and know to keep an eye out for him."

She glanced at Garrison, then back at this man. These total strangers, these cops, were on her side? They were going to help her protect Red?

She didn't have to do it alone.

Tears welled in her eyes. She tried to blink them back, to hide the emotion that bubbled up inside of her. "Sorry. I'm just... Thank you."

"Just doing my job," the man said.

The other cop, Eric, snatched a couple of tissues from a box on a table, stood, and handed them to her. "Here you go, ma'am."

Ma'am. He almost sounded like home.

She dried her cheeks and reined in her emotions. "Thank you."

"I'm a little curious, though." The chief looked from her to Garrison and back. "Why would you need a lawyer?"

Garrison stood. "Part of that long story."

"Sounds like a story I need to hear now," the chief said.

Garrison just laughed. "Thanks for coming, guys. I'll take it from here." He shuffled the two cops out the door.

After they walked out, Sam walked in. Garrison closed the door while Sam sat beside Harper. "I'm working on putting together a group of people who can sit with Red. I'll help, of course. And Jack suggested Ginny, his real estate—"

"Wait." Harper leaned away. What was she talking about? "That's my job. I don't need help."

Garrison sat on the other side of her. "You have to go to Maryland and get this cleared up."

"What?" She turned to him, tried to figure out what he'd said. "I can't do that. I have to stay. He had a heart attack. He needs me."

"The hospital is keeping him for a couple of days. You can get to Maryland and back before he's released."

"But what if they arrest me? What if they throw me in jail?"

On her other side, Sam took her hand, but Harper snatched it away and stood. She turned to face them. "No. I can't."

A knock sounded, and then Jack stepped in.

She stared at him. Did he know what was going on?

Whose side was he on? She hadn't done anything wrong, but they were all against her.

"Why aren't you with Red?"

"A couple of cops came in to take his statement." He turned to Garrison. "Friends of yours?"

Garrison nodded. "She met them."

"What'd you tell them?" Jack asked.

"Nothing about the murders," Garrison said. "Just about Derrick."

Jack stared at the man a moment, then focused on her. "You okay?"

"He wants me to leave Gramps here and go to Maryland."

Garrison rose, too. They seemed to be in some sort of three-person stand-off. Garrison blew out a breath. "What did you think, that you were just going to be able to pretend it didn't happen? Two men have been murdered, Harper. You have information about those murders. They have evidence—"

"I didn't do anything. What evidence could they have?"

"I don't know," Garrison said. "I do know that as we speak, technicians are combing the Burns house, looking for more."

"Why? How would they—?"

"I called them," he said. "I told them the Cadillac likely belonged to Red Burns."

Panic rose like a tornado in May. "They didn't die at the house!" Her voice was too high, but she couldn't control it. "I didn't do it. I didn't kill anybody."

Jack took her hand. "Until you go and tell them your side of the story—"

"I can't! They won't believe me. They'll throw me in prison. And then Red—"

"He'll be taken care of." The words came from Sam. She stood and walked to Harper's other side. "We'll take care of him until you get back. That's what I started to tell you. Somebody's going to stay with him, either in his room or outside his door, constantly until his grandson is located. And hospital security will be watching out for him."

So Red would be protected. At least for now. And she'd turn herself in. She could already feel the handcuffs. "But what if...?" She looked at Garrison, at Sam. Then she focused on Jack. "What if they don't believe me? What if I don't come back?"

"If the worst happens," he said, "I'll hire you the best attorney money can buy. You didn't do it. They won't convict you."

"But what about when Red gets out of the hospital?"

"I'll take care of him," Jack said. "God forbid you end up in jail, I'll take him back to Maryland. I'll stay with him until you can again. And I'll be close."

"What? You can't—"

"And I'm going with you tonight."

Tonight.

They wanted her to go now.

To face the nightmare she'd left in Maryland.

To tell the police everything.

To trust that this time, this time, the justice system would get it right.

And then, his words registered. "You're coming with me?"

"Of course." He stepped closer, kissed her forehead. "We're in this together."

CHAPTER THIRTY-SIX

Derrick cursed himself again.

Why had he let up? Another thirty seconds, a minute at most, and Gramps would have been dead. There would have been no autopsy for an eighty-five-year-old man with health problems. Nobody would have questioned it.

Derrick could have slipped out the back door, returned to Maryland, and been there to receive the sad news that his grandfather had passed away.

And then he would have inherited everything. He wouldn't have had the money within a week, but knowing the inheritance was coming would have satisfied Quentin.

Now... Now he had no idea what to do. Because now Gramps knew how desperate Derrick was. And Harper had already known. Had they told the police? Were they looking for him?

Derrick had been in his rental in the hospital parking lot for hours. He'd followed the ambulance here. Then, he saw Harper arrive with a man. Was it Jack, the man Gramps had told him about? Were they together now?

The anger rose again. Harper belonged to Derrick. He'd

rescued her from that dreary life in Vegas, wiping geriatric butts for a living, working two jobs just to make ends meet. He'd loved her, provided a home for her, given her gifts. He'd tried to be the man she wanted, the man she needed. And she'd betrayed him. And apparently, she'd already moved on.

As if Derrick had never mattered at all.

But he did matter. He did! If Harper didn't see that... Why didn't Harper see that? Why didn't she realize what kind of man Derrick was? How important he was?

Well, if she didn't, who cared? He'd show her. He'd show them all.

He itched to hit a casino, to prove his worth once and for all. To fix this with one hand of cards. He'd do it, too. Except right now, Quentin had no idea where Derrick was. If he set foot in any casino in the country, Quentin would hear about it. And the last thing Derrick needed was to have another run-in with the loan shark and his goons. He had nothing to give them. The cash he'd gotten from Roger was nearly gone, thanks to the wild goose chase he'd been on this week.

So a casino was out. Derrick could run, far and fast. Except Quentin would eventually find him. Derrick knew how Quentin dealt with people who tried to skip out on their debts.

He rubbed his eyes, as he'd done a thousand times since Vegas, to assure himself they were both there.

No, running away wasn't an option. He had to get the money to pay Quentin back. And he only had a couple more days to do it.

Assuming Gramps remembered what happened, would anybody believe him? Nobody had seen Derrick in town, and the dementia sometimes made Gramps say crazy things. Maybe if Harper hadn't figured out about the poison, nobody would believe Gramps now.

Except Harper would believe him. And if she hadn't put

two-and-two together about the Gatorade before, she probably would now.

So... Derrick would come up with a plan. He could deny he'd been at the other man's house, deny he'd smothered his grandfather. He could admit to having been in New Hampshire, tell the police he'd come to find his grandfather. That Harper had stolen him away, and he'd been searching. All that was true. And plausible.

He could say he'd gone to the food bank where Gramps had called him from and watched, but the place was deserted by the time he got there. So he'd planned to go back the next day. He'd been watching for them. That made sense, right?

It would be Derrick's word against Gramps's.

Without evidence, nobody could convict him.

But they could arrest him.

He'd seen two men arrive earlier who looked like cops. Their dark sedan was still parked against the curb near the ER doors. They were probably taking statements right this moment.

Derrick had to get out of there.

He had to figure out how to keep tabs on Harper without following her too closely.

He mulled the problem over. Would she stay with the guy in the pickup? Would that eventually lead Derrick to where she lived? Maybe he could duct tape a cell phone to the bottom of the truck, then use an app to track it.

There had to be a cheaper option. He pulled out his cell and searched for ideas. Yes, a GPS tracker that would report their every move, and it was on sale at a store in town. It was a risk to leave here, but surely Gramps wouldn't be released from the hospital anytime soon. Harper would stay by his side. So Derrick should have time.

He backed out of his parking space and drove down the aisle where the pickup had parked, snapping a photo of its license plate, just in case. If the truck was gone when Derrick returned, Tank could track it for him. The private investigator had sworn off helping him, but the man could be persuaded.

He pulled out of the parking lot and headed for the store, where he bought two trackers, just in case he needed one for Harper's car, too, assuming he ever found it. He was back in thirty minutes. The pickup was still there. Derrick parked close to it, downloaded the app he'd need to track the devices. When he had a strong signal, he made sure nobody was watching and duct-taped the tracker to the underside of the pickup. Not exactly the way the instructions had written it up, and if the truck went through puddles, the device would likely be ruined, but he had no other choices right now.

Derrick climbed back into his rental and drove away. At least he had that problem solved. By the time he figured out where Harper was staying, he'd have made a plan.

He could still make this work. He had to get the money out of Gramps. Derrick had failed to kill him, and now Gramps would change his will. Which meant Derrick would have to find a way to compel Gramps to hand over the money.

Gramps wouldn't do it to save Derrick's life. He'd already made that clear. But he'd do anything to save Harper's.

That was Derrick's only hope.

CHAPTER THIRTY-SEVEN

Harper watched as Jack settled her suitcase into the backseat of his pickup and thought about the contents inside. What was the proper attire for surrendering to the police? Should she plan to wear slacks and a nice blouse, try to show them that she was a normal person, a trustworthy professional? Or would that make it look as if she were trying too hard?

Did it matter what she wore? What she said? When she walked into that police station, would they see a twenty-eight-year-old healthcare worker who loved the old man she cared for as if he were her own grandfather? Would they see a woman who'd done everything in her power to protect him?

Or would they see an ex-con who'd run?

She couldn't think about it or she'd melt into a puddle of fear.

Jack's phone rang, and he walked away and answered it.

She and Jack had already been to his house so he could pick up a few things. He'd insisted she stay by his side, just in case Derrick was close. She hadn't argued. Derrick *was* close. As stupid as it would sound if she said it out loud, she knew she was being watched. Eyes on her burned like the Vegas sun. Somebody was watching her. She'd forgotten the way she'd always felt, as if danger lurked around every corner. Back in Vegas, and even in Maryland, it had been so frequent that the anxiety had felt like it was part of her. And then she'd come here to this idyllic little town, and she'd felt safe.

For less than two weeks.

She could hear Jack talking quietly on the phone. Probably making arrangements for this last-minute trip.

She leaned against the side of his truck and inhaled a deep breath. The fresh country air was perfect. Just what she needed. So unlike the stale recycled air in prison.

Harper couldn't go back. She couldn't.

Was she really doing this? Was she really going to walk into a police station and tell them her story? And trust they'd believe her?

They wouldn't. And then she'd end up behind bars. Again. For a crime she hadn't committed. Again.

Her gaze shifted to the forest behind the house. She could run, just take off into the woods.

Right. How long would she last on the run? Hiding from Derrick had been one thing. But hiding from the police and... Garrison was former FBI, so they'd be on her trail. She probably wouldn't last a day. And when they caught her, they'd never believe her story.

Anyway, even if Jack and his friends would take care of Red, Red would never understand why she'd abandoned him.

After what Derrick had done, her leaving might just kill the old man.

She had no choice. She had to go back to Maryland. She had to face whatever was coming and trust that the police would at least listen to her side of the story. This time, she wouldn't go alone. Garrison had already compiled a list of defense attorneys.

She'd make calls while Jack drove. An attorney on her side... This time, they'd believe her.

She told herself that, but nausea rose anyway.

Jack hung up the phone and walked toward her. "You okay?"

She crossed her arms against the chill in the air. "I'm ready."

He studied her. "You're white as a sheet."

"I'm scared."

He raised his eyebrows. "Did you kill those men?"

The question threw her. She blurted, "No."

"Were you trying to kill Red?"

"Of course not."

He leaned in and kissed her cheek. "Let's trust the Lord on this one, okay?"

She had no idea how to do that.

Jack added, "Jesus said, 'The truth will set you free.' Do you believe that?"

The truth hadn't set her free before. It had landed her in prison. But... she'd been guilty before. Not of murder, but of plenty of other stuff. She'd been guilty, and she'd served two years. As awful as it had been, prison had changed her. She'd come out determined to live right. She'd emerged sober, wiser about men and all the relationship issues she'd had before. She'd given up her dream of fame and fortune and gotten the job at the nursing home, where her favorite patient had told her about Jesus. Then she'd met Derrick. She'd been fooled at first, but when he'd shown his true colors, she'd ended that relationship. And through Derrick, she'd met Red, who'd told her more about Jesus. She'd believed in her Savior, and she'd been set free from her past because of Him. Prison had been awful, but it had been the beginning of this walk of faith.

"I do believe it," she said. "Maybe I won't be physically free, but He has set me free from my past."

Jack stepped nearer. He took both her hands, looked into her eyes, and smiled. "I believe He means to set you free from all of it, right now. On the other side of this storm, you're going to find peace. And I'm just happy to be along for the ride."

She let out a short laugh that surprised both of them. "You might be a little bit crazy."

"I've been called worse." He wrapped his arms around her.

When his lips touched hers, those worries floated away like vapor. He tasted of confidence and love. How could she not trust this man who'd done so much for her already? Who was willing to go on this journey with her, to keep her safe, to stand by her through all the ugliness that was surely to come.

Maybe Jack was right. Maybe this was the beginning of the end. Maybe, soon, she would be safe.

Maybe this time, the truth really would set her free.

III

BEAUTY IN BATTLE

For my uncle, Tracy Freeny.
You impacted the world one person at a time. The fragrance of
Christ lingered wherever you went.
You will be missed.

CHAPTER ONE

Darkness swallowed Harper's rental home even before Jack navigated his pickup around a corner. She leaned against the cold window and restrained the sigh that wanted out. To quote Yogi, it was déjà vu all over again.

When she'd first navigated the streets of Nutfield, rain and fear and exhaustion had made the little town seem scary, even sinister. Now that she was leaving, she knew better.

She'd like to tell herself she'd see the house again, see this town again, see Red again. But she'd fallen into that trap before.

When she'd hugged her parents good-bye, taken off to Los Angeles to see her name in lights, hadn't she been sure she'd go back home to Kansas someday? Go back to flaunt her glorious success? What a naïve, foolish girl she'd been. She hadn't been home, and now she'd never go, never have the opportunity to beg her parents for their forgiveness, to rebuild the bridges she'd torched with her own stupid choices.

When she'd left LA to take a job in Vegas, the move should have been temporary. Once she had some stage experience, she'd told herself, she could return to LA and resume the auditions that, she'd been sure, would lead to that big acting job. But somehow the dry landscape of Vegas had sucked her in like quicksand, and she'd never seen LA again.

When she'd realized fame and fortune weren't in her future, she'd gone to nursing school. She'd quit after receiving her certificate as a nurses' aid, but she'd been sure she'd go back. As soon as she got her life together, found a better job, and kicked the bad habits she'd picked up, she'd achieve her new dream of becoming a registered nurse.

But she'd never return to that, either.

When she'd left Emmitt and Barry sleeping after discovering she'd unwittingly been part of a robbery—and murder—she'd gone to the police station to tell the truth. She'd been sure she'd return to their shared apartment. After Emmitt and Barry were arrested, she'd foolishly thought she'd have a chance to pack her things and go home to Kansas. She'd long since given up on her dream of fame and adventure. Then, all she'd wanted was freedom.

Instead, she'd landed in prison.

And now she'd found a new home in this little town of Nutfield, New Hampshire. She'd found friends, a job, a life here. She'd found Jack. But the senseless cycle of her life continued.

Red, the man she'd claimed as her grandfather, was in a hospital after a heart attack had almost killed him, and she wasn't where she should be—by his side.

Beside her, Jack checked the rearview mirror.

Bright November stars twinkled beyond the trees and hills that surrounded this idyllic place. At the junction of the main road, Jack turned toward the highway, not toward town. The farther they moved from Nutfield, the more her anxiety heightened. She clenched her fists and relaxed them, trying to settle her nerves.

"It's going to be okay," Jack said.

"Based on what?" Harper hadn't meant the words to sound so harsh. But really, what did Jack know about anything? He'd only discovered her true story by digging around and running a background check. Yippee for him, he'd found out about her felony record. Had it really been that very day that he'd led Garrison—former FBI—right to her door?

His hand left the wheel and reached toward hers. She readjusted her position and slipped her fingers beneath her thigh. He'd brought the feds, or the almost feds, into the picture, hadn't he? Maybe not on purpose, but he'd led them right to her door. If she'd packed and picked up Red, Derrick wouldn't have gotten to him, nearly suffocated him.

Although, maybe Derrick would have followed Harper. Maybe she and Red would both be Derrick's victims by now. Maybe Jack had saved their lives.

She didn't know what to think.

Just thirty minutes before, Jack had calmed her with a kiss, a kiss that had made her feel both secure and loved. But that feeling had flitted away like all the dreams she'd ever carried.

He blew out a long breath. "We've talked about this. You don't want to keep running, do you? Eventually, the police will catch up with you. It'll be better if you tell them what you know."

"That's the problem, Jack. I don't know anything. I have no idea who killed those men. I have no idea how they ended up in the living room of Red's house. I have no idea who they were working for. The police should be looking for Derrick. He can tell them a lot more than I can."

"Be that as it may"—he cut a glance at her on the curvy, tree-lined road—"they're looking for you."

"I didn't do it."

Another deep sigh. "I know you didn't."

They'd been over this, over and over it. She didn't want to talk about it anymore.

Jack checked the rearview mirror again.

She swiveled in the passenger seat and looked behind them. Beyond the glow of the taillights, nothing but black. She faced Jack. "What are you looking for back there?"

"Making sure we're not being followed."

Acid flooded her stomach, and she looked behind again as if headlights could be conjured from his words. Still, they were alone on the country road.

"And?" she asked, almost afraid of the answer.

"Nobody's back there." He glanced at her and offered a quick smile. "We're safe."

Safe. What would that feel like? On the other hand, that skin-crawling feeling she'd had off and on since Vegas had vanished. For now.

"It's too late to drive to Maryland. We should at least wait until tomorrow." She threw the words out there, though she'd been making the same argument for hours.

"I agree," Jack said.

Her head snapped to face him. "Since when? You insisted we get on the road."

"I didn't want to say so at the house. With Derrick in town, I wasn't sure... I mean, it's crazy to think he knows where you live, but he did find your... find Red, so he could have found the house. I was afraid he might be listening. Which is ridiculous, maybe. I'm no spy. I'm no good at all this cloak-and-dagger stuff. I just wanted to get you out of there."

She nearly smiled, but then the words penetrated. "You think Derrick could have been nearby?"

Jack shrugged. "Seems stupid now. He's obviously not following us." He checked the rearview again. "But at the time..."

She shook off the thought of Derrick watching her and focused on the other thing he'd said. "So we're not going to Maryland?"

They reached the junction to Route 101, and he merged onto the highway toward Manchester, sliding in among the line of cars, trucks, and SUVs. After one more glance in the rearview, he repeated, "We're safe."

Wouldn't safe be nice?

"We are going to Maryland, Harper." He reached for her hand and squeezed. "But I'm with you. In all of it."

She didn't pull away. She couldn't bring herself to because, as afraid as she was of what was coming, she couldn't imagine doing this without Jack by her side. How had he become so important, so vital to her well-being in the short time they'd known each other? Frustrated as she was at the situation, at least she had Jack believing in her.

"We're not making the whole drive tonight," he said. "I wanted to get you out of Nutfield and away from Derrick. I'm sorry I didn't tell you before, but I wasn't really sure what the plan was. Garrison's been in touch with the police department investigating the murders, and we're meeting with the detective tomorrow at two p.m. I figure if we can get three hours of the drive in tonight, we can take our time tomorrow."

"Three hours will put us where?"

"About New Haven."

She and Red had driven through New Haven just a few weeks before, but they hadn't stopped. She'd been desperate that day to put as much geography between herself and any Maryland cops as possible.

"It's going to be okay." How many times had Jack repeated those words? Ten, fifteen, fifty?

She huffed. "It's not like I have a choice. Now that the cops know where I am."

"If you'd been honest with me from the get-go—"

"If you hadn't decided to do a background check on me, none of this would have happened."

He released her hand and gripped the steering wheel. "You can't be on the run for the rest of your life. I'm trying to help you get free of it."

Free. Jack Rossi knew nothing about freedom, nor did he understand the cost when it was taken away.

Harper knew. She'd been in prison once before. Was she about to go back?

CHAPTER TWO

Derrick Burns checked the locator app on his phone screen. He was about three miles behind the pickup truck, three miles behind Harper and her new friend. He'd asked Tank to run the man's license plate. So, Harper's latest victim was one Jack Rossi, owner of a real estate management company in Nutfield. Small-time loser.

With a face like Harper's—and a body to match—Derrick wasn't surprised she'd found some patsy to help her. Men tripped all over themselves when she batted those blue eyes or swished those hips. Even his grandfather had succumbed to her spell. And, sure, Derrick had fallen for her tricks, too. Moved her from her crappy little studio apartment in Vegas to his grandfather's home in Maryland. From poverty to luxury, all thanks to his own stupidity.

He'd cared for her. He'd loved her. And all he'd asked was that she help him impress his clients, put in a good word with Gramps. She'd done exactly the opposite, screwing up his career and turning his grandfather against him. And then, when his life had fallen apart, she'd just moved on. Moved on to a healthier host like the parasite she was.

After Derrick planted the device on Rossi's pickup, he'd tracked them to a little neighborhood in Nutfield. He hadn't stayed close, but he had driven by a few minutes after they'd gotten there, and he'd seen Harper's beat-up VW Jetta in one driveway, the pickup in the next. Apparently, they were neighbors, Harper and Rossi. He watched from down the street, saw Rossi toss a suitcase into the back of his truck. Together, they'd gone to Harper's house. Seemed they were going on a trip together.

With the address saved on his phone, Derrick had headed to Manchester, found a pawn shop, and used almost the last of his money to purchase a handgun. He knew very little about firearms, so he'd picked the cheapest pistol in the case and grabbed a box of ammo to go with it. He hadn't been thrilled about the paperwork, but the man behind the counter didn't raise an eyebrow at Derrick's Maryland driver's license, and he didn't enter the information on any computer. Maybe he would later. Maybe not. All Derrick knew was that, in order to pull off his plan, he needed a weapon. He'd deal with the fallout later.

The red dot on the tracker had alerted him just as he was getting ready to head back to Nutfield. They were moving toward him. His heartbeat double timed. Yes, sir. Let them come.

He grabbed a burger and fries, which he ate in the car not far from the on-ramp. As they neared, he slid right in behind them. Eventually, they'd stop, and he'd make his move. Once he snatched Harper, he'd make a phone call to Gramps demanding money.

If Gramps had only given Derrick what he'd asked for, none of this would be necessary. He could still see the suspicion in that wrinkly face when Derrick had asked him for money a few months back. Gramps hadn't believed Derrick had an investment opportunity, as if it were ludicrous that Derrick could actually make him money. Because Gramps had zero faith in Derrick and his abilities as a stock broker. Never mind that he made money for his clients every day. Never mind that he'd started with next to nothing and made himself a wealthy man. Gramps just saw him as a screw-up. This was Gramps's fault.

Of course, Harper held her share of the blame for what would happen next.

And then there was Rossi.

Jack Rossi had better stay out of his way. Because Derrick had to get that money, and the only way to it was through Gramps. And the only way to get Gramps to loosen his fist on the money was through Harper.

If Rossi—or Harper—tried to stop him... Well, that's why he'd bought the gun.

CHAPTER THREE

Jack checked behind them again. They were outside Worcester, Massachusetts, and the traffic was thick, even at nearly nine o'clock at night. Nobody had followed them out of town, and only dumb luck would have Derrick stumbling across them now. It hadn't been luck that pointed Derrick to the rec center and Red. That had been Red's phone call to his grandson.

No, Derrick had failed to kill the old man. If he had half a brain, he'd already be on the far side of the Canadian border.

That's what Jack kept telling himself. But he'd learned over the years that it paid to be cautious. Hence his continued vigilance and his plan to get Harper out of Nutfield. He wasn't about to give Derrick access to her.

They'd driven nearly a hundred miles, and he figured he could let down his guard. They were safe. He planned to keep them that way until they arrived at the police station in Maryland. After that, it would be the job of the cops to find Derrick and bring him to justice.

He'd hoped Harper might relax on the journey, maybe even

drift off to sleep, but she was sitting erect and staring at the tail-lights in front of them.

"You okay?" he asked.

"Sure."

There was a lie if he'd ever heard one. "You don't seem okay."

"Just wondering where I'll be this time tomorrow."

"Do you want to stay at Red's house tomorrow night? Or will that be too scary after the last time you were there?"

Her silence lasted so long, he chanced another glance. She was looking at him as if he were crazy. "I was thinking more like would I be in jail."

"You're not going to jail."

Another long pause. Then, "I hope you're right. I'm just going to say this one more time. I know you think I'm crazy, but I'm telling you, there's a very good chance they'll lock me up."

"On what charge?"

"Murder."

"Garrison doesn't think you're going to have any trouble."

She muttered something that sounded like, "Only if my luck changes."

"Harper." He glanced toward her to make sure she was listening. Her eyes were wide, her mouth pinched at the corners. She had the look of defeat as if nothing he said could make a difference. That didn't mean he wouldn't try. He shifted into the middle lane and fell in behind a sedan. "Harper, honey, you're going to tell the truth, get free of the suspicion surrounding you, and move on with your life." He paused to let that take hold. "I don't know what that new life is going to look like—what you want it to look like."

He knew what he wanted—Harper with him in Nutfield. But she was so attached to Red, and Red's home was in Maryland. Would she return with the old man to be his caretaker? Where would that leave Jack?

Could he go with her? Would she want him to?

He didn't know, but he wasn't about to lose her. Angry as she was at him right now, angry and frightened and defensive, he'd seen her heart. He knew just what kind of woman Harper Cloud was, and he wasn't about to let her go. Not now. And if he had his way, not ever.

He forced himself to gloss over all those unanswered questions. "Whatever you want, your future's about to open up wide. You don't need Derrick or Red to take care of you. These last few weeks, you've proved you can take care of yourself and then some. You're going to make a fresh start."

"Jack." He didn't miss the frustration in her voice. "People like me don't get fresh starts. There are no new beginnings for former strippers and ex-cons. Only baggage and more baggage until life looks like... like the back end of a Beverly Hillbillies' truck."

Nice visual, but he'd never associate it with the beautiful woman beside him. He didn't know how to convince her she was wrong. He hoped by this time tomorrow she'd at least have begun to believe in her future. In their future.

"I know I can't," she said, "but everything in me wants to just... just run away."

He thought back to that afternoon, to the sight of her tossing her suitcases in her car, preparing to do just that. To leave without saying good-bye. At the time, he'd been so guilt-ridden about getting Garrison involved, his other feelings had taken a backseat. But now, anger had him tightening his grip on the steering wheel. "That's what you do, isn't it? Run away. First sign of trouble in Maryland, and you run to New Hampshire. Before that, things got hard in Vegas, so you ran to Maryland. Same with LA and Vegas. What was so awful back in Kansas that you took off to LA? Have you ever stuck out anything difficult?"

"You know nothing about me. You have no idea—"

"Because everything with you is a secret!" He clamped his lips shut, took two deep breaths, and started again with a gentler tone. "I want to know you. But you haven't allowed me to. You didn't trust me with the truth."

"I didn't know you. How could I have known how you would react? What you would think? You don't know anything about my life, about the things I've been through."

"Maybe my life isn't as complicated as yours, but at least I've shared it with you." The tires rumbled beneath them, filling the silence. After a minute he added, "At least I've been honest with you."

"And how would that have gone over? 'Hi, I'm Harper. Former stripper, ex-con, and running from the law. Nice to meet you.'"

"At least it would've been the truth."

She uttered a soft *pfft* and faced forward, arms crossed.

Excellent. That had gone well.

He was right.

And he was totally wrong.

Why would she have confided in him? She hadn't known him, and she'd had a lot of experience with untrustworthy men. Even if Jack had started their relationship well, he'd ended by doing a background check on her and then thinking the worst.

He was the jerk here, not her.

He let a few more miles slide beneath the wheels of the truck before he said, "I'm sorry. I know it hasn't been easy for you."

In the silence that followed, he wondered if she'd given up speaking to him altogether. And then she said, "You've done nothing but try to help me. I'm just scared."

He reached across the front seat and took her hand in his. It was cool and tense. He lifted it to his lips and kissed her knuckles. "I know. And although I can't make any promises, I know the One who does make promises. Let's keep trusting God to work it out."

CHAPTER FOUR

———————

Trust God. That seemed like Jack's answer to everything, but Harper wasn't sure how to do it. Oh, she'd heard the stories. The Bible she'd bought was full of stories. Red had more stories about how God had been faithful in the trials Red and his family had faced. He'd convinced her to trust God. What good had it done? What if God let her down the way everybody else did? God was a *He*, after all.

On the other hand, if God wasn't going to help her, she had no hope at all. She needed Red and Jack to be right about God.

"I need to stop for gas," Jack said. "Do you mind fast food?"

"I'm not really hungry."

She didn't feel hungry, but her stomach rumbled at the thought. Had she eaten lunch that day? She didn't think so. Didn't think she'd eaten since toast that morning.

He pulled into a service area and parked, then walked around to open Harper's door. The place was empty but for the folks working the counters and an older, gray-haired woman, who was spraying and wiping down tables and chairs. There was a retail area on the far side filled with souvenirs and travel accessories and everything one might find at a convenience store.

Jack led her past the kiosks filled with travel brochures and around the many tables to the counters, where they found a plethora of choices. Auntie Anne's pretzels, D'Angelo's sandwiches, and Papa Gino's pizza, not to mention a coffee shop and an ice cream shop. "What sounds good?" he asked.

None of it, but she knew she'd eat once food was in front of her. "You pick."

"The pizza smells delicious, but I don't want to wait. Let's do grinders."

Grinders? "Where I come from, a grinder is a power tool."

He grinned. "You'd probably call it a sub, but you'd be wrong."

"If you say so. Let's split something. Anything. Just no olives. Or hot peppers."

He ordered a large steak-and-cheese and two drinks, and they sat at one of the many empty tables. The grilled sub was good, but that feeling had come back, the feeling that she was being watched, that she wasn't safe.

She looked toward the doors, the windows, the hallway leading to the bathrooms. Paranoia wasn't her best quality.

She was hungrier than she'd realized and continued working on her sandwich and sipping her drink, trying to focus on the meal and not how exposed she felt.

People came in, wandered through the store, used the restroom. Most stayed away from the food court. It was late for dinner. She looked at every person who walked in. Of course Derrick wasn't among them.

"What's wrong?" Jack asked.

She rubbed her arms. "Nothing. Why?"

"You've looked over your shoulder about ten times."

"Oh. Nothing. Just…" She glanced toward the windows and

the gas pumps beyond. Unlike the restaurant and store, the pumps were busy, crowded with travelers. There was nothing out of the ordinary. Nobody watching her.

He looked out there, too, eyes narrowed. "You seem spooked."

"Just a feeling."

He said nothing—probably didn't think it was worth the effort to argue with her—and finished his portion of the sandwich. When she'd eaten all she could, he gathered their trash and dumped it in the can.

She stood. "I need to use the bathroom."

He nodded toward the restroom sign. "Just come out to the pumps when you're done. I'm going to fill the tank."

He was leaving her alone? But what if... She looked down the hall beyond the restrooms. There were a couple of doors, one beneath an exit sign. Who knew where the other led. But wherever it was, she was safe. Jack had assured her they hadn't been followed. She didn't need to be afraid.

"I can wait for you," Jack nodded toward the bathroom. "We're in no hurry."

"No." She forced a smile. "I'll meet you outside."

He studied her a long moment.

"Really, I'm just being paranoid. It's fine."

He nodded and turned toward the door.

She used the facilities and washed her hands, smiling politely to the young mother and little girl beside her. After they stepped out she looked at herself in the mirror. She looked tired, haggard, and older than her years. She considered putting on lipstick but figured if she did, then she'd look tired and haggard and like she was trying too hard.

As she stepped out of the restroom, an alarm sounded.

The old woman who'd been cleaning rushed toward her

from the dining room, her focus beyond Harper. "Hey! You can't go that way."

Harper turned toward the exit door at the end of the hall. A man, barely visible in the dim light, turned and stepped back out. Harper barely glimpsed him, yet something about him—the height, the build... Her heart thundered in her chest.

The door slammed, and the alarm silenced.

The woman brushed past Harper, shoved open the door. Over the sound of the again-screeching alarm, she screamed, "Stop!"

A moment passed while Harper stared at the woman, told herself to run.

The woman stepped back in, swiveled, and stomped toward Harper. Behind her, the door slammed again, and silence again filled the space.

"Thieves," the old woman muttered. "Wonder what that one got away with."

The entire thing happened in less than thirty seconds. Not until the woman was out of sight did the panic rise. Harper stifled a scream. She ran down the hall, through the store, and out the door into the chilly night.

Jack was twisting the cap onto the gas tank.

"Jack!"

He hurried to meet her.

"He's here. Derrick is here. I just saw him."

"What?"

"He's here!"

"Okay, okay." He shuffled her to the passenger door and settled her inside. As soon as she slid into the seat, she slammed the door and locked it. Jack ran around and climbed in. "Tell me what happened."

"Drive! We have to get out of here!"

Jack started the pickup, exited the truck stop, and merged onto I-90.

She recounted the events, forcing herself to sound rational, not crazy.

"So you're saying a man was going out the back door, and you think it was Derrick?"

"It *was* Derrick. I swear, it was. And I think he was coming in, not going out."

"Tell me again what he looked like."

"I didn't get a good look at his face." Any look at his face. Just the back of his head. "But I swear it was him."

"Okay, but..."

The *but* said it all.

"You don't believe me."

He swallowed and cut a glance at her. "It's not that I don't believe you, it's just that—"

"You don't believe me. That's exactly what it is."

"Harper. It's dark out." He gestured toward the windows, in case she was too thick to understand the word *dark*. "Isn't it possible you saw a man who looked like Derrick?"

"I know it sounds crazy, but it was him. I'm..." She wanted to say she was certain, but was she, really?

At least a mile rumbled beneath them before he said, "What was he wearing?"

Wearing? She had no idea.

"Jeans? Slacks?"

She closed her eyes, tried to picture the scene. All she saw was dark clothing. "I think jeans. Maybe."

"Did he have on a jacket?"

"I wasn't paying attention to that."

"Okay."

Again with the *okay*. The sure-you-saw-him-except-I-think-you're-crazy okay.

But she wasn't crazy. She wasn't. It had been Derrick.

Or, maybe she was crazy. Maybe she was seeing Derrick everywhere now. Maybe her mind had finally slipped its last gear. Maybe she couldn't trust her eyes anymore. Her ears. Her brain.

Jack reached for her again. This time, she didn't bother to pull away. Jack was right. She'd conjured Derrick's image in her panic. She hadn't seen the man's face at all. Hadn't seen his hair color, hadn't seen glasses, hadn't seen eyes. She hadn't seen anything except the back of a head in a dark night.

Anyway, how in the world could Derrick have tracked them down at a truck stop off the highway?

They were safe. *Dear God, please let us be safe.*

CHAPTER FIVE

Derrick pounded the steering wheel until his fist ached. He'd chosen to step in through the back door rather than the front because he hadn't wanted to be seen. He figured eventually she'd go to the bathroom, and that's when he'd make his move. They'd been on the road for hours. Surely she'd have to go. No guarantees, but it had been the only plan he could come up with on short notice.

All that studying of the doors while Harper and Rossi ate had come to nothing. Derrick had seen an old lady take the trash out the back. The door had closed behind her, then opened easily when she'd returned from the dumpster, so Derrick knew it wasn't locked, and no alarm had sounded. Maybe she'd disabled the alarm before she'd stepped out.

If he'd known about the alarm, obviously he'd have gone in through the front and forced Harper out the back. Yes, the alarm would have sounded, but they'd have stepped out, gotten into his waiting car, and been gone before anybody would have seen. By the time Rossi realized she wasn't coming out, they'd have been long gone. By now, Derrick would have called the hospital, asked for Gramps's room, and made his demand.

Gramps would have transferred the money right away, and then...

Derrick didn't know what would happen then. He'd let Harper go, of course. He wasn't a killer. But Harper had held out on him. For months she'd held out on him. Her and her beautiful face and her perfect body, a body he knew wasn't pure and innocent. A body that had been touched by plenty of guys. Just not Derrick. After he'd cared for her, gotten her a job, found her a place to live, she'd still held out on him. So he wouldn't kill her, and he wouldn't take anything from her he wasn't owed.

He was owed plenty.

Once he finished with her, he'd have to make sure she wasn't found before he'd had a chance to escape, just in case Gramps and Harper decided to turn him in.

Which they would. Of course they would. And the fact that Gramps had claimed to love Derrick, the fact that Harper had claimed to care for him—those facts wouldn't matter one bit to them.

So Derrick would have to pay Quentin back and then run.

That was fine. He'd been gone from his job so long, he figured they'd already given his clients to other brokers. His firm wasn't known for loyalty. He was upside down on his condo and his car, so it wasn't as if he really had anything of value to lose. Derrick would be better off getting a new identity and starting fresh somewhere else. New name, new home, new friends, new job. Maybe not as a stockbroker—too hard to fake that license. But a stockbroker was just a salesman who dealt in paper money, and Derrick could sell sand to a beach bum. Cars, houses, computers—he could sell anything.

Yes, that was the answer. Snatch Harper, get what he was owed from Gramps and from her, then stow her away long enough to escape, get on the far side of the country. Maybe San Francisco or Seattle. Somewhere near the ocean.

A new life. That's what he needed.

First, he had to focus on paying back Quentin, his psychopathic moneylender, before the man lost his patience.

Thank God Harper hadn't seen him. He'd caught sight of her stepping out of the restroom—if not for the alarm, his plan would have worked perfectly—and he'd shifted before she'd turned toward him. No way she could have recognized him.

Fine. He'd bide his time. Eventually, he'd snatch her and get Gramps to hand over the money. Between now and then, he needed to come up with a plan of escape once he got his cash.

CHAPTER SIX

J ack was almost certain Harper had been wrong about
seeing Derrick at the truck stop.

Almost.

While he drove, he tried to convince himself they were safe.
But his gaze kept drifting to the rearview mirror. Something in
his gut told him to trust her instincts.

Maybe she wasn't being melodramatic. Maybe she was right
about Derrick following them. For that matter, maybe she was
right about the police. Maybe they would throw her in jail.

He glanced at her, but her gaze was fixed on the side mirror,
watching behind them just like Jack.

She was terrified.

Finally, they made it through New Haven, and Jack pulled
off the highway after a blue sign promised a host of hotel
options. He found two side-by-side, parked the pickup in the
darkest corner of the lot at what looked like the dumpier of the
two options. "Let's go."

She climbed out of the truck before he could run around to
open her door.

He reached in the back, got their suitcases, and walked

beside her into the lobby. The man behind the counter was on the phone, so he passed through the small space and looked around. There was a restroom down a short hallway. At the end of that hall was a door that led to the parking lot on the opposite side of where his truck was parked. Perfect. "You need to use the bathroom?"

She nodded and headed that direction.

Jack walked to the counter, set Harper's duffel bag on top of his suitcase, and tried to figure out how to play this. When the man hung up. Jack said, "Have John and Sally Stansfield checked in yet?"

The man behind the counter narrowed his gaze. Then he tapped on his computer. "Don't have anybody here by those names."

"Huh." Jack took out his phone, pretended to look at something. "I swear they said they'd be here."

"Don't have 'em here, don't have a reservation for 'em," the man said. "You have a reservation?"

"No. We were hoping to be in the same hotel as my brother." He smiled at the man, shrugged. "I'll just give them a call. Thanks."

He hoped that had been enough time to make it look as if he was getting a room, on the off chance somebody was watching from outside.

Maybe all those spy movies he'd seen hadn't been a total waste of time.

He pulled the two suitcases down the hallway toward the bathrooms. He stopped just out of sight of the man at the counter.

When Harper stepped out, Jack put his finger over his lips.

Her eyebrows rose, but he just nodded toward the side door.

She followed, no argument, and stepped into the cold night. After the door closed, he said, "We're walking to the hotel next door. If you're right and Derrick is nearby, I figure he'll be watching for us in the hotel where our truck is parked. At least we can sleep without worrying."

"Oh. That's..." She shook her head and held out her hand. "Let me get my bag."

"I've got it." They crossed the parking lot and climbed a short, grassy hill to reach the neighboring lot. He couldn't help looking around. Was Derrick near? Even if he'd followed them somehow, Jack hoped his focus was on the front door or on Jack's pickup. He wouldn't have been watching the far door. Surely.

Finally, they made it to the neighboring hotel and stepped into the lobby. Behind this counter was a forty-something woman in a crisp uniform. "Can I help you?"

"Any chance you have adjoining rooms?"

After a few clicks and a swipe of his credit card, he was handed two room keys, and he and Harper made their way to the elevator.

"I'll find a way to pay you back," Harper said, "for all of this."

Pay him back? Was she serious?

Didn't she understand how much he cared for her? Did she really think he was worried about the money? He tamped down the quick flash of anger. "You don't owe me anything."

"I do. And I have no idea how I'll ever pay—"

"You don't. Stop talking."

He didn't bother to look to see her reaction. He'd been rude. Well, she'd started it.

On the third floor, they followed the signs to their rooms. He handed her a key. When she opened the door, he followed her and set her duffel on the bed nearest the bathroom, figuring she'd prefer the one near the window. "I'll be right next door."

She stood in the middle of the room, arms crossed. "You're angry with me."

He saw the defensiveness for what it was now. Fear. The thought that she might be afraid of him, of what he might think of her, killed his frustration. He stepped close, kissed her forehead. "It's been a very long day. I'm not angry with you, and I hope you're not angry with me. I care about you, so I have a vested interest in your safety—and your freedom." He stepped back. "Okay?"

Her smile was tired, but it was there. "Okay."

He nodded once, stepped into the hallway, and opened his door. His room was a mirror image of hers. Once he'd closed and locked it, he knocked on the adjoining door and then opened his side.

She opened hers. Her smile was a little wider. "There you are again."

Wow, that smile, that real smile, nearly knocked him off his feet. It had been days since he'd seen it. He desperately wanted to step into her room and take her in his arms. But with all those beds, no old man right down the hall... He'd better stay in his own space.

"I'm going to keep my door unlocked," he said. "Go ahead and close yours. Lock it if you want. If you need me, don't hesitate to come in. I mean, knock first, just in case."

She nodded. "Okay." Her smile faltered, and she glanced toward the window. "All that parking next door and walking... Why?"

"Just because you didn't see his face doesn't mean it wasn't Derrick. Someone coming in the back door... It's suspicious."

"So you believe me?"

"I know you're sane, and I trust your instincts. If you think that was Derrick, then maybe it was. I don't know how he could have found us, but I'm not willing to bet your life on it."

She stepped into his room and slid her arms around his waist. A very platonic move that had his heart racing anyway. "Thank you."

He hugged her back, then stepped away before he turned the hug into a kiss and then into something they'd both regret. He rubbed her arms. "Do you need anything right now?"

She shook her head. "Just sleep, I think."

"Okay. Knock when you get up and don't hesitate to wake me if you need anything."

She stepped into her room and left the door between them cracked about an inch. Maybe she felt better knowing he was near.

Knowing how close by she was would only be torture for him.

He brushed his teeth and changed into pajama pants and a T-shirt. He read his Bible on his phone, trying to find some peace, some certainty, in his suddenly very uncertain life. He was reminded of the God who held the world in His capable hands. It felt out of control, but God wasn't worried, so Jack would try not to be, too.

When Harper's light went off, he reached for the switch on his own.

He didn't know how long he'd slept when his eyes popped open.

Derrick couldn't have followed them. Which meant if that man at the truck stop had been Derrick, he had to be tracking them.

But how?

Maybe he'd found a way to hack into the GPS on Jack's pickup. Except the man was a stockbroker, not a computer programmer.

He sat up and was reaching for the light when something stirred in the room.

He turned on his phone, and in the glow of the screen, saw Harper in the adjoining bed.

She was breathing steadily, sound asleep. Maybe she'd been afraid next door. Maybe she'd not been able to sleep. He was glad she'd decided to come in. Very glad she'd felt comfortable enough to do so. But not glad that he'd discovered it, because now there was no way he was going back to sleep.

His phone told him it was almost four a.m. Not quite morning, but close enough.

He dimmed his phone as low as it would go and typed in the search engine, *how to track a car*.

The answer was so obvious, he had to stifle the *duh*. A person could buy a tracker at any electronics store.

He stood, slipped into the bathroom, and dressed. Then he tiptoed through the room, found a pad of paper and a pen, and took them back to the bathroom, where he wrote a note for Harper that he'd be right back. He left the note on his pillow, grabbed his parka, and slipped out through the adjoining room so as not to wake her, pocketing her key on the way.

The overnight dew had turned to frost on the cars. He sprinted across the dark parking lot, down the grassy hill, and across the other hotel's parking lot. He walked behind the building on the off chance Derrick was watching the front door. But if Jack's guess was correct, Derrick was sound asleep somewhere, waiting for the tracker to tell him they were on the move.

He reached his truck, eyes open for people in the other vehicles. Just his luck Derrick would be close by and whack him over the head with something. But the lot seemed empty.

Jack turned on the flashlight app on his phone and crawled under his truck. He shined that thing all around the edges until...

And there it was. A little black box that had been adhered to the underside of the frame with duct tape.

The man at the rest area had been Derrick.

If not for the alarm on the door, he'd have snatched Harper. And done what with her?

The question had Jack's hands clenching into fists, his stomach churning. He closed his eyes, breathed a prayer of thanks to God for protecting her, and set about removing the tracker. Carefully. He didn't want to let on to Derrick that he'd discovered it.

When he had the tracker off the car, he rolled out from beneath it and taped the tracker to the underside of the sedan parked beside him. Maybe that would throw Derrick off for a little while.

Derrick. Who had to be close. Who was just waiting to make his move.

Should Jack move the pickup? No. Not until they were ready to leave. He didn't want Derrick realizing the tracker wasn't on the pickup until they were long gone.

Jack stood, looked around the dark parking lot one more time, and sprinted back to his hotel. Impossible as it seemed, he imagined Derrick at Harper's bedside, forcing her up and out while Jack was out here playing in the parking lot.

By the time he reached the lobby, he was out of breath, but he kept running, past the quiet elevators to the stairs, then bolted up to the third floor. He sprinted to her room, slid the key in the lock, and let himself in.

The door slammed behind him, but he didn't stop until he'd stepped from her room into his. He stopped by her bed.

She sat up, eyes wide.

Afraid, but safe.

Thank God.

CHAPTER SEVEN

Harper's heart pounded as she stared at Jack, who was dressed and wearing his jacket. Even in the dim light coming from the other room, she could see enough of the look on his face—wide eyes, tense jaw—to have her scanning the room for danger.

"What"—she cleared her throat—"what happened?"

"You were right. About Derrick." He sat on the other bed and took a deep breath. "I'm sorry I didn't believe you."

"Where have you been?"

"I went out to check the truck." His gaze met her eyes, then slipped down and popped back up fast.

She pulled the blankets up to cover herself. She was wearing those same ugly, fluffy pajamas she'd put on the night they met, but still. "I'm sorry," she said. "I couldn't sleep, and I just—"

"I'm glad you felt comfortable enough to come in. Should I step out?"

"Just tell me what happened. Please."

He gave her a quick rundown. She wasn't crazy—he'd found

a tracker on the pickup. Just to be sure, though... "So you're saying Derrick was tracking us?"

"I'm guessing he was at the truck stop last night. I'm sorry I doubted you."

She shook her head, worked to form words. Derrick had been so close. So close. And what would he have done if he'd gotten to her? What did he want from her? She didn't have any money to give him. She couldn't help him out of his debt, and she wasn't with Red. So why would he be following her?

It didn't make sense. But the way he'd come after her, through the back of the truck stop...

"I'm sorry," Jack must have taken her silence as anger or frustration with him. "I should have—"

"You didn't do anything wrong. But what does Derrick want with me? Why would he be following me? I knew he wanted to get to Red, but why me? I can't do anything for him."

"I don't know." Jack looked past her. After a moment, he shook his head. "Maybe he thinks you'll be able to talk Red out of his money."

"But he knows I won't," she said.

Jack nodded slowly, then offered a slight, joyless smile. "Maybe he doesn't intend to *ask* you this time."

She didn't want to know what Jack meant, but Jack continued anyway.

"Would you have gone with him willingly?"

"Of course not."

"He had to have been planning to force you into his car. A threat. A weapon. Maybe he planned to use the same thing to get the money."

"Oh." It made sense. Derrick must have decided to... what? Hurt her? Kidnap her at gunpoint? And the only thing that had stopped him was the alarm and that woman cleaning the tables.

The truth of it soaked into her like a cold rain. Derrick

would have shoved her into his car and used her to demand the money from Red. A ransom. And Red would have paid, no doubt. Because he loved Harper just as Harper loved him. And then what would have happened?

She imagined the two men she'd found dead in Red's house weeks before. Bullet holes in their heads. Then, the image shifted, and it was her body lying on the carpet, her head with the bullet hole.

She shuddered and folded her arms, squeezing her eyes closed. All this time... She'd been beaten up by men who'd ended up dead. She'd known she was involved in a dangerous game. But she'd run, and she'd pretended, and she'd grown comfortable.

Every interaction she'd had with Derrick flashed into memory like images in a slideshow. The night she'd met him in Las Vegas, their subsequent dates. The way he'd shown her around his grandfather's house, proud of his home, proud of her. The way he'd held her, kissed her, made her promises. That weekend at the beach, the way he'd come into her bedroom, leaving only when she'd demanded it. The flashes of frustration, of anger. The certainty that his problems were her fault.

He blamed her for his grandfather's refusal to hand over what Derrick considered his due. Now, he planned to use her to extort what he'd been denied.

"Hey." The bed shifted beside her, and Jack's arm slipped around her shoulders.

She turned toward him, buried her head against his neck, and tried to still her trembling limbs.

"You're okay," he said. "You're safe."

Surely, she was. On some level, she believed it, but that was right now in this moment. Still, the feeling remained, the conviction that Derrick was right outside, watching, and no matter what they did, Derrick would eventually catch up to her.

And he would win in the end.

She never won. Never. And she'd pulled Jack into her nightmare. Jack, who even now was rubbing her back, his work-roughened hands surprisingly gentle. He was whispering, cooing, making promises he couldn't keep. Because she wasn't safe, not really. She'd never been safe, not from the moment she'd left her parents' house in Kansas.

She might never be safe again.

But oh, how good it felt to pretend. Here, in Jack's arms, she could pretend there was nothing outside the door. No Derrick. No police. No Red in a hospital room. Just the two of them. Here. Alone. Protected.

She lifted her gaze and stared into his eyes. His gaze shifted from comforting to smoldering in an instant. She angled toward him, desperate for a kiss, for something to make all her terror fall away, even for just a moment.

He met her lips with his, and the passion she felt set her on fire.

She slid her arms around his neck. His fingers dug into the hair at her nape. All her worries, all her fears disappeared until all she thought of was Jack. Holding her. Wanting her.

And then he pulled away and stood, leaving her chilled and alone.

She hadn't known a person could move that fast.

He crossed his arms and moved several feet across the room. "Um... yeah." His voice was gruff. At least he, too, seemed to be breathing heavily. He ran one hand through his hair, stepped into the adjoining room, then came back into his own room and stopped at the door. He looked stricken.

"I'm sorry," she said.

"No." He shook his head. "I'm sorry. You were scared. I was only trying..."

Only trying to comfort her, and she'd practically thrown

herself at him. And he'd rejected her. The shame, the embarrassment, heated her cheeks and made her want to hide. She'd never met a man who wouldn't have accepted the invitation she'd just offered.

Maybe Jack knew what she'd known all along. He was too good for her. Too good to be sullied by her and her history.

She'd run from the room and never see him again if she weren't wearing bright yellow pajamas.

Jack chuckled, and red crept up his neck. "Yeah. That was—"

"I'm so embarrassed," she said. "I don't know what I was... Can you just...? I'm so sorry. I don't want this to change anything. You've done nothing but help me, and I've—"

His laugh had her clamping her mouth shut. "Seriously. Don't apologize. That was..." He shook his head and chuckled again. "Indescribable, apparently. But now's not the time for us to"—he gestured to the bed—"not that you were... but I was definitely... And I respect you too much, care for you too much, to take advantage of... whatever was going on. In your head, I mean. Not that you were..." He laughed again. "Holy smoke. I'm going to shut up now."

All her doubts dissipated like vapor. He hadn't rejected her. He'd protected her from her own fear and stupidity. The thought warmed her all over again, made her giggle.

And he groaned. "I hate to be rude, but maybe, if you go into your room and I stay in here and take a nice cold shower, we can get back to normal."

"Oh." Right. She was in his bedroom. She stood and straightened her pajamas.

He stepped toward the window and pulled the curtains back and stared outside.

She slipped into her own room.

"Make sure your door is double locked." He stepped into

the doorway. "Derrick could be anywhere. We need to assume he's watching us."

Oh. Right.

"Knock if you need anything." Jack stepped back into his room and closed the door.

She checked the hallway door and collapsed on her bed to relive the kiss and the sweet, sweet man who'd sent her away. And who'd done it because he cared about her, because he respected her too much to take advantage.

Wow. She'd never known a man like Jack.

Neither Derrick nor Emmitt had put her first and protected her. In fact, every man she'd ever known would have taken full advantage of her weakness.

But Jack...

Jack was exactly the kind of man she wanted.

No. Jack *was* the man she wanted. Not a man like him. Because there was no other man like him in the world.

Harper stepped into the shower, thoughts of Jack still in her mind. Until thoughts of Derrick intruded, along with the fact that she'd be turning herself in to the police later today, where she'd be arrested and processed and handcuffed.

And for all Jack's kindness today, what would he think of that? Could this fragile relationship they'd built survive the image of her being led away and thrown in jail?

Or would that be the moment he realized she wasn't the woman for him?

CHAPTER EIGHT

Derrick shoveled the breakfast sandwich into his mouth, his gaze riveted to his phone. Harper and Rossi were still at the hotel. The little blip that indicated the tracker on Rossi's truck hadn't moved.

He could imagine them now, lounging in bed together, giggling and touching and laughing at him. At him, for being one step behind them.

But he wasn't.

He was right down the street. And as soon as they got on the road, he would, too. Rossi couldn't stay by her side twenty-four seven.

Derrick would have to be bolder this time. He'd bought a baseball cap emblazoned with the Boston Red Sox logo to keep his face off cameras and a too-big jacket with the same hideous logo to camouflage his size. Derrick wasn't the type of guy to wear any sports apparel, and certainly nothing depicting the Red Sox, considering he'd been an Orioles fan since diapers. He remembered how his father had cheered for the team, elated when they won, devastated when they lost. Now, of course,

Derrick knew there was more than team pride on the line. Dad usually had a sizable bet riding on the game.

Gambling hadn't killed his parents, not directly. But it would kill Derrick if he didn't get the money. That cheap fast-food breakfast churned in his gut. He tossed the trash in the can and rushed to the bathroom, his bowels as weak as his self-control. When he'd finished ejecting the disgusting breakfast, he drove the couple of blocks back to the hotel. Surely Harper and Jack would be leaving soon. He wasn't sure exactly what they were up to, and he didn't like the direction they'd driven the night before. Seemed they were headed back to Maryland, where Harper would likely go to the police and tell them everything she knew.

He had to get to her before that.

The next time Harper and Rossi stopped, Derrick would make his move. He'd snatch her, get his money, and get out of town. Yeah, the authorities would probably put it all together eventually, but by the time they did, Derrick would be long gone. New home, new name, new identity. And with Gramps's money, he didn't need to limit himself to the West Coast. Why not Europe? He'd always wanted to visit Monaco.

And why not dream big? Derrick was no longer content to just get the two hundred thousand. Nope. Gramps would be forking over everything he could scrape together. A million, at least. Gramps had plenty. He might have to work to gather it from his many accounts, sell some real estate fast, but he could manage it. He figured Harper was worth at least a million to the old man.

Derrick had thought she was worth that. But that was before she'd betrayed him and stolen his grandfather, turning the old man against his only living relative.

Derrick pulled into the hotel parking lot and looked toward the spot where Rossi's pickup had been parked.

The spot was empty.

He opened his phone and studied the map in the tracker's app. It showed the tracker still at the hotel.

He refreshed the screen. Maybe, it just needed to re-sync. He watched as the screen focused, but the little dot didn't jump.

Harper and Rossi had figured him out. They were gone.

CHAPTER NINE

"This is it?" Jack peered at the rusty sign that hung from the front of a rundown brick building. This wasn't the ending to the morning he'd envisioned. After they'd left the hotel, no sign of Derrick following them, they'd driven for hours with nothing in their stomachs but gas station coffee. He'd been looking forward to a delicious lunch.

"This is where she told me to meet her," Harper said.

He peered at the sign again. He wasn't that big a fan of Tex-Mex, and this place looked a little too authentic. But their upcoming meeting wasn't about food—though he was starving. It was about Harper meeting the defense attorney who'd agreed to accompany her to the police station in the small town in Western Maryland, where together, they would tell her story.

He found a spot and parked, then ran around the truck to open Harper's door. When she stepped out, he caught a whiff of her shampoo, and the memory of the kiss they'd shared that morning hit him full-force, hit him enough that the cold breeze suddenly felt welcome. He forced himself to step back when what he really wanted was to taste those lips again.

Get a grip, Rossi.

His body wasn't listening to his brain, and when she smiled up at him in that shy way of hers, all his whys for keeping his hands and lips to himself blew away with the falling leaves in the autumn breeze.

He took a deep breath of the chilly air, forced a casual smile, and held Harper's hand as they walked together. It was ten past eleven, and they were early for the eleven-thirty meeting, not having known exactly how long the trip from New Haven would take. He opened the door to the little hole-in-the-wall the attorney had suggested and was hit with the scents of garlic and peppers and meat, not to mention the sound of a mariachi band playing over the speakers somewhere.

His stomach growled.

Harper said, "Reminds me of Vegas."

He turned to her. "Really? When I think of Vegas, I imagine swanky casinos and fancy dining."

"Sure, for tourists. But the locals know the best places to eat. There are lots of authentic Mexican restaurants."

Made sense.

A dark-haired man met them at the stand. "Two for lunch?" His accent was strong, his smile contagious.

"We're meeting someone," Jack said. "She'll be here—"

"The lawyer, Ms. Banks?"

Jack glanced at Harper, and she said, "That's her."

"Follow me." The man led them through the dining room. Even though it was early for lunch, especially on a Saturday, most of the tables were filled. He glanced at the food, and his stomach growled again. He might have to rethink his aversion to Mexican food.

The man stopped beside a woman in a booth in the farthest corner. She stood and faced the host first. "Thanks, Pete. You call me if you have any more trouble with that neighbor."

Pete the host nodded, said, "I will do that," and left them

there.

The lawyer turned to them. "Harper Cloud?"

At Harper's nod, the woman stepped forward and pulled her into a hug. It was odd and should have raised alarm bells, but something about this woman felt comfortable, homey. "Seems when you're having a really bad day, you need a really big hug, am I right?"

After Harper had returned the woman's embrace, she uttered a short laugh and stepped back. "I never turn down a friendly hug."

"Smart lady." She focused next on Jack and held her arms wide.

He offered his hand. "Jack Rossi. I'm having a pretty good day."

The lawyer shook his hand. "Why do the handsome ones always refuse?" Before he could think of a good answer to that, she indicated the table. "Sit, sit. I ordered us some queso. Best cheese dip this side of the Rio Grande."

Harper slid into the booth first, and Jack followed. Before he'd even gotten settled, a dark-haired beauty in a bright red flowing skirt and a white peasant blouse slid glasses of water on the table for Harper and him. "*Hola*, friends of Ernie. You want soda, tea? Margaritas?"

Predictably, Harper ordered sweet tea. "I'll stick with water," Jack said.

The lawyer already had a drink, Coke, it looked like, so the waitress left to get their drinks.

"I'm Ernestine Banks," the lawyer said, "but everybody calls me Ernie."

The name sank in. Jack said, "Ernie Banks, as in—"

"Dad was a big Cubbies fan." She turned to Harper, and he did, too, to find Harper's expression blank. "Ernie Banks—aka, Mr. Sunshine—played for the Cubbies for about two decades."

"Oh."

"I look just like him." Ernie said the words with the laugh. "Except my skin's a little paler, I'm about a foot shorter, and I have a bit more hair."

Jack couldn't help but like this woman. She was short and squat and had a square face and a head full of brown frizzy hair. She wore a business suit that had probably fit a few sizes back. But her smile was contagious, and based on the way the people at the restaurant treated her, she was one of the good guys.

Of course, that didn't mean she was a good attorney. But Garrison had recommended her, and Jack trusted him, despite the man's behavior the day before.

The waitress returned with their drinks. Before Jack had even opened a menu, Ernie said, "You guys trust me?" And then laughed. "How could you? You don't even know me. But you're gonna have to start, so"—she turned to the waitress—"we'll share the number three, the number seven, and the number twelve. And bring us three plates, so we can eat family style. And the potatoes, not the rice, on at least two of the meals."

The woman nodded, took the menus, and disappeared.

Ernie focused on Harper. "Let's see how much of the story you can tell before our lunch gets here."

"Oh." Harper glanced at him, a trace of fear in her eyes.

He squeezed her hand under the table and nodded.

She turned back to Ernie. "Okay. Um..." And then she began the story she'd shared the day before. The move to Maryland to care for Red. The discovery that Red's grandson was a gambling addict and in too deep to get out on his own. The conversation she'd overheard when Derrick had tried to swindle his grandfather out of two hundred thousand dollars. The men who'd attacked her in the parking lot. The way Red had gotten sick, and how, eventually, she'd realized he was being poisoned by his own grandson. The decision to call the police about the poisoned bottles moments before she'd found the two bodies on the floor in her living room.

"Whoa." Ernie had a chip dripping with queso halfway to her mouth when she froze. "Dead bodies?"

Harper nodded, fear in her eyes.

Jack set his chip down—he'd been enjoying the salty crunch with the warm cheese dip—and slipped his arm around Harper's shoulder.

"Tell me about the bodies." Ernie had been taking notes between bites, but now she focused all her attention on Harper, scribbling furiously as Harper recounted the details. The bullet holes, the lack of blood or anything else.

"You're saying someone left them there, in your house?" Ernie asked.

"Red's house, but yeah, it's where I lived."

"Just lying there on the floor?"

"On their backs," Harper said, "side-by-side, like... Like an offering."

The woman made a note, then stared beyond them for a moment. She shook her head, took a breath, and said, "Okay, then what?"

"I panicked, I guess. I mean, someone murdered those men. I had no idea who or why they'd been left there. I did know Derrick was trying to kill Red. And so, I just got him into my car, and we drove away."

"Just left them there? What if they'd been alive?"

"They weren't alive. They weren't..." She shuddered. "Trust me. If they'd been alive, then blood would have been pumping, and their wounds would have been bleeding. They were pale. Eyes open. They were dead."

"Still," Ernie said, "you didn't call the police?"

"I did, sort of. When we were safely away, I called 911 and told them I'd seen a disturbance at the house. Like a concerned citizen. I told them to hurry over there, that I thought I'd seen someone prowling around. I left the back door unlocked. Figured the police would come, see the bodies through the back windows, and go in."

Ernie was nodding.

"But then—"

"Hold on." Ernie wrote something down, then flipped back in her notebook. "Yeah, your friend Garrison told me to look into 911 calls related to the address. I did, and a call came in that night, but when the police checked it out, they didn't find anything."

"I don't understand how that could be."

"Cops made a note that they looked through the windows. The lights were on inside, but they didn't see anything."

"The bodies would have been visible," Harper said.

Jack stated the obvious, because somebody needed to. "Whoever killed those men left them for you to see, then moved them after you left."

Ernie focused on him. "Yeah. But why?"

That was the million-dollar question. Or in this case, the two-hundred-thousand-dollar question.

Harper ran her fingers through her hair. Her hand was shaking. "Anyway, I thought they'd find the bodies, but they didn't. The bodies were found last week in a hotel parking lot in this town."

Ernie pulled a sheet of paper from her file. "Yeah, I got the newspaper report and the police report. They were found in a Caddy—"

"Probably Red's," Harper said, "but the VIN number was filed off and the plates missing."

Ernie made a note and studied what she'd written. "Doesn't make a lot of sense."

"No kidding," Harper said.

Ernie ate a couple of chips. "So you ran. Where'd you go?"

Harper gave the lawyer the rundown on where she'd been while Ernie munched more chips.

When she finished, Ernie was quiet again. She ate some chips, and Harper did, too. So Jack helped himself, wishing their meals would come.

Finally, they did. Three gigantic, steaming plates of food. Flour tortillas filled with chicken and smothered with sour cream sauce, steak covered in grilled vegetables, and poblano peppers bursting with meat and cheese.

After the ladies helped themselves, he forced himself to take polite portions, keeping himself from mmm'ing and moaning with every bite.

He would have to learn how to make this. What fool didn't like Mexican food?

Even Harper, who'd claimed to be too nervous to eat, was enjoying her share. He poked her in the side. "Looks like you were hungry after all."

"Might be my last good meal for a while," she said. "I figure I better enjoy it."

Jack looked at Ernie and waited for the woman to argue. Instead, she set down her fork. "Yeah. About that. I'm not gonna lie to you. It looks bad."

"She didn't do anything wrong!" Jack hadn't meant to shout and knew he'd been too loud when diners at other tables glanced their way. He lowered his voice and added, "She was the victim."

"I know." Ernie gave him a look that told him she'd seen his brand of naïveté before, and she could indulge it for a moment. "But she's an ex-con. The cops aren't going to take her word for anything. We just have to wait and see what kind of evidence they have against her."

"Can't you find out? Don't they have to share it with you?"

"Not unless they charge her with something, which they haven't yet."

"They can't charge her," Jack said, "She hasn't—"

He quieted when Ernie pointed her fork his way and gave him a look that said, *Shut it.*

Ernie focused on Harper. "You know the drill, hon. You've been to this party before. What aren't you telling me?"

Harper set her utensils down and clasped her hands together in her lap. "I swear, that's all I know. Except, one of the dead men was a cop."

"Keith Williams," Ernie said.

"I knew him. I'd met him at a party with Derrick."

"So you were personally acquainted with—"

"I barely spoke to him. His wife and I became friends, though. So yeah, I mean, I guess I was acquainted with him."

"Why didn't you turn him in when he attacked you?"

"He was behind me. I didn't know it was him. He never spoke. And anyway, the men wore masks."

"You had no idea it was him when he attacked you?"

"How could I?"

Ernie made another note before she looked at Harper.

"There's nothing else," she said. "I swear."

Ernie's gaze didn't falter. Even Jack started to get nervous after thirty seconds or so. What was the woman thinking? Finally, she set her pen down, picked up her fork, and nodded to the food in front of them. "So, did I do good or what?"

"Delicious." Harper nodded but didn't resume eating.

Jack pushed his plate away, too. He'd managed to stuff enough food in to keep him full until well past dinnertime. And now, the food settled like lead. He focused on the lawyer. "What do you think?"

Ernie looked at him a moment, then focused on Harper. "I think you have to tell your story and hope for the best."

CHAPTER TEN

T he drive to the police station took far less time than Harper had hoped. They followed Ernie into the lot and parked outside a two-story brick building surrounded by a chain link fence.

Jack opened her door, but she couldn't seem to make herself move.

She'd done this once before. As a naïve twenty-four-year-old, she'd marched into the Las Vegas PD and told them what she knew about a robbery and murder. It had been hard, one of the hardest things she'd ever done, to turn in her boyfriend and one of her closest friends, but she was sure they'd committed the crime. A man had died, and she'd played a part. Sure, she hadn't known they were going to rob that liquor store. She'd had no idea Emmitt even owned a gun. But she'd driven the car and helped them get away. A man had died.

Died.

She'd seen his wife on TV that morning, weeping and holding her children and lamenting about her children growing up without a father, about the monsters who'd done this to her beloved husband.

Harper had refused to be a monster, so she'd summoned all her courage and walked into that police station and told them what she knew.

And she'd ended up in prison for two years as an accessory. Guilty by association.

Emmitt and Barry hadn't exactly been upstanding citizens. They all used illegal drugs, and illegal drugs were, well, illegal. She'd known that. But that was a harmless crime, or so she'd told herself. Who—besides herself—had she hurt by smoking pot and taking pills? Except Barry and Emmitt had been addicts, and when they'd run out of money, they'd needed to find a way to feed their habit.

They'd gone to the store to buy liquor, to take the edge off. She'd believed them. And she'd told the police detectives everything she knew because of that grieving woman and her beautiful children. She'd told the truth, and she'd paid for her honesty with two years of her life and all of her future. Because ex-cons couldn't be registered nurses. Ex-cons couldn't get good jobs. Ex-cons were the dregs of society, relegated to the jobs nobody else wanted.

She'd told the truth, and she'd paid with her freedom.

And here she was again.

She couldn't do it. She couldn't go in there and tell the truth and have them slap handcuffs on her and lead her away and throw her in a cell with a bunch of other women who'd resent her because of her pretty face and claim of innocence. She'd been there. She couldn't go back.

Jack stepped into the space between the open door and the seat and pressed his hand against her cheek. His palm was rough and warm and real, and she leaned into his touch, relished it. Would she ever feel his hands again, or would he see her for the loser she was and walk away?

She'd worked so hard after prison to rebuild her life. And she was about to risk everything. Again.

Jack didn't say anything. Just held her gaze and waited.

And she remembered why she was doing this. Because she couldn't take care of Red unless she was free of these charges. She couldn't protect Red from Derrick unless she told her story and got the police looking for him. She couldn't be free unless she surrendered her freedom.

Could freedom come through surrender?

That's what she'd discovered in her relationship with Christ. Surrendering to Him made her free—of her guilt and shame and fears and addictions.

Maybe, true freedom could only be found on the far side of obedience. And trust.

She'd trusted God with a lot, but she hadn't trusted Him with this. She was terrified. But fear could only defeat her if she let it stop her.

Jack's gaze still didn't falter, and she realized something else. She couldn't be free to love Jack unless she risked losing him. If he didn't stick, then he'd never been meant to be hers. If he did stick... If he kept his promises and stayed with her no matter what happened next...

She'd never known that kind of love.

She wanted to, though.

She swallowed, took a deep breath, and reached up to cover Jack's hand with her own. "I can do this."

"You can do this."

He stepped back, and she got out of the truck and faced the building.

Ernie had parked and was waiting on the sidewalk.

Jack laced his fingers with Harper's, and they followed the lawyer inside.

The building was nicer than she'd imagined, though she

didn't take comfort in the padded chairs as they waited. They didn't have to wait long before a uniformed officer called Harper's name. The three of them stood, but the officer told Jack he had to wait in the lobby.

She turned to him, wanted to kiss him, but didn't. He squeezed her hand, kissed her cheek, and said, "I'll be here when you're finished."

She turned and followed Ernie through the door.

They were led to a small, windowless room, where they sat on the far side of a wide Formica table. A moment later, a woman walked in, followed by a man. The woman had her brown hair pulled back in a severe bun, not a great look to accompany her wrinkled skin, but she didn't seem the type to care about her appearance. She looked to be in her mid-fifties. The man was younger, maybe thirties, with a round face and kind eyes. They both wore slacks and button-down shirts.

"I'm Detective Whitney," the woman said, "and this is Detective Finnegan."

Ernie rose and shook the female detective's hand. "Nice to meet you." She turned to the other one and shook his hand, too. "I know we'll be fast friends."

The male detective shook her hand, cutting a glance to his partner as if he wasn't sure what to think of that. They all turned to Harper.

She remained seated, hands on the table. She'd learned that the best way to get decent treatment was to behave as meekly as possible. Project *I'm not a threat.*

Ernie said, "This is Harper Cloud."

She nodded to the detectives, neither of whom offered to shake her hand. Of course. She was the suspect. In their minds, she was the guilty party.

Funny how just being here made her *feel* guilty. Inside this little room, the weight of every sin she'd ever committed seemed to settle on her. Was her chair sinking under the burden?

The detectives and Ernie all sat. The female detective, Whitney, took the lead.

"Why don't you start by telling us what happened on Thursday, November second."

Harper took a deep breath and repeated the same story she'd told Ernie earlier that day, the same story she'd told Jack and Garrison and Garrison's pretty wife, Sam, the day before. Her voice shook, her hands trembled, and a couple of times, she faltered, afraid. But she spoke the truth. There should have been no fear in the truth.

As she spoke, she studied the faces of the two detectives across from her. While the man's features seemed to soften, the woman's hardened until her lips were pursed, the wrinkles on her cheeks deeper with the pressure of keeping her thoughts to herself.

Unfortunately, the woman seemed to be in charge.

"I had no idea I was wanted in connection with those men's murders," Harper explained as she finished up. Ernie had coached her to add that right away. "Obviously, if I'd known, I'd have come in immediately."

Harper let the story stop there. She glanced at Ernie, hoping to get some indication that she'd done well, but the lawyer was focused on the two detectives.

It was the female detective who broke the silence. "That's not so obvious to me," the woman said. "In fact, it seems to me that you knew we'd be looking for you. That's why you ran."

Harper started to respond, but Ernie rested her hand over Harper's clenched fists, and Harper kept quiet.

"She called 911, as you can see from the paperwork I gave you."

The woman kept her focus on Harper. "*Someone* reported a prowler, but we have no evidence it was you."

Ernie made a note on her notepad. Harper glanced at it and read *get recording from 911*.

A good idea, but it wouldn't convince this woman of anything.

And then the real questioning began. Both detectives fired them at her, and she answered truthfully, over and over, sometimes answering the same question two, three, four times.

Why didn't you report that someone was trying to kill the old man?

"Like I said, I didn't realize it until right before I found the bodies."

Why not report it afterwards?

"I was afraid of the men who'd beaten me up, and whoever killed those men."

Why not take Mr. Burns to a hospital?

"I was afraid."

Why didn't you keep the Gatorade?

"I went to grab a bottle, but the bottles were gone."

Which, of course, they didn't believe, even though it made perfect sense. Derrick had been there that night. Whoever had murdered those men had been there, too. Maybe Derrick, maybe someone else. But the point was, others had had access to Red's house that night.

"According to you." The lead detective's sneer made her already unattractive face downright ugly.

This wasn't going well. This was going very badly. Worse, even, than Harper had imagined. Because the detectives in Las Vegas had been kind when she'd spilled her story about the robbery-gone-bad. They'd been gentle and made promises.

Of course, the promises had been lies. At least this woman

was straightforward. She made no bones about the fact that her goal was to throw Harper in prison for the rest of her life.

Harper forced herself to hold the woman's gaze. She'd learned in prison not to meet the eyes of the craziest prisoners. Like alpha dogs, they took on every challenge and put it down. But here, she had to hold her ground. She wasn't guilty. She wasn't. And she wouldn't cower.

She just hoped they couldn't see how badly she was shaking.

The questioning continued. Rarely did Ernie advise her not to answer. The truth wouldn't hurt Harper, couldn't hurt her, because she hadn't done anything wrong.

That seemed irrelevant to the woman across the table.

Harper glanced at the man, Detective Finnegan. He looked more confused than suspicious at this point. Maybe he believed her. Maybe he'd be an advocate.

A few minutes later, he piped in with a question. "Why New Hampshire?" The question threw her off, not because it was a strange question but because of the way he asked it. As if he were genuinely curious.

"I picked it randomly," Harper said. "I'd have preferred to be in a city, but the rents are higher, and I didn't have much money. I came from the southwest, so I figured I'd head northeast. I thought people would be more apt to look for me in Vegas or Kansas and never think of New Hampshire."

The man nodded, wrote something on his notepad, and slid it to his partner.

She read what he'd written and scoffed. "You would."

Would what?

He wrote something else, and the female detective actually laughed. She focused on Harper. "He thinks you're innocent. Probably because he can't imagine someone with a face like yours committing murder. You probably get that a lot, people falling all over themselves to help you." She rolled her eyes and focused on the man. "Pretty women commit murder, too. And they get away with it because of men like you."

The man wilted under the woman's stare. When she was satisfied, she turned back to Harper. "You're a cop-killer."

Before Harper could defend herself, Ernie said, "Don't respond to that." Then to Detective Whitney, "Williams might've been a cop, but it sounds like he was working on the side for some shady characters. Maybe one of them did this."

Whitney's smile was cruel. "He was involved with a shady character." She leveled a gaze at Harper. "You." The smile widened until she showed all her teeth. "Your fingerprints were found on one of the dead men's shoes."

Harper said, "I didn't—"

"Just listen." Ernie focused on the detective. "Go on."

"Today, we found out the bodies were found in your car."

"Red's car," Harper said, "and you only know that because I told Garrison, and he told you. I have nothing to hide."

The woman's expression didn't shift. "But we didn't find your fingerprints in that car. Why would that be?"

Before Harper opened her mouth, Ernie grabbed her hand and shook her head.

Fine. This woman was going to believe what she was going to believe, and there was nothing Harper could say to dissuade her.

Whitney continued. "We found a gun hidden in a bedroom at the house."

What? Red owned a gun?

"Once ballistics tests are performed," Whitney continued, "we'll be able to prove it's the gun that killed those men." The woman leaned forward, and her smile turned to a sneer. "You're a cop killer, Harper Cloud. And you're going down for it."

Whitney stalked out of the room.

Harper, Ernie, and the Detective Finnegan sat in silence. Less than a minute passed before Whitney returned, two uniformed police officers in tow. One carried handcuffs.

Harper looked at Ernie, but again, Ernie wasn't focused on her. "You're arresting her? On what charge?"

Whitney glanced at her watch. "We've got until tomorrow at three-thirty to finalize all the charges. Until then, she can just cool her heels in our fancy facility."

Harper stood, turned around as if on autopilot, and allowed the police officer to slide the handcuffs into place.

They felt icy and familiar and brought back memories she'd hoped to forget forever.

She wasn't even surprised.

CHAPTER ELEVEN

J ack glanced at the time on his phone. Hours had passed since Harper and Ernie had disappeared through that door into the bowels of the police department. He'd known it would take some time for her to tell her story, but this was ridiculous.

He'd tried to pass time with a magazine, but that had proved fruitless. He wasn't a man accustomed to sitting around. He always had a project. A wall to paint, a meal to cook, a drain to clear. Between his work as a property manager and his own fixer-upper, he was never without something to keep his hands busy. Being here with nothing to do but worry was making him crazy.

Maybe he should ask if they had any leaky faucets he could repair while he waited.

The door opened, and Ernie stalked out, wearing a scowl. He'd only known her a few hours, but in that time, he'd never seen anything but kindness, laughter, and understanding on her face. Right now, she looked furious.

Harper wasn't with her.

Jack nearly tripped over the chairs in his rush to get to the lawyer's side. "What happened?"

"They took her into custody."

"No." He'd been so sure, so sure they'd believe her. Garrison had believed her. This was all Jack's fault. If only he'd kept his stupid mouth shut and never told Sam and Garrison about her, she wouldn't be in this situation.

It didn't make sense, though. She'd turned herself in! Why would she have done that if she were guilty?

How could they have thought that Harper, his beautiful, sweet Harper, could be involved in a murder?

Before he could voice any of his questions, Ernie answered them all with a simple statement. "They were sure she'd done it before she walked in the building."

"But—"

"I know." She crossed the room so fast, he had to rush to keep up with her. A moment later, they were outside in the chilly evening air. A brisk wind blew through his jacket, and he shivered.

Ernie continued to her Audi and pressed the button so the doors would unlock while Jack followed. Surely the lawyer wasn't going to leave without...

"Get in," she said.

He pulled open the passenger door and climbed inside. Nice car. Maybe it meant she was a good lawyer. Maybe all wasn't lost yet.

Ernie cranked the engine, backed out of the spot, and pulled onto the main road.

"Where are we going?"

"For a ride."

Jack turned and looked at the brick building as it got smaller behind them. Harper was there. How could he leave her?

The woman drove for five minutes and then pulled into the

lot beside a coffee shop. "Let's get something warm to drink. It was freezing in there, and it's freezing in this car."

"You think Harper is cold? Should we bring her something?"

Ernie laughed, though the sound was dark. "They don't let us bring the prisoners take-out." She climbed out of the car, so he did, too. But it felt wrong, so wrong, to be here without Harper. Everything felt tight. Uncomfortable, as if he'd grabbed a too-small shirt that was pinching and pulling on his skin.

Inside, the scent of coffee made his stomach churn. He followed Ernie to the counter and ordered. They waited at the counter while their drinks were prepared, then found a table in the far corner.

Ernie sipped her coffee, then set the cup on the table.

"Are you going to tell me what happened," he said, "or are we just going to sit here looking at each other?"

"I was optimistic, but I knew there was a good chance they'd take her into custody. The detective, Marsha Whitney..." She sighed. "I've never met her, but I made some calls this morning before you guys got here. She's tough, but she's fair. She's got it in her head that Harper's guilty, and she'll move heaven and earth to prove she's right."

"But she's wrong."

"I know. You know. Harper knows. Eventually, Whitney'll know, too. Until then..."

"We have to get Harper out of there."

"They have evidence. Her fingerprints were found on one of the dead men's shoes. The bodies were found in Harold Burns's car, which she drove. Somebody wiped the car down— no fingerprints."

"So they can't prove she drove it."

"But she did drive it, all the time, and she told them that. So wiping the car just makes her look guilty."

"That still doesn't—"

"And they found a gun at the house. Whitney thinks ballistics will prove it's the murder weapon."

Jack sat back and ran a hand through his hair. A gun? The car was wiped down?

Either Harper was the greatest liar on the planet, or somebody was trying to frame her. But if so, then why take the plates and file the VIN number off the car? Why wipe off all the fingerprints, if hers would be all over it? When he voiced the questions, Ernie just frowned.

"They don't have all the pieces put together yet, but they're pretty sure they have their killer. All they need is a positive ballistics test, and they'll charge her."

"What about the fingerprints on the shoes? How did she explain that?"

"When the men were beating her up, she said she tried to crawl away and grabbed one of the men's shoes by accident."

Made sense, but it also made her look guilty. He sipped his coffee. It was hot and bitter and not the least bit enjoyable. But he needed to think, and after a nearly nonexistent night's sleep, the caffeine wouldn't hurt.

"What if we prove she's telling the truth?" Jack asked.

Ernie leveled a look at him. "What did you have in mind?"

He didn't have anything in mind, not yet. But there had to be a way to prove Harper hadn't killed those men.

"You think the old man can help?" Ernie asked. "If he would swear that she was with him that whole night, at least she'd have an alibi."

"I don't think he remembers." Jack thought back to the story Red had told him. Had that just been two nights before? Seemed like weeks. But Red's memory of the night of November second was fuzzy. He'd been ill, and he knew

Harper had left and come back roughed up. But would Red be able to tell anybody how long she'd been gone?

Jack doubted it. Especially since, according to Harper, Red had seen the two dead men that night, but he had no memory of it.

No, Red would be no help.

"There's no way Harper could have murdered two people, put them in a car, and driven them here," Jack said. "How would she have gotten them into the car?"

"I think Whitney figures she had an accomplice," Ernie said.

"Who?"

"Whitney didn't tell me her suspicions, but if I had to guess, I'd say her boyfriend, the grandson."

Jack's stomach twisted. "He wasn't her boyfriend anymore."

"According to her. I'm guessing Whitney will be looking into him and the grandfather now that they have names. But you're saying the grandfather's been gone since the night of the murders. And maybe the grandkid, Derrick, has, too. So, that makes him look guilty. I'm guessing Whitney believes Derrick is in on it."

"But why?" Jack resisted the urge to yank his hair out. "Why in the world would Harper kill anybody? What could her motive possibly be?"

Ernie shrugged. "They'll charge her and figure out the motive later, if they have means and opportunity."

"But they don't have either."

"They think they do. If the ballistics report proves that gun killed those men, they'll have enough to charge her."

"Do they know whose gun it is? Is it hers?"

"Whitney didn't say who it was registered to. I'll get all that information when they charge her."

When they charge her. As if it were a foregone conclusion.

"Let's talk through the timeline," Jack said. "Harper sees the bodies and takes off. She goes to Newark and gets a hotel room."

"Yeah. But the police think—"

"That she drove a good thirty, forty-five minutes west of Baltimore. The opposite direction. I wonder if—"

"If we can prove she was in Newark when the bodies were left." Ernie grabbed her phone and dialed. A moment later, she walked away, phone pressed to her ear.

Fine, then. He'd just sit there and do nothing.

Again.

Except... He'd been paying attention when Harper had told her story earlier. He knew Harper had stayed in Newark, and he even almost knew the name of the hotel. Economy something.

He pulled out his phone and searched. She'd have chosen a hotel near I-95... And there it was. An Economy Sleep right off the interstate in Elizabeth, New Jersey.

Two and a half hours away.

It was now Saturday night, and Harper had arrived on a Thursday night. So maybe it wouldn't be the same person working tonight who'd worked that night. But maybe it would.

At least it would give him something useful to do.

Ernie slipped back into the booth. "I talked to Detective Finnegan. He seemed a little less convinced that Harper was guilty. He said the Cadillac went into the parking garage at just before midnight on Thursday, November second. Now, if we can put Harper somewhere else—"

"I'm driving to the Newark hotel tonight," he said.

She scrunched her eyes and shook her head. "Bad idea. I'll hire an investigator to look into it. If she used a credit card—"

"Great. Do that. Definitely. But I want to go, to talk to someone who saw her there. Maybe someone remembers her, so it's not just a paper trail but an actual human trail. And anyway, how soon could that investigator look into it?"

She shrugged. "Probably Monday."

"She's not staying in custody until Monday."

"You need to accept that they might charge her."

"She's innocent!"

Ernie offered the first genuine smile she'd given since they left the police station. "I know she is. And soon enough, they'll know, too."

He loved her confidence. He just wished he shared it.

CHAPTER TWELVE

Jack stared at the sign for the Economy Sleep Hotel just outside Newark, New Jersey. It looked like the kind of place where a person could rent a room by the hour. Why would she choose this place?

The cost, for one thing. He'd bet money this was the cheapest place she could find. Maybe this hotel didn't demand a credit card but took cash up front. Maybe it was the kind of place where clerks and guests looked the other way. If so, then this had been a fool's errand.

After a deep breath and a quick prayer, Jack walked in the front door. The foyer was just big enough for a tall counter and maybe two or three guests with their luggage. A glance in the corners revealed no cameras—bummer, but he wasn't surprised. It reeked of stale smoke and something Jack didn't want to identify. He approached the counter. Nobody was behind it, but on the other side, a door was open about a foot, revealing what Jack assumed was an office. He could hear the sound of a football game and see the flickering of a TV.

"Hello?"

"Coming."

A moment later, a young man, maybe late teens or early twenties, stepped out. Jack wasn't sure what he'd expected, but not this. Clean cut, hair trimmed, Polo shirt and khakis. "Sorry. Florida State's driving for a TD. You a football fan?"

"I don't watch a lot of college ball," Jack said, "but I'm a Patriots fan."

The kid's face split into a grin. "Ha. They call them a dynasty, but my Giants beat 'em twice in the Super Bowl."

Jack forced himself to chuckle as if he cared. "You were lucky. Twice."

"You looking for a room?"

"Actually, no. What's your name?"

A slight pause, then, "Chet."

"Nice to meet you, Chet." Jack reached across the counter with his hand held out. "I'm Jack. I'm wondering about one of your guests."

Chet released the handshake and leaned back. "I can't give out information on our guests."

"I understand that." He looked around, then leaned in and lowered his voice as if the walls of the dingy lobby could hear. "The thing is, this guest needs to prove she was here. An alibi."

The man's eyes widened just a bit. "Seriously? What'd she do?"

"She's in jail because they think she killed someone, but she didn't. She was here." Jack straightened up and shrugged. "Or so she says. Anyway, the police will probably be calling on you eventually, but I'm investigating myself. I think the cops are... let's just say they want to prove she's guilty."

Chet chewed the inside of his mouth for a minute, thinking. "When was she supposed to have been here?"

"She'd have checked in November second or early in the

morning on the third, and she'd have stayed a couple of nights. Did you work that weekend?"

"I work every night. Saving money to go to school in January. My mom owns this place. She says if I pay for my first year's tuition and make good grades, then she'll pay the rest."

"Where do you want to go?"

Chet nodded toward the back room and the TV playing there. "Florida State, man. Beaches, beautiful girls. And a good finance program."

The kid was kind, reasonable. Hopefully, he'd be helpful, too. "If you were working, then you'll remember this woman." Jack swiped open his phone, scrolled through the photos, and found the only one of Harper. He'd taken it at the beach the one time they'd gone. They'd been halfway to the car, and she'd been walking beside Red, talking to him, helping him navigate the gravel parking lot. Jack had run ahead to open the doors, and as they'd approached, he hadn't been able to help himself. He'd snapped their photo. He looked at the picture now. Red wore an open smile. Harper's was tight, nervous. Jack hadn't understood at the time, but it was clear now why she'd been concerned about having her photo taken.

He turned the phone so Chet could see. Before the kid spoke, Jack knew he'd seen her by the look on his face.

"Someone thinks *she* killed a guy?"

"Two guys, actually," Jack said.

Chet shook his head. "Idiots." He tore his gaze from the photo. "Yeah, she was here, and the old dude was, too."

Thank You, God.

"I guess he's her grandfather," the kid continued. "Old dude was wicked sick. I know because I have to clean the rooms, and theirs was..." He waved his hand in front of his face. "Bad. Guy must've had it coming out both ends. I offered to call an ambulance, but she swore she had it under control. Said she was a nurse. Said they were on a trip to see his other grandkids when he got sick, so she stopped to try to get him well. They were here all weekend." He looked around and lowered his voice. "Thing was, she had a bruise"—he tapped his cheek—"right there. I wondered if maybe she was like, running from an abusive boyfriend or something." He straightened up. "None of my business, of course."

"You remember when she checked in?"

The kid looked toward the ceiling. After a long pause, he focused on Jack again. "It was the night the Browns played the Jets. That new QB played great. I was watching the postgame when they came in, so it had to be"—another long pause—"about eleven, eleven-thirty? Something like that."

A Thursday night game, and the kid even had a good memory of the time. Still... "Can you tell me why you remember *her* so well?" Jack asked.

Chet tapped Jack's phone screen with his fingernail. "Look at her. If the old dude hadn't been sick, I'd have asked her out. As it was, I offered to get them food or whatever, but she said she had it covered. She came with sacks of stuff, so I guess she knew what she was doing."

"Would you be willing to testify that you saw her?"

The kid's face lit up. "Heck, yeah. Happy to. I'd love to see her again."

Jack forced a smile, even though what he really wanted was to tell the kid in no uncertain terms that Harper was not available.

"You a PI or something?"

"Just a friend," Jack said.

"Oh. A *friend.*" Chet waggled his eyebrows.

Yes, Chet. That kind of friend. So don't even think about it.

But Jack didn't say any of that. "Just a friend, but I wouldn't mind if it were more."

"I bet."

"Listen, the police will probably be calling here soon. Tell them everything you told me, and if you have any record of her being here—credit card receipts, paperwork, whatever—maybe get that for them."

"Sure thing, boss."

Jack reached across the counter and shook Chet's hand. "Good luck at Florida State."

As soon as Jack got into his pickup, he called Ernie.

She answered on the second ring. "You know what time it is?"

He glanced at the clock on his dash. Nearly ten o'clock. "It's Saturday night. Surely you aren't asleep already."

"Some of us go to church on Sunday mornings."

If life were normal, Jack would probably be planning on church in the morning. But nothing about this situation was normal. "I found the hotel where Harper stayed and talked to the clerk who checked her in. He remembers her and even remembers when she got here. She was here when Red's car pulled into that parking garage."

A long pause was followed by, "All right. I'll make a call tomorrow. Good job."

"Tomorrow? Why not now?"

"They're not going to let her go until they get the ballistics report, and even if they might, they sleep, too. It's Saturday night."

"But—"

"I know you wanna get her out. I do, too. She spent two years in prison. One night in jail won't kill her."

Jack wanted to reach through the phone and throttle Ernie, then track down those idiot detectives who'd put Harper in jail and throttle them, too. But, as usual, he was powerless to do anything.

Despite the fact that Jack had uncovered proof that Harper couldn't have been driving the car that left the bodies in the parking garage, she'd stay in jail tonight. He prayed she'd stay safe.

CHAPTER THIRTEEN

Jack woke to the ringing phone Sunday morning. He glanced at the clock on the nightstand of the cheap hotel where he'd found a room the night before. After nine, but his eyes were scratchy with fatigue. He snatched his cell and looked at the screen.

Ginny? Why would his Realtor be calling him on a Sunday morning?

He cleared his throat, sat up, and swiped to connect the call. "Hello?"

"Sounds like we woke you," she said.

"I should be up," he said. "Who is we?"

"Mr. Burns—"

"Red." The old man's voice was clear in the background. "I told you a thousand times to call me Red."

Jack chuckled. Red sure sounded better. Not happy, but healthier. That was news Harper would be glad to hear.

The thought of Harper brought back the lump that had been sitting in his stomach since she'd been taken into custody. Had she slept? Had she eaten?

When would they release her?

How could he have been so certain the police would believe her story—and so wrong?

"Sorry, Red." Ginny's voice held a hint of amusement when she spoke to the old man. "Red's been trying to call Harper, but she won't pick up. He's worried about her and insisted I call you."

Crap. He'd hoped to avoid talking to Red until Harper was out. "Put him on the phone."

A moment later, Red said, "Where's my girl?"

"She's fine," Jack said. "Just... It's sort of a long story."

"Well, they're keeping me hostage in this stupid hospital, so I got nowhere to go and nothing better to do than listen to your long story."

"There's been a mix-up." Jack had no idea how to tell Red that Harper was in jail, but he wasn't about to lie to the man, either. "We had to come to Maryland because the cops think she was involved in a crime."

"Yeah, I know all about it. Had the police here questioning me yesterday, asking me about my gun."

"You own a gun?"

"Just a handgun. I keep it in my nightstand. Not loaded, though. With my memory the way it is, doesn't seem safe. But I like to think I could still defend myself if I had to."

So, the gun was Red's, and the cops knew it. Did that matter, though? Harper could have used his gun to kill those men. Nobody would believe Red could have done it. "What else did they ask you about?" Jack asked.

"They showed me some pictures of a couple of men, but I'd never met 'em. And they wanted to know what I remembered from the day we left the house." His voice shook a bit, and he blew out a long breath. "Problem is, I don't remember much. Just being sick and then leaving. It's all fuzzy."

"You remember that some guys roughed her up that night?"

"I remember the bruises."

"The guys who hurt her—probably the guys whose photos you saw—were killed that night, and the cops think she had something to do with it."

"Killed? Well..." A long pause. "She couldn't have," Red said. "She was with me."

Except Red didn't remember everything. So his assurances wouldn't convince anyone. But Chet-the-night-manager's memory of that night was excellent. "We're going to get it taken care of today." He spoke the words and prayed they were true.

"Put her on the phone."

"She's not with me right now."

"Well, go get her, then. I'll wait."

"I'll tell you what. I'll have her call you—"

"Listen, Jack." Red's tone was serious as the heart attack he'd had two days before. "I wanna know what's going on, and I wanna know now. She hasn't called me in almost twenty-four hours. That's not like her. I want to talk to her. Right now."

Jack blew out a long breath. "Harper's in jail."

Red was silent a moment. Then, his words burst out as if from a cannon. "What did you do? How could you have let that happen?"

"I didn't have—"

"I trusted you to take care of her. You promised when you left here the other day you wouldn't let her out of your sight, and now you're telling me she's in jail? On what charge? For God's sake, man, get her a lawyer. Get her out of there!"

"Red, calm down."

"Don't you tell me what to do."

Jack could hear voices in the background, all telling Red what to do. *Remember your heart. Relax. Settle down.* As if telling a person to calm down ever led to that person actually calming down.

Jack forced a steady, confident tone. "Listen, Red. You there?"

"Yeah, I'm here. Just fending off Ginny and all these nurses who're afraid I'm gonna blow a gasket." Then to the people in the room, "I'm fine. See. Deep breaths." He took a deep breath, and Jack did, too, and added a prayer for the man's health.

"Harper won't be happy if you get yourself worked up," Jack said. "And if you do it on her account, she'll feel guilty."

"Fine." A long pause, more voices in the background. "There," he said to someone else. "You happy? My numbers are fine." He said into the phone, "Do I need to send you some money to get her a lawyer?"

"She has a lawyer." Jack filled Red in on everything that had happened since they'd left Nutfield—everything except the fact that Derrick had been tracking them. He didn't figure Red needed to be reminded of his grandson's treachery. He finished with the story of his trip to Newark the night before.

"Yeah, I remember the hotel. I was sick as a dog. So you're saying you got proof she's innocent?"

"I have it, her attorney has it, and by now, I'm sure the police have it, too."

"Okay, then." Red's voice sounded so much more relaxed. Small favors.

"How do you feel, Red?"

"Fine. They adjusted my meds, and I feel strong. Ready to get out of here."

"I bet. We're going to stop by your house when Harper's free." Assuming the police would let them. Would it be considered a crime scene?

"Grab my photo of Bebe," Red said. "Don't care about anything else."

"You're probably ready to get home."

The man snorted. "There's nothing for me back there. Ever

since my grandson quit coming around, the big old house is too empty. Without Harper, I'd probably have moved into one of those retirement villages. After losing Bebe and George and my daughter-in-law, and now..." Derrick's name hung between them, his name and his evil deeds. "Anyway, Harper's the only family I have left. I don't care about going back to Maryland. I care about Harper. I love that girl."

Jack swallowed a lump of emotion that lodged in his throat and spoke the truth that had been planted and growing in his heart for days. "Me, too."

"Yeah. I sorta figured that out. So, what are you waiting for? Go get her."

Jack hung up the phone, determined to do just that.

CHAPTER FOURTEEN

Derrick was a fool to be back here, but he was running out of options. He'd lost track of Harper, and this was the only place he knew she'd eventually come.

He stared at the house that had been his home for years. He'd moved in after his parents had died and lived here off and on with Gramps all through college and for his first few years of working. It had been a good place. A safe place. He'd always believed Gramps loved him, but it turned out Gramps loved his money more than he loved Derrick.

He should have killed the old man when he'd had the chance.

He was sitting in his rental, staring at the house and wondering if Harper was there when someone stepped beside his door.

All he saw was a torso.

He reached to click the lock, but he was too late. The door opened, and Derrick was yanked from the car. He got a glimpse of the man. Rambo, the goon he'd met in Vegas. Before Derrick could utter a word of protest, Rambo punched him in the stomach, and he went to his knees. The pain in his middle was unbearable, and he kept his gaze down, focused on the asphalt.

Rambo must have been watching the house, waiting for Derrick to be stupid enough to come back. He yanked a handful of Derrick's hair and forced his head back. "Long time, no see."

He tried to get breath to answer. Not enough air.

"Not such a big shot now, is he?" Rambo spoke to someone else near the front of the car, but Derrick couldn't see the person he was talking to. Probably the smaller guy who'd been Rambo's sidekick in Vegas.

"Quentin wants his money," Rambo said.

"I'm working on it." His words were raspy.

"Boss wanted an update."

"I'll have his money tomorrow."

Rambo leaned close. His breath smelled as if his teeth hadn't seen a brush in years. "If you don't, I'll be back. You think this hurt?" The man let go of Derrick's hair and punched him in the nose.

His face exploded in pain. His eyes clouded with tears.

The man covered Derrick's mouth and bloodied nose with his meaty hand, kept him from breathing. Derrick struggled, but Rambo's grip was an iron vice. He couldn't breathe. His vision blacked on the edges.

Rambo said, "I'm not even breaking a sweat." He let up, and Derrick sucked in a breath, collapsed on the asphalt, and rolled into the fetal position.

Rambo and the little goon strode away. The whole thing couldn't have taken more than two minutes.

With a grip on the car door, he pulled himself to standing. When he did, he looked around at the quiet street, the huge homes, many of which were decorated for Thanksgiving. Not a soul had seen what just happened. Not a soul would care.

Gramps had betrayed him.

Harper had betrayed him.

Quentin was going to destroy him.

Derrick had to take care of himself.

He wiped the blood dripping into his mouth on the sleeve of his dress shirt. He managed to get back into the car, grabbed his handgun and his keys, and then climbed out. He was going in. If Harper was there, he'd take her captive now. If not, Derrick would grab valuables to pawn, steal the man blind. And he'd wait. Because, eventually, Harper would be here. She wouldn't come all the way back to Maryland—and he had no doubt this was where she and Rossi had been headed—without coming to the house. When they got here, Derrick would be waiting. If he had to kill Rossi, then that's what he'd do. And if he had to hurt Harper... Well, he was looking forward to that.

CHAPTER FIFTEEN

Harper had no idea what time it was when she heard the slam of the heavy metal door on the far end of the small collection of jail cells. Funny how time didn't follow the rules when a person's freedom was taken away. Time became both a bitter enemy and a dear friend. The clock—a clock she couldn't see—dictated when to eat, when to sleep, when to exercise, when to work. At least in prison, there was work. In prison, she'd had more than these four walls with nothing to do and nobody to talk to and nothing to think about except everything she'd ever done wrong.

What amazed her was how different these hours behind bars were from the years she'd spent in that Nevada prison. Because now she had God, and she'd been talking to Him all night. And He'd answered her.

That thought still shook her right to her core. He'd reminded her of the truth she'd learned in church with Red and in her Bible, that greater was He, the One in her, than all the bad guys out there. That she was saved, redeemed, and forgiven by the blood of the Lamb. That she was learning the truth, and the truth would set her free.

Free.

She could be in jail and still be free. It was a matter of choosing love over hate. Choosing truth over lies.

And during that conversation with God, she'd chosen once again to trust Him. He'd promised that even if it looked as if all the world were aligned against her, He wouldn't leave her. He was there. And He was a God of miracles.

"Please, God," she whispered.

She didn't sleep, but she found a measure of peace.

And then her brain kicked in, and rationality warred with the spiritual. She figured the best-case scenario would be to hear nothing for as long as possible. If they didn't get enough to charge her, eventually they'd have to let her go. Any news before three-thirty—another five hours, she guessed—would be bad news.

But the footsteps coming down the hall neared, and a moment later, her cell door opened and a uniformed officer motioned her forward. A sinking feeling of despair settled in her middle. They really were going to charge her.

It was all so familiar, the feeling of being utterly helpless and hopeless. She tried to shake it off. Because this time, she had hope.

The female guard was shorter than Harper, thicker all around. She'd be terrifying except for the gentle expression on her face. "Time to go."

The woman led Harper out of the cell, down the long hallway she'd walked the day before, and into a small room. She was given her shoes and her ID.

"That's everything," the guard said. "You're free to go."

Free to go?

The relief was so sudden and so surprising, Harper had the urge to throw her arms around the guard and hug her. The thought brought on a laugh. The guard didn't laugh with her, but the corners of her mouth twitched as if the expression were right there, trying to get out.

The woman nodded toward a closed door, and Harper pushed it open and stepped into the police station's anteroom.

Jack was just a few feet away and held his arms open. She rushed forward and fell into them.

"I'm so sorry," he said. "I'm so stupid. I thought for sure—"

She cut off his foolishness with a kiss. Because none of this was Jack's fault.

After too little time, he broke away, leaned back, and studied her face as if searching for clues. "You okay?"

"I'm free to go."

He turned her toward the glass door and the bright sunshine beyond. They were nearly there when she felt a hand on her shoulder. She turned to see Detective Whitney.

"We may have more questions for you, so don't go far."

Harper forced a deep breath so she could respond with patience.

Jack said, "Listen—"

"I got it, Jack." Harper focused on Whitney. "I am Red Burns's caretaker, and I left him in a hospital in New Hampshire to come in and talk to you. I'll be happy to tell you where I'm staying, and you already have my cell phone number. But I have to take care of Mr. Burns. It's my job."

The woman's eyes narrowed.

Harper decided to just ask. "Why did you let me go?"

"Your alibi held up." She flicked a glance at Jack. "Hotel clerk remembers you and the old man checking in that night."

"Oh. Good."

"And it turns out Mr. Burns's gun didn't fire the bullets that killed those men."

"It was Red's gun you found at the house?"

Whitney's face was still as stone, which Harper took for a yes. She'd had no idea he even owned one.

"We're going to dig until we find out exactly what happened," Whitney said. "We haven't proved it was you yet—"

"And you won't, because it wasn't." Harper's fear had burned off somewhere between the cell and here. Now, she felt confident. She was free, and the evidence the cops thought they had against her was falling apart. "I assume you're looking for Derrick Burns."

Again, Whitney's face revealed nothing.

"He'll be able to tell you who those men were working for. Derrick's loan shark, I think, but I don't know his name. I'm not saying I think Derrick did it, but he'll be able to tell you a lot more than I can." When Whitney still didn't speak, Harper added, "I didn't know Keith Williams very well, but his wife was kind to me. Nobody deserves to have her husband murdered. I hope you find out who killed him."

"Don't worry." Whitney seemed to be trying hard to keep the sneer off her face. "We'll figure out who did it, and when we do, they'll pay."

Harper offered a smile as sweet as her iced tea. "Happy Lord's Day." She turned to leave, then turned back again to see Whitney still there, arms crossed, watching. Harper kept her smile in place. "We're planning to go to the house—Red Burns's house—to pick up a few things today. Is that all right?"

The woman's eyes narrowed slightly. She paused, then nodded. "They finished processing it yesterday."

"Okay. Thanks." Harper turned and pushed through the glass door before Jack could open it.

Outside, she stopped and pulled in a deep breath. The sky was blue, the air was crisp, the sun was shining. She barely resisted the urge to throw her hands in the air and spin like Julie

Andrews in *The Sound of Music*. She closed her eyes and breathed, *Thank You, God.*

"You okay?"

She popped her eyes open. "It's beautiful, isn't it?"

Jack's gaze scanned the little downtown, all the squat buildings and cars and rundown storefronts. She tried to see it from his point of view. Maybe it wasn't beautiful in the traditional sense. He took her hand and gazed into her eyes. "You're beautiful."

She kissed his cheek. "You need to learn to appreciate your freedom. It's a wonderful thing." She started toward his pickup, pulling his hand when he didn't keep up, and then waited for him to open her door. He did, and she slid in and shivered against the cold seats. A moment later, he was beside her. He cranked the engine, started the warm air blowing, and drove.

"I figured you'd be hungry," he said.

"Famished. They need to discover spices in that place."

The little amusement he'd had on his face faded. "What sounds good?"

"Steak? Burgers? Anything."

Jack pulled into a Chili's, and Harper requested a table by the window. She wanted to be close to the sunshine, away from the reminder of prison darkness. There, the darkness had come not only from prison walls, but also from her own poor choices. They'd been dark, sinful choices, and they'd colored her whole life with a gray crayon.

She and Jack made small talk until the waiter took their orders. Then, Jack's almost smile faded to a deep frown. He reached across the table and covered her hand with his. "Seriously. Was it awful?"

"I've endured worse."

"I'm so sorry I didn't take your worries more seriously. I truly never thought they'd put you in jail."

"Of course not." She studied him closer, the bloodshot eyes, the tightness in his lips. This sweet man had never experienced the ugly side of life—murder and crime and police stations and jail. He was naïve in all the best ways, in ways she wished she still were. "I'm not upset with you, Jack. I love the way you look at life. I love your hope, your optimism. You told me I should trust God with it. I was afraid to do that, afraid God didn't love me enough to protect me. Last night, I was in a cell all by myself, and I was beating myself up for going there, for turning myself in. But then I started praying, and I realized God was with me. He hadn't forgotten about me, and if He could speak to me through those ugly walls, if He could still see me there, then there was nothing He couldn't do."

She placed her free hand on top of Jack's, curled her fingers around to grip his palm. "Jack, you are naïve and innocent—"

"I'm not." His eyes had narrowed. "Innocent, that is. I've committed plenty of sins in my life. Just like you, I've been saved by grace."

"Okay." She couldn't help the smile she felt crawling across her face. "You're not innocent, but you have this... What is that expression from the Bible? Innocent as doves?"

"And shrewd as snakes," he said.

"That's how I mean it," she said. "I've lived shrouded in cynicism for too long. Believing nobody had my back. I had to take care of myself because nobody else would take care of me. Anyone who tried—well, I knew they wanted something from me. The world proved that to me over and over. Look at Derrick. He offered me a job, and I took it, and for that, he had these expectations. Never mind that I love his grandfather and I've taken good care of him. Derrick thinks he saved me, and, therefore, I owe him."

Jack opened his mouth to speak, but she cut him off.

"You... You've been kind to me. You've helped me. You've

given me things and fixed me meals and helped me with Red, and you did it all expecting nothing in return. I didn't think that kind of selflessness truly existed in the world. At least, not for me."

"I'm sorry you've had so many bad experiences," Jack said. "Especially with men."

She considered that, then shook her head. "My path was my path. I wouldn't choose it for somebody else, but God was with me even before I acknowledged Him. And He led me to you. I won't ever be sorry for that." She squeezed his hand. "I won't be sorry that I met you. You taught me to hope again. I was right in the short run—they did throw me in jail. But in the long run, in the ways that matter, you've been right about everything. We do have a God, and He is the God of hope. And I can trust Him. Thank you for helping me see that."

Jack swallowed hard and nodded slowly. "I don't know what to say."

Their waiter headed toward them with their meals. "You don't have to say anything." She pulled her hands away and made room for her bacon cheeseburger. It smelled heavenly.

After the waiter left, she snatched a french fry, but Jack cleared his throat. She looked up to see him reaching across the table again. She took his hand, and he bowed his head and prayed.

His words of thanks for their meals, but mostly for her freedom, brought tears to her eyes. She added her own silent prayer. *Lord, thank You for this man.*

CHAPTER SIXTEEN

Derrick crept into the house, gun drawn. It was silent except for the hum of the heater. Nothing had changed since the last time he'd been there. After peeking into the empty living room, he stepped into the kitchen and picked up the faint smell of something over-ripe. Sure enough, a bowl on the counter was filled with apples. He left it there and went upstairs.

When he knew the place was truly empty, Derrick moved his car into the garage and searched for valuables.

He started in Gramps's room. Gram's jewelry box rested beside a crystal paperweight shaped like a house, an award Gramps had won years before for service to some real estate club he belonged to. Because Gramps was awesome and always had been. Derrick had never been good enough for the old man.

He left the worthless paperweight and focused on Gram's jewelry box. All of her jewelry was still there. He emptied it into one of the plastic bags he'd grabbed from the kitchen. He'd sort through it later to separate the real stuff from the costume. Gramps didn't have many pieces of jewelry, but what he did have looked real and valuable. A gold ring with a stone Gramps had once told him was a star sapphire. Another gold ring, which, if Derrick's memory served, had been handed down from his father.

Derrick added those to his plastic bag, then scoured the rest of the bedroom. There was a box of old coins, an envelope with some kind of paperwork—financial information?—and a shoebox of baseball cards.

He looked through that one and found cards from way back, maybe from Gramps's own childhood. There were some from the years when Derrick's dad would have been a kid, and at the very back, the baseball cards Derrick had collected.

He'd forgotten Gramps had bought them off him. At the time, he'd thought the old man was off his rocker to offer him money for the cheap pieces of card stock, but now... Did Gramps think the cards were worth something? Or were they just valuable to him because Derrick had collected them?

He shook off that thought. If Gramps really cared about him, he'd have given Derrick the money he asked for.

Derrick added the shoebox to his growing pile.

When he'd thoroughly searched the master bedroom, he moved past the room that had been his since his folks had died and headed into the spare bedroom. Nothing of value in there. Finally, he pushed open the door to Harper's room.

Her bed was made but rumpled, as if she'd set something heavy on it. Her jewelry—most of which he'd bought her—was strewn haphazardly across the top of the bureau. He grabbed an empty plastic bag from his back pocket and scooped all the pieces into it. Nothing very valuable, but it would collect a few bucks.

The attached bathroom still had some of her things in it—a bottle of perfume—which he'd also given her—a can of hairspray, a headband, and various other useless items. Nothing worth a second glance.

In the closet hung most of Harper's nicer clothes. Slacks, blouses, dresses, leather shoes, scarves. In fact, everything he'd bought her was there. She must've only taken the crappy clothes she'd brought from Vegas and the cheap stuff she'd bought since she'd moved to Maryland. Apparently, she hadn't been planning to attend anything that required her to look decent.

Back in the bedroom, he opened her nightstand drawer and found a Bible and a journal. He flipped through the journal looking for his name, but all he found were weird questions and Bible references.

Proverbs 3—How do I trust You with all my heart?

Psalm 1:1-3—Teach me not to stand in the way of sinners, Lord.

Isaiah 30:21—Help me hear Your voice in my ear telling me which way to go.

He closed the journal, dropped it and the Bible back in the drawer, and slammed it shut. Such a waste of time, all that Bible stuff. As if those verses could help Harper now.

She'd need more than a few Bible verses when Derrick got his hands on her.

He turned his attention to the bureau, pulled open the drawers, one by one, telling himself he was looking for valuables. But mostly, he hoped to find Harper's bras and panties. He'd never had the opportunity to see them on her, but he couldn't pass up the temptation to touch them now, to imagine...

Except for socks, running shorts, and T-shirts, the drawers were empty. He dug through each one anyway, just in case she'd stowed something valuable, but of course Harper hadn't owned anything of value that Derrick hadn't given her himself.

Harper's value didn't come from what she wore or how

much money she had in her bank account. Harper's value lay in that perfect body and that beautiful face. A man would pay a pretty penny for a woman like Harper.

If Gramps didn't turn over the money, that would be plan B —once Derrick had finished with her.

CHAPTER SEVENTEEN

How could this creature be sitting across the table from him? How could normal, ordinary Jack Rossi be dining with a woman like Harper Cloud?

Harper pressed her phone to her ear as she reassured Red she was all right. Jack stared, mesmerized. She'd been beautiful before. Beautiful, but also haunted and guarded and suspicious. Somehow, a night in jail had freed her. She laughed with total abandon, smiled widely, and exuded joy as infectious as a baby's giggle. She seemed like a new person. Or maybe this was the real Harper, the one no longer cynical and afraid.

She ended the call when the waiter delivered the brownie-and-ice-cream dessert. Throughout lunch he'd told her about being the middle child sandwiched between two sisters, and she'd told him about life with two brothers. She'd just taken her first bite of dessert when he gently mentioned her parents.

Her smile faded, but it wasn't replaced with the fear or the defensiveness he'd seen before. No, she looked sad but genuine. "I miss them."

He speared a bite of pie, going for casual. Maybe she

wouldn't see right through him. "You could call them. You never know. They may miss you, too."

She sipped from her steaming cup of coffee and took another bite of dessert. She turned to look out the window. But she didn't answer.

Did he just ruin the moment?

But when she turned back to him, she offered a tender smile. "I've been afraid all this time that they'd reject me again. I thought I had to prove something to them. Prove I was worthy of their love. I don't know. After this, after everything that's happened the last two weeks... I've handled it, right? I mean, maybe not the best way, but I'm still alive, Red's still alive, and the police are looking for whoever murdered those men. And for Derrick. It's just a matter of time before this is all over. All sorts of terrible things were happening all around me, but I kept myself out of it. Not alone, of course. I couldn't have done anything without you—you and Garrison and Sam and all those nice people I don't even know who are watching over Red for me. But... I didn't let Derrick suck me into his mess. I didn't let everybody else's sins drag me down. And part of me wonders... will that be enough to prove to my parents that I'm worthy of their love?"

"Isn't it possible your parents are longing for you as much as you're longing for them?"

"Maybe," she said. "My dad told me never to call again, but... That wasn't like him. He was disappointed, of course. But maybe I just took him off guard. Maybe I needed to prove to myself that I was worthy. Because a few years ago, I would have just run away at the sight of those bodies. And this time I could have, you know? I could have abandoned Red and taken off. Heck, when I got beaten up, I could have run, never gone back to the house, never faced Derrick."

"Did you consider that?"

She shook her head. "Funny. It never crossed my mind. But a few years ago, I'd have taken off and not looked back because I didn't care about anyone as much as I cared about myself."

She stared out the window again, though at what he didn't know. He couldn't take his eyes off her face.

"I was so focused on me, me, me," she said, "and I was miserable. Now, I'm trying to do the right thing. I'm focused on keeping Red safe and healthy, on making sure the bad guys are brought to justice, and even though I'm still in this huge mess"—she turned to face Jack—"I'm happy. Who knew doing the right thing could be so satisfying?"

"I'm proud of you, Harper. A lot of women would have folded under the pressure."

"I would have, too, if not for Red. I love him, and that love kept propelling me forward. Not that I did it right. I should have gone straight to the cops the night I found the bodies."

"But you didn't avoid them for your sake. You did it for him."

"I did it for him." She met Jack's eyes across the table, opened her mouth, and closed it again. Her cheeks turned the most alluring color of pink he'd ever seen.

"What?"

She looked down, took another bite of dessert.

"Okay, then," he said. "I'll say it."

She swallowed the bite, eyes wide.

"What you did for Red, I've been trying to do for you. Protect you. Care for you. Help you. And for the same reason."

Her tiny, "Oh," had his heart racing and gave him courage to continue.

"I know just enough about you to know I care for you very deeply. Maybe it's too soon to use the L-word."

Her blush deepened. "Maybe it's not."

He lifted her hand over the dessert, kissed the back of her hand. "Maybe it's not."

"I'll just leave this." The clueless, obviously too-busy-to-care waiter slid their check onto the table. "You guys need anything else?"

Harper pulled her hand back, looked at her plate, that shy smile tugging at her lips.

Jack turned to glare at the waiter. "We're fine."

"I'll be your cashier whenever you're ready."

As he reached for his wallet, Jack muttered, "Hope you weren't counting on a big tip."

Across the table, Harper giggled, and Jack looked up and winked.

They could continue the conversation in the pickup. Or the next day. Or the day after that. As far as Jack was concerned, he and Harper had the rest of their lives together to declare their feelings to one another. This was just the beginning.

CHAPTER EIGHTEEN

J ack parked in the circle drive in front of a beautiful home just a few blocks from the bay. "Wow."

"Yeah." Harper gazed at the house. "Red built it for Bebe after he made his first million."

Jack looked at Harper. "Romantic."

She shrugged. "It's just a house. What's romantic is how much they loved each other. She died years ago, but he's still so devoted to her." She focused on Jack again. "So the most important thing we have to get here is—"

"Her picture," he said.

"Don't let me forget."

"What else do you need?"

"The rest of my clothes, some more of Red's things. Not a whole lot."

"Let's go, then. The sooner we're on the road, the sooner we'll be back in New Hampshire." He stepped out of the truck and ran around to open her door. She dug in her purse, then pulled out a set of keys. She kept them in her left hand and took his with her right. He loved the way her smooth skin felt against his palm.

She unlocked the oversize door, and he pushed it open, then stepped aside to let her step in first. When he followed, he let out a long whistle. "Wow." He looked up at the two-story foyer, the chandelier hanging from the high ceiling. A bear to clean, but it was pretty. Through the wide opening on the left, he spied the dining room with a table long enough to seat ten surrounded by heavy, carved chairs. Red's office was beyond glass-filled French doors on his right, and straight ahead, he got a glimpse of the living room.

She shoved her keys in her pocket. "It's grand, but it's homey, too. Come on."

She led him up the stairs and down a long hall. They stepped into what had to be the master bedroom. On his right was a bureau that had a lamp, an open jewelry box, and a crystal paperweight. On his left, a dark blue comforter lay over the king-size bed.

She gasped, and he turned to her, saw her wide eyes, her open mouth.

His heart thumped hard, realizing before his brain registered it that something was wrong. He lowered his voice. "What?"

"Someone's been here." Her words were whispered but urgent.

"The police."

"Someone else." She nodded toward an open jewelry box. "Bebe's jewelry is gone."

So, Derrick had come here and cleaned the place out. He was desperate for money, so that shouldn't surprise him. But what if...?

A shadow moved in the hallway. He pulled Harper into the room, propelling her away from the door and toward the bed.

Jack swung the door closed, but whoever was on the far side

of it stopped it with a foot, shoved it toward him. Off balance, Jack stumbled back.

The door swung open.

A man stood there. Short, dark brown hair, receding hairline, brown eyes ringed with bruises. Blood on his shirt.

Gun in his right hand, pointed at Jack.

"You must be Rossi," the man said.

Behind him, Harper said, "Derrick."

Derrick. By the look in his eyes, he was dangerously angry. And he was armed.

Jack held his hands out to the side in an I'm-not-a-threat stance and backed up.

Behind him, Harper shifted, and he put himself between her and the man in the doorway. He reached behind to ensure she was there, as protected as he could make her under the circumstances.

"Well, well, well," Derrick said. "If it isn't the little betrayer and her latest sucker."

He felt movement and reached to make sure she was still behind him, but he didn't look. He couldn't tear his eyes away from that gun. "Look, nobody has to get hurt."

"Sure," Derrick said. "Let's try that. First, both of you toss your phones over here."

Jack lifted his right hand and reached slowly into his jeans' pocket with his left. He grabbed his cell and inched it out, careful not to spook the man with his finger on the trigger. He tossed it across the hardwood to Derrick's feet.

Derrick stomped on it, over and over, until the glass splintered and cracked.

The sound was deafening in the silent room.

Derrick leaned slightly to the side, eyebrows lifted. "You, too, babe."

Behind him, Harper said, "I'm not your babe."

"No. You discarded me for this guy and never looked back."

Jack could feel Harper's anger and frustration warming his back. He worked to sound even and confident when he said, "Just give him your phone, Harper. It'll be okay."

He didn't turn to look but felt her moving. He heard the jingle of keys, then watched as her phone skidded across the hardwood.

Derrick caught it with his foot, then stomped on it, too.

They were unarmed and had no way to call for help, and they were at the mercy of this man.

"Babe," Derrick said, "I need you to step out from behind your boyfriend and come to me."

"No." Jack felt her step to the side and matched the movement, staying in front of her. He kept his eyes on Derrick. "She's not going with you. Just tell us what you want, and we'll do whatever we can to help you."

Derrick ignored him and focused on Harper. "I'm afraid at this range," he said, "if I shoot your boyfriend, the bullet may go right through him and hit you. I don't want you to get hurt, but I don't have time to negotiate."

Jack wanted to tell her to run, to go into the bathroom and lock the door and open the window and scream for help. Or lower herself to the ground and jump. Anything to get her away from this man.

But he couldn't say any of those things. So he reached for her hand behind him. She took it, and he squeezed.

He focused on Derrick. "I know you're frustrated. You need money, and you think Harper can help you get it. And you're right. She can. Nobody has to get hurt here. I can tell you where your grandfather is, and—"

"I know where he is," Derrick said. "And I'm going to get what I need from him." An ugly sneer crossed his features, and

Jack saw evil glint in the man's eyes. "And she's going to help me."

"Jack," Harper said. "Derrick won't hurt me. I'll be okay."

Standing behind Jack, sheltered by his body, Harper couldn't see the hunger in Derrick's eyes, the hate, the lust.

"He will hurt you," Jack said. "You're not going with him."

"Fine." Derrick lifted the gun and aimed. "I'll aim for your head, and we'll hope she survives."

"Go for it." Jack sounded much more confident than he felt. "You hurt her, you won't get anything out of your grandfather."

Derrick shrugged. "I like my odds."

"Don't!" Harper let go of Jack's hand.

"No!" Jack shifted to grab her, but it was too late. She'd taken a step to the side.

Derrick flashed a wicked smile.

Jack dove toward his legs.

The gun went off.

Pain shot up Jack's calf as he barreled into Derrick's knees.

The man went down, and they both fell into the hallway. Derrick backed to the side, kicked, connected with Jack's shoulder.

He ignored the pain and tried to reach the weapon, but Derrick scrambled farther away. He lifted the gun and brought it down hard against Jack's head.

His skull exploded in agony.

CHAPTER NINETEEN

Harper had scrambled into the bathroom as soon as Derrick went down. She had to get out of the house and call an ambulance.

Her hands were shaking, but she managed to get the window unlocked and was trying to force it up. Her only hope was to jump from the second story window and hope she wouldn't break her leg when she landed. Then she could run for help, call 911.

"Open the door, Harper!"

She managed to get the window halfway up. Just a few more inches...

A bullet ripped through the door and into the tiny room. Then, the door crashed open.

She chanced a glance as Derrick stepped inside. His eyes were wide. The gun was trained on her, trembling.

"Get over here."

The cool, fresh outside air beckoned her, but she stepped away from the window and walked toward him. As soon as she was within reach, he gripped her arm and yanked her back into the bedroom. Then he pushed her away.

She stumbled, kept her feet. She was trapped between Derrick and the wall.

He ran his free hand over his head.

Adjusted his glasses.

Stared at her.

Maybe someone had heard the gunshot. Maybe the police were on their way right now.

The wild look in Derrick's eyes shifted. They narrowed. And then, a slow smile spread across his face. "We're alone."

"Is he dead?"

Derrick glanced at Jack's body in the doorway. She looked, too. All she could see was a portion of Jack's legs. The hardwood floor was smeared with blood, and more blood pooled beneath his calf. A gunshot to the leg shouldn't have killed him. But what if the bullet had hit an artery? He could be bleeding to death at that moment.

She looked back at Derrick. "What did you do?"

"I wasn't planning to shoot him." He glanced at Jack again, then focused on her. "He shouldn't have interfered."

"He was trying to protect me."

Derrick took a step toward her. "Do you think you need to be protected from me, Harper?"

"I didn't. But now..." She glanced at the gun, and he pointed it at the floor. His finger remained on the trigger. She forced herself to look into his eyes, to see his reaction. "You killed those men?"

"What men?"

"Keith and... and the other guy. The men who beat me up."

"They're dead?" he asked. "I didn't know."

"I don't believe you."

"Believe what you want. I don't care anymore." He took another step toward her, then another.

She stepped back and hit the wall between the closet and the bathroom. If she could dive into the bathroom...

He lifted the gun. "Don't move, Harper. I'm feeling a little jumpy."

She froze, her gaze darting from the gun to his face.

He stepped forward again. She fought to stay in place, though everything in her wanted to run, to hide, to scream for help.

But he'd shot Jack. He'd actually aimed the gun and pulled the trigger. If Jack hadn't moved, would Derrick have fired?

He would have. Everything in his expression confirmed that.

She focused on Derrick's face. His lips were pulled back in a sneer, and his eyes were wild and hungry.

Oh, God. Please... No more words came, but God knew. He knew she needed Jack to be alive. She needed to be saved from Derrick.

And she needed a happy ending to this story.

Right now, she couldn't see any way from here to that fairytale.

Except, maybe, her knife.

When she'd pulled out her cell phone, she'd brought her keys with it. While Derrick had been crushing her phone, behind her back, she'd opened the little Swiss Army knife that had been a gift from Estelle, the old woman who was always so concerned about Harper's safety.

The knife was in her back pocket. She'd use it if she had to. And if he shot her, he shot her. She'd die before she became a victim of the lust she saw in Derrick's eyes.

He lowered the gun as he took another step in her direction. They were so close, she could feel his breath against her cheek.

He lifted his free hand, tugged a lock of her hair and wrapped it around his finger.

She pressed against the wall.

Derrick lifted the hand holding the gun and rested it against the wall beside her head. He slid his free hand behind her back. "Here we are." He pulled her toward him. "I'd pictured this in your bedroom." He looked around Red's room, and his eyes sparkled. "I wonder what Red would think."

Red. Not Gramps. "You know exactly what your grandfather would think."

His eyes lost their gleam. They were lifeless and cold. "He should have given me the money. You... you should have been on my side." He lowered his gaze to her lips. "You should have given me what I wanted."

He leaned down, tried to claim her lips. She leaned away, turned her head.

The cold steel of the gun barrel pressed against her temple. "Now, now," he said gently. "I think we've learned what resisting gets you."

How could she have been so stupid? How, in the months they'd spent together, could she have not seen this side of Derrick?

He slid his hand up her back, gripped her hair in his fist, and held her head in place. Then, he kissed her, his lips dry and hungry.

She kept her mouth closed, her teeth clamped shut.

His body pressed against hers.

She wanted to fight, but would he shoot her? Was she really willing to die to avoid this?

She was a survivor. She'd survived all the stupidity of her past. She'd survived prison. She'd survived getting beaten up by two masked men in a parking lot. She'd survived running.

She didn't know if she could survive this.

She had to try to get away, to help Jack. Even if it meant she got shot in the process. Except... Derrick needed her to get his hands on Red's money.

Derrick wouldn't kill her.

She had to fight.

She pushed against Derrick's chest with one hand, hard. He didn't back up or slow down. With the other hand, she slipped the knife from her pocket, blade pointed down.

Where would the knife do the most damage? From this angle, she could reach his back or his side but little else. Which would hurt the most? Which would stop him?

She didn't know. She knew she could get him in the side easily.

The blade was only a couple of inches long. If she stabbed him hard, maybe she could get away. Their only chance for survival would come if she could escape and call for help.

She could do this. She had to do this.

CHAPTER TWENTY

S lowly, Jack's vision cleared. It was too quiet in the bedroom. He didn't have to look to know what the man had planned. He'd seen the intent in Derrick's eyes.

Father, give me strength. Help me rescue her. I need You.

He pulled in a deep breath and sat up, careful not to jostle his legs in case Derrick was looking through the door.

The hallway spun, slowed, and Jack was able to focus. Blood was smeared all over the hardwood floor. It still dripped from the wound in Jack's leg, but not too badly.

He shifted the leg just a little. That he could move it was a good sign. He wouldn't be running a marathon anytime soon, but the leg would support him. It had to.

By the sounds of things, Derrick was taking his time. Drawing out Harper's torture. Jack visualized the room. What could he use as a weapon? Something heavy. Something close to the door.

The paperweight.

If he could grab it and hit Derrick with—

Footsteps sounded downstairs. Quietly. Maybe someone had heard the gunshot. Maybe the police were here. Except...

only a few minutes had passed. And wouldn't the police announce themselves?

Jack considered calling for help, but a clear thought stopped him.

Play dead.

It was nearly a command. Everything in him wanted to rush into that room and rescue Harper. But Jack trusted the voice in his head—whether it was God or his intuition, he didn't know.

He glanced behind him and saw more blood near where his head had landed. The sight made him woozy, and he closed his eyes and lay back down just as someone crept up the stairs.

In the next room, Derrick let out a pained sound, almost a scream. Then a curse.

Harper gasped. Footsteps neared.

Jack nearly moved, but the new person bounded up the staircase and jumped over Jack and into the room.

If the new guy didn't help Harper right now, if that man was working with Derrick, then Jack had just made a fatal error.

CHAPTER TWENTY-ONE

She was a survivor.

Not a decoration on a man's arm.

Not a plaything.

Not a victim.

A survivor.

So she stabbed him in the side, hoping to hit an organ.

He screamed, jerked away, and swiped wildly with his hand. It hit her arm, and she lost her grip on the knife.

He looked at her with murder in his eyes.

He lifted the gun, brought it high to hit her.

She lunged for the bathroom, but Derrick grabbed her and yanked her back.

She stumbled, nearly fell.

A man shouted, "Hey!"

Jack?

Derrick turned.

Before Harper could form a word, before relief could fill her spirit, a gunshot split the silence.

Derrick fell forward, and she jumped back to keep him from falling on her.

She watched as blood seeped from the back of his head.

Had Jack...? Her gaze traveled to the open door. Jack's legs weren't there. Then she looked at the man standing before her.

Shook her head. It couldn't be.

"Barry?"

"Harper." He breathed her name, stepped around Derrick's body, and pulled her into a hug. "Thank God I got to you in time."

She angled away, wanted to step back, but she was too close to the wall. She shook her head again. Maybe she'd been hurt. Maybe this was a hallucination. Because it made no sense for Barry to be there.

She'd left Barry in Las Vegas. She hadn't seen him since the night someone had been waiting for her in the alley behind her apartment. The night Barry had run off a dangerous man.

Because he'd just *happened* to see her.

Except he hadn't *happened* to see her. He'd been watching her.

He pulled her against him, wrapped one arm—the one holding the gun—behind her back. His other hand pressed her head against his jacket.

She didn't fight the embrace. This was wrong, terribly wrong, but the fact that Barry was here...

"I'm so sorry," he said. "I had to take care of the men who were following him or I'd have been here sooner."

She fought to understand his words. "Him?"

"Derrick Burns. When I lost track of you a couple of weeks ago, I started tracking him. I knew he'd lead me to you, eventually."

She pushed away from his embrace, and he let her.

So maybe he wouldn't hurt her.

But he didn't step back, and she didn't have the courage to

sidestep him. Because Barry was here, and Barry wasn't sane. Barry had just killed a man.

At least with Derrick, she'd known what to expect.

She filtered through all he'd just told her. "How...?" She couldn't even form the question.

"I design apps." He stood a bit taller, shrugged with false humility. "I designed one to keep tabs on you, make sure you were all right. I emailed the file to you. All you had to do was open it—and of course, you did. I designed it to look like it came from your bank. The app downloaded onto your phone."

"All this time, you've been watching me."

"Watched you take up with that..." His gaze darted to Derrick. "I almost killed him once before. You two were arguing on the front step outside. You were holding your own, and then he stepped toward you like he might lift a hand to you. I was ready then." He shook his head, seemed disgusted with himself. "I got out of my car. Maybe the sound of the door slamming was what made your boyfriend step away."

She remembered that day. It was the day she and Derrick had ended things for good. She remembered how aggressive he'd become. She even remembered the slamming car door that seemed to bring him to his senses. That had been Barry?

"When you and the old man took off that night, I didn't worry about following you. The tracking app would tell me where you went. So I stayed, disposed of the bodies. I thought I'd catch up with you later. But then, your phone..." Barry's expression looked stricken. "I found it in a trash can at a truck stop. You were gone."

Yes. She'd dumped the phone not long after they'd left the house. She'd been afraid the police would track her down with it when they found the bodies. She'd had no idea Barry—

"So I sent the app to Burns and tracked him. I knew he'd catch up with you."

"But why?" she asked.

Now, his smug look shifted to a gentle smile. "Don't you know yet?" He brushed his knuckle down her cheek. "You and I are supposed to be together. We should have been together all this time, but you were with Emmitt. That's why I talked him into robbing that liquor store that night."

Wait, what? "I thought it was his idea."

"Everybody did. He had a record, and I was a computer geek. I brought Emmitt's handgun. He didn't even know I had it. He carried that little revolver, but I had the pistol. I wore gloves, so only Emmitt's fingerprints were on it. His fingerprints were on the bullets that loaded it. I shot that man, but everybody thought Emmitt did it."

No. It made no sense. "You murdered—"

"He wasn't supposed to die." His voice was pleading, his eyes filled with sadness. "That clerk—he had a heart condition. That's what killed him. The wound shouldn't have killed him."

"But it did."

Barry kept talking, moving on as if he couldn't dwell on that inconvenient fact. "I'd planned to go to the police the next day, confess my part in it, and tell them how Emmitt had plotted the whole thing, how I'd just thought we were going to buy liquor. I was going to tell them where the murder weapon was. I figured they'd let me off in exchange for my testimony. But you..." A flash of anger, and then he smiled. "It was our fault. We never should have put you in that position. And both of us ended up in prison. I'm so sorry about that, Harper. I should never have involved you."

The police had given Emmitt twenty years for that murder, and here was Barry, free. The mastermind of the whole thing, the one who'd murdered that man. "Why?"

"To be with you, of course." He pressed his hand against the side of her head. It was hot, and she flinched, but he didn't seem to notice. He ran his fingers through her hair. "You've let it grow a little longer. I like it."

She angled her head away from his hand. "You set my boyfriend up to go to prison?"

"He was no good for you, Harper."

She couldn't help it. She felt her eyebrows lift. "And you are? You're a murderer."

"All the men I've killed, everything I've done, I did for you."

And then she understood. Finally, everything made sense. "You killed those men and left them downstairs."

His eyes filled with rage. "I was late getting to you. I saw you were at the grocery store, but I'd gotten out of work late, and by the time I got there... I watched the men move you, talk to you. I knew you were alive." He swallowed, shook his head. "I'm so sorry. I didn't know what to do. I was torn between taking care of you and taking care of them. What they did to you"— and just like that, his eyes darkened with rage again—"I had to take care of them."

Barry's moods shifted by the second. She needed to tread very carefully.

She forced a tender tone. "Who else? Just"—her gaze flicked to Derrick's body—"just him, right? There wasn't anybody else?"

"There were a couple of goons outside. They beat up Burns, and I couldn't let them get their hands on you. Not after what the last two did to you. That's why I was late saving you just now."

"What did you do to them?"

"Shot them. Left them in their car." He tugged a lock of her hair, the corner of his lips tipped up in a smile. "Don't worry. They'll never trace it back to me. We'll be safe."

She thought of Jack. He'd been gone when she looked. She

was afraid to ask the question, afraid to learn the answer, but she had to know. "And Jack?"

His eyes narrowed. "The dead guy in the hall? Is that Jack?"

The dead guy...

Her eyes filled with tears.

Barry's gaze hardened. "He was nobody," Barry said. "You're mine."

She nodded as if she agreed, anything to keep Barry from losing his temper with her. To stay alive.

Jack would want her to stay alive.

"It's been you, all along." His features softened, and his eyes crinkled with a smile. "I love you, Harper. I can take care of you. I have all the money we need. We can live wherever you want. Here, Kansas. Back in Vegas. We'll have kids. We'll be happy."

She should nod, should agree with him. But the truth bubbled out as if from a fountain, and she blurted the truth. "I love Jack."

His eyes hardened. His gun clattered to the floor, and he pressed his hands against the sides of her face. "No. You're meant to be with me.

His hands were like fire, pressing.

"Say it. You belong to me."

She tried to nod, but she couldn't move. She couldn't speak for the terror bubbling in her throat.

"You are mine."

"Yes."

"Say it!"

She couldn't form words. "I'm..." But the rest was caught when his hands pressed against her cheeks, her mouth.

He wrapped one hand around her neck, pushed the palm against her windpipe. "You're mine. You were always mine."

Desperate for air, she couldn't think. She'd tell him whatever he wanted to hear, but the words were caught, trapped by his fingers squeezing her neck, the other hand over her mouth. She was a fool. She tried to nod, to agree, to do anything that would convince him, anything that would allow her to pull in air.

She pushed against his face with one hand. With the other, she tried to pry his fingers off her neck. If only she'd held onto the knife.

She prayed for help. But Barry was strong. Much stronger than she.

She was a fool. A fool who'd die at this man's hands because of one moment of honesty.

Then, she heard a sickening thud.

And Barry collapsed.

CHAPTER TWENTY-TWO

Jack stared down at the man's body, the bloody paperweight shaking in his right hand.

Harper was frozen, eyes wide.

She was safe.

Thank God.

The room spun, his vision darkened, and he reached out to grab something, anything to keep himself from falling.

Harper grabbed his upper arms, held him steady. "We have to go, now, before he wakes up."

Jack's vision returned, fuzzy but better. He forced himself to focus on the man crumpled on the floor.

The stranger stared, unseeing, at the ceiling. He wouldn't be waking up.

He'd done it. Jack had done it, though he'd doubted every second he could.

After the man had shot Derrick, Jack had forced himself to his feet. It had taken too long, far too long, to make himself move, to feel steady enough to cross the floor. He'd listened to his confession. Barry. Harper had called him Barry.

And uttered three words that could have gotten her killed.

I love Jack.

He'd grabbed the paperweight. It was heavier than he'd expected, solid etched glass the size of a softball. Jack had stepped over Derrick's body and brought his weapon down as hard as he could on Barry's head.

Now, all the adrenaline seeped away, and Jack stumbled toward the door. He sat, landing on the remains of their crushed cell phones, and leaned against the jamb.

In the distance, a siren wailed.

"Let's just wait for the police," he said.

"But what if...?" Harper glanced behind her at the dead men and gasped. "Oh, God. Oh, God."

Jack tugged on her hand. "Don't look. Honey, look at me."

After a quick shake of her head, she crouched beside Barry, gently pulled a cell from his pocket, and dialed 911.

While she talked to the dispatcher, she sat beside Jack, her back to the dead men. Her voice trembled until finally she set the phone on the floor and leaned into Jack's waiting arms.

He pulled her against him, relished the feel of her. She was safe.

She was safe.

Thank You, Lord.

She wept against his chest. He ignored the pain in his leg and the throbbing in his head and rubbed her back and whispered in her ear. "It's over. They're gone. Nobody's going to hurt you." He repeated the words until she quieted, and they held each other and waited for the police to arrive.

CHAPTER TWENTY-THREE

The sirens cut off, and a moment later, there was pounding on the door, then a call of, "Police."

Harper shifted out of Jack's embrace, and his arms fell as if he didn't have the energy to hold them up any longer. He collapsed against the wall behind him.

His face was so pale. "Up here!" she called. "Hurry!"

She studied his face. His skin was deathly pale, his eyes ringed in black circles. His breathing was shallow.

She heard heavy footsteps. "They're coming," she said. "Just hold on."

A moment later, a tall, thin uniformed police officer stepped in, gun drawn. A second shorter man came in behind him. The first checked both bodies while the second crouched beside her and Jack. He met Harper's eyes. "You hurt?"

She shook her head. "He needs help."

"Paramedics are right behind us."

People poured into the room. A paramedic helped Harper stand, settled her on the bed, and wrapped her in a blanket.

Other men surrounded Jack. Within minutes, he was laid out on a stretcher and on his way out the door.

She stood. "I have to go with him."

The female paramedic who'd been checking her vitals pushed her back down. "He's in good hands."

Harper threw off the blanket and stood again. "I'm going with Jack." She followed the stretcher down the stairs and outside, the paramedic's hand tight around her upper arm.

She froze on the doorstep at the sheer volume of emergency vehicles. A fire truck, three police cars, two ambulances, and a few other unmarked cars were lined up and down the street.

"Ma'am," the paramedic said. "You're in shock. You need to sit down."

Jack was being loaded into the back of an ambulance.

She needed to get there. But the woman was right. Harper couldn't think straight, couldn't figure out how to get from where she stood to where Jack was.

The woman settled her on the porch steps. The blanket came around her shoulders again.

"I have to go with him."

"We'll get you to the hospital where he's going. Don't worry."

The next thing Harper knew, she, too, was loaded in an ambulance.

"I'm fine." But nobody paid her any attention. The paramedics gave her gentle smiles and patted her shoulders and told her everything would be all right.

"But Jack. I need to know if he's all right."

The woman smiled. "Your friend lost a lot of blood, but he didn't have any life-threatening injuries that I saw. He'll recover."

Harper felt tears bubble up, sobs building. "You promise?"

The woman's eyes were kind. "I don't know what happened back there, but it's over now. I promise."

CHAPTER TWENTY-FOUR

Jack's vision was clearing, though his head pounded. "You're sure she's—"

"I promise, your friend is not injured." The ER doctor studied the screen that displayed Jack's vital signs, then turned to him. "We're more worried about you."

"I'm fine." But Jack wasn't fine. His leg throbbed. They told him it was just a flesh wound. Which should have made him happy but mostly irritated him. *Just* a flesh wound, he wanted to snap. *You try having a bullet rip at your flesh, see how it feels.*

But he didn't let any of words out, because these people were stitching him up, and none of them had shot him.

Anyway, his head hurt too much to speak.

After far too many tests to check on his concussion, Jack was transferred—flat on his back—to a room to spend the night. He complained all the way down the hall, in the elevator, and down another hall, desperately trying to convince them he was fine and needed to find Harper.

But when they rolled him into the room, she was there.

She approached him as the orderlies locked his bed in place. Tears filled her eyes.

Except for red marks that were already turning to bruises on her neck, she seemed fine.

Those bruises made his stomach ache, and he swallowed once, twice, thinking of what could have happened. But he didn't tell anybody he felt ill, not after swearing up and down he was fine.

When she smiled at him, he felt much better. She stepped close and took his hand. Hers were cold and soft and shaking.

"You're all right?" he asked.

She nodded, swallowed. "I'm so sorry."

He pulled her closer, kept tugging until he could reach her face. With his free hand, he pressed his palm against her cheek. "I don't know what you're sorry about, my love. I'm not sorry you're here. I'm not sorry you're safe."

"I dragged you into this."

He slid his hand around to the back of her head and pulled her closer. "No. I volunteered." Then, he kissed her.

The door swung open. "Knock, knock."

Harper stepped away, a blush creeping into her cheeks, that shy smile on her face. She looked to see who'd come in, and he forced himself to turn that way. The concussion was definitely not giving him extra patience. "I don't need to be here," he said to the plump woman who'd interrupted.

"Nice to meet you." The woman was extra cheerful, maybe just to irritate him. "I'm Marjorie, and I'll be your nurse."

He flipped the blanket off his legs. "I'm not staying."

Harper pulled the blankets back over him. "You are staying."

"But we need—"

"There's absolutely nothing we need to do," she said. "So just get comfortable."

He huffed, but he leaned back against the bed.

"Good," Marjorie said. "How you feeling?"

Jack opened his mouth.

"Be nice," Harper said. "This isn't her fault."

He took a deep breath. "I'm fine. Thank you."

The nurse wrote her name on the whiteboard, washed her hands, and checked his blood pressure. After she left, Jack turned to Harper. "At least they're leaving us alone for a minute. Tell me the truth. Are you hurt?"

She smiled, though the tears were right behind. "I'm okay." After a thick swallow, she added, "I'm just glad you're all right. I thought you were dead."

"I did too for a minute there."

"What did the doctor say?"

Jack had spoken to the doctor, but he didn't remember what he'd said. Maybe that blow to the head had been worse than he'd thought. "He said I'll be fine. They just need to keep me overnight because of the concussion."

"Okay, then." She'd barely settled in the chair beside him when the door swung open again.

A man and a woman walked in. Jack had seen the woman at the police station a million years ago. Except, it had just been earlier that day.

They both pulled out badges to show him. The woman spoke. "Detective Whitney. This is Detective Finnegan." She focused on Harper. "Step outside, please."

Jack said, "I'd rather—"

"We need to ask you some questions," Whitney said.

Harper kissed his cheek. "It'll be fine. I answered their questions already. Ernie came and stayed during the questioning."

"That's good," Jack said. "She still around?"

Harper shook her head. "She said to tell you to get well soon. Now, I'm going after a cup of coffee. You need anything?"

He wanted to convince her to stay, but with her so close, her pretty blond hair brushing against his cheek, the words flitted away. She kissed him again, this time on the lips. "I'll be right back."

And she was gone.

But not for long. Not forever. Because she loved him. And he loved her. And they had the rest of their lives to be together.

CHAPTER TWENTY-FIVE

Tuesday morning, Harper awoke to sunlight streaming through the window. It took her a moment to remember where she was.

Jack's house.

Since Red was still in the hospital, she'd slept on the couch in Jack's living room so she could be there in case he needed her. He hadn't, of course, but he also hadn't put up much of a fight about her staying. He seemed to like having her under his roof, and she didn't mind not sleeping in her little rental house alone.

She was safe now. With both Derrick and Barry gone, surely she was safe.

But she wasn't taking any chances.

After she showered and dressed, she knocked on the door to the master bedroom. At Jack's soft, "Come on in," she stepped inside.

He was up, dressed, and coming out of his bathroom. "Good morning."

"What are you doing up already? You're supposed to let me help you."

"I've been dressing myself for a long time." He winked. "I had it under control."

He limped toward his bed. She rushed across the room and took his upper arm. "You were shot, Jack. You shouldn't be walking without that crutch."

"It's just a flesh wound." But the pain in his expression as he shifted to sit on the bed belied the words.

"A bullet went completely through your calf muscle. It's not *just* anything."

He looked up at her. "Are you ready for this?"

She sat beside him and stared across the room at the doorway. Today, they had to tell Red his only living relative was gone. She would never have guessed that Barry—sweet, chubbyfaced, awkward Barry—could be capable of such violence. She and Jack had both told Detective Whitney about Barry's confessions. Whitney had promised to contact the DA's office in Vegas. With Barry's confession, Emmitt's prison sentence might be reduced.

As if he knew the path of her thoughts, Jack said, "And Emmitt's incarceration isn't your fault, either. He didn't have to rob that liquor store."

"I know."

Jack's arm slid around Harper's back, and he pulled her close. She rested her head on his shoulder. "Derrick is dead because of me."

"Derrick is dead because he was hurting you. He was going to..."

His words trailed off, but Harper knew what Derrick had planned. *You should have given me what I wanted...* She could still feel the cold steel of the gun against her forehead, Derrick's hot hands through the fabric of her shirt. "I know."

Jack leaned away. "Look at me."

She turned, and he took her hands. "All that time you were

with Derrick, Barry never hurt him. He watched you two together. He probably saw you hugging, maybe kissing. Right?"

She nodded.

"And Barry never lifted a hand against him."

"That's true."

"He got Emmitt out of the way, but he didn't kill Emmitt. He could have, must have had plenty of opportunity. But he didn't. Right?"

"He was always so docile," Harper said.

"Derrick is dead because he was hurting you. Barry... He was crazy, no doubt about it. But he was protecting you. He killed those two men who beat you up."

"He killed the men who were outside the house that night."

"Remember what he said, though. He killed them because he was afraid they would hurt you."

She thought back to those few moments with Barry. *I couldn't let them get their hands on you.*

"He was crazy," Jack said, "but he was devoted to you. I don't think he would have killed Derrick if Derrick hadn't been forcing himself on you."

Those last few words made her shudder. She pushed the memory away. "We don't know that."

Jack leaned his forehead against hers and focused on her eyes. "None of this was your fault, Harper. None of it."

She tried to believe Jack. Right now, her thoughts were too jumbled, the grief and fear too fresh. One day, maybe she'd believe the truth Jack had spoken. The truth Detective Whitney had spoken. The truth even Garrison had spoken when he and Sam had met them at the house the night before.

This wasn't her fault, and she was free.

CHAPTER TWENTY-SIX

R ed and Harper had been back at their little rental house for two days when Jack walked up the ramp to their door Friday morning. Before he knocked, a car roared behind him. He turned to watch as Ginny parked her little red Chevy sedan in the driveway. He waited until she joined him. "What are you doing here?"

She shrugged, but he could tell by the gleam in her eye she knew exactly why she was there.

Weird.

He knocked, and Harper opened the door with a smile. It faded to shock when she saw the woman next to him. "Hey, Ginny. What are you doing here?"

"Mr. Burns asked me to come by."

"For the tenth time," the old man called from inside the house, "call me Red!"

She giggled and lowered her voice. "I just do it to annoy him."

"I heard that," he yelled.

Jack couldn't help a laugh as he followed Ginny into the house.

The living room looked like it was supposed to. Not like the empty shell of a home Harper had left when she'd planned to take off without saying goodbye. It looked lived in with Red in the chair in the far corner, his Gatorade on the end table beside the photograph of Bebe. A newspaper lay folded and draped over the arm of his chair. On the coffee table, Harper's novel had a bookmark sticking out of it. The TV was on but silent.

"Come in," Red said. "Everybody sit down."

The couch was only big enough for two to sit comfortably, so Jack grabbed a kitchen chair and set it beside the TV.

Harper perched on the far end of the couch. "What's going on, Red?"

He turned his eyes to her. "I'm gonna tell you. Just hold your horses."

Ginny sat beside Harper, closer to Red. She looked as serene as could be, so whatever was coming, she knew all about it.

Interesting.

"The other day," Red started, "when you were talking about what happened to... to my grandson." He sniffed, shook the emotion off. "You said something about going back to Maryland when I'm strong enough."

He closed his eyes against the thought. *Please, not yet.* Jack wasn't ready for Harper to leave, and he had a lot to do before he could go with her. How would their relationship stand the separation?

They'd talked about it all week, and the only option was for him to go, too. But he owned a business here, and he had a real estate deal in the works. He couldn't take off. It would be a month or so before he could turn over the properties he managed to another company and back out of the contract on the apartment building. He'd hoped Harper and Red would stay until he was ready.

Harper's voice was patient. "I'm not sure you're there yet, Red."

"First, I'm strong as an ox. But I'm not going back."

Harper looked at Jack, then back at Red. "What do you mean?"

"What's there for me? What do I have in Maryland?"

"Your house," she said. "All your memories."

He tapped the side of his head. "My memories are just fine right here. Don't need the house." After a glance at the photo of Bebe on the end table, he focused on Harper again. "With Derrick gone, you with Jack—"

"But we're going with you, of course," Harper said. "We would never—"

"I know that," he said. "I know what you're planning, and it's ridiculous. You two both gonna move to Maryland so an old man can feel comfortable in his own home? I can feel comfortable right here."

Here? Red wanted to stay here?

Jack could hardly believe it.

Apparently, Harper couldn't believe it, either, because her mouth was open, her jaw slack.

"You're catching flies, girl." Red winked at Jack.

Harper closed her mouth before opening it again to speak. "Are you serious? You want to stay here?"

"I've made more friends in the last week in New Hampshire than I've made in Maryland in a decade. All my friends there are dying off, and the ones who're still alive are old as dirt." He chuckled. "You young people are good for me."

"Oh, Red." Harper glanced at Jack, and he caught the sheen of tears in her eyes. Because Harper didn't want to go back to Maryland. She'd told him her fears about being in that house again, stepping over the places where Derrick and Barry had died. Maybe Red understood that.

Maybe he didn't want to be in the house where his grandson had died, either.

Ginny cleared her throat, and Red said, "I'm getting to it."

She grinned and sat back.

Red turned his gaze on Jack. "No offense, son. This is a nice house and all, and I'm sure you'll fix it up real pretty, but it's not exactly what I'm accustomed to."

"I've seen what you're accustomed to," Jack said, "and I'm impressed you've been here as long as you have."

"Well, I didn't make all that money to live my last days in a place like this." He turned to Harper again. "I'm going to buy a house, a big house. And I hope you'll stay with me."

Harper stood and knelt at his feet. "I'll stay with you, Red. Always."

He patted her shoulder. "You're the only family I have left now. Would you please call me Gramps?"

She gave him a hug while Ginny pulled a bunch of papers out of her huge purse. They were MLS sheets, real estate listings. She went over each house with Red and Harper, and the three of them narrowed down which homes would be worth touring.

Jack sat back and watched, amazed and overwhelmed with gratitude. Because Harper was staying. And Red was happy. And Jack had acquired a new and amazing family.

CHAPTER TWENTY-SEVEN

Harper stared at the house she'd grown up in. The white trim looked freshly painted against the dark red brick on the two-story home. The bushes were more mature, the oaks surrounding the house taller than they'd been before, beautiful in their winter starkness.

The front porch was decked out for Thanksgiving. Straw bales on the porch, mums and pumpkins placed artfully all around. Mom's handiwork, no doubt. The family was just beyond that door, preparing for a Thanksgiving feast. And they didn't know Harper was coming.

This was a terrible idea.

"Maybe it's too soon." Harper turned to Jack, who waited patiently in the driver's seat while she tried to get up her nerve. He'd been on his phone, doing what, she had no idea. "Will you hate me if I chicken out? We can come back at Christmas instead."

Jack slid his phone into his pocket, leaned across the console of their rental, and kissed her cheek. "I love you, and nothing's going to change that."

Anxiety leaked out of her like air from a leaky balloon.

But then Jack stepped out of the car. He leaned down and met her eyes across the front seat. "We're going in." He slammed the door and walked around to open hers. "Come on."

"But what if they don't want me?"

He didn't bother to answer. They'd had this same conversation a thousand times in the last week. So Jack just held out his hand and waited.

What choice did she have? She slipped her fingers across his palm, and he closed his hand around hers. Hanging on, she stepped out of the car.

The car door slammed, and she nearly jumped out of her skin.

Then the front door opened. A man stepped out. A man she barely recognized.

Her little brother.

Braden jogged across the grass, wrapped his arms around her, and lifted her in a hug. She started to laugh, then cry, as she held onto him.

He set her down and leaned back. "You look good."

"You look..." But she could hardly talk for the tears. She took in the sight of her baby brother. He'd been an awkward teen. Now, he was tall and broad and sporting a scruffy beard. "You look grown up."

"Well, duh. It's been years."

Nearly a decade. Her baby brother had become a man.

He focused beside her and held out his hand. "You must be Jack."

What? Harper faced Jack, who shook Braden's hand. "Great to meet you in person, Braden."

"How do you two...?"

Jack rested his hand on her back. "You were afraid to call, but I wasn't."

"They know I'm coming?" Harper looked at Braden.

He shook his head. "I told Robert, but we agreed it should be a surprise for Mom and Dad. Mom would've stressed out every single second if she'd known you were coming."

"Oh." Harper couldn't think of anything to say, so she just squared her shoulders and faced the front door.

"You're just in time," Braden said. "I've been watching from the window. Another minute, and I'd have come out and dragged you inside. Only reason I didn't was Jack texted to tell me to be patient."

She glanced at Jack again, and he shrugged.

The front door creaked.

A woman stepped out and called, "Braden, invite your friends to..." And her words cut off.

Harper swallowed the lump in her throat and stared at the figure in the doorway.

The screen slammed behind her mother. She looked just like Harper remembered. Beautiful. Noble. She stepped forward, and Harper said, "I'm sorry. I should have—"

"Dean!" Her mother shouted behind her. "Our baby's home!" She sprinted across the yard and wrapped Harper in an embrace.

Harper fell into her mother's arms. A moment later, the screen squeaked, and more arms came around her. She didn't have to look to know it was her father as he enveloped her in his strength and his scent.

Everything about him said she was home.

"I'm so sorry," he said.

"No." She fought to control her emotions. "I'm sorry."

The door opened and slammed again, and then someone was patting her arm. "Hey, do I get a turn?"

She peeked over her mother's shoulder to see her older brother, Robert. He turned to shake hands with Jack, then wrapped her in a hug.

And before she knew it, Harper was ushered inside as a hundred questions came at her and a million happy tears streamed down faces. She met a new sister-in-law and a niece she hadn't known existed.

Everybody seemed to love Jack, the man who'd brought her home.

Two more places were set at the table while turkey was carved and yeasty rolls were transferred to a basket. The fine china, the good crystal, the silver serving dishes were set out. But the riches were in the people, these people she'd longed for and treasured.

The family gathered around the table and joined hands. Mom insisted Harper sit beside her. Her hand was thinner, though her grip was strong.

Daddy prayed, his voice shaking with emotion. He cut the prayer off quickly and snatched a napkin to wipe his eyes.

All around, her family sniffed and smiled through tears. Only the little girl's eyes were dry as she stared at Harper with open curiosity.

And then they passed the food and chattered and behaved as if everything were normal. Harper knew they'd have a million more questions for her. They'd want to know where she'd been and what she'd been doing, and she would tell them everything. But right now, her family seemed content to have her home.

She tried to eat her dinner, but she was so full of love and joy and emotions she couldn't even name that there was room for nothing else. She watched her family—her family!—eat and talk and laugh and joke, and everything felt right with the world.

Last spring, Estelle, her favorite patient in the nursing home, had told Harper to return to Kansas and her family. But Harper had been afraid her parents would reject her. She'd been afraid of so many things. Since then, she'd faced trials and danger, but she'd also met kind people, people who'd pointed her to the God who stitched up wounds and mended broken hearts.

The God who healed and saved and reconciled people to himself. She looked around the room and realized that He reconciled people to each other, too.

Jack took her hand under the table, and she turned to meet his eyes.

There were so many things she wanted to say, but all she could manage was, "Happy Thanksgiving."

He kissed her forehead. "Happy homecoming, my love."

If you enjoyed Harper and Jack's story, you're going to love the next book in the Nutfield Saga, LEGACY REJECTED. Turn the page for more on LEGACY REJECTED.

She's not giving up her home, no matter what threats come against her.

Realtor Ginny Lamont's family has abandoned her, leaving her with nothing but a warning that she's in danger. But Ginny's built a home in New Hampshire. After a childhood of nomadic living, she's not running again, certainly not because of some nameless, baseless threat.

Real estate developer Kade Powers is thrilled to go out with Nutfield's beautiful new real estate agent. But the prowler they surprise after their first date offers a glimpse into Ginny's past and the legacy of lies her parents left her with. She brings a mystery, one he's determined to help her solve.

With Kade's help, Ginny searches for the truth of her parents' criminal activity while her enemies close in. When mobsters show up in her quaint New England town, will she find a way to bring them down, or will she lose the home—and the man—she's come to love?

Legacy Redeemed

Amanda Series

Chasing Amanda

Finding Amanda

Standalone Novellas

A Package Deal

One Christmas Eve

Faith House

ABOUT THE AUTHOR

Robin Patchen is a *USA Today* bestselling and award-winning author of Christian romantic suspense. She grew up in a small town in New Hampshire, the setting of her Nutfield Saga books, and then headed to Boston to earn a journalism degree. After college, working in marketing and public relations, she discovered how much she loathed the nine-to-five ball and chain. After relocating to the Southwest, she started writing her first novel while she homeschooled her three children. The novel was dreadful, but her passion for storytelling didn't wane. Thankfully, as her children grew, so did her writing ability. Now that her kids are adults, she has more time to play with the lives of fictional heroes and heroines, wreaking havoc and working magic to give her characters happy endings. When she's not writing, she's editing or reading, proving that most of her life revolves around the twenty-six letters of the alphabet. Visit robinpatchen.com/subscribe to receive a free book and stay informed about Robin's latest projects.